AN EXTRAORDINARY
PASSION

By the Author

An Independent Woman

An Extraordinary Passion

Visit us at www.boldstrokesbooks.com

AN EXTRAORDINARY PASSION

by

Kit Meredith

2025

ISBN 13: 978-1-63679-679-6

THIS TRADE PAPERBACK ORIGINAL IS PUBLISHED BY
BOLD STROKES BOOKS, INC.
P.O. BOX 249
VALLEY FALLS, NY 12185

FIRST EDITION: AUGUST 2025

CREDITS
EDITOR: RUTH STERNGLANTZ
PRODUCTION DESIGN: STACIA SEAMAN
COVER DESIGN BY INKSPIRAL DESIGN

Acknowledgments

Thank you to my editor, Ruth, and everyone at BSB for supporting me in developing my writing and putting it out there. I've already learned so much.

Thank you to my sensitivity reader, Meg Elison, for your thoughtful feedback and tips. Yours and Marianne Kirby's Writing Fat Characters master class helped give me the confidence to write a non-binary character who doesn't look like the usual rep. Thanks also to all the fat, queer activists and authors who helped inspire me, including Aubrey Gordon and Sofie Hagen, who first raised my awareness through their podcasts.

Thanks to my LGBTQIA writing group for the encouragement and accountability. It's been an honour to see everyone develop their craft and inspire each other. I feel so lucky to have this space we're created and to have you all by my side.

And thank you to everyone who has helped me become more me than I've ever been. Every moment of acceptance and queer joy we have shared has made a difference. Thanks for giving me the courage to start to write characters who share those parts of my identity that feel most in need of being loved and seen through a kinder lens. You deserve all the happy endings.

For everyone who needs to see
that there is love and happiness ahead of us

Queer joy is our rebellion

Chapter One

Hannah shuffled back into the wardrobe, letting the soft fabrics drape around her. She allowed herself a moment to enjoy the sensation of being tucked away in a soft, quiet space apart from the world. The nest she'd built out of cushions in the bottom of the wardrobe meant she could rest comfortably for a while. Except she wasn't there to rest.

She reached out and tweaked the position of her microphone. The mic sat on a little coffee table inside the home-made recording cube she'd constructed out of a cat bed and foam—not an invention she could take credit for, though she'd tweaked the imperfect design from an online tutorial. It might not look professional, but she felt more secure having the expensive mic buried in its own little bed safe from clumsy limbs. Plus it did its intended job of improving her acoustics so she sounded professional. It was probably for the best that her audience never saw her set-up.

She glanced down at her printed prompt sheet again. She had a feeling she wouldn't need it for that episode's guest, but as she'd never spoken to them before, she couldn't really know. It was a struggle to get much out of some guests—or at least much relevant to the podcast—while others needed very little prompting to monologue on their area of interest. Experience had taught her not to do a pre-recording chat, as otherwise some of the best material could go unrecorded, and even with prompting some people were reluctant to repeat themselves. Though that wasn't something anyone ever accused her of.

It was time. She checked the silent fidgets were in place to her left, so she could stim without risking messing up the recording, and tested her sound levels. She could predict them from experience, but it was a calming routine, and the one time she didn't check it was bound to go wrong. She let her plosives pop and sibilants hiss naturally and was reassured she was far enough away that the mic didn't pick up too much of the excess sound. Maybe she should buy one of those mic guards, but whenever she tried researching online, the number of options and differing recommendations made her dizzy. It was safer to stick with her well-established system that had served her well so far.

A pop-up on the computer screen behind the mic-bed informed her that her guest was waiting in the lobby. Not that the lobby really existed, even in a virtual sense. It would be cool if she could create the illusion of one, with relaxing furnishings to help them feel at ease, instead of just an automatic message and whirling circle that might or might not indicate it was working properly. She stayed in position and clicked to let them in.

A round, smiling ivory face with short, asymmetrical spiky blue hair appeared on the screen. There was something about that smile that made her want to reach out and stroke the edges of it. She waited a few seconds for the audio to connect and checked her own presentation on the video feed before hiding it so she didn't get distracted by her reflection. She didn't usually worry about her physical appearance, more about whether she was giving the social cues she meant to and not projecting any emotions she shouldn't be. Including a desire to stroke her guest.

"Hi. Thanks so much for joining me."

"Glad to be here." Drew continued to beam at her, looking out of her screen with a keen gaze as if they were attempting to read her soul.

The volume of interest and all the potential insights Hannah could read in their eyes was overwhelming. Luckily, remote recording meant she could look at the camera instead and still seem like she was looking directly at Drew. Her family and friends accepted that wasn't the way she operated, but she only had one chance to connect with her guests and didn't want to risk them misinterpreting her lack of eye contact as lack of interest.

Which it definitely wasn't. This guest in particular had grabbed her interest from their first message and kept it in the flurry of emails that followed as arrangements were made. She'd even been curious enough to check out their socials—something she tried to avoid, as the rabbit holes social media led you down were not usually good for your sanity, though it was sometimes necessary when prepping for the show. Maybe the hours she'd spent scrolling through their commentary and studying clips of them to try to understand their draw wasn't strictly necessary, but it gave her some idea of who she'd be working with. Of course, the carefully curated and flattering content Drew chose to post didn't mean they'd hold up in a live interview.

"How are you doing? Any tech issues or anything we need to bear in mind?"

The second phrase proved useful in case someone thought it was a prompt to start their life story. Some questions were too open to give a clear idea of the type or level of information required, and time was limited.

"I'm good. Buzzing. This is my first official podcast interview, but I figure I'm in safe hands." Their rolling, drawn-out West Country accent became clear as Drew started to say more, but it wasn't so strong that anyone should have trouble following them.

Then the glint in their eyes, when Hannah dared to glance directly into them, made her wonder if that last part was supposed to be in some way flirtatious.

Don't get distracted. Sure, Drew was cute and queer, but that was not why she was talking to them. Well, the queer part was significant: That month's book was one starring a non-binary lead, the first she'd come across in mainstream fiction, and she was keen to get an insider perspective on record. Initial reviews from within the community showed a severe split in opinion, some rejecting it without even reading the book due to it being written by an outsider—a perspective she got, having been burned before, but that lacked the nuance and depth required to make an interesting episode. Drew's response had struck her as being from someone open to give the book a chance and who had read the whole thing with mixed feelings. In fact, they'd been the one to contact her asking to discuss it, apparently being an infrequent listener to her show and keen to take their opportunity to make an expert appearance.

It didn't matter that Drew wasn't famous, though their decent social media following could help give her show a boost from the queer community if all went well. She'd stuck with her pledge not to chase famous people but to carry on with her blog's structure of talking to real people about the realities behind the stories she consumed. It was part of the charm of her moderately successful show. You could hear from people you wouldn't hear broadcast anywhere else and could see yourself sitting across from her one day, as Drew was now.

While she fiddled with the settings to ensure Drew was also going to sound good on playback, she went through her introductory script, finishing with the most important part as far as her guests were concerned. "I will be editing afterwards, so if we go off track or you need to stop and try explaining something again, that's fine. And I will give you a chance to review the recording too. If there's anything you say that you wish later you hadn't, I'll cut it for you."

It was the massive plus of podcasting over live radio, which had always terrified her with its unforgiving nature and was part of why she'd only blogged until other options allowing editing emerged. In some ways recorded conversations were easier even than everyday life, where you couldn't so easily cut out an awkward moment or misjudgement and pretend it never happened.

"Ideal," Drew replied. "And if there's anything you think I shouldn't have said, probably best cut that too." Drew followed this with a laugh, which made it unclear whether that was a serious request.

It was a good sign that they didn't seem worried about how Hannah would spin things. She couldn't blame people for being suspicious, but if Drew trusted her, then they'd be more likely to speak freely.

"Same goes if I cut something you wish I hadn't. I don't want to misrepresent you."

She'd been nervous about this interview in particular, given the toxic mess the media tended to make of the topic of gender diversity, and she didn't want the trans community facing any additional backlash because of her. She didn't usually focus on representation of vulnerable groups, partly due to her fear of getting it wrong…and even if she didn't, it could mean exposing herself to mean-spirited internet scrutiny. She also didn't want to make Drew speak for all trans people or make out that was the most interesting thing about them. Of course, her guests were often from marginalized groups. Although Hannah didn't speak about her own queerness, she intentionally platformed members of her communities even when topics like gender, sexuality, or relationship diversity weren't the focus of conversation.

"I get that. But from what you've said and done so far, I think we're on the same page," Drew replied.

"Me too."

Hannah glanced down again to meet Drew's gaze and return their smile. The curve of their lips was enticing, and she found herself drawn in to the detail of their unpainted face. She preferred the look of someone wearing little or no make-up, so they always looked the same rather than like different portraits of themselves. A human face without pores or blemishes seemed eerie to her, like a mask that she couldn't peek underneath. Not that what Drew looked like mattered—it wasn't a video recording, and they were just there to talk about a book. Which was what she should be focusing on. Staying on track wasn't usually an issue for her, especially since she'd steered clear of any romantic entanglements following the disastrous end to her marriage. Books were a safer bet than people: You usually knew from the start whether you were being set up for a traumatic or happy ending.

She pulled her gaze away from Drew's face to the equipment they were wearing. It looked like standard earphones with a built-in mic, which should be good enough. The downside of recording remotely was not being able to control the guest's set-up, but at least Drew seemed to have taken her tips on board. There was a mishmash of fleece hanging from what she assumed was a clothes rail behind them, set up to dampen any echoes.

"I don't want to miss anything exciting, um, interesting you might say"—she fluffed her usual script but tried not to let that or Drew's smile throw her—"so I'll hit record now. We can do a little warm up before we start the book discussion, though."

"Go for it."

Hannah resisted looking for any additional non-verbal cues that might accompany their words. She needed to focus. "So, can you tell me about your day so far."

"What do you want to know?" Drew chuckled, a rich, enveloping sound, then continued before she had time to sink into it or overinterpret the question. "My morning started as it usually does, being woken up by the cat kneading me and aggressively purring in my ear. I don't know why I bother with an alarm clock, as whatever time I set it for, he decides is too late for his liking."

It was Hannah's turn to laugh, and she was left smiling. This was a guest that she'd have no trouble making entertaining, and she had a feeling it would be an interview she'd thoroughly enjoy. Not that she didn't usually enjoy them, but there was something special about Drew Barker.

❖

Drew pulled up behind Alex's van and jumped out to help her. She was dragging a large box out of the back that looked like a two-person job, and her sister appeared to show no intention of assisting. Phoebe was staring resolutely at her phone, large headphones hanging around her neck, and Drew could hear a faint blast of music as soon as they opened their car door.

"Here, let me." Drew took the other end of the box and most of the weight.

Alex didn't like people making a fuss, but she'd never fully recovered from the motorcycle accident that had crushed her leg, and she shouldn't be putting that much pressure on it. Drew was used to hefting around bags of soil and compost that were far heavier so probably could've carried the box alone but knew their friend better than to push it that far.

"Cheers," Alex grunted. "You gonna get anything, Bee?"

Phoebe peered into the van, put her headphones back up over her ears, and picked up one light-looking bag. Alex rolled her eyes but didn't protest any further. She had warned Drew not to let themself become Phoebe's willing servant while she was away, but everyone knew she ran around after her little sister whenever there was a hint Phoebe was in need.

"I thought you'd already moved everything in?" Drew started edging backwards towards the Hawthorn View flats. "Or does Salem not pack light?"

Alex laughed. "Nah, we took his bits in first, so he could get himself settled. He's not a fan of being in the van."

"As much as I'm team cat, if you wanted a furry friend who would be happy riding around with you, then you probably shoulda got a dog." Drew could say that while they were out of Pebbles's hearing—he probably wouldn't understand, but best not chance being massacred in their sleep for the slight.

"I'm happy with my choices. Dogs are too needy—I prefer a

housemate who can entertain himself and doesn't care too much what time I get home. Though I do wonder how he'll cope in a new place without me. He might just figure I've abandoned him, leaving him here for months..."

"I'm sure Bee will give him plenty of fussing and make sure he doesn't. And I'm here to make sure she doesn't forget to do the less fun parts."

The supported accommodation bosses had been unsure of Phoebe taking on responsibility for Alex's cat alone, in one of their recently refurbished flats, and Drew had been the obvious choice of a backup caretaker. Their own moggy might be suspicious when they came back smelling of another feline but thankfully wasn't too bothered about sharing them. Drew had long suspected Pebbles also had backup humans to ensure he wasn't neglected, and they were just happy he deigned to—mostly—reside with them.

"So what's all this then?" Drew had spied plenty more boxes and bags in the back of the van.

"Just some extra bits for the flat. She only had a single bedroom in her old place, and they don't provide anything more than the basics here." Alex narrowed her eyes at the block of flats ahead, as if she suspected the housing might be lacking in other ways too.

"Least that means she can put her own stamp on it and make it feel like a real home."

Alex smiled at that. "She was well excited about finally getting her own place, hence all the extra shit. I just wish I'd had time to help her get properly settled in before I took off, but Willow's dates are all booked"—Willow and Alex were a longtime couple—"so we couldn't delay. Maybe I should join her later instead and—"

"No way. You've been looking forward to the Europe tour for ages, and I'm sure Willow is looking forward to having a groupie with all the benefits going along with her." Drew flashed her a knowing grin.

The couple deserved some quality time together, as well as the chance to see other parts of the world. Phoebe would miss Alex—they all would—but she had plenty of other people in her life now to help out if needed. Including Drew, who was officially just there to help with Salem but knew Alex was trusting them to keep an eye out for any dodgy goings-on.

"Yeah, you're right. Willow would understand, but I'd still have a lot of making up to do, and I don't know if she could manage all the driving herself. We've planned to take turns to cover more ground."

"Glad you're not gonna try to be a hero and do it all yourself."

"I'll be sensible, I promise. When it comes to the driving anyway. I'm hoping to fit in some adventures along the way." She winked at Drew, finally getting into the spirit of things, then turned back to her sister. "You got the doors, Bee?"

Alex mimed turning a key to her. She probably couldn't hear anything with those headphones on.

Phoebe pulled out a key on the chain hanging from her right pocket and overtook them. So the chains weren't just part of her aesthetic.

She was in her standard rock-chick garb, including a band T-shirt that bordered on obscene. Phoebe wasn't the image you usually saw of someone with Down's syndrome, but Drew didn't look like people thought they should either, and it was hard to know who folk were double-taking at when out together. Phoebe's visible disability and style of dress might draw attention, but Drew's currently blue short hairstyle, multiple ear piercings, and unapologetically round belly and thick thighs turned heads Drew's way as well. It could be hard to tell whether the second looks were approving or not, but Phoebe didn't seem bothered, and for their part Drew liked to think at least some onlookers shared pride in their queer non-conformity.

The supported living flats were tucked down the end of a quiet residential dead-end street on the outskirts of town and didn't stand out among the other housing. There were apparently at least a couple of care staff on site, but the residents had their own keys and came and went as they pleased. Less promisingly, there were also no signs of the trees or hedgerows that lent Hawthorn View its name. Probably cleared out to build the place. Hopefully there were still some left standing in the fields behind—Drew hadn't taken a look yet, partly out of worry what the support workers keeping an eye on the place might think they were up to snooping around back. There were times when it would be handy to be able to go unnoticed.

As soon as Phoebe got her flat door open, a furry whirlwind streaked through the hallway and wound itself around all their legs.

"Hey, Salem." Drew manoeuvred around the black cat to dump the box before bending down to give him a scritch behind the ears.

Phoebe dumped her own smaller load, then plopped herself down on the sofa in the open-plan living area, and Salem rushed over to join her. It seemed he'd already accepted his change in caretaker.

"Are you gonna help us get the rest in, or do you want to make us all a cuppa? I've got time for one before I need to get going," Alex prompted.

"I'll make the tea," Phoebe said and dragged herself up with a dramatic sigh.

She still seemed to be adjusting to no longer living in a care home where most everything was done for her, having only just moved in fully thanks to a load of bureaucratic delays.

"I think it's quiet time soon, so we can't build the furniture now anyway. Though I'm not sure, what day is it?" Phoebe called over her shoulder.

Alex froze in the doorway, and Drew nearly bumped into her. She'd already turned to head back out, so Drew couldn't see her face, but her back had gone rigid.

"They have a set quiet time here?" Drew said what Alex must be thinking.

The point of Phoebe moving there was that she got full control over her own home and didn't have to follow restrictive rules, just with some care staff on hand in case she needed help with the more complex parts of independent living.

"Only my next-door neighbour. She makes a podcast, so I have to be quiet when she's recording. I don't mind, it's cool."

"Ah, that's all right then." Drew gave Alex's shoulder a squeeze to help ease her sudden tension, then grabbed for the lighter topic. "What's her podcast about?"

Seemed just about everyone had one these days. Maybe Drew should start one…if they could ever settle on a single idea for long enough.

Phoebe shrugged. "I dunno."

"Didn't you ask?"

"Not everyone's as nosy as you."

Drew laughed. "You got me."

They wouldn't have put it that way, but it wasn't the first time they'd been accused of nosiness. It wasn't that they wanted to know everyone's business for idle gossip, but how were you supposed to support and understand someone if you didn't know what was going on for them?

"And I did ask. But she said it's *a-non-y-mous*." Phoebe stumbled over the word with a hint of uncertainty. "That means no one's supposed to know it's her."

"Sounds a bit suspect. What do you think it's about?" Alex pressed.

"I dunno. I don't listen to podcasts."

Given Phoebe was planning around her neighbour's schedule, you'd think she'd have a little more curiosity. Maybe the podcast was something outside the status quo that the neighbour didn't want the support staff to know about. That was an intriguing thought.

"There's lots out there, mind. I bet you could find some you'd like," Drew said. "Speaking of, I was just interviewed for one."

"Really? You didn't say! What's it about?" Alex had finally unfrozen and shaken off whatever had stopped her in her tracks.

Drew must've forgotten to mention the recording to her with all the focus being on getting everyone ready for her big trip. At least it had shifted her attention off worrying about her sister's living situation.

"It's a books podcast—"

"You read?" Phoebe said.

The bookcase next to Phoebe contained well-thumbed copies of a number of YA series as evidence of her own ability. At a glance, they looked to be the more brutal kind.

"Yes, I can read! Okay, so it's not my first choice to sit quietly with a book. But I listen to plenty while I work."

"That doesn't count."

"Hey, don't be a snob," Alex told Phoebe, then turned back to Drew. "But I must admit, that's not what I thought you were into either."

She surely didn't mean it as an insult, and Phoebe was probably joking, but the comments hit a nerve. Drew might be a little paranoid about people looking down on them just because they hadn't been to college or university like most of their friends. Even if a lot of the queer people they knew seemed to have only gone as an easy way out of home and an opportunity to explore themselves. Drew wasn't sure how much academic learning was done there, but they definitely came out having learned some things.

"I'm not a snob." Phoebe stuck out her tongue at Alex.

"Good." Alex returned the gesture.

"Anyhow, I'm on the pod as their non-binary point of view. She likes to get someone on with real life experience to see how it tracks. I read the book. And I had thoughts."

"Cool. I'll have to give it a listen," Alex said.

"I'll send you the link. If it's any good."

It was the first time Drew had been interviewed on mic, and you never knew how you'd come through in the edit. It was why they generally stuck to their own socials—unedited, unfiltered—when they wanted to put their voice out there. Putting themself in someone else's hands had been a risk, but an exciting one with a chance to get a glimpse behind the curtain. At least there seemed to be chemistry between them and the host. There was nothing worse to listen to than an awkward interview where it sounded like the presenter would rather be talking to someone, anyone, else. Hopefully Matilda didn't regret choosing them.

CHAPTER TWO

Drew hadn't known what to expect. The recording hadn't just been their first podcast interview—it was also their first chance to catch sight of the elusive host who was behind it.

It had come around so fast. They'd sent their proposal on the spur of the moment after finishing the audiobook—okay, so Phoebe was right, they didn't usually *read*-read books, but they did consume plenty while at work and able to let the narration wash over them as they tended to the earth. They hadn't really expected a response, let alone enthusiastic acceptance.

Unusually, the podcast had no social media presence at all. Zero. They'd assumed it was an exaggeration when the host mentioned it, but on digging they hadn't found it on any of the usual platforms. There was just the podcast and an old-school blog—which might count, but the style of writing took you back to a time before social media was even a thing. There was also nothing about the creator online. Drew couldn't even find her real first name, and in emails she'd signed off with her pseudonym. There was no need for a deep dive to figure out why she'd called her bookworm alter-ego *Matilda*.

Despite their earlier fruitless search, Drew still found themself scouring the internet for clues in-between refreshing their emails—in case they'd missed the notification—to see if Matilda had sent the edited recording through yet. She had said to give her a week, and it had only been three days, but Drew couldn't wait to hear what they'd created together.

A furry face squeezed under their arm where they were nestled on the couch, nudging their scrolling finger away. Pebbles gazed, or more accurately glared, up at them while pawing at their thigh hard enough to distract them completely.

"He says cyber stalking is a crime," Leigh translated.

"It's not really. It should be, though, you're right." They scratched Pebbles behind the ears, as if he really did care about anything other than whether he was getting the attention he deserved.

"True." Leigh sighed and leaned over from the other end of the sofa to join in the fussing, resulting in Pebbles's purr rising to a deafening level. "In which case, you can tell me who without fear of punishment."

"I'm not stalking anyone."

Though if they had been able to find a trace of the real Matilda, how far would they have followed it? After meeting her, their desire to know more had ramped up from idle curiosity to something more intentional. Not that they had any set intentions, but they couldn't deny that their interest in her had reached new levels since seeing her in action. The image of her intense yet warm gaze was stamped in their mind as if they'd taken a picture and made it their screensaver. Which they hadn't—that really would be creepy.

Leigh waited them out. Having known them so many years, she knew full well that additional prompting wasn't needed to get Drew to spill the beans. Not that there were any beans to spill.

"Fine. I was just seeing if I could find out any more about the podcast host while I'm waiting for the edit to come through. But no dice."

"Ah, the mysterious Matilda. What was she like?"

Despite being married and living together, their busy lives meant it could be days before they had the chance to slump on the sofa together and catch each other up on the various goings-on in their worlds.

"She was…like she is on the pod. A bit bossier maybe, she's proper organized, not in a bad way. Very easy to talk to and seems genuinely passionate about what she's doing."

That wasn't a given. The amount of popular podcasts out there and the potential income stream meant there must be a risk someone could be in it just for the chance of fame and fortune.

"What does she look like? How you imagined her?"

Drew had tried not to paint a picture in advance so they wouldn't be thrown when they saw the real face behind the voice.

"She's cute," they admitted, not worrying how their wife might react. "Looks to be white and straight-sized. Long dark hair which she had in plaits—"

"Plaits? How old is she?" Leigh seemed genuinely shocked by this revelation.

Had Leigh ever worn plaits? Drew couldn't picture her chestnut curls ever being tamed to that degree, and back in their schooldays she hadn't had the chance to grow them out. Would she have had schoolgirl plaits if people had understood that was who she was, rather than the buzz cut that had tried and failed to make a man out of her? Back then, the two of them had often joked about trading looks, far beyond a basic wardrobe swap. Drew's look hadn't changed as dramatically as Leigh's since school, since Drew hadn't medically transitioned, but they were determined not to remember if their own hair had ever been forced into plaits.

"I dunno, maybe forty? Our age or thereabouts. Not everyone's a fashionista like you, mind. And they suited her." Drew jumped to her defence despite only having met the mystery woman once. They felt like they knew her better than the time they'd spent talking together justified.

"I'm sure they did." Leigh gave Drew a sly look but didn't ask any more about what they thought of her. "So, what happens now?"

"I spend the next week obsessively checking my emails until I get the edited recording from her. Then I have to check she's cut it in a way that doesn't make me sound like a monster before giving her the okay to post it."

"I doubt you have anything to worry about. She's not presented people badly before, from what I've heard."

"Oh, I'm not worried about her. I more want to check I didn't say anything that could get me into trouble."

"Good point. That is where it could all go wrong." She leaned over and gave them a kiss, softening the point.

"Yup."

They both knew Drew's big mouth could cause trouble without them ever meaning to—it was why Drew usually drafted posts off-platform, to give them a chance to reconsider before sending anything out into the world. There was enough toxic BS out there—they did not need to add to it. They did need to try to balance it with a more humane, real view, which was what they hoped they'd achieved. Getting heard and understood on a mainstream podcast could make more of an impact than all their personal posting, petition signing, and protest marching combined. It was torture waiting to find out if they'd done a good enough job.

"I'm sure you did great, my love. I'm proud of you." Leigh gave their arm a rub, then moved back to petting Pebbles before he could protest.

She might not be when the results came out. "You haven't heard what I did yet."

"Don't need to. I know how I feel about you. I always have."

Despite their continuing anxious wait, Drew's heart beat easier at the words. Leigh had always been wonderfully romantic and their staunchest cheerleader. And good at smoothing over any mess they did make.

"Thank you." Drew matched her sincerity and shuffled closer so they could wrap their arms around her.

Hopefully they would do her proud. Hopefully they would do all their community proud. Sure it was a high bar to set, but trans lives were on the line, and media rep had a big part to play. Drew couldn't let everyone down, including *Matilda*, who had taken a chance on them. Maybe she would even invite them back if they'd done a good job—it wasn't how the podcast generally worked, but they couldn't help fantasizing about the chance to see her again.

Hannah sliced through the packaging tape with great care and a satisfyingly smooth *whoosh*, then peeled back the cardboard flaps. Inside she found exactly what she'd been waiting for. The glossy cover was even more beautiful in real life. She traced the embossed lines swirling across it with the tips of her fingers.

"Is that the new Elliot Hall? Thank God, people will not stop asking for it." Her supervisor, Tracy, bustled in and broke the spell of the moment. "Make sure to check the pre-order list before you start putting them out. You can clear room and display them on the *New In* stand."

She walked out again before Hannah could respond.

Which was fine. It wasn't like she needed the instructions,

she'd been at Barnaby's Books long enough, though she appreciated confirmation of the system. She woke up the computer in the corner of the stockroom to check the list, even though she was pretty sure who would be on it. She'd fielded a lot of requests herself plus knew their regulars well enough that she could predict what they'd be interested in. She loved when she was able to give them news of an exciting new release, even better when she could show them it without them having any prior knowledge and watch their faces light up with glee, like small children being presented with an unexpected gift.

Then there were eagerly anticipated releases like this that their customers knew about before they even appeared on the delivery schedule. It would still be a pleasure to ring them up and give them the good news. This was done automatically by email, but when she found the time, there were some people who greatly appreciated that call—particularly some of her older and single customers who seemed to come by the bookstore for the real-life human interaction as much as the books. It was at least partly what kept Barnaby's open amidst the thriving internet book business.

Phone calls were not her forte, and she outright avoided them in other circumstances, given the unclear audio and lack of visual cues, but this was different. Once she had given the basic information in her usual script, then they just needed her to listen, without seeming to care how much of their monologues she was able to follow. The pre-order list contained half a dozen familiar names, plus several she didn't know and so could make do with the automatic notification. At the top was one of her favourites: a retiree who had devoted himself wholeheartedly to reading on a mission to make up for all the years when he was too tired after work to indulge.

She checked her watch. She should probably do the display first otherwise he'd have her chatting—or more accurately, listening—until the end of the shift, and her supervisor would have her staying late to get the shelves stocked. As much as she loved her job, she tried not to stay late given she was only on minimum wage and wouldn't get paid for the overtime. Though it was minimum wage plus massive discounts and the occasional free advance proof copy, which given her reading habit made up for the low pay.

Plus it meant she was kept in the loop about what everyone was talking about, without risking social media. The conversations in the shop provided inspiration for her podcast even when they weren't about books she would ever cover. Somehow she had managed to turn her passion for reading into a career, something neither she nor her parents had predicted when they'd argued over her spending her childhood with her head in a book away from the chaotic outside world. So much that happened in real life had no rhyme or reason, but in the stories she read there was always a reason. And a reckoning. While the world seemed to be drifting towards dystopia, inside the pages justice was served.

She itched to take a peek inside the new arrival, which promised to be full of wonderful adventures and satisfying truths, but reading on the job was a step too far. Despite the unlikelihood that the customers would judge her negatively for it, reading while on shift was explicitly against the rules. Before heading out front with the remainder of the box, she slipped a copy onto the desk and stuck a Post-it on it with her own name. The new friends it contained would wait for her.

It also meant someone would likely be kind enough to remind her to purchase it before she left. Sure enough, when she was doing the rounds at the end of the day, politely but firmly ushering people to the till or the door, her supervisor appeared and placed it by the till.

"You better get your purse before we cash up."

She tapped the book in what, if Hannah didn't know better, could've been read as impatience. Thankfully—though not for her bank account—Tracy encouraged Hannah to take full advantage of her discount. They'd developed an understanding over the years: Tracy kept a closer eye on everything that was out there, but read far more reviews than books, and Hannah brought the in-depth knowledge from fully committing to each text she opened.

"I'll be expecting your thoughts next week. I'd like to be able to put up a personal review as soon as possible, and I'm sure the regulars will want to discuss it with you."

"No problem."

Now she had it on orders, she wouldn't need to find an excuse to curl up with the novel instead of tackling her mounting chores. There had been no advance copies, for fear of leaks, so she'd been waiting for its release as eagerly as the rest of the author's fans.

The bus ride home gave her the opportunity to make a start, and she nearly missed her stop at the other end. Thankfully someone with a buggy clattered around for a while, propelling her out of the story, and she managed to rush off the bus before she was taken beyond.

As she opened the front door and started down the corridor, vaguely familiar voices grew louder. She froze, then shook herself: There was no real need to avoid her neighbours or the staff who supported them. When she'd first moved into the supported living block, she'd been wary of the other residents, especially after spotting emergency services vehicles parked right outside more than once on arriving home. It wasn't that she judged or feared them, but she didn't need to be pulled into someone else's personal crises and trauma while recovering from her own.

That was eighteen months ago, and she'd become more relaxed around the place, though not completely off guard. Her new neighbour who lived across the hall seemed nice and stable and had even brought round freshly baked cupcakes to introduce herself. Hannah hadn't asked too many questions, not wanting to be overly friendly and invite her in, but was glad to hear she'd moved in as a step-down from a care home. As opposed to a step-up for those no longer able to cope in a regular household without professional support and potentially on the verge of hospitalization. Hannah herself fell into that latter category, though she was always quick to point out that it was the breakdown of her toxic relationship that drove her there more than a personal breakdown. Not that there was a clear line between the two.

Her focus on not following her instincts to hide meant she clocked who the voices belonged to far too late. Not that she would've been likely to guess who her cupcake-baking neighbour was talking to, given how out of context they were, until she was facing them.

Drew, her last podcast guest, was inexplicably walking towards her with Phoebe. If she hadn't heard their distinctive accent, maybe she wouldn't have recognized them at all. Except it wasn't every day she was faced with a vibrant, blue-haired, plus-sized person who made her question everything society had taught her about what was beautiful. And desirable. Hannah stopped in her tracks and just blinked, suddenly understanding the phrase *rabbit caught in the headlights*. She was trapped in the path of their dazzling presence and could only wait for the inevitable, hoping she would survive. Which she clearly would, given Drew was coming towards her armed with nothing more than a bright smile. They also stopped and stared as recognition dawned in their eyes.

"Hi, Hannah." Phoebe appeared oblivious to her discomfort.

Or maybe she should give her more credit and assume she was trying to help bridge the awkward moment.

"Hi," she said, in a slightly strangled too high pitch. She cleared her throat and tried again, this time directing her greeting at Drew. "Hi."

Drew didn't respond straight away, instead screwing up their forehead in a cute expression of concentration. "Oh, hey. Didn't expect to see you here."

"Me neither."

It was a blunt response but the best she could manage, and at least she'd said something. In overpowering moments, speech had been known to completely fail her.

"I'm just visiting a friend." They gestured to Phoebe. "So, is this your day job?"

"Hmm?" It took too many seconds for her to process and interpret their mistaken assumption. "Oh no, I don't work here."

"Oh, do you have friends or family here too?" They said it with a smile and complete innocence, as if the real reason did not even occur to them.

She took a deep breath. Best get it over with, then she could retreat to the safety of her flat, the front door of which she focused on over Drew's shoulder, and process their unexpected appearance. And their response to her reality.

"No. I live here."

"Oh." The wrinkles on their forehead appeared again, and she couldn't help interpreting them as more judgemental than cute this time.

"Hannah's my neighbour, the one I told you about who does the podcast," Phoebe stage-whispered.

"*Oh...*" Drew let out a softer echo, the pieces seeming to click into place agonizingly slowly.

"Hang on, was I supposed to say that?" Phoebe turned to her.

"It's fine. Drew already knows."

It wasn't fair to leave Phoebe out of the dawning understanding.

"Hannah"—Drew pronounced her real name with a slight question mark, looking to her as if for confirmation—"is the podcast host who interviewed me the other day."

"Cool." Phoebe paused, then her face lit up with an eager grin. "Now I know what your podcast is!"

Usually this would concern Hannah, but she was relieved to have moved to a safer topic. "Just don't go telling anyone else that you know…or posting it on social media. Please."

"I won't. I can keep a secret." Phoebe mimed zipping her mouth closed.

Hannah laughed, mostly to relieve some of the tension in her body and the air. "Thank you. I trust my secret is safe with you." She turned to Drew. "And you."

They were the bigger risk in terms of breaking her anonymity, given the amount Drew interacted online and their link to her show.

"Of course. I wouldn't share anything you didn't want me to."

Drew seemed sincere, and hopefully her direct plea would prevent them leaking it as gossip.

"Thank you." Not knowing what else to say, Hannah pulled her keys back out of her pocket and let their jangle speak for her.

Drew understood that signal at least.

"Sorry, we're in your way." They moved behind Phoebe so she could pass. "It was good to see you again."

"You too," she mumbled, speeding past so that they couldn't read the mixed emotions on her face.

It was good to see them again. Or it would've been in different circumstances. Hannah didn't mind them knowing who she was—in fact, she'd idly daydreamed about telling Drew, so they could connect beyond the podcast—but she didn't want them knowing where she lived. At least not until they'd had the chance to get to know her first. Her living situation brought too many possible assumptions and judgements about what she was and could be.

She hadn't wanted Drew to look at her like they did—with that hint of pity and puzzlement in their kind eyes.

CHAPTER THREE

The problem isn't that it's a false picture—it is true of some non-binary people. The problem is that it's the only picture we see.

Drew smiled as they reread the tag line on the draft episode intro. It was a fair summary of what they'd discussed—it didn't tell you everything, but it was only supposed to be a taster. It would also work well for their own post sharing the episode and blog with the world. Which got their heart thumping as the release date grew nearer. They were really doing this.

They had only listened to the full cut once, which maybe wasn't enough, but it was too cringy listening to themself talk for that long. It wasn't like their voice made them shudder IRL, but when hearing it back on a recording, removed from the context of their body language and visual presentation, even *their* brain couldn't help classifying it as female. It wasn't a cause of soul-crushing dysphoria and they could cope with the thought of other people listening to them. It was more an uncomfortable prickling, giving the sense that something was not quite right. It wasn't like they wanted to sound male. It would be better if they couldn't so easily be put in one too small box or the other.

It was the same issue with their figure: Their full curves painted a picture that was considered too womanly to be seen as anything but female, unlike the slim androgyny that people were used to seeing in non-binary people. Drew had *umm*ed and *aah*ed about including a pic of themself, but the image Hannah had put together using it told the story. The thin, flat-chested, Hollywood-beautiful cover model was placed next to a full shot of Drew in all their fat, messy glory. Their well-worn gardening overalls showed off their soft underarms and did little to disguise their substantial chest but were baggy to accommodate their wide hips and allow them to move freely. Not every non-binary person looked like them either, but that wasn't the point. It had been hard to find a photo they were totally happy with, especially as they'd decided it should be unfiltered, unlike the professional print it would sit next to, but if they took a step back and imagined their younger self seeing it, then they couldn't not smile.

The blog was more comfortable to read, and Hannah had managed to pick out quotes that didn't make them sound like a judgemental arsehole or ignorant clown. She'd cut out their rambling and turned their contribution into clear points, using the balance of real-world lived experience instead of the so-called balance of some spiteful hypocrite who didn't believe non-binary people like Drew existed. Who believed they shouldn't be allowed to exist—it was the same thing at the end of the day. But Hannah had kept her word, and the opposing views she'd quoted were all from other non-binary people, which was fair enough. It should pass the online queer world's scrutiny, though it was hard to predict sometimes what would be taken out of context and wielded against you.

Drew still had a few days to review the edits. Truth was, they'd gone through it all on the first night and made their decision then. It wasn't the content that was holding them back, though they told themself that's what it was—they did need to be as sure as they could be that it was helpful rep. They tried to pretend it had nothing to do with how they'd humiliated themself and Hannah when they'd met afterwards in real life, in what they could believe was fate if it hadn't gone so badly. At least Hannah hadn't held it against them in a way that showed in her work, which could mean Drew was still redeemable in her eyes.

They reluctantly stopped scrolling and picked up their mug to slurp the remains of their lukewarm coffee. The temperature was a hint that they'd taken a long enough break.

Outside the sun was still peeking through the clouds, and the air wasn't yet heavy with the threat of rain. Hopefully they had another hour at least before the skies opened. It was the opposite problem to many of the pros they followed from the other side of the globe who battled dry soil and water shortages on a regular basis. They eyed the grey-tinged clouds above them. Drought was not something they need worry about on the little island of Great Britain.

A padded mat lay waiting for Drew in the middle of the patch they'd been weeding. They told themself it was more professional than kneeling in the dirt, though in reality they'd finally made the purchase to relieve some of the aching in their hips and knees. Sometimes they missed feeling the rough ground beneath their shins, but at least they could still press their bare hands into the earth.

Drew deliberately didn't don their gardening gloves before they sank to the ground and pushed their fingers into the soil. The earth welcomed them without judgement, not caring what they looked or sounded like, just how they cared for it. They sank into the earth and let go of the social scrutiny that followed them in the human realm. Their dirt-caked hands were strong and sure as they carefully divided weeds from the roots of intentional growth. They allowed themself to get lost in the quiet pleasure of tending to a world that didn't question their intentions, even if it didn't always grow according to their vision. There was only so much they could tame it, and when it rebelled, they didn't take it personally. They respected the freedom it claimed.

They kept digging until the air turned heavy with moisture and the first drops started to patter around them—time for another coffee break. The homeowner was out, but was one of their regular clients, so they were fine to help themself. There was a plate of biscuits and occasionally a freshly baked cake on the side waiting for them whenever they arrived. Like back in the day when they'd been a teenage babysitter. They'd managed to start both careers before any qualifications were required and always built business by word of mouth. They'd got enough clients that way to have a steady stream of work and not worry about potentially catastrophic online reviews. It seemed best to keep their business away from the reach of the trolls.

That day had brought the treat of a lemon sponge waiting for them on arrival. They hadn't been able to resist a bite before they started, and it was melt-on-your-tongue delicious, the sponge airy and the lemon tang balanced with sweet icing. They'd promised themself the rest of the slice later, and it was finally time to indulge. *Not that cake has to be earned.* Even they still had to remind themself sometimes that enjoying a sweet treat wasn't a wicked indulgence. Cake was cake, made to be eaten.

As Drew waited for the kettle to boil, they pulled out their phone to check their emails. There was a dating app notification waiting, and they clicked it absent-mindedly with no strong hopes. They kept a regularly updated profile on the most poly-friendly platforms but didn't spend much time on them these days. In fact, they probably hadn't looked through the deck of profiles on QSpark in several months, having grown bored of seeing the same faces pop up over and over—highlighting the insular queer and poly community.

The notification took them to a profile belonging to one of the key demographics: unicorn-hunters. Ugh. You'd think the couples searching for a hot bi babe to join them would at least check Drew belonged to that category before messaging them. Okay, so Drew kind of did, but their profile made it clear that they weren't all woman and they had no interest in cis men. They had dated some men when younger, but the only person it had really worked with had turned out to be a trans woman who just wasn't out yet, which said everything. Like their gender, their sexuality wasn't completely boxed in, but they'd gotten a good idea of who they wanted to be with. And it definitely wasn't a previously hetero-mono couple looking for a disposable selfless woman to broaden their horizons with some no-strings fun.

Drew reflexively started flicking though the stack of profiles, barely pausing to read the opening lines as familiar faces whizzed by, while they enjoyed their cake. Then they saw her and coughed on a crumb. Was her profile new, or had they just never paid attention, not knowing who was behind it? Surely they would've at least taken a peek: She was undeniably cute and a strong match as far as the algorithms were concerned.

Hannah's profile stated she was bi and non-monogamous. But she wasn't looking for a relationship, only flings or friends-with-benefits, which explained why Drew would have passed her by if they had ever come across her profile before. They weren't judging her for it, but that was not their style…they were notoriously no good at keeping emotional distance and had a tendency to fall hard for anyone they got intimate with. It figured Hannah was queer, given how many of her podcast guests were, and there had been speculation online.

Drew had been writing and scrubbing out emails to her, wanting to apologize for their cringeworthy ignorance when they'd bumped into each other, but fearing bringing it up could make it worse. At least they hadn't said anything offensive, or at least they hoped so, but they had blatantly jumped to the wrong conclusions. An email wouldn't allow for the kind of casual apology they wanted to make. If they could get to see Hannah again in real life, they could show her that they weren't that kind of judgemental arse usually and maybe find out more of her story. A low-key, planned meetup would be the best bet: one-to-one and unrecorded, on neutral territory.

It would be nice to have a real conversation. There would be no pressure, and both their profiles stated they were looking for friends as well as anything else. If Drew hadn't put her off getting to know them already.

Hannah needed a second opinion. Luckily, she knew someone else with an inside perspective who she could trust to tell her plainly.

Cass sat in the armchair in Hannah's living room, headphones on and legs curled up next to them on the squishy chair. Every now and then, they nodded or smiled or even laughed out loud. There were frowns too, and head shakes and sighs, and Hannah couldn't know if these were in agreement with or in opposition to what she and Drew were saying.

She could've played it out loud, but the idea of listening back to her own recording with someone was shudder-worthy. She wouldn't be able to help logging every facial expression as concrete judgement of her work and would have the urge to throw it all out and start again afterwards. Realistically, that probably wasn't necessary. At least she hoped not.

To distract herself while her friend finished listening, she checked her emails and read various virtual newsletters that she only got round to occasionally, though she enjoyed them when she did. The newsletters counted as research—she didn't do social media, but she did deliver a steady stream of mail to her own mailing list, mainly announcing the release of each new episode, and it was useful to see how others did it. Her newsletter seemed to get read, or at least opened, by the majority of subscribers, and it funnelled their responses direct to her. The podcast got a lot more feedback than her original blog ever did—most of it supportive, and sharing more insights and ideas—which became part of her research too. She'd ended up creating a separate account for the podcast to save her inbox overflowing and any other important mail getting buried in the avalanche. Not that she got important emails.

She was about to switch over to the podcast box to buoy herself up with the last episode's responses, when she spotted an email notification from QSpark. She'd dipped her toes into the world of dating apps following her divorce but, as she still wasn't ready to face another doomed romance, didn't check in often. The apps had brought her a few fun dates and one-night stands, and even a couple of semi-regular friends-with-benefits who also weren't looking for anything heavy. To be honest, calling them *friends* was a stretch as that signified a depth of connection beyond enjoying each other's bodies and the way they fit together. Whatever they were, they fulfilled her wants and needs in terms of her sex life, so she wasn't actively looking for anyone else to add to the mix.

Her finger hovered over the unread message. Was there any harm in looking? Curiosity enticed her to at least take a peek at whoever had sent the intro, even if she had no intention of replying. But what if she was tempted? Then it was worth remembering that she wasn't exactly overwhelmed with attention at that moment. Besides, it was probably just someone looking for an uncomplicated hook-up, or hopefully it was and they'd read enough of her profile to see that she wasn't after anything romantic. Not yet. Maybe not ever again.

It wasn't that she was expecting anyone in particular, but she definitely hadn't been expecting Drew's charming grin to pop up on her screen. For a moment she was sure she must be imagining it, being focused on their interview, and it was just someone vaguely resembling them. But no, not unless it was someone with the same first name who also had something to apologize for.

Hey, good to see you again. I realize I might have come across as a bit of an arse last time we met and want to recover both our senses of dignity. How about I buy you a coffee? No strings attached.

Hannah snort-laughed at the message, earning her a curious look from Cass despite the headphones. Cass had sensitive enough hearing that it took much more than that to protect them from disruptive sounds, a trait they had in common. At least Drew seemed to have read her profile properly and knew she wasn't looking to cultivate an attachment. Though that could've been their plan anyhow—*no strings* was hardly a distinct phrase, so Drew's use of it could be coincidence.

More than a little curious, she opened their profile. They'd seen hers, so it was only fair that she got to take a look. What she found was less unexpected: They hadn't explicitly said they were polyamorous in their interview, but they had used some common phrases that clued you in if you were familiar with the lingo. It seemed like every pocket of society had its own language and it had taken a while for her to get the hang of that particular segment's. Thankfully, she'd found podcasts to help and when she'd first discovered poly had binged them to the extent that she had felt part of the hosts' extended polycule. You had to watch out for those parasocial relationships. That was part of why she shared so little of herself, not wanting to encourage attachments she had no intention of reciprocating.

Drew was different, though. Weren't they? They weren't just some random fan that had tracked her down. They had met naturally, and Drew already knew more about her than most people. The fact that she lived in supported accommodation wasn't something Hannah usually chose to share. Most people didn't need to know, and it risked inviting overly personal questions she couldn't hope to dodge.

What story had Drew constructed for why she was there? Their incomprehension was understandable to some degree given the differences between Hannah and her neighbour. Unlike Phoebe's Down's syndrome, her autism was considered invisible, and some people didn't click no matter how much time they spent with her, unless they happened to witness a full-on meltdown. And the ones who got it straight away? Well, it wasn't coincidence that they were neurodivergent themselves. She glanced over at Cass, who seemed to have gone back to being fully immersed in the recording, the only sign of life a light rocking and twisting of the fidget they held in their lap.

There was no mention of neurodivergence in Drew's profile or any of the alternative terms people used to signal it. But one phrase did catch her eye. She was still unsure if it was a deliberate code for *I like autistic people* but indicated an interest in autistic-type communication at least: *I love hearing people talk about what they're passionate about.*

Most people she clicked with were neurodivergent, even if undiagnosed as such, but there was a small contingent who just liked her style of relating.

Drew's poly identity could do with a bit more explanation for her to be confident she understood where they were coming from. They described themself as Kitchen Table Poly which could cover a range of approaches from *I want all my partners to at least be on speaking terms* to *Everything must be decided as a group and your individual wishes are not so important* to *Welcome to our cult*. Not that it would be a date or she would end up being a part of that arrangement. But she liked to know the facts especially given her own experience in the polysphere. To be fair, her ex had already been controlling, and opening up their relationship had only given that side of her more room to shine. She shuddered and refocused on Drew's pics before she fell down that dark memory hole.

She was still gazing at Drew's profile when Cass finally removed their headphones and rejoined her in the moment. She met their eyes briefly, then scanned their face for further sign of what they thought, while unintentionally holding her breath.

"It's great. And you picked a charismatic guest. They were a good choice. I love the realness of their perspective, they seem…genuine."

Hannah let out her breath and sank back into the sofa. The tension from waiting for Cass's judgement dissipated into the soft cushions. She could always trust Cass to get to the point and tell her what they really thought, not try to bury their true opinions under layers of social niceties which delayed understanding. Sometimes she wished she lived somewhere more invested in honesty and less obsessed with what was considered polite.

At least she still had Cass living close by to call on when she needed someone to speak with, unfiltered. Though Cass's housemates meant it wasn't easy to hang at theirs, and Hannah inevitably played host. Which wasn't a problem but didn't encourage her to leave her flat as much as she maybe should, according to the support staff anyway.

"Yes, they were great." She glanced down at Drew's image on her tablet, noticing a warm feeling spreading as she let herself remember how much she'd enjoyed their conversation. "Anything you think needs cutting? I struggled to get it down to the usual length, they had so much interesting stuff to say, but I can easily cut or swap—"

"No," Cass didn't hesitate to answer, "I love it as it is."

"Thanks." Hannah ducked her head and smiled, not used to taking complements face-to-face.

"Thank you. I really am glad you're doing this. We need the boost."

Cass wrapped their arms around themself as they spoke and gave themself the literal hug that she hoped her contribution felt like.

"I was glad to have the chance. I can't take the credit—Drew approached me with the idea, though I was very happy that they did."

"I did wonder about that. So, what were they like? Were they as charming in real life, or did you just pick the best bits?"

Hannah felt the warmth rise to her cheeks and hoped Cass wouldn't notice. "They were just like that, no editing needed."

Unlike some of her guests who she'd struggled to get enough decent snippets of to fill an episode. If they were all like Drew, it would make her job easier, in some ways. But it had been genuinely tough to cut any of Drew's contribution, and she'd spent hours more than usual re-listening to parts and trying to force herself to make choices. Because Drew wasn't like her other guests. There was something more... appealing. She glanced down at their profile. Was it something worth investigating? She didn't usually meet up with her guests afterwards, but plenty of hosts were friends with theirs, and Drew had gifted her the excuse. Maybe she could make an exception for them.

CHAPTER FOUR

It was release day. Drew had been twitchy all morning, even though Hannah had told them the episode wouldn't go live until four p.m. They hadn't been able to settle to anything and had ended up in their back garden, trimming and weeding to help the hours pass. It was a good thing they'd arranged to see Rebecca, otherwise the garden might have ended up bare by the time four finally came. Instead of stripping the flowerbeds, Drew could focus on supporting Rebecca.

"What do you wanna do today?" Drew couldn't make that decision in their distracted state, but hopefully Rebecca had an idea.

"Maybe just lounge around here? Ishani is away for the weekend, and I don't fancy heading out." Rebecca snuggled into their side, clearly intent on staying there.

"Sounds good to me."

Though going out might be more of a distraction, Drew never liked to turn down the opportunity to be home alone with their non-nesting partner. It was the practical side of their polycule that tended to be most difficult to manage. As they both lived with other partners, alone time required advanced planning and coordinating multiple calendars. Luckily Rebecca seemed to enjoy the organizational side of things.

"There's a new series of *Sex Education* out, we could watch that."

"Ideal. I thought you might want to watch it, so I've been resisting starting without you."

"Aw thanks, sweetie." Rebecca twisted round in their arms to plant a gentle kiss.

"My pleasure."

It was nice to have things that were specifically theirs as a couple to share together. Plus Drew had guessed a box set marathon might be all Rebecca was in the mood for.

Rebecca's phone buzzed, and Drew felt her tense, but she made no move to reach for her mobile. Drew laughed gently.

"You can check that. I don't mind."

"Are you sure? I know we don't usually do phones, but Alex said she'd message me when they arrived at their next stop safely."

Drew shifted to allow her to sit up. The phone thing wasn't meant to be controlling, just that considering they only got to see each other once or twice a week, time together was precious and carefully cordoned off.

"No worries. I guessed it was her. Say hi from me."

They'd received updates from Alex themself, though probably not as many as Rebecca who had developed a deep romantic bond with Alex, despite swearing she wasn't interested even after everyone else had figured out where things were headed. She was clearly missing Alex terribly already, and it was going to be a long couple of months before she returned. Then Drew might not get to see Rebecca for a spell while the lovebirds made up for lost time.

"She's arrived."

Rebecca twizzled her phone to show Drew the shot of a picturesque Spanish vista with a sun-kissed Alex and her other partner, Willow, in the foreground. Rebecca smiled to herself as she composed a reply.

"Great." Drew grabbed the TV remote while Rebecca tapped at her phone and set about cueing the programme. "So, how much are you missing her on a scale of one to ten?"

It was obvious in the way she'd been moping about, but Rebecca hadn't talked about it. At least not to Drew—maybe she didn't want to burden them with talking about her longing for someone else. But they could take it. Alex had become a close friend of theirs, even while she and Rebecca had still been dancing around their clearly mutual attraction, and it was a relief when they'd both finally admitted to their feelings and gotten together. Drew had struggled not to push them and might have overstepped the line a couple of times, but who could blame them? Everyone could see the sparks flying, and there was only so long they could all live in denial-land.

Was that what it was like for monogamous couples if one of them fell for someone new? Were you permanently stuck in that place unless you made the tough choice of ending a relationship or slipping into a non-consensual affair? Drew was lucky to have discovered poly early and to have never been in that position themself. They couldn't be doing with the secrecy and lies, and couldn't stop themself falling hard and fast when they met someone who ignited *that* feeling.

"Um, seven?" Rebecca glanced sideways at Drew before burying her head in their shoulder and whispering, "Eleven."

Drew chuckled and held her close. "You got it *baaad.*"

"Yep," Rebecca mumbled.

"So has she, mind."

"You think?"

"I know. She's on the adventure of a lifetime with her long-term lover, yet she still hasn't stopped texting you."

"True." The edge of a smile peeked out from Rebecca's buried face.

"One hundred percent. It's a good test, seeing if you're still interested after a few months apart. Not that I ever doubted it of either of you."

"Yeah."

Rebecca clearly wasn't in a talkative mood, but she never had been one for thinking out loud, unlike Drew. They tried not to push her too much, but at the same time…it wasn't great for her to internalize everything, and they needed to know where her head was at.

"She'll be back." They planted a kiss on Rebecca's head. Then their train of thought was interrupted by the buzz of their own phone. They sought out a clock, despite knowing there wasn't one in their living room, needing to check if they'd reached four p.m. finally.

"You can get that," Rebecca said but didn't move from her place resting against them. "I know I'm not a great date right now."

"You are always a wonderful date. But I will check as it might be about the podcast. My episode's out today."

"That's today? Why didn't you say! You should be out celebrating, not moping around with me."

"I'm fine here. You're the best distraction from sitting worrying how people are gonna take it."

"I'm sure they'll love it. Unless they're determined not to, and in that case there's nothing you could've done. Anyone with an open heart will love you." Rebecca sat up as she took her turn to provide reassurance.

"Thanks, lovely." They accepted her kiss, then reached over to check the notification.

It wasn't about the pod, at least not directly. Probably. It was from QSpark, saying they had a message from the host. They went to open it, then paused, remembering who they were with. Looking at a dating app while on a date with someone else surely wasn't cool, whatever your relationship style.

"What does it say? Is it bad news?" Rebecca gave their thigh a squeeze. Their hesitation must've been visible.

"No. It's not to do with the pod."

At least they assumed not. Surely Hannah would still contact her through Matilda's official channels if it was.

"If it's something you need to deal with…"

"It can wait."

Drew wouldn't want to appear too eager by replying straight away anyway. Though they'd never been any good at waiting the prescribed time before replying to messages from a potential date, especially given the app was sitting there on their phone and it would be so easy. Not that Hannah was a potential date. She was a potential friend, and it was best not to contemplate anything different. They didn't need to be getting carried away with their imagination. Hannah's profile made it clear that she wasn't looking for any romantic relationships, and Drew's made it clear that they were no longer interested in casual hook-ups. So sex and romance were not on the cards. Which was fine. It really was.

The numbers were good. Really good. It was two days post episode drop, and the listens were already above most episodes and still climbing. Plus the responses had started pouring in. Thankfully almost entirely positive—it might have helped that trolls didn't seem so into email, presumably as it lacked the attention they sought, and they also didn't have the sense to be subtle about the purpose of their emails, so even Hannah could bear to delete them without reading and let the spam filters do their job. If she looked for it, she could probably find people having a tantrum somewhere online about the subject matter, but she'd learned long ago not to go there.

Besides, the emails she received were much more her style in terms of length and depth, as they gave her more than a throwaway comment to make sense of others' perspectives. There were suggestions for other LGBTQIA books and characters she could cover, and she was soon compiling a spreadsheet. Replying to all the emails was already looking like an immense task. She should give each a personal response—especially given how heartfelt their missives were—but the week would be overtaken. For once, it was a good thing it wasn't all down to her. It soon became apparent many messages were more aimed at and better answered by Drew, so after checking permission, she'd started to forward the majority on. It had left her a little twitchy, but Drew was copying her into their replies and proving perfectly capable of handling the correspondence.

How much of the episode's success was down to Drew? It wasn't just the book or topic people were responding to—it was their nuanced take and easy charm. There was no judgement or gatekeeping from them, and they'd been quick to point out that not everyone would relate to any single specific portrait of an enby. It had been tempting to follow the track into critiques of anti-fat and weight loss culture, but that hadn't been the focus for the episode or in the book they'd covered. Maybe they could pick up that thread another time.

As she scrolled through the podcast inbox, pulling out more messages to pass on, her phone buzzed with a notification. It was the star of the show. She smiled as she opened the pic of a ginger cat stretched over Drew's lap, almost completely masking the book underneath him.

This is why I don't read so much.

This is why I don't have a cat. Hannah paused, then added a winky face before sending her response.

Having initially messaged through the dating app, she'd prompted them to move to WhatsApp sooner than usual after the first exchange. Drew already knew where she lived, so it was hardly risky to give them her phone number, and QSpark wasn't for platonic conversations, as far as she was concerned anyway. Cass had pointed out that she didn't need to make excuses. If she wanted to connect with Drew, then she should do so.

And she did want to. It just wasn't that simple, as the flutter in her chest reminded her every time a message from them popped up on her screen. It was important she not give them the wrong impression and lead them into thinking that their upcoming coffee date was anything other than a literal coffee. Or tea, in her case. It wasn't that she was in denial about her attraction—it was that she wasn't looking for any kind of romantic entanglement, and Drew's profile made it clear they wouldn't be satisfied with a sex-only or even friends-with-benefits type arrangement. And Drew's connection to her next-door neighbour and podcast meant there were already strings attached. Which brought the risk that, even if she and/or Drew didn't want to see each other again, they might not have the option to slip out of each other's lives entirely.

The dread that overcame her when considering that lack of escape route was something to explore with her therapist.

Maybe once the episode was out and her audience had moved on… maybe then there could be options. But at that moment, the only thing on the table was a friendship of the purely platonic variety. Besides, there'd been no further mention of the awkward misunderstanding at the centre of their previous in-person meeting, and who knew what conclusions Drew had ended up drawing. It was tempting to check and explain her situation by text, without the pressure of eye contact and the need for instant responses, but it might make it into an even bigger deal. Better wait for it to come up in natural conversation—something she found herself scripting in idle moments.

Not that she'd had many of those. Hannah had developed a strict schedule for podcast work after it had quickly become apparent that podcasting required far more hours than those she spent on the mic. She usually gave herself a week post-release date to respond to feedback and enquiries, including confirming details for the next recording, and—in theory—a rest after a week of intense editing. Sometimes, especially early on before she'd picked up many listeners, she got that rest, but this month she would be lucky if she finished reading through the mail. It was a good thing her day job wasn't too intensive, though there were still only so many hours in the day.

When she'd first moved to Hawthorn, after her breakup, she'd been extremely glad of something to fill the long hours spent alone in an unfamiliar place. The podcast had allowed her to bury herself in work and books, without too much time to think about how it all went wrong. Time was something she was keen to fill, and her weekly therapy sessions were when she stopped to process in the safety of a professional's presence. Since then, it had got easier to trust her mind not to wander into any dark caverns she couldn't find her way out of alone, and the therapy had become a fortnightly check-in to help ensure she wasn't just avoiding any issues that could still arise with the right trigger.

When she'd mentioned Drew to her therapist, she had instantly regretted it, as Min had leaned forward in her seat with interest. But there was no need to make a big deal out of it. It wasn't like she hadn't been on any actual dates recently, though fitting them in was hard, even when she had the urge, and it was a good thing she'd not ended up making any big commitments. Min had brought up the whole work-life balance idea, but the podcast wasn't her work. It was her life, even if that hadn't been her initial intention, and that wasn't about to change. Hopefully. The show was unlikely to go on forever but definitely wasn't at the point of winding down, and she had no wish to push it in that direction.

She glanced at the clock, and her breath hitched when she processed it was already one o'clock. Where had the whole morning gone? She was supposed to be meeting Drew at two, taking advantage of her day off to make their meetup a more casual time of day. It also meant if they wanted to hang out after their coffee, she wouldn't have to worry about leaving enough time to wind down properly before bed and an early start. Or any misinterpretation about what *coffee* meant— she had learned the awkward way that at night an invitation for coffee was not to be taken literally.

Drew had named the meeting place, and Hannah had managed to pop in and scope it out a couple of days before, as despite being only a little way out of the town centre, she'd been unaware of its existence. She did tend to stick to known favourites, but maybe it would become one. The coffee shop was big enough that they should be able to sit well enough away from the obnoxiously loud coffee machines, which made it sound like you were in some kind of steam-punk factory. The plush sofas and chairs would provide some assistance with absorbing background noise, or at least not make any more through rattling frames and squeaking legs as they were pulled in and out. The lights were cushioned by floral lampshades that looked like they belonged in another century but were an improvement on modern too bright strip lighting that required personal protective equipment. It should do nicely.

The outfit she had picked out was hanging on the back of her bedroom door, waiting for her. As she headed to the bathroom to shower before slipping on the clean clothing, she stroked the soft fabric for reassurance. If only clothing wasn't expected to say so much about who you were and wanted to be and could just be about simple comfort and protection. Drew might not pay any attention to what she was wearing, but she'd still picked out the cardigan that best brought out the colour of her eyes and gave her pale skin a warmer look. Well, Cass had picked it out, seeing Hannah was struck by decision-making paralysis, and they kindly managed not to mention that Hannah didn't usually worry about what to wear when meeting a friend.

It was a good thing they had, as she was at risk of being late as it was. Being slightly late was usually socially acceptable, but she didn't want Drew thinking she had stood them up. She was looking forward to seeing them and turning the many messages they'd exchanged into a deeper conversation. There was so much they'd not had the chance to dive into during the podcast discussion, and she planned to take full advantage of the opportunity to follow up on the many paths left unexplored. It would be interesting to get to know more about Drew, and not just their experience of gender—there was of course more to understand about their relationship with their body, and about their body, but she would only need to know about that if she was going to have sex with them. Which she wasn't, so didn't need to ask. Or imagine.

Drew got home just in time to decide between a shower or lunch. They chose the shower after taking one look at their dirt-streaked and sweaty appearance in the mirror. Even though it wasn't a *date*-date, they couldn't show up looking like they'd made minus effort for Hannah.

The steamy shower also drained away some of the aches of a morning of hard labour. They were glad to have a physical job where they could be outside instead of stuck sitting in a dull office, but they weren't a spritely twenty-something any more and needed to readjust their limits. Or just get some—their days of working until they were worn out seemed to be coming to an end, if they wanted to be able to get up in the mornings without groaning. Like they were now as they let the shower massage their lower back and hips. Reluctantly, they slammed the water off and nearly took the shower curtain with them as they stumbled back out of the tub.

By the time they reached the wardrobe, the bedroom clock was insisting they would be late. Drew grabbed a casual shirt and smart joggers—the closest thing they could find to casual trousers in their size—and checked their reflection briefly. No, something wasn't right. They didn't have time to mess about, but they dragged the top and sports bra back off and opened the wardrobe again. The binder they pulled out was a light beige that wouldn't show through the cotton shirt. They wriggled into it with practised patience and layered their outfit back on top. That was better. They smiled at their reflection as they smoothed the shirt down over the single curve of their torso, their chest flattened down to meet the rise of their stomach without any straining buttons. Okay, now they really were late. A quick squirt of hair gel and dodge of Pebbles, who seemed to assume they'd come home to entertain him, and they were out the door.

When they arrived, Hannah was already seated in the back of the cafe. She had a book in her lap and didn't seem to notice Drew's arrival. Unless that was her way of making a point. They had texted her with their ETA, and she'd claimed to be fine entertaining herself with the book she inevitably had in her handbag. They stayed in the doorway gazing at her as she fidgeted with one plait, engrossed in the page in front of her, wondering whether they should go over and interrupt or join the queue at the counter. And trying to ignore the squeeze in their chest that had nothing to do with the stiff fabric hugging it.

"Excuse me, mate." Someone bustled in behind them and broke the spell.

It did mean Hannah finally looked up, and on seeing Drew she broke out a warm smile that made them move towards her without further thought. She was wrapped in a cosy-looking cardy buttoned over a loose tee that added to the librarian look. In a good way, a her way. She was probably still a few years away from reading glasses, but they could imagine her slipping a pair out of one of the deep pockets to balance on her nose.

"Hey." Drew lifted a hand in a half wave as they reached her.

They'd failed to check if she was a hugger, and it was best not to risk making her uncomfortable with possibly unwanted physical contact, especially after putting their foot in it repeatedly on their last meeting.

"Hey." Hannah echoed their greeting, then slid a bookmark into her novel and closed it but didn't put it away. Instead she laid it in her lap, lightly clutching it as if it was a talisman.

"What are you reading? Is that next month's book?"

They took a seat on the sofa opposite, relieved Hannah had chosen the spacious sofas rather than leaving Drew to squeeze themself into a small armchair or ask to move to better seating. It was one of the reasons they choose that cafe—plenty of wide seats so they didn't have to worry about finding one they could relax on.

Hannah scrunched up her eyes for a moment before replying. "Oh, for the podcast? No, it's just for me." Her fingers stroked the glossy cover. "I read next month's before confirming with the guest, though I'll re-read to review it before the interview so it's fresh in my mind."

"You read them all twice!"

How did she find the time? Drew struggled to squeeze in any reading regularly, though to be fair it wasn't something they usually made an effort to prioritize. Book reading, anyway—they managed to spend plenty of time reading posts and articles online, but that was easier to dip in and out of without losing track of who everyone was and where they'd got up to. Was Hannah someone who'd consider listening to audiobooks cheating? They were probably better off not knowing—there was always the risk of discovering something off-putting when getting to know your idols. Though so far the woman behind Matilda had not been a disappointment.

"I try to. And don't you find when you read a book again, knowing how it wraps up, you notice threads that you didn't consciously the first time? I always think that's the sign of a good book, when you get more from it the second time around."

"You're right." Drew couldn't help smiling at the passion in Hannah's voice and the way she hugged her book to her chest as she spoke. "And the bad ones?"

"I don't like to label any that way, but I'll admit the opposite can be true. You read it again and spot all the ways it doesn't add up."

"I've been there, or at least from flipping back and going *hang on a minute*."

Hannah laughed. "I don't know that I could do any better. At the writing, at least. I always have had an eye for picking up on others' mistakes."

"I bet that made you popular." It was out of their mouth before they had the chance to predict Hannah's wince.

She quickly covered it up with a wry smile. "I've learned to rein it in, or at least not point out errors without invitation."

"You're clearly meant for a career as a critic. Those guys don't seem to worry about reining it in." Drew managed to twist their fumble into a compliment and was glad to see the tension sink back out of Hannah's shoulders.

"Or being popular," she added. "I wonder if their acquaintances all fear their sharp eyes and words, or if they're complete sweethearts in real life."

"You've got a better imagination than me. I can't picture them as anything other than snobby, arrogant, well-off, cis het white men. But maybe that's my outdated view."

Hannah laughed at that, a delightful tinkle that seemed to surprise her when it escaped from her mouth and surprised Drew with the warm tingle it sent through them.

"I need to get a drink." Drew stood up to deliberately break the spell. They had settled down and started talking without realizing they'd skipped that step of their coffee date. "Can I get you a top-up?"

There was a moment's silence as Hannah studied her nearly empty cup, seeming to do some kind of calculation of whether she wanted another and possibly whether she wanted to owe Drew one.

"No pressure to buy the next round. I invited you, and I owe you for letting me on your show."

"You don't owe me anything," Hannah countered, "but thank you," she continued in a softer tone.

"So, is that a yes? Same again?"

She nodded. "Just a pot of regular tea, please."

"No problem."

Drew joined the queue at the counter and looked over to see that Hannah had re-opened her book. They pulled out their phone, which they hadn't checked since sending their last message to her, saying when they'd get there.

The only message waiting for them was her reply. They opened it to view the attached image: a selfie of Hannah sitting on the sofa, declaring she was here and making herself comfortable. Without overthinking it, they clicked on the image and reacted with a heart.

Hannah must've been keeping an eye on them as she'd tucked her book away before they got back to the table. As they laid the tray down, they noticed something glinting inside her ear. It didn't seem to have any tech involved to make it a hearing aid and could be mistaken for jewellery, but they'd seen neurodivergent friends wear—and discuss— similar before.

"They're ear plugs with filters to take down the background noise." Hannah must've caught them looking.

"Soz, didn't mean to stare. I guessed that was what they were. Some of my autistic friends rave about them."

"Yeah, they can make a big difference to us."

So that confirmed their hunch, or at least part of it. "Tell me to butt out if it's none of my business, but is that why you live at Hawthorn? Because you're autistic?"

"Yes. Well, partly. I only moved in after a bad break-up that left me in a difficult place." She poured a stream of steaming tea and, still looking down, added, "Mentally and practically."

"That makes sense."

There was clearly a story there, but they should resist prying too much given they were barely more than a stranger still. It did potentially explain something else too, though, and they couldn't resist following that other hunch.

"I guess that explains why you're taking a break from romance too," they said, then hurried to add, "unless you're aromantic and just not into it at any time."

Hannah smiled, but it was a sad, lopsided expression that tugged at their heartstrings. "Yeah, it does. I'm not aro, and maybe one day I'll be ready to put myself out there again—but not yet."

It was good to know why she was taking that stance, not so Drew could wait for that day, of course, but so they could try to avoid putting their foot in it and accidentally triggering some unhealed trauma.

"Well, I reckon that's sensible. If only more people took the time to work through their shit before diving into another relationship, there might be a lot less trauma to pass around. Not that I expect anyone to not have baggage going in, we've all got a past, but at least knowing what you're carrying can make all the difference."

"Definitely. I learned that lesson the hard way."

"At least you've learned it." They lifted their mug and raised it towards her. "Here's to lessons learned the only way they truly stick."

Drew had always tried to learn from others and had got a lot from the poly community, but there were some things that you could only take to heart if you'd been there. They tried not to repeat the mistakes of those who'd thrashed it out beforehand. They really did. It was just that it was so much easier to advise *others* and see clearly where they were going wrong. Like warning someone to guard their heart from a captivating woman who was clear from the start that she had no intention of letting them into hers.

Chapter Five

A argh!" Hannah pushed her phone aside and flopped over her desk, pressing her forehead into the cool wood.

"Grr...aargh. Grr...aargh," she repeated, the simple words and echo of an old favourite programme soothing her triggered brain. She let herself stay there for a few minutes, letting the pressure of the smooth wood contain her thoughts and stop her spiralling. She had to go to work soon—she did not have time for a total meltdown.

This is why you give yourself all this time. She turned her head to watch as she traced the patterns of the wood grain with her right hand. As much as you prepared, late-notice changes were something you could never entirely avoid. She'd had a prickly feeling about the upcoming guest even before they cancelled, perhaps picking up on signals that he might not be taking it entirely seriously. She should've trusted her gut instinct and called it off herself instead of waiting for him to let her down.

Her phone buzzed briefly and sent the vibration through the wood into her head. Despite the bad news weighing her down, her chest still gave a little flutter as she reached across to see who was messaging her, and a little more when she saw it was Drew.

Hey, how's things. It was good to see you yesterday :) Maybe we can do it again sometime x

At another moment it would've made her smile, but it did at least make her lift her head off the desk to attempt a reply.

It was good :) I would like to do it again, when I have the time. Things are less good today. My next guest just cancelled :(

Typing it out made her predicament just seem more real, and she almost slumped back down again. Instead, she forced herself to get up and dragged herself over to the kettle. She just about had time for another cuppa before her shift started and she wasn't going to be able to force down a full breakfast now. She stepped away once she'd turned on the kettle. Its escalating rumble would grow too much for her in that state.

*That's rubbish. Need me to go sort them out for you? *strong arm emoji* ;)*

The emoji made her ninety-five per cent sure it was a joke. It did make her smile, once the images that flashed up in her brain of what *sorting them out* could mean had passed and she pressed down on the message to laugh-react. It wasn't exactly representative of her response, but overdramatic emoji made it clear how things were to be taken, so she worked with the system.

So what's plan B? Do you have someone else lined up?

She did have a list of potential books, a few with names attached, but didn't know what or who to bring forward. Her brain was overwhelmed by the detailed web of all the possibilities and knock-on changes that she'd have to make.

Not exactly.

Her brain also wasn't up to putting that into words and explaining it fully to anyone else.

*What about all the suggestions of queer books you got after our episode? Maybe we could do a mini Pride series! It is the season *rainbow emoji**

It was a good suggestion and worth proper consideration, once her melty mind was up to it. The emails and book nominations had continued to flood in since the episode went live, and the accompanying blog post's comments had turned into a recommendations list. Some contained suggestions of guests to go with them too.

The *we* in Drew's message needled her—were they imagining guest-hosting the whole series or helping her put it together in some capacity? It was one thing to consider Drew's ideas, but that didn't mean she wanted to make them an ongoing part of the show. She didn't have recurring guests and had deliberately chosen not to bring a producer or anyone else on board, despite acknowledging that would make it more manageable in some ways, because the lack of full control and introduction of office politics didn't seem worth the trade-off.

That might work. I'll have a think. Thanks.

It hopefully came across as grateful, and still non-committal enough to not hurt Drew's feelings. The idea of doing more episodes with them was tempting given how well they bounced off each other. It was unusual for her to establish that good rapport with someone, especially on a personal level, so quickly. But if she did decide to go with the series, she would need to make it clear first how much she did and didn't want Drew involved.

The kettle clicked off, and she went back into the kitchen to pour her drink. She breathed in the steam that rose from the cup. She would need to leave soon, but as she was on closing duty, she didn't have to get to work early to open up the shop. She could afford to take a moment to lie down and let more of the strain dissipate. Drew's support had taken an edge off, but she still needed to give her brain the chance to process and get back on track. She grabbed her weighted blanket and headed back to her bedroom.

These things happened, and maybe it would turn out to be a good thing—the Pride concept was already starting to take root and flourish in her imagination. Once she emerged from her blanket cocoon, she could consider it properly. And once she'd managed to get herself out to work and through the day. She settled the heavy fabric on top of her and let the deep pressure work its magic. It smothered the fire shooting through her mind which threatened to melt all the connections and encouraged her nervous system to calm down and recognize it wasn't a life-threatening situation. The tea went cold on the nightstand.

When she made it to work, fifteen minutes late and still not up to making eye contact, her supervisor clocked without needing an explanation that it was one of those days and put her on stocktake duty. It didn't officially need doing as the stock database was automatically updated by sales on the tills, but it was useful to check manually from time to time. Useful and soothingly simple, what Hannah needed to help regulate herself. The task was a welcome distraction from her messy thoughts, as it came with clear instructions and a straightforward system. It was up for debate whether any missing books were due to thievery or accidental errors on her colleagues'—and maybe even her own—part, but she tried not to worry herself with that part of the equation. It wasn't her job to figure out why.

She managed to pass the majority of the day that way, working methodically through the shelves and noting any discrepancies. The tablet she used for the task thankfully behaved itself, so she didn't have to juggle piles of paper and she could reduce the contrast to suit her tender brain. It did mean she was exposed on the shop floor for customers to easily approach, but a colleague generally swept in if customers asked her for anything more than simple directions.

As the hours ticked by in gentle toil, her mind started to drift back to Drew's earlier suggestion. Was that the way forward? She did theme books and episodes based on the time of year, but only individually. Would she need to release episodes more regularly if it was to be a season? Would that be possible? Even with Drew supporting to respond to feedback, it would still mean significant extra pressure on her to finish more than one episode a month. Given how sparse her life outside the podcast was since her marriage dissolved—before that, to be honest, as Georgia had gradually became more possessive of her and her spare time—it wasn't like she had much else to do.

It would be a good excuse to dive into the promising list of queer titles that she was itching to read. Some she'd already sampled, of course, but her store didn't stock much outside mainstream bestsellers especially in—quote, unquote—*niche* categories, so she was yet to get her hands on a lot of them. Maybe she could even recommend some to her manager that got good responses and that were good quality as well as good representation, which unfortunately didn't always go together.

As long as she could do it without flagging her connection to the podcast. It was fine for everyone at work to know she was bisexual, but knowing about her role in *Beyond the Books* might make them want to become involved. The fewer people that knew, the easier it was to seek advice and feedback only when she wanted it. It had taken several months before she'd told any of her colleagues she was autistic, fearing the potential pity and disabling assumptions, and now that they did know, it was important to maintain a balance in how much assistance she accepted so they still saw her as capable. She did not want them pushing in thinking they needed to help her run her show.

What would Drew be like to work with longer term, if she took that option? They might have been clueless when she first bumped into them at the flats, but they'd been better since and not shown any signs of looking down on her. It most likely helped that they'd followed her work and seen what she was capable of before finding out how her brain was wired. She shouldn't have to prove herself to people, but it was necessary sometimes to escape being dangerously underestimated. Sure she had these bad days, but when well regulated she could do a lot more, and some things she did better than others—she wasn't just assigned the stocktake to allow her a break.

Hannah resisted checking her phone and emails at lunchtime to avoid toppling back over into overload, a heightened risk when getting over a fragile moment. So it wasn't until she finished work that she got Drew's stream of messages and realized she might have made a mistake. One included screenshots of a post they'd made and the responses to it.

What do you think of us doing a mini Pride series on #BeyondTheBooks?

The level and tone of responses left little room for doubt that it was a popular idea. Which was why Drew should've checked with her before posting and attaching her to a project she hadn't decided if she wanted to—or could—embark on. And the *us* made it sound like they'd not only locked her to it, but with them.

That month's poly meet was turning out to be a popular event. Drew scanned the busy back room for a place to set down the tray as they carried another round of drinks over. They found a spare spot on a small corner table occupied by a couple of newbies. The couple appeared to be in that common state of overwhelm for those first dipping their toes outside of fantasy and into the world of consensual non-monogamy. They were practically cowering in the corner, eyes darting, and clinging to each other.

"Hey, how are you doing? Sorry I didn't get the chance to do intros when you got here. I'm Drew, they/them, your host for today."

Drew gave a mini bow that managed to elicit a smile from the woman. Her husband—judging by the matching rings—still looked terrified and like he expected to be bundled off into some dank basement where all manner of things he could never tell his friends about might happen.

"This is your first time here, right?" Drew directed this at him, hoping to start to bring him down to earth with a simple question.

"Yes." He nodded sharply as if to reassure himself that was indeed the right answer. "I'm Nick."

"And I'm Olivia. Um, she/her. It is our first time at an in-person meetup like this, but we've been researching online and have some personal connections in similar...communities." She said most of this with a rising tone, like it was a question. Or she was Australian, but there was no hint of an accent to point to that explanation.

"Ah, cool. So you know some swingers?" Drew took a punt, having met enough newbies to have a good idea where they might be coming from.

Nick's stiff spine seemed to melt with relief at their understanding. He was clearly not someone used to having to explain why he was in the room. "Yes, we know some. But we haven't really...taken part."

"It didn't seem like it would suit us. Not that we're judging anyone"—Olivia raised her hand—"but we're wanting more of a deeper, ongoing connection."

"Yeah, swinging suits some people, but it's not for all of us." Drew paused, knowing their next question could take them into murkier territory. "So are you looking to meet someone together, or separately?"

The couple exchanged a shifty look. *Crap.* What's the bet they were unicorn hunters.

"We think it would be best for us to date together. At least to start with." Nick mumbled the second part as if it was a throwaway line he wasn't even pretending to seriously mean.

Sure you do. "That's a common place to start. Just bear in mind it can be tricky to find someone that way, and most people like to get to know someone one-on-one first, though it can lead to a triad naturally, further down the line." They may well have been told this already, but it was best to help them have realistic expectations. "Not that this is a dating event, mind."

"We know, we weren't just coming unicorn hunting!" Olivia laughed as if in on a shared joke. "We thought it would be good to meet other people in the same position. In real life."

"Great, that's what we're here for. Do you want me to introduce you to some other couples?"

Drew looked around the room for anyone who might be a good match. Best avoid anyone attending alone, in case the newbies didn't stick to their declared intentions. Over the other side, they spotted a cluster of couples that had been in the community long enough to hopefully give some useful perspective. "Follow me."

Nick raised a questioning eyebrow to his wife but obediently stood and let Drew guide him over to the others.

Drew didn't have a chance to do introductions before someone tapped them on their shoulder.

"Those our drinks?" Nancy, one of their favourite regulars, drew their attention back to the tray of drinks they'd left behind undelivered.

"Oh yeah, soz. Give me a minute." Drew turned back to the group, to find someone else had already taken on the task of integrating the newbies, who were settling into a cleared space in the cluster. Apparently their work was done.

"I can get them." Nancy took off to rescue the abandoned drinks, leaving Drew to rejoin their original social group.

"Unicorn hunters?" Ishani muttered to them as they slid into the chair next to her. She had abandoned her wheelchair in favour of one of the well-stuffed large armchairs that she and Rebecca were treating as a love seat.

That wasn't why Drew had chosen a place with that seating, but they couldn't blame Ishani for taking advantage of it. A benefit of being the organizer was that Drew could ensure the meetup was somewhere where the chairs fit them. Trying to find a bookable, free space that didn't require navigating any steps had not been an easy task either, but Drew had found somewhere they and Ishani could both comfortably access.

"They claim not to be." Drew exchanged a look with her that acknowledged they both knew better. "I emphasized it's not a cruising ground, and they said they're not on the pull."

"Good job. There's still some tension from last time."

Drew cringed, remembering the last new couple who'd attended on the prowl and seemed mortally offended when they kept getting knocked back. Eventually Drew had to step in and tell them to cut it out, which had not gone well either. At least that pair had left once it was clear they weren't going to find what they were after. And possibly had noted that Drew had a few pounds on the guy and didn't seem afraid to use that strength to their advantage, if it came down to it. Thankfully it hadn't, but the encounter had still left a bad taste.

"Hopefully they'll be chill."

The newbies seemed to be relaxing in the company of the group and were chatting away. There shouldn't be any trouble.

"Did they say if they're looking to date separately or together?" Ishani wasn't so easily reassured.

Drew didn't get to say anything. The look on their face must have been enough as Ishani groaned. Her scepticism came from a place of experience, not idle judgement, and Drew got it. Not only had the previous newbies hit on any potentially available able-bodied, cis, white women, but the guy had kept commenting on Ishani's guns. Drew had stepped in there too when it looked like even the usually measured Ishani might end up punching the dude. His complete failure to realize she hadn't built those muscles down at the gym and might be a tad self-conscious about her top-heavy frame was another strike against him. Not that it was something she should be self-conscious about, but they had some common understanding about what it was like having a physique that didn't fit societal expectations.

"Let's give them a chance to prove themselves."

It wasn't like there weren't plenty of couples in their community going against that trend, including themselves. Okay, so none of their polycule had come from a straight relationship, but both Ishani and Rebecca, and Drew and Leigh had opened up from their respective monogamous couples. None had done the trying-to-date-as-a-couple thing either, but if Leigh had suggested they start there, then maybe Drew would've given it a shot. It was the set-up people were used to seeing, so you could hardly blame new couples for thinking it was the way to go. It was a nice fantasy, a shared partner who loved and wanted you both equally, plus all the threesomes your loins could desire. Drew had never fancied the idea of just being an add-on to an existing relationship, but there were some elusive women who were interested in that role, or so they'd heard.

"Of course," Ishani said, but the tilt of her head said otherwise.

"I'll keep an eye on them."

"Keep an eye on who?" Rebecca turned from her conversation with Nancy to join them.

"New couple." Drew nodded to the pair in an attempt at discretion. "Ish thinks they could be trouble."

"I just believe we need to be cautious in order to keep this a safer space."

It had taken years to bring their local community together and establish a regular friendly meetup with decent attendance, where everyone respected each other's boundaries, mostly. Not everyone had the supportive family—of origin or chosen—that Drew had, and they especially wanted to provide a nice space for those that didn't. The meetups meant far more to some than an outsider might realize. Which was why Drew was still running the group, despite being way past the point personally of needing to get out there to find their people.

"I'll step in if I have to."

It was something they'd done to one degree or another many times in their role of organizer. Usually it just took a gentle nudge, or sometimes a more direct word, to bring anyone in line. Drew preferred to keep it friendly, but they'd do what they had to do. They were comfortable in the fact that they were not easy to push aside, and people figured that out sooner or later.

"They appear to be behaving themselves." Rebecca peered round to study the newbies.

"See? Don't worry, Ish. It's nice to have some new faces, and we can help steer them in the right direction." Fantasy and reality could be jarringly different, and it was hard enough to predict how you yourself would respond, let alone anyone else. "They'll probably fuck up along the way, but don't we all?"

Rebecca blushed, and they reached over to squeeze her hand. She had been the most recent one to bring drama into their polycule, but they hadn't been aiming the comment at her. And that had all worked out, with Drew gaining a new bestie as well as Rebecca getting all properly loved up again for the first time since they'd got together. You never could safeguard your heart completely. Not that Drew had ever really tried. They were a proud romantic, and nothing they'd witnessed had ever managed to change that.

"We are only human," Ishani added and planted a quick kiss on Rebecca's cheek. "I didn't mean to be judgemental."

"I know."

It wasn't in her nature, and it wasn't that Drew was naive either. They knew full well what went on within the community, better than most, as their position meant access to the inside scoop on many members' personal lives. They believed people would find their way… but some just needed more directing than others.

They scanned the room again for any other new faces or, if they were being honest, one in particular. They'd not seen Hannah at any meetups before, and her current relationship status meant it was unlikely she'd show, but there was part of them that still checked the door whenever it opened, wondering if she might be about to walk in. She'd said she wasn't ready for new relationships, but who was to know when she would be. And they would be there if and when she wanted to step back out. Not to take advantage, of course, but to be that crutch if she needed it. Okay, and maybe more if that was what she wanted. But given that Hannah hadn't replied to their messages for the last few days, as they were reminded with a sinking heart every time they glanced at their phone, that seemed unlikely.

❖

"Pass the potatoes."

Hannah put down her knife and fork to pick up the serving dish, but by the time she'd processed what was said and done so, Josh had already grabbed it. She returned to her meal, attempting to saw apart the Yorkshire pudding without pinging it across the table or knocking anything else off her plate.

"Do you need help with that?" Her mother leaned over with her cutlery poised to intervene.

"I can do it."

There was no way she was going to let her mother cut up her food as if she was a child. No matter how long it took her to delicately tear it apart.

"I heard your podcast yesterday," her mother added. She leaned into Hannah's side, invading her space again, as if this were hot gossip.

Hannah resisted pausing her chewing to ask what she thought. If her mother wanted to tell her something she would, whether Hannah wanted to hear it or not. Hannah wasn't the only straight talker in her family.

"I thought it was interesting. Yes, it wasn't a perspective you hear every day."

Hannah tensed, unsure whether that was a compliment or the start of a rebuttal.

"It was enlightening. Your guest was very charming, weren't they? You sounded like you had a nice conversation."

"I did. They were easy to talk to." Hannah smiled down at her plate, unable to contain the smile but not wanting to share it with anyone.

"Were they hot?" It seemed her brother had caught the expression and jumped to conclusions.

"Josh!"

Her mother's horrified response would've given the impression to an outsider that his question was out of character. It was not.

"Were they?" she added in a stage whisper.

"Mum!"

Now it was her turn to act horrified, which was handy as hopefully it would explain away the heat that had risen in her cheeks. She looked around the table to find her family all staring at her as if seriously expecting an answer.

"I will not be answering that inappropriate question."

"Spoilsport," Josh shot back.

She poked her tongue out at him. No amount of jibing would get her to confide in them how hot she found Drew. After her parents had stuck by Georgia, right up until the break-up, and even then questioned Hannah's decision to leave, she had vowed not to trust them with her personal life. They might be okay with her being queer, but they hadn't understood her being polyamorous and still blamed her for having an *affair*, with Georgia encouraging this view when it suited. It was one of the many reasons she hadn't moved back in with her parents afterwards. That, and they all got on better when they only experienced each other in small doses.

"So what's next?" Thankfully her dad steered the conversation away. Or at least attempted to.

"That's the question. My next guest cancelled, so I need to figure out how to fill the gap soon."

"Oh no, that's frustrating. Are you okay? Is there anything we can do?" her mum said.

"It's fine, I can handle it." She took a breath. There wasn't anything, and her mum probably realized that, but it was meant as a kind gesture. "Thank you."

"If you're sure." She went to squeeze Hannah's shoulder but realized just in time that she had gravy on her fingers and veered off to grab a napkin.

Hannah appreciated that gesture more than she would the squeeze.

"Can you shift someone else forward in the schedule?" her dad suggested.

"That's one option, although it would knock out the seasonal links, and they might not be available early. Plus I'm truly in trouble if they also drop out or don't respond in time."

"What's the other option?" Josh asked. He knew her too well to not realize she must have an alternative if she hadn't pursued the obvious.

Hannah placed down her cutlery and folded her arms. It was too difficult to manage her food and the topic, especially when both made her stomach twist—for different reasons. "Drew suggested a mini Pride series."

"That sounds like a wonderful idea." Her mum clapped her hands once, then nudged Hannah's elbow. "Elbows off the table."

Hannah pulled her arms back to wrap around herself instead. "Maybe."

It did, but she was still pissed about Drew advertising it before she'd had the chance to think it over properly.

"Have you got guests in mind?" her dad asked.

That was the part she really needed to figure out. She picked her fork back up and toyed with the remaining scraps of her roast dinner. "Drew seemed interested in cohosting it themself."

"Gotta be hot if you want to bring them back."

Hannah kicked Josh under the table and he let out an exaggerated yelp, which everyone chose to ignore. You'd think he was still a horny teenager. Being back home seemed to make him temporarily regress to that state, and to the sibling drive to wind her up whenever possible. Hannah tried not to let herself revert back to child status, apart from the odd kick, as difficult as that could be in her family's company.

"Your mother's right—they were very charming. You worked well together. Might be worth seriously considering, and it'll save you having to find anyone else at short notice."

"Yes, exactly." She couldn't deny it.

Despite the social media boo-boo, the idea of working with Drew again was appealing. And not for hormonal reasons. It would surely be the easiest and safest option, only having to coordinate with one guest who had already proved reliable, if a little overenthusiastic. They were also easy to get hold of, and she wouldn't have to worry about waiting around for a response while the prep time slipped away. She shouldn't let one minor incident put her off entirely—it wasn't like *she* never got carried away when she was passionate about something.

"You have to admit, as brilliant as you always are, they brought even more life to the podcast," her mother added.

So it wasn't just her own, potentially biased opinion. Drew was special, and apparently it had been obvious to everyone listening. They could enliven any discussion and have plenty of interesting things to say, which would take pressure off her.

"I'll see what they think."

She had avoided replying to Drew since they'd sent the evidence of going ahead behind her back, not wanting to make out it was okay and not wanting to push them away either. But time was pressing on, and she didn't have the luxury of a long decision-making process if she was going to stay on schedule. Maybe she should just take the easy option for once and go along with Drew's idea. It wasn't like she was locking herself into a long-term partnership with them. She would go back to regular programming and full control afterwards. It was only one short season.

CHAPTER SIX

The email inviting Drew to cohost the *Beyond the Books* Pride miniseries was surprisingly formal. Maybe it shouldn't have surprised Drew, given how dedicated Hannah was to her side hustle, but it didn't fit with the more casual messages they'd been exchanging since the pod recording. Though it could explain why those had trailed off.

Please refrain from sharing anything about this project on social media until we have finalized the details.

Hannah hadn't responded to their message showing the reaction to the proposed Pride series, not even an emoji. And here was the evidence that she hadn't been happy with them for posting about it. *I knew it.* They'd messed up, though at least not badly enough to put her off working with them completely.

The Pride idea started as a spur-of-the-moment suggestion, which had quickly blossomed into a plan in their mind. And now it was actually happening. Despite the pointed socials boundary, it still gave Drew a buzz to have been chosen as cohost and to have the chance to make one of their daydreams come true. They tried to block other imagined scenarios with Hannah from making a bid for attention. The invitation clearly wasn't a request for any kind of personal connection.

Drew clicked on the attached list of possible books to cover and when the document opened felt a cold sweat creep across their brow. Some serious work had gone into the chart, which didn't just contain the names of the authors and titles. There were columns for LGBTQIA status, genre, content notes, popularity, cost, and then some. The mass of data swam before their eyes. Did they really need to think about it all? Sure, Hannah would need to know at least some of it, but Drew hadn't been planning on doing deep research. They were more into the chatting about queer creations with the cute host part.

At least Hannah was giving them options, and they wouldn't be stuck trying to claw their way through some boring fancy text that was more about the author showing off their education level than telling an interesting story. Pretty words could only get you so far, at least as far as Drew was concerned. You needed a real connection and characters. At first glance, there didn't seem to be much in their preferred genre—romance, they were a sucker for a guaranteed happy ending—but they were open to delving into other queer stories. There were a few they'd read, and a lot more they'd heard of and had thought about getting round to reading someday.

Despite all the data, there was nothing to hint at Hannah's own preferences. Did she always leave it completely up to the guest? There was no way Drew was going to be able to narrow it down enough alone. They flicked back to the email. Hannah was proposing they cover eight or more books in total over four fortnightly episodes. That made it one book a week, right? What had they got themself into.

Staring at the spreadsheet was not going to help. Before they could talk themself out of the whole project, they gave Hannah a call.

"Hello," Hannah answered after several rings.

"Hey, it's Drew. I got your email."

"Good."

She didn't seem in a chatty mood, but maybe she was tensing for them to let her down too.

"It sounds like a plan. I'm gonna need help narrowing down the book choices, though, and it would be good to hear more about what you wanna do."

"That's fair enough."

They left a pause to give her a chance to offer more, but nothing came, and they did not enjoy the silence.

"Have you got time to chat now?" Maybe they'd caught her at a bad time.

"Umm...I was about to make dinner."

"No problem, soz, I can call back later."

"Um, that wouldn't work well either." A sigh crept down the line. "To be honest, I'm not good with phone calls at the best of times."

"Ah. No problem." That tracked and maybe they should've predicted it, but emails weren't going to cut it. "How about I come round yours instead and grab us a pizza on the way?"

It wasn't like they needed to ask her address, and they could check in on Phoebe afterwards.

There was a long pause, and Drew chewed their lip to stop themself butting in while Hannah thought it through.

"Not having to cook would be nice and save me spoons. And yes, we do need to talk about it in more depth. Okay, you're on."

"Ideal." They glanced down at the worn old polo shirt they were slouched in. "Give me ten to make myself decent. You can text me your order and where you want me to pick it up from."

"Great." A smaller sigh drifted over, which seemed more like relief this time. "Are you sure you don't mind me choosing? Feel free to get something different for yourself."

"I'm happy with whatever you want. Pizza's pizza."

Hannah laughed. "I do not agree, but if you really don't mind, I will pick for us. And prove you wrong."

"Ha. I'll trust you to make a wise choice. See you shortly."

Drew bounced up from the sofa and tucked their phone away. Leigh was out for the evening, and they'd not got any plans other than flopping in front of some uninspiring TV. Chatting with Hannah over pizza was a big improvement.

Something brushed their calf, and they looked down to see Pebbles winding his way between their legs, reminding them they'd better get his dinner before going anywhere.

"Don't worry, I've not forgotten you."

They bent over and picked him up, letting him rest his head and front paws on their shoulder as they carried him through to the kitchen. It wasn't entirely true, he had slipped their mind when they proposed their evening with Hannah, but they would've remembered before getting out the door. Their head wasn't so full of her that they'd forget he was their number one priority. Generally they were a big fan of reciprocal relationships, but cats had other ideas. You were their willing servant, and in return you got the joy of their company…when they felt like it. On their terms. It was a pattern Drew at least tried to avoid in their relationships with humans.

Drew gently extricated Pebbles from their shoulder, without his claws gaining purchase and taking part of it with him, and set him down on the kitchen side. This earned them a head rub as Pebbles knew as well as they did that he was not meant to be there, but while Leigh was out, he got away with it. She believed cats shouldn't jump on up furniture, particularly surfaces where human food might go. Even Drew could see this was a losing battle and didn't consider it a cause worth fighting for.

Once Pebbles was happily munching away, Drew headed to the bedroom to get changed. A buzz in their pocket turned out to be Hannah's pizza order. *Lush.* Maybe they should ask Phoebe if she wanted one too. It seemed cruel to walk past her door with a steaming pizza without offering her any. Plus Alex had asked them to keep an eye on if Phoebe was eating as she'd never been responsible for feeding herself before. As far as Drew could tell, she was keeping on top of whatever they brought back from their weekly supermarket trips, and her support staff sometimes helped with meal prep. So eating better than takeaway pizza, but it would be a nice treat.

"Hi, Drew." Phoebe picked up quicker and sounded much more pleased that they'd called.

Not that Hannah didn't want to speak to you. She had explained her initial reluctance, and they were going to see her.

"Hey, Bee. Just a quick one, I'm gonna pick up a pizza to take to Hannah's, you want me to get you one too?"

"Yes, please!" There was a pause before she added, "Why are you hanging with Hannah?"

"Just podcast stuff." They probably shouldn't say more. They didn't need to annoy Hannah again by leaking the plans to her neighbour.

"Uh-huh." Phoebe didn't sound convinced. "She seems cool. Are you friends?" Another pause. "More than friends?"

"We are simply meeting to discuss a business arrangement."

"Uh-huh."

"And there's no relationship more important than friends."

It was a common phrase that people said without thinking about it deeply, but it still irked them whenever they heard it, and they couldn't resist correcting. As if friendship should automatically rank lower than sexual or romantic relationships. Sure, they loved romance, but they also loved their friends. It was just a different kind of love. Not everything was a competition, especially when it came to relationships—something it might have taken a while for them to unlearn, but that was down to their insecurities.

"I know. Oh, maybe Faye wants to come over for pizza. The staff here said it's okay for her to hang, as they can do her meds if there's an emergency. She needs a lift, though…"

Drew rolled their eyes. "As in Faye from your old home? Sure, I can pick her up on my way, it's not far out. Long as she's okay with me."

"She'll be fine. She's not had a seizure in *aaages*, not since her new meds. You're the best."

"Give her a call now, then let me know if she wants to come. I'll text you the link for the menu."

Despite claims that her bestie would be able to see Phoebe as much as she liked, the care home staff seemed reluctant to actually take her to visit. Phoebe had been complaining about missing Faye since moving out to her own flat, and Drew suspected she missed her even more than she let on. It must be weird living alone for the first time. Drew had never done it and had never wanted to. They couldn't imagine not having someone there to cuddle and moan with after a rough day, or ridicule crap TV with. Many things were much less fun alone.

As they stood in front of the open wardrobe in their boxers, trying to figure out what level of casual to go with, they tapped out a quick update to Hannah. They had told her they wouldn't be long, but surely she wouldn't resent them helping Phoebe out. And with Phoebe's absent sister being one of Drew's closest friends, there was space in their life for Phoebe to take advantage of. Not that she was taking advantage—they would happily do pretty much anything for anyone in need. They weren't a complete pushover—they had their own principles and plans. It just never hurt to give someone a lift, literally or metaphorically, on their way.

❖

They were late. At that rate, Hannah could've cooked and eaten dinner before Drew even got to hers. Her stomach grumbled.

She'd used the extra time to get her flat ready for a visitor. She didn't usually have people round, apart from Cass, partly because that would involve having to explain how she lived in supported accommodation. How and why. It wasn't that she was ashamed. She just didn't want it to shape people's view of her. Drew's accidental discovery of where she lived and casual acceptance of her situation meant there wasn't anything to worry about in that regard—she could be completely open with them. That realization sent a tingle through her.

Hannah didn't want to risk putting the Hoover on and missing the buzzer, especially as she usually wore ear defenders for that job, so she paced around with a dustcloth instead. While she paced, she practiced points to say to Drew, scripting different versions depending on how they might respond, and tried not to let the scenarios extend beyond words to what else might take place when an attractive person came around. This wasn't a hook-up—this was work. Occasionally she picked up the intercom phone in case she had missed the alert. By the time Drew arrived, every surface was blissfully shiny, and she'd resorted to lining up ornaments and coasters.

She peeped through the aptly named peephole before opening the door, despite buzzing them in to the building moments before. The only other people it was likely to be were the staff or her neighbours, the former dangerous to ignore in case they overanalyzed her reason for doing so, and the latter likely to hang around long enough to see her answer to Drew, so just ignoring them would come across as clear rejection. When she'd first moved in, she would ignore any knocking as she didn't want to encourage random drop-ins. She still didn't but had learned a downside of living there was that visitors couldn't always be avoided, and it was best to just check who it was so she could school her face to welcome unwelcome visitors, as briefly as possible. With Drew it was the opposite. She took a few breaths to calm her racing heart and try not to look too happy to see them. *They are late.* The reminder did the job, but she also needed to be careful not to look too annoyed. Drew had a good reason.

They also had a too-cute sheepish grin when she opened the door, and they were holding extras as well as a large pizza box.

"Hey, thanks for letting me come over. Soz about the delay. I brought warm cookies to make up for it."

"In that case, you are forgiven." She took the boxes from them and stepped back so they could come in.

Drew took the cue and strolled in. She closed the door behind them on the blinking security camera, which reminded her that she hadn't texted whoever was on duty to let them know she had a guest. Apparently you had to report visitors for fire safety reasons, but she suspected there was more to it than that. Another reason she didn't invite people over—having to give their details felt intrusive and like something she should ask permission for. At least Drew was probably already aware of the system from visiting Phoebe. She placed the warm boxes on the kitchen counter where the grease wouldn't leave a trace and sent a quick text in case someone decided to investigate why Drew had gone through a different door.

When she headed back into the hallway, Drew was bent over, removing their boots, and she tried to avoid staring at their butt. It was good to see they were housetrained. She had the same instinctive response as her mother to people walking into her place in dirty outdoor shoes and had to hold back from echoing her mother's pointed words on that matter. Though as she hadn't vacuumed, could she really judge if they hadn't de-booted? Hopefully Drew wouldn't judge her. She guided them through to the lounge.

"This is a nice place. A different layout to Phoebe's."

"It's a conversion rather than a new build, so they must've worked with what they'd got. Otherwise we probably all would be living in identical ergonomically designed pods."

Drew laughed. "You're better off with a bit of individuality, mind."

"Yes. It feels more like my own home this way."

"You have got it looking cosy." Drew glanced around the living room at the overstuffed bookshelves which served as the main source of character. "Phoebe's place is pretty bare. Maybe we should help her get more bits."

"I'm sure she'll fill it soon enough. Your belongings seem to fill whatever size space you have."

Hannah had worried about how she'd fit everything into a small flat after moving out of her house, but it turned out a lot of stuff didn't need to come with her, and she'd not had the energy to fight or beg her ex for anything unnecessary. It had been the right decision, and Hawthorn View had provided the basics, which she had slowly replaced and added to while making it her own. Not having to eat off crockery that reminded her of tense mealtimes with Georgia was a blessing. But she didn't want to think about that. She scrambled to come up with another topic to shift the direction her mind was going in. "So, how do you know Phoebe?"

Was that too personal a question? She had been speculating ever since she'd seen them together. Her best guess was Phoebe's drama group—Drew seemed like they could also have a flair for the dramatic and had taken to it like a pro during their recording.

"She's a close friend's little sister. In fact, my metamour's sister." They paused and looked her in the eye as if trying to see whether she understood the term. "She's travelling at the moment so asked me to check in on Phoebe, as it was obviously bad timing with her having only just moved in. Though so far the only thing she seems to need me for is an unpaid taxi service."

"Ah okay, that explains it."

Partially anyway. Was Drew that close to all their partners' other partners? How did their polycule work? Did they all like to be that close? Maybe that was what they'd meant by Kitchen Table Poly. It was very tempting to ask her questions out loud, but that wasn't what Drew was there to talk about, and it was none of her business. *Focus.*

"I'll just get plates, then we can eat before it gets cold."

She edged back into the kitchen and pulled out a couple of large plates. On her way, she opened the windows. The warm summer breeze shouldn't have much impact on the temperature of the food, but it would dissipate some of the smell.

When she stepped back into the lounge, Drew seemed to have made themself comfortable on the sofa.

"Do you want to eat there or at the table?"

Drew eyed the rickety wooden dining chairs with suspicion. "Here would be better, if you don't mind."

"No problem. I'll get lap trays."

When she returned, she handed a tray to Drew, then hesitated as she tried to decide whether to sit next to them or in the armchair opposite. Drew took the other tray too and placed it down next to them with an inviting smile. So, cosied up on the sofa together it was. That shouldn't be distracting at all.

"Books!" she declared, and Drew gave her a look like they were wondering if she also had Tourette's. Heat rushed up her neck. It would be nothing to be ashamed of if she did, but she didn't. "You wanted to talk about book choices. For the podcast."

Drew's eyes twinkled as they finished their mouthful, as if they were sensing the instincts she was pulling back from. Or they were just really enjoying that pizza.

"Yes, books." They smiled and wiped their fingers on the kitchen towel she'd provided before picking up their phone. "I'll be honest, I'm gonna struggle to know where to even start. You said eight, two an episode, right?"

"Right. I know it sounds like a lot, but we need a decent amount to cover a range of identities and experiences. It's only one a week to read."

She usually got through more than that, so it sounded realistic, although it might be tight to read them all twice like usual. It was fitting all the post-recording work in that would be tough—her plan to manage that was to keep the conversations on track so the editing could be minimal. It wasn't like Drew had needed much last time. Cutting it down to time was the only difficulty.

"Or two if you're reading them twice." This had also occurred to Drew apparently. There was a teasing tone to their voice, but light enough she couldn't be sure it wasn't a serious concern.

"I don't expect you to do that. And I expect I'll have read some of them at least once already, especially the classics."

They laughed. "Good to hear, cos I might struggle to fit in one go-through. Though if they're available on audio, so I can listen at work, I stand a good chance."

Hannah slowed her chewing to consider this. She was used to only having to fit reading all the books in her own schedule. Maybe it was too much to ask of Drew.

"We could stick with one an episode if you like. I just thought it could be interesting to compare older portrayals to modern ones. Or I could try to get a different host for each episode…"

"No need. I do want to do it. And that sounds like a great idea—I reckon it'll provoke lots of discussion, and I really should know the queer classics."

"Okay, if you're sure." They definitely sounded sure, but Hannah wasn't convinced if that was because they were determined to stay at the centre of the project or if they actually could manage it all. "We could stick to those available as audiobooks given how many are these days. I can add another column to the spreadsheet."

"Is there room for more?" Drew tilted their head in apparent amusement.

"There's always room for more," she quipped back, grabbing another slice of pizza. Feeling emboldened by Drew's easy company, she added, "And I could maybe record the odd book that isn't available."

"I like that idea. I can just imagine you reading to me as I lie down after a hard day's work."

Hannah lifted an eyebrow over her pizza slice. She was glad her mouth was full as she didn't trust herself to respond appropriately.

"Doing all the voices..."

That made her snort into the end of her slice. "I wouldn't go that far."

She was starting to regret the suggestion already, although she did like the idea of Drew closing their eyes under the power of her voice. Would they enjoy submitting themself to her like that? *Bad brain: not what they're here for.*

"So that's how you're going to read them. Now we need to think about what. Tell me, what do you usually like to read?" She steered them back on topic.

"I'm a big fan of romance." They locked eyes with her and smiled shyly before continuing. "In the current climate, I reckon we need all the happy endings we can get."

"Romance isn't the only genre with happy endings," she countered. There was no way she could deal with reading romantic lines to Drew, let alone the sex scenes, without ending up out of her depth.

"True, but it's the only one where it's guaranteed for the queer leads, and you don't have to worry about them being tortured or sacrificed to appease our conservative overlords."

"Well, when you put it like that...we could cover something at least in that category." How could she deny them that slice of happiness? "You'll see I've included content notes on the spreadsheet, where I could find them, so we can avoid anything particularly tragic if you wish."

"That would be good. There's enough tragic news stories to get bogged down in. Though I get if we're covering older books, that might be unavoidable."

"Yes, it could be tricky. But we can at least choose our preferred version of the queer tragedy."

They both laughed at this. Because you had to, didn't you, or you might get overwhelmed by torturous emotions like the doomed protagonists.

"What about you? I wanna know what you like when you're not worrying about what will work for the show."

The question brought her pause and a fuzzy feeling. None of her other guests had asked her that, or not with any real interest besides filling space with small talk and the question being easy picking given what she did. It was like Drew actually wanted to get to know her.

"I genuinely enjoy all sorts. I like imagining and learning about different worlds and cultures. Especially characters who feel real and aren't wholly defined by a marginalized group they're meant to represent."

"I'm with you there. We need real, messy characters who show our humanity and wholeness."

"That's a beautiful way to put it." Hannah grabbed some kitchen roll and dabbed her mouth, resisting the urge to squeeze them.

"It's true. We're more than we're made out to be."

Drew didn't seem to feel the same need to hold back and squeezed Hannah's knee in a move that from someone else would've seemed too forward and intrusive, but from them felt just right. A warm tingling heat spread out from their fingertips. Hannah nodded but was unable to find the words for what their observation meant to her. Hoping that she was included in that *we* as the hand on her leg seemed to infer.

It had been a long time since someone had made her feel worthy so easily. She was clearly still recovering from being made to feel worthless. Not that she could blame that completely on Georgia—the wider world had always made it clear that her configuration was not what it recommended. She reached down and laid her hand on top of Drew's, squeezing back for a moment before pulling away. She could allow herself that small amount of comfort. She didn't know Drew's intentions, outside of wanting to be on the podcast, and she didn't dare ask in case they weren't what she hoped. Or in case they were.

CHAPTER SEVEN

The promised week to read a book—which was pushing it for Drew, as it was—turned out to be more like one week to read two. That wasn't Hannah's fault, or theirs—it was down to the late cancellation of Hannah's original guest. At least they'd managed to find two books they'd both already read to cover in the first episode, and Drew would get the full two weeks to read before the next one. If Drew had also been involved in the editing, there would be no way they'd keep up, but Hannah seemed confident in her reading speed. It was tempting to question, but they had to trust she knew what she was doing.

Drew had managed to snag copies of both titles from the library to flip through. There was no need to stress themself out studying them thoroughly, as long as they made some notes of points to raise and had thoughts on the key themes. Plus they could look up reviews from others. Hannah's social media aversion was their gain as they could count online research as their contribution to the show—instead of worrying that it was sucking up their little free time, then keeping on scrolling regardless but feeling bad about it.

Phoebe had offered to accompany them on their trip to the library to stock up on her preferred genre of angsty fantasy. The woman had a thing for broody vampires, which Drew had never quite got, but who were they to yuck someone else's yum? Unless someone was getting hurt, and there didn't seem any chance of Phoebe getting with a blood-sucking creep in real life. They'd headed back to Phoebe's with their prizes, but the cuppa Drew had been promised was yet to appear.

"What's up with you today? You seem like you've got ants in your pants."

Usually Phoebe would be flopped on the sofa with them after a trip into town, but her butt hadn't touched the seat since they got back.

"I gotta get ready for Callum to come over."

"That explains it." Drew shut the book they were flipping through. "Is he just gonna hang out here, or have you got special plans?"

From what Alex and Rebecca had told them, Phoebe's boyfriend was not the brooding type but was utterly devoted to her—doting but not dangerous. They'd not heard it directly from Phoebe, though, so this was their chance to find out where things were at with the couple.

"Staying here. He's gonna stay the night." Phoebe's tight smile hinted at nervous excitement.

"Is this the first time he's stayed?"

Did Drew need to give out safe sex advice, or could they trust she was already clued in? Maybe they should text Alex to check, but Phoebe was a grown woman and that definitely would be invading her privacy.

"Yeah. They didn't want me having overnight guests for the first month or two. But we agreed I could after six weeks. Which is today!"

They chuckled. She wasn't hanging around. A woman after their own heart—they never had been good at going slow when they were attracted to someone. Although, hang on, did that mean Hawthorn View got a say in who residents could have over and when? How did that work for Hannah? This they did need to investigate. Just in case.

"Do they get to vet your guests? As in, say who's allowed to stay?"

Phoebe paused mid-pace and crinkled up her nose at this. "No, it's not like that. At least I don't think so."

"I'm sure it's not."

They weren't but they didn't want to worry her more. They'd been pretty cosy at Hannah's last night. What if she'd asked them to stay after it'd got late? Not that anything was likely to happen, but she hadn't seemed to want Drew to leave any more than they'd wanted to go.

"It was only while I settled in, they said. Now I just have to let them know."

"That's alright then."

Although surely it could be awkward if you were someone who liked to bring unplanned guests home with you. It might be simple for

Bee with her one steady boyfriend, but from Hannah's dating profile it seemed she was more into hook-ups—they hadn't established yet if this was just while she was steering clear of romance or her usual style. Either way, it was what she wanted and sounded like it might not be approved of by the management. Did she have to sneak people in and out like a horny teenager? But this wasn't about Hannah. They refocused on Phoebe.

"So, when you say it's the first time, does that mean it's your first time…"

Drew wasn't sure how much of a chance the couple had before to spend quality time in privacy, given Phoebe had been living in a care home and Callum with his parents.

"I don't mean sex. That's definitely not my first time." Phoebe shrugged off the assumption like she was way past that stage in her personal life.

"Soz, didn't mean to judge either way."

They probably should've guessed that one. Especially given there'd been that whole drama the year before where Phoebe and Callum had run off together out of fear someone would stop them being together, like with Phoebe's previous boyfriend. Okay, Drew seriously should've known.

"I don't mind you asking. Long as you don't try to stop me." Phoebe crossed her arms and gave them a look that made it clear they didn't stand a chance if they did.

"Hell, no. I have no interest in stopping you enjoying yourself and your man."

Phoebe beamed at this and her arms dropped. "Good. Cos that's one of the big reasons I wanted my own place," she said with a wink.

"Fair enough. So, what's the plan? Home-cooked romantic dinner for two?"

"I was just gonna order takeaway. Although I did have that one last night."

"You want to do something more special than that. Celebrate your freedom finally having your own flat to snuggle in." It maybe wasn't total freedom, but it was much more than Phoebe was used to having.

"That would be nice." Phoebe worried at her nails.

"I can help," they offered without thinking.

"Really?" Phoebe dropped her hands and looked back up at them.

"Really. I could prep the ingredients while you get tidied up." They were in no rush, and Phoebe deserved a special night.

"That could work. Thanks. I have some nice recipes from my cooking class. We could try one of those."

"Ideal. I reckon we've got time for me to pop out to the shops if you don't have everything in. Is there anything else you need? Wine? Candles?"

"I don't know." Phoebe began chewing on her nails again.

"No problem. We'll make a list for the perfect romantic dinner, and anything you don't have I can get while I'm at the shops."

"Okay. I won't tell Callum, and it can be a nice surprise."

"I'm sure he'll love it. Right, let's get to work. We have, what, three hours to prepare for the perfect romantic evening."

"Is that enough time?"

"With me helping, you bet. I am a pro at this." Drew cracked their knuckles. There was nothing they loved more than wining and dining a special someone, and making them feel even more special. They were happy to coach Phoebe to bring that joy herself.

"By the way, have you got Hannah's number?"

"Sure, why?"

Was this the part where Phoebe attempted to pry into their own private life? They didn't mind, although unfortunately there was nothing to tell. Not in a personal sense anyway. Hannah would be dropping the teaser for their upcoming series any moment, and then they could tell the world about their working partnership.

"Cos you could warn her that she might need headphones tonight."

Drew couldn't restrain their cackling laugh. Phoebe clearly didn't need their guidance for the latter part of the evening. "Maybe you can take her some of your baking to make up for it."

Not that Hannah was likely to complain, unless she was recording an episode, which Drew knew for a fact she wasn't. She lived across the corridor anyway so shouldn't be disturbed even if Phoebe and Callum did get carried away. Her hearing was sensitive, but surely not that sensitive. One test would be to ask if Phoebe had ever heard her when she had a date over, but that would lead them into dangerous territory. They did not need encouraging to think about what Hannah got up to in the bedroom. It was hard enough to keep things professional between them, and they had just locked themself into another two months working together, which was starting to sound like a very long time.

The books lay abandoned on the sofa.

❖

"You got pizza without me?!"

Cass must've opened the kitchen bin and spotted the box.

"I did. Please forgive me." Hannah's reply was only partly in jest. Curling up with a takeaway pizza in front of a movie together was their thing.

"Only if you tell me who you were cheating on me with." Cass returned from the kitchen with a couple of cups of tea and a jar of biscuits.

"I thought you didn't believe in the concept of cheating." Hannah made a pass for the biscuits after Cass had put the tea down, but they lifted them out of her reach.

"Nice try. It is cheating if everyone hasn't given informed consent. Which I haven't." Cass pouted in an exaggerated fashion that helped clarify they were at least partly joking and put the plate down. "And you can't distract me that easily. Who are you hiding?"

Hannah had clearly made it worse for herself by even attempting to withhold. Maybe she could still convince them—and herself—that it was no big deal.

"It was just Drew. They came over to discuss a podcast related project."

"You invited them over?" Cass sounded a mix of shocked and delighted by this news.

"No, they invited themself. They already knew where I lived and pop in regularly to see my neighbour, so it was no big deal."

"It's no big deal that you had your most alluring guest over. I'm assuming alone?"

"Of course alone. No one else is involved in the project."

She attempted to take a sip of tea without revealing that her hands were shaky at the memory and inquisition. Sometimes she wondered if she needed a therapist too or if she could just rely on Cass to push her to confront the truths of her situation. And her brewing feelings.

"True. But be honest, would you have let anyone else come round?

With pizza, which means it wasn't a quick visit or a particularly formal one."

"Well deduced, Sherlock," Hannah grumbled into her cuppa. But she couldn't blame them for following up their hunch—she expected no less. "They offered to bring pizza because it was dinnertime and neither of us had eaten yet."

"And it couldn't have waited until after dinner? Or been discussed in a video call?"

Hannah opened her mouth to explain why but found she couldn't. It wasn't just that she couldn't find the words—she had no answer. Why hadn't she just suggested they switch to video and called them back later?

"Exactly," Cass continued. "You know why I don't think you did?"

"Why?" She could guess where this was going, but she might be wrong.

"I think you wanted to spend time with them and get to know them in a more intimate setting."

"We stayed on the sofa eating pizza. Me and you do that—would you call that intimate?"

"We are intimate. Just not sexually."

It was a line they'd agreed to draw not long after Hannah's marriage opened up, to not complicate an important, enduring friendship. It had been the right call.

"We weren't—"

"And we don't curl up on the sofa together. I sit here." Cass tapped the armchair they were seated in. "And you sit there."

"Now you're just being pedantic."

And she was getting defensive. Cass again had a point. When she'd been tucked up on the sofa with Drew, it had felt intimate. The warmth of their body next to hers and the occasional casual touching of limbs felt like it meant something.

"When do you let someone be that physically close to you? Someone that you aren't fucking. Or planning to fuck."

This made Hannah snort her tea and then splutter it over herself. She grabbed a tissue to dab her top. Damn. It would need rinsing ASAP to ensure it didn't stain. Which at least gave her an excuse to exit the conversation. "I need to clean myself up."

Hannah took her time selecting a clean top as she let Cass's question sink in. She'd always preferred plenty of personal space. It wasn't socially acceptable to say once you were an adult, but people smelled, amongst other disruptive sensory output, and could get in the way of her flapping. Even more so since her marriage turned sour, and she tended to only breach that space when she really wanted to touch someone. Which, as Cass noted, tended to be around sex. Or kink, which wasn't always sexual for her—she could get lost in sensory play without wanting anything else. Though was that admitting she'd only let Drew close because she wanted to have sex or play with them? That really hadn't been her conscious intention when she'd agreed to them coming round.

She carefully removed her soiled top and slipped on a replacement before heading to the kitchen to rinse it. Cass met her there.

"Don't think I'm gonna let the subject drop." They leaned against the kitchen counter, hovering on the edge of her vision.

"I know." Hannah put the top in the sink and ran the tap, letting the sound of the gently running water flush away her resistance. "You have a point, I concede. But I wasn't planning on anything happening. And nothing happened."

"Do you think Drew wanted anything to happen?"

Hannah paused her squeezing of the fabric. Did they? They had seemed happy to be close to her, and there was that twinkle in their eyes. "I'm not sure."

Okay, so they asked her out on a dating app, but they had been clear it was in a platonic way.

"I suppose it only matters if you want something to happen…"

Hannah felt the heat blooming in her cheeks and her lips turn up into an involuntary smile.

"I'm going to take that as a yes. Now we're getting somewhere." Cass was practically bouncing off the sideboard.

"We've just agreed to do a two month miniseries. I don't want anything to mess that up."

"That's only two months. After that…?"

Hannah shrugged in an attempt to make it feel casual, as if it didn't really matter what happened next. "We'll see."

It wasn't like it hadn't occurred to Hannah that there could be possibilities there, but she needed to remain focused until then. There was a moment's silence, except for the sound of water splashing and escaping from the sink. She turned to Cass to see them looking at her with a curious expression.

"What?"

"They're poly, right? Polyamorous and married. Would that be an issue for you?"

Cass really wasn't holding back. But that was why she loved and trusted them.

Would it be a problem? She'd hooked up with poly people recently, though not people she'd known or wanted to get to know. Some of them were married, though she wasn't with them long enough to get the fine details, except when she was joining both parties. They just helped her scratch that itch.

"No, not for me. I've been with poly, married people, and it's been fine. Drew already has more than one long-term partner, so seems happy and settled in it."

She hoped so anyway. Not everyone was like her ex, even if they did have some wobbles while figuring out how multiple relationships could work.

"That's a good sign. Being the first can be rough."

Cass had their own experience, though from a different perspective, as they had been the new partner walking in without realizing they were being put in the middle of a marriage meltdown. Hannah had heard enough from them, while she comforted them during and afterwards, to be wary of putting herself in that position. Even before she'd been part of a couple opening and breaking up…and hurting other people in the process.

"So you'd be open to dating them, or someone like them? You've not been put of poly entirely?"

It was a subject they generally steered clear of as Cass was very aware of Hannah's wish to take a break from relationships and the reasons why. She'd never want them to feel that they had to hold back from telling her about their own dating dramas and happiness, but she probably wasn't their first choice of a confidante any more. It wasn't just her own romantic life that she'd ended up taking a step back from, and she missed being the friend Cass turned to. Given how they'd stuck by her, surely she owed them better than that.

"I'm still not looking to date in the romantic sense. But when I am, yes, I'd want to date poly people. Poly wasn't the problem with my marriage. Despite how that went down, I still believe in it."

"I'm glad she didn't wreck your hopes of non-monogamous happiness completely. Can I give you a hug?"

"Yes." Hannah dropped the top and dried her hands before opening her arms to welcome them in.

It was a raw subject, but she was slowly healing. Having a friend like Cass helped, a friend who wasn't afraid to talk directly about things but never pushed her to move faster than she was ready for.

When she was ready to put her heart out there again, she had no plans to go back to monogamy. She'd been enjoying the freedom to explore sex and kink connections with whoever she wished, rather than expecting one person to meet all her needs. Why would she give that up if she didn't have to? And it had never entirely made sense to her that you could only love one partner, when you could love more than one friend, parent, or sibling. It was illogical. Take Drew—they were someone who clearly had so much love to give, and to constrain that would be a waste of such a passionate soul. She had no doubt that they had the capacity to love both their partners wholeheartedly and have room for someone else.

Maybe even someone like her, if she let them.

CHAPTER EIGHT

Drew was tempted to stick the big announcement straight on their socials, but there was someone else they wanted to tell first. Plus if they did, they'd soon be bogged down engaging with the responses and didn't want to delay their visit.

Their mum lived a good couple of hours away, having moved towards the coast when she retired. Although Drew had initially disliked her not being close enough any more that they could pop round to see each other regularly, Fran was happy there, and it did have the advantage of being near the beach. It reminded them of the seaside holidays they'd taken when Drew was a kid, just the two of them, hanging out on the pier playing the 2p machines and building elaborate sand castles which drew praise from passersby. Sometimes their creations would draw helpers and would become a large communal project, making up for Drew's lack of siblings. Good times.

It was lunchtime when they arrived, which meant fish and chips on the beach. As it wasn't yet school holidays, the car park was only half-full when they got there, and they spotted Fran's car easily. It was empty—she must have decided to take a wander while waiting for them.

A cool sea breeze tickled their ears when they stepped out of the car. They grabbed a light beanie from the door where they kept it for these times. The beach was beautiful, but it could be nippy even in June. They called Fran while weaving through the car park towards the waterfront.

She picked up within two rings. "Hello, my love. Are you here?"

"Hey. Yep, I'm heading to the beach. Where you to?"

"I'm in the queue at the chippie. It was building up, and I figured you'd be hungry when you got here."

"Great, I'll head over. See you soon."

They didn't need to ask which chippie or give their order. This was their little ritual since Fran's move. And they'd managed to reach a compromise years before that she wouldn't question what they ate—no hinting they should be on a misery-inducing, slimming diet to at least show willingness to conform, despite having been fat their whole life without any fad diet changing that fact—so they could safely tuck in without enduring heckling. It had taken a few months for Fran to sample the numerous offerings close to the beach and settle on the best Newbay had to offer, but once she'd found her favourite, there was no turning back, and she'd probably be heading there weekly until the day she died.

Which shouldn't be any time soon. Drew couldn't imagine a world without her. Although little Drew had sometimes asked for a sibling—before they fully understood what they were asking of their single mum—they had been happy being the centre of her world and wary of any potential step-parents. None had stuck, and their mum had seemed content without a romantic partner. She'd filled her life with work and child-rearing, and art and friends. But once Drew was all grown up and she gave up paid work, she'd re-evaluated and announced her intention to move away.

At least she'd picked somewhere scenic where they could still easily visit. Despite being ten minutes late, Drew couldn't rush their stroll along the beach and took in great gulps of the salty fresh air. By the time they'd made it to the shop, Fran was at the front of the queue collecting their lunch. *Ideal.* She beamed when Drew entered, a little bell announcing their arrival and causing all the locals to turn their way. Her residence and Drew's regular visits meant they weren't counted as a tourist, and they exchanged cheery greetings as they passed the queue to join her.

Fran put the paper wrapper in her hands down, and Drew enveloped her in a hug and gave her a big squeeze, lifting her slightly off the ground, having long been the bigger of the two of them.

The pier was less busy than the chippie, and there was a free bench at the tip, where they could stare out at the water with nothing else in sight. It was their favourite spot, and they headed there by unspoken agreement. The lapping waves against the reinforced wooden posts beneath them added a peaceful soundtrack to their meal.

Drew captured a chip on their wooden spork while keeping an eye out for hungry seagulls. It was the disadvantage of eating al fresco, but those childhood beach trips had prepared them well.

"So, what's new with you?" They were dying to tell Fran all about the podcast series, now that it had finally been announced, but held back, so as not to risk missing out on hearing about her life once they started in on that news.

"Well, there is something I've been wanting to tell you."

Drew paused with a chip half to their mouth. This sounded juicy.

"You're dripping!" She pointed to the chip with her own spork.

Ketchup was escaping back to the tray in their lap. "It's fine, didn't get me. What do you want to tell me?"

Drew couldn't let her get distracted from whatever she'd been wanting to share. They had regular phone calls but saved bigger news for when they were together in person. And this sounded like something bigger.

"I've started seeing someone."

"That's great. Is he a local? Where did you meet?"

As much as she had seemed content without a partner for a long time, Drew did worry about her getting lonely in a new place without even workmates to hang around with.

There was an uncharacteristic pause before she answered. "Yes, *she* is local. I met her at my book group."

This time the whole chip dropped off their spork, and they put it down rather than looking away to respear it. "She!"

This was the first hint—like *ever*—that their mum might be queer too. How had they not known? How had she never told them?

"You don't have to announce it to the world." She patted their knee and looked around. "Don't you always say it doesn't matter what gender the person is you fall in love with?"

"You're in love?" Their voice rose to almost a squeak, and they took a breath to bring it back down before continuing. "And you're right, I'm just surprised as you'd never mentioned any interest in women before. How long has this been going on? Why am I only hearing about it now?"

Maybe it wasn't something every mother would tell their offspring, but they'd always been friends too, and Drew was way old enough to know.

"I'm not interested in women. At least, not that I'd noticed. I'm just interested in Viv. It came out of nowhere for me too."

They sat in silence for a moment while that sank in.

Fran looked down at her tray to spear another chip with a shy smile. "And yes, I think I'm falling in love with her. It's wonderful and terrifying. I was scared I wouldn't know what to do but..." Her smile grew.

"Ha! Yeah most people worry about that, it's totally natural, but when you get down to it you know what feels right."

Which was good because as close as they were, giving their mother sex advice might be a step too far even for them. But that clearly wasn't why she was telling, and now that she finally was, they didn't want her to regret it.

"Sorry, I am really happy for you, it just caught me by surprise." They pressed a kiss to her cheek, a hug being too risky around the chip papers. "So, tell me all about her. You met in your book group..."

"Yes. I'd noticed her and we got on instantly, but I thought it was just a friendship. Then we read one of that Sarah Waters's books, and I kept picturing her, us, in the story..." Her cheeks flushed, and she paused to take a drink. "Then when we discussed it, Vivienne shared a hint of her past with women. She's a widow, see, was married to a man, and I hadn't realized he wasn't her only love."

"As in she was with someone else beforehand, or they were poly?"

This was getting more interesting by the minute. Drew had to nudge themself to keep eating before their food got totally cold.

"Not quite. Or that's not what she calls it, and it wasn't the same as with you. He was actually gay too, it turns out. They both knew about each other from early on, but it still made sense for them to marry. They loved and respected each other and could be safe to do what they wanted while appreciating the home they built together."

"Sounds like it was a good thing they found each other. I bet they weren't the only people to make that choice, and who knows, I might've done the same thing if I was born in a different time."

They didn't know how common it was, but it was a story

they'd heard before and weren't about to judge. And it sounded truly consensual, unlike many other versions they'd heard. It must've helped that they were both closeted gays. *We always find each other.*

"And I'm glad you found each other too," Drew added.

"Me too. I'm happy with her. We're happy. Ridiculously so. We're like two infatuated schoolgirls at times."

"Aww. I can't wait to meet her. Though maybe once you're past the not being able to keep your hands off each other stage." They winked.

She reddened, and the sea breeze clearly wasn't to blame. Had they ever seen their mum blush before?

"I'm sure you'll get to meet her soon. She's keen to meet you. I've told her all about you, of course."

She gave Drew's knee a squeeze as if they still needed that reassurance of their place in her world. Despite being nearly forty, they did appreciate it.

"Anyway, enough about me for now. What's new with you?"

It was tempting to pry for more information on the mysterious woman who had sent their mum all aflutter, but they did have big news also.

"Well, I am now safe to tell you that I'm gonna be doing a Pride miniseries with *Beyond the Books*."

"That's wonderful, my love. You must have impressed everyone last time. I listened with Viv, and she was very impressed. She regularly listens to the show and said you were one of the most charming guests they'd had on. I'm so proud of you."

Fran put her arm round them and gave them a squeeze despite the risk of splatter.

It figured her partner might listen, given how the couple had met. Maybe they could find a way to slip that story into a recording somehow. Hannah was sure to be interested in a queer book bringing two retirees out and together. Drew did smile to themself at how quickly Fran brought it back to her new romance, but they couldn't resent her for it. It was hard not to get swept up in a new love. And Viv's backstory made it all sound like a novel—the new kind, where they could be allowed to live and love happily ever after.

❖

Hannah was curled up with a book, engrossed, when her phone buzzed. For the third time. Or was it the fourth? The earlier alerts had merely tickled the edge of her consciousness as she moved through the story. The only reason she was more aware this time was that she'd just gotten to the end of a climatic chapter and was ready for more tea.

She took her phone with her as she padded through to the kitchen to put the kettle on. Who was that interested in getting hold of her? She could make a guess but didn't want to get her hopes up. Or acknowledge that she wanted their attention. It could be marketing spam or unnecessary notifications. She tried to turn off and unsubscribe from as much as possible, so when her phone buzzed it meant something, but some junk inevitably got through.

It was only after she'd swished out the kettle, refilled it, and turned it on that she let herself look. She didn't want to be drawn out of the fantasy world she was currently occupying but could risk a peek while she was waiting for the water to boil.

There were indeed four messages, and they were all from Drew. Her stomach did an uninstructed flip. Since their cosy night in together, they'd been exchanging messages every day, and only some were related to the podcast. There was a connection building between them that she couldn't ignore or stop. She didn't want to. It didn't need to turn into the type of connection she'd sworn off. Drew could be a good friend…and friendship could have many benefits.

The first was a beach photo of the fully clothed, look-at-the-beautiful-scenery kind. What would Drew wear in the other kind anyway—she could hardly imagine them in a string bikini, though she wouldn't describe all their clothing as definitely not womenswear. Would they be comfortable stripping down in public? They didn't seem the self-conscious type generally but hadn't shared whether there was any body dysphoria that might get in the way. Not that it was any of her business. Maybe they'd be into the nudist approach, given that then they wouldn't have to worry about gender-affirming clothing. It was her own preference, rather than wearing tight uncomfortable swimwear that dug in at pressure points. Okay, thinking about Drew getting nude was not what she should be doing. Where had that even come from? The photo was perfectly innocent.

The second photo was another selfie on the beach, but unlike the first which starred the scenery, this one starred two beaming people holding ice cream cones. The woman sitting next to Drew seemed faintly familiar, and the accompanying message explained why. It was Drew's mother. There was a definite resemblance in the shape of their facial features and their open expressions.

Had a lovely day visiting my mum. She's excited about the series and can't wait to meet you—her new girlfriend is a big fan of the pod!!

That was a lot of information to take in. Their mother couldn't wait to meet her? Had she agreed to that or accidentally indicated an interest in getting to know Drew's family? She shook her head to clear the many more questions crowding in regarding how Drew might be viewing their connection. It was probably just a turn of phrase and not meant to be taken literally. Though the girlfriend being a fan might mean they would try to make it happen. Hannah didn't usually meet her fans, but was Drew expecting her to make an exception for them?

The two mothers, or mother and female partner, were also a revelation. Not that it mattered that Drew's mother was queer, but it was interesting to note. Maybe in exchange she'd be willing to talk to Hannah about her experiences being sapphic and what it was like for her generation. It would add depth to her understanding of the older queer titles. Hannah made a note on her phone with this idea before remembering she should probably respond directly too.

The next message broke that thought chain. Apparently Drew had also moved to thinking about the podcast, but in their case not about the content.

We were wondering why you don't have some kind of loyalty programme. It's clearly popular and other shows make a good income off their patrons, without having to let any advertisers on. You make good content and you should get paid for it!

This was followed by another long message with ideas about bonus content to provide for these imagined patrons.

It was tempting to just ignore the suggestion rather than diving into a discussion where she'd have to justify not doing what they suggested. It wasn't like the idea had never occurred to her, and she'd already weighed up the pros and cons. She didn't need to rethink it. The podcast already took up a huge chunk of her life, and she didn't have the spare time or brainpower to do more. She'd already doubled the production and therefore her workload for their series. It wasn't like she was hoping to quit her job and make it her main focus—she loved her job and her *hobby*. She wasn't about to fall into the trap of overcommitting herself just to earn some extra money that she didn't need. Clearly none of that had occurred to Drew despite their inside knowledge.

It would be best to not engage until the tension had left her head and she wouldn't be tempted to snap at them. But given what happened last time she took time to respond to a bright idea of Drew's, she couldn't afford to leave it unanswered or say she would think about it. She did not need them galvanizing her audience to put pressure on her to do it. Hopefully Drew had learned from last time too, but she couldn't be sure. Best not risk it and be direct. Which handily was her forte.

I had considered it but decided against it. I don't have the resources (time, energy, etc) to run it and I don't need the extra money.

That should clear that up.

The kettle must've boiled already as the light had gone off and the switch was back up, but she hadn't heard the click. She put her hand to the body to check. Yep, it was very hot. And she'd taken a moment too long to register that fact. She pulled away and stuck her hand under the cold tap. It wasn't burned, but the heat smarted, and the cold water calmed her angry skin and prickly thoughts. She left her hand cooling under the running water, though used the other to put the teabag in her mug and pour the water over it. At least she'd had the sense to test it with her non-dominant hand.

Her phone buzzed again as she carefully patted the scorched skin dry. Ugh. She slid the device back out of her pocket, genuinely hoping this time that it wasn't Drew. It was.

What if you had someone to help? You wouldn't have to set it up yourself and it would mostly manage itself once running. It could produce a decent revenue for little extra work each month. I'd be happy to lend my expertise from running my own business.

She pressed her lips together. They clearly weren't getting it. Was this another attempt to stay involved and/or get some control? She'd only known them for a short while and wasn't ready to trust them with her baby, or commit to working with them long-term. It was her passion project, not theirs, and she'd put a lot into it over the years. It wasn't like she was slacking off or missing out on opportunities she wanted.

That's not the point. I would still have to produce the bonus content, interact, and have ultimate responsibility. I don't need that extra work. And the show doesn't need it.

Okay, that might have sounded harsh, but it was the truth. She didn't need them pushing her in a direction she didn't want to go or wheedling their way into *helping* manage her business. She'd had enough of that from her ex. Before Drew could come back with any more suggestions, she followed up with a final message.

I need to get back to my book, so I'm finished ready for the recording. Please do NOT post that idea as I don't want to raise people's expectations. Speak to you later.

The last part hopefully softened her dismissal. And even if it didn't, maybe that was for the best. She didn't regret sending it as she carried her mug back to the armchair and deliberately left her phone on the kitchen side where it wouldn't distract her further.

Her notepad still sat where she'd left it on the arm of the chair covered in scribbled notes of possible discussion points. Yes, she had enough to do and was already wondering whether committing to the extra shows—and cohosting them with Drew—was a mistake. Could she persuade them to rein it in enough to keep things running smoothly and come out the other side without anything having majorly changed? She wouldn't usually want someone to rein in their enthusiasm and disliked it when people tried to dampen her passion, but this was different. Wasn't it? She wasn't trying to diminish them as a person or prevent them from taking up space. She just wanted to retain control of the project and ensure she didn't take on too much.

This must be why everyone said not to mix business with pleasure. She couldn't help enjoying getting to know Drew, but it was proving tricky to enjoy that personal connection and stop them getting over-involved in the podcast. She needed to get her priorities straight. Starting with figuring out what those were.

CHAPTER NINE

Drew's apology went unread. *Crap.* They hadn't meant to be pushy about setting up financial support for the pod. It was just a thought…but one Hannah was clearly not open to.

"What do you think, am I the arsehole?"

They directed this at Pebbles, who was curled up in their lap. He kneaded their thigh in what they decided was meant to be a reassuring way—he had retracted his claws first.

"Thanks, buddy. I was only trying to help. Is it so wrong to think someone should be rewarded for their hard work?"

They scratched behind his ears, and he purred loudly, nuzzling into their hand.

"Not that you know the meaning of hard work, eh?"

The furball didn't appear insulted by this. Instead he nudged them to keep fussing him. He knew his place—he was there to be worshipped. And his affection, when he felt like bestowing it, was enough reward.

Was that the real issue, that Drew didn't know their place? It wouldn't be the first time they'd been told off for overstepping. It wasn't like they did it deliberately, and definitely not maliciously, but their tendency to be a backseat driver could be misread as an attempt at a coup. Not everyone appreciated their dedication, but once they were invested in something, they gave it their all. Wasn't that something Hannah should be able to relate to, given how much she gave to her passion project?

Pebbles rolled over so they could rub his belly. At least *he* had no complaints about the level of their attention.

Maybe this was one of those situations where someone felt like

Drew was taking over instead of supporting. Hannah was clearly still raw from when Drew had posted about the series before she'd decided if she wanted to go ahead. Personally, they didn't see it as a big issue—it was just a bit of market research, seeing if there was a thirst for it before they put any effort into planning. But to Hannah apparently it felt like pressure. Would she keep on holding that against them, or could she let it go? The fact that she'd planned a whole series with them surely meant something.

They would have to smooth things over again before the next recording in two days' time. Text clearly left too much room for misinterpretation of tone and intent. They needed to speak to her properly. It was unlikely Hannah would appreciate them just turning up at her door, though.

Finally, their phone buzzed, and they scrambled to grab it, almost dislodging Pebbles from his perch on their lap. It wasn't a full reply, but it was a response from Hannah at least—an okay reaction to their last message. It would have to do for an opening.

Sorry again if I overstepped earlier. Let me buy you dinner to make it up to you and we can NOT talk about it?

That would have to do. They didn't feel like begging her to forgive them as if they'd committed some unspeakable betrayal, but dinner would give them the chance to get past it. Drew put their phone down on the side table again so they wouldn't just keep staring at it, willing her to accept. She probably wouldn't even read it immediately. In the meantime, they could make it up to Pebbles for not being home much all week. He seemed happy with this plan, and his purrs increased to a ferocious level as Drew rubbed his fluffy belly.

They jumped when their phone buzzed again only a minute or two later.

Thanks, but I've already got dinner sorted.

They sank back into the sofa with a heavy sigh. Oh well, hopefully the offer helped. They were about to reply and say not to worry, when they noted she was typing more.

But you could treat me to dessert?

They broke out in a grin that was probably wider than necessary. She was still typing, so they forced themself to resist jumping in and let her finish.

Fancy heading out to that new ice cream parlour in town? I've been meaning to try it.

Ideal. They had already been with Rebecca, as part of their attempts to cheer her up in Alex's absence, but had no issue going again. The private booths allowed for easy conversation, and the wide, solid built-in benches meant no worries about cramped or flimsy seating.

You're on. Shall I pick you up or meet you there?

It was tempting to insist they'd chauffeur, but best not push it. Hannah took a few minutes to reply.

A lift would be great, thanks. Can we say about 8pm or is that too late?

That was fine by them. It would give them time to grab dinner first too, though they wanted to leave plenty of room for dessert so they could enjoy the outing. Sometimes they got self-conscious eating junk food around people they didn't know well or trust not to judge them, especially in public. There was the risk that their companion would feel the need to make pointed diet talk and insinuate Drew was guilty of the sin of gluttony for not starving themself to holy thinness. Hannah wasn't like that, though. There'd been no sign of judgement when they'd enjoyed takeaway together the week before. She didn't seem uncomfortable with their body size—in fact they could've sworn they'd caught her checking them out more than once, turning to find her gaze on their round butt with a look that was hard not to interpret as admiration, but maybe that was just wishful thinking, and the venue was her suggestion, after all.

Maybe they should've invited Phoebe to join them, but instead they found themself hoping that she wouldn't spot them at the block of flats, as not including her would be impossible then. They waited in the car after texting Hannah to say they were outside—they were on a double yellow so shouldn't get out and risk a parking ticket anyhow. It wasn't that they didn't want to see Phoebe, just…they wanted one-on-one time with Hannah to ensure they were all good.

Hannah emerged not long after they texted. She was wearing a light flowing cardigan that curled around her hips. Drew forced their eyes up as she approached and popped upon the door.

"Hey," she said as she climbed in next to them.

"Hey."

They smiled at each other for a moment, and Hannah fiddled with one of her plaits.

"Wanna put your seat belt on and we can get going? I shouldn't hang around on the double yellow."

"Yes, of course." Hannah blushed lightly and fumbled for her seat belt.

Drew wasn't sure whether to bring up their disagreement or not so focused on edging out of their temporary spot on the parked up street.

"So, you had a nice time with your mother? Does she live near the seaside, or did you take a trip?"

Hannah seemed to have decided rehashing things wasn't necessary, and Drew's hands relaxed on the steering wheel. It also gave them the chance to discuss their mum's big news. By the time they'd reached the car park behind the high street, they'd caught Hannah up on the main details and backstory.

"I must admit, I'd be interested to hear more of her partner's story. It sounds fascinating and like it could give real insight into a subgroup of older queer people's experiences."

"I thought the same. She could make a good guest or at least research subject, if there's a book you can link it to." They bit their lip. "Not to say you have to—"

"It's okay. I was thinking the same thing. I'm glad you didn't take it as me being uncaring and just wanting to use her as research." Hannah gave a short laugh to shake off that concern, then smiled and gave Drew's hand a quick squeeze where it rested on the handbrake. "I'm sorry if I seemed short with you yesterday. I just know that's a path I don't want to go down, and I didn't want you to get carried away…"

"No worries, I get it. I didn't mean to push. I should've figured you'd already thought it through."

"Yep. That's generally a safe assumption."

Hannah laughed and they joined her, relieved that there wasn't any big tension between them. They were a fan of talking shit out, not being scared of confrontation, but that relied on the other person also being okay with disagreeing sometimes. They didn't need their friends to agree with them all the time or never put a foot wrong. No one was perfect, themself included.

"Hopefully the ice cream will make up for it."

"I'm sure it will. I had a look at the menu, and I've narrowed it down to two options but may need your help making the final selection."

"If you don't object to sharing, I'm happy for us to order both, and then you can test which is best."

Sharing sundaes in a private booth would make it seem more date-like, but Drew tried to shrug off that thought. *Friends can share dessert too.*

"That would save me making the decision. Except I haven't told you what they are yet—you might not want either."

"I'm willing to take the risk and trust your judgement again. I don't think you'd lead me too far astray." They turned and winked at her while they were stopped at a light.

Hannah's smile spread, and the glow reached her sapphire eyes. Drew found themself staring into those eyes for a moment too long and had to resist the urge to lean in towards her. Were they imagining the spark there, or was Hannah feeling the charge between them too? And if so, would she want to act on it? Sure, she wasn't looking for a romantic relationship, but maybe their friendship was destined to have some added benefits. If Drew could enjoy that without wanting more.

It had been many years since they'd gotten intimate with someone they weren't romantically involved with or at least dating, but they had enjoyed sex outside relationships when they were younger. That had stopped once they'd discovered romance also didn't have to be shared with only one person. Maybe it would be worth reopening that door before Hannah slipped out of their life again. Once the series was over and Alex was back so not needing them to drop in on Phoebe, they'd have to decide if there was something personal between the two of them that meant they wanted to stay in each other's orbits. Hannah didn't seem to want Drew sticking around to help with the show longer term, but she might like to keep them around for other reasons.

❖

Hannah scooped up the last piece of brownie. The gooey chocolate cake swam in a puddle of ice cream, a texture and temperature combination that was somehow so good, once you knew what to expect.

"Did you want the last piece?" She held the long spoon out towards Drew.

They smiled, eyes twinkling, before they waved it away. "No, you go for it. I've had plenty."

Drew had stuck with their offer to split the desserts, allowing her to sample both options, and had seemed satisfied with her choices. It had been a bit awkward at first as they clashed spoons and leaned in close to sample from the same tall dishes, and more than once it had resulted in nervous laughter. It wasn't that she didn't want to get to close to them—it was the opposite, and that made her jumpy. She kept having to remind herself it wasn't a date. It was simply an opportunity to clear the air before they next worked together and to ensure they could still talk comfortably as required for the podcast. There didn't seem to be any issue with that. Drew was very easy to talk to in person, especially with all the extra signals to guide her that texts didn't contain. After the initial joyous sampling of the desserts, they'd both slowed down to chat as they made their way through the sundaes.

"Mmm. This was a very good idea." It had been her own idea, but it was still true. The brownie melted in her mouth, the rich dark chocolate balanced by the not-too-sweet vanilla ice cream.

"Agreed." Drew pulled the other dish towards them to scrape out the remnants.

Hannah followed their lead and shifted the once-brownie sundae in front of her, so she'd have less chance of dripping the melted remains everywhere. She had somehow managed to avoid any major spillages so far. She checked her watch. She'd need to leave in the next five minutes if she was going to get the next bus.

"Did you need to be getting off?" Drew must have noticed the gesture.

"Only if I want to catch the nine fifteen bus." She'd wondered if it had been a mistake to accept their offer of a lift so had planned her options beforehand in case she wanted to leave before Drew was finished or didn't want to be trapped in a car with them after. But she'd felt no urge to escape their company.

The parlour was fairly busy—she'd failed to take into account it was a Saturday night when she'd suggested it—but the layout of the booths meant it didn't feel crowded once they were seated. She'd managed to successfully request one away from the entrance and the counter, tucked up against a wall and with tall Perspex sides that reached the ceiling creating a protective bubble. The only issue was the glaring strip lighting, but she'd brought a cap which took care of that, and Drew hadn't questioned why she put it on when they came inside rather than taking it off.

"No need, I can drop you back." Drew didn't look up as they dredged the bottom of their glass.

"Only if it's not too far out of your way."

She didn't relish the idea of getting the bus at that time, but she had her earbuds and MP3 player in her pocket, which would make it more bearable. She didn't want Drew feeling obliged to help her or thinking she wasn't capable of getting around by herself.

"It's not too far. And I'm happy to. I wouldn't just take you somewhere, then abandon you and expect you to make your own way back."

"Good to know." She laughed. It was a fair point. "Thanks."

Drew leaned back and rested their hand on their belly. "Though I might have to let this go down a bit before I'm up to moving."

Hannah suddenly wished that she was seated next to them and it was her hand pressing on the soft curve of their body. She held on tighter to the cold glass in front of her.

"That's fine by me. I'm in no rush if I don't have to worry about buses."

She didn't have any other plans for the evening, except for her usual night-time routine, and hanging out with Drew was a nice way of filling the gap in her schedule. That was all.

"Cool. I may just pop to the bathroom, although…" They looked towards the gendered doors with suspicion.

"I never got why toilets have to be labelled with stick figures. I used to get confused when I was a kid. I did get that the figure with the skirt was supposed to represent women and girls, but I still questioned which one I should use given I wasn't usually wearing one." She shrugged. "Why can't they just label them all with what they actually contain—cubicles, urinals, sanitary bins, baby changing stations…It would be more logical."

It must be infinitely more difficult for someone like Drew who was fully aware that they didn't fit either option on offer and not just because of their clothing choice. Hannah didn't know what their body looked like under their clothes but also didn't know why it would matter to her in terms of sharing a public space. She couldn't entirely relate but hoped they would see her story as the attempt at empathy that it was.

"That would make going out a lot easier. If only everyone was that logical. Though it's not just the gender thing. I've also gotta make sure it's not too much of a squeeze." They held their palms up close together, indicating a narrow space.

"Ah, okay. There's a gender-neutral disabled toilet over there if that would be a safer option." She pointed behind them at the separate door.

"I know, but I don't like to take that up in case someone needs it."

"You need it." It was tempting to add that she was disabled and had no problem with them using it, but she was never certain if she had the right to claim that term. If the world didn't take issue with her way of being and was built to suit people like her, she might not be.

"I guess." Drew continued to stare at the main facilities behind her.

It was strange seeing them so unsure of themself. Hannah glanced over and noted the group of people hanging around near the toilet doors. It would probably be fine, but she knew better than to reassure them that no one would care which one they used because she couldn't be sure that was true.

She sighed in frustration. "People shouldn't get so hung up on these things. Everyone should be able to pee in peace."

Drew cackled. "That should be our motto."

"I can go with you if that would help." She could wait until she got home and didn't tend to trust the cleanliness of public facilities, but if it would help Drew feel safer, then she could face it.

"I don't think it's that kind of establishment." They winked at her.

Hannah laughed. "I didn't mean it like that!"

"Shame." They laughed too, then flopped back in their seat. "I try not to overthink these things and just get on with my life. I won't let it stop me going anywhere I want to go."

That was more like the Drew she'd got to know.

"Yeah. Sometimes the world isn't built for us, but avoiding it completely isn't the answer. We'd miss out on so much otherwise."

Though she wasn't going to pretend it was always easy to put herself out there.

"We gotta do what we can to make things more accessible, mind," Drew said, "but we can't wait for everything to be perfect. I reckon the best way to revolt sometimes is to enjoy our lives."

Hannah leaned towards them. "Definitely. I've struggled in autism spaces online because of the focus on trauma and everything wrong with the world. I get we need to talk about those things in order to know what needs to change, but…"

"I get it. Trans spaces can be the same, and there's only so much of that anyone can take. Sometimes you gotta focus on what brings you joy, not what takes it away." They reached over and took her hand, then chuckled. "Shit, I sound like one of those cheesy mindfulness memes. Maybe I'm spending too much time online."

"Probably." Realizing that might sound too harsh, she added, "But if it leaves you quoting motivational loving-kindness memes rather than conspiracy theories, I think you're doing okay."

"Glad you don't think I'm a lost cause." They smiled and met her eyes, as if challenging her not to agree.

She turned over her hand, careful not to slip out of their grip, so she could return their hold. She had always been too honest for that kind of banter.

"I could never think that. You give me hope for the world. You're so open and caring and offer so much, and you deserve to receive all that kindness back too."

Drew's smile wobbled, and their eyes took on a filmy sheen. "Now who's being cheesy."

She had to laugh and let the tone lighten. But she didn't want to let their moment of intimacy pass so soon. "Want to order a drink while we let our food go down?"

"Definitely." Drew pulled their hand back slowly, as if reluctant to break contact, and took the menu from the stand. "Do you need to let anyone know when you'll be back?"

"No."

It was an odd question as Drew knew she lived alone, didn't they? Unless they were thinking the accommodation staff tracked her movements.

"I come and go as I please. I don't have to tell anyone anything."

"Cool. I wasn't sure how it works at Hawthorn."

"It's not restrictive at all. Which is part of why I moved there instead of back in with my parents. They probably would've wanted to know a lot more."

Plus she didn't want to put everything on them, considering the state she'd ended up in. She'd tried to shield them from the worst of it and keep her independence, though the flipside of that was her parents didn't totally understand why she'd needed to leave her ex.

"As much as I love my mum, I couldn't imagine moving back in with her and having her keeping tabs on what I was up to," Drew agreed.

"Exactly. I wanted to move forward, not backwards. My parents are supportive, but they don't entirely get me. Including my desire for alone time. Plus there are some things they don't want or need to know."

The idea of having to explain her sexual partners to her parents was a nightmare even in her imagination. There was no script that would easily persuade her mother it was no big deal. She was an adult. She shouldn't need to justify her private life.

"It does take some juggling when you live with anyone. Leigh, my wife, doesn't even want or need to know everything. Though she fully consents, mind." Drew held up a hand in the stop signal as if to stop her even thinking anything untoward was going on.

"I get that. It is so much easier now that I live alone." Especially given what her ex was like. Hopefully Leigh was nothing like that. Or Drew. Drew might get a bit overenthusiastic sometimes, but they wouldn't be controlling or possessive of their partners, would they? They seemed like a relaxed and empathetic person.

But people weren't always what they seemed, and she'd learned a long time ago not to trust people at their words. It turned out that not everyone was as honest and upfront as her, or even wanted to be. Only time would tell if Drew really was as genuinely lovely as they seemed.

Chapter Ten

A re you seriously abandoning us to stay at home with a book?"
Drew looked up from said book to find Leigh had put on
her jacket, then returned once again to check she'd understood what
was happening. At least she seemed surprised rather than offended, and
there was a smile tugging at the corner of her mouth.

"I want to get this finished before the recording tomorrow."

Or nearer finished anyway. The reality of their deadline was
setting in.

"Okay. But we'll miss you. If you're finished later, you can always
join us for a drink or two after the quiz." She walked back over, clearly
in no rush to leave them.

"We all know you're the brains of the operation. You won't miss
me in the scores."

It was something they'd come to accept early on in their relationship, before they even *had* a relationship. Although it occasionally
brought on a twinge of self-doubt, mostly Drew was proud of Leigh's
wits. They had always had a thing for smart women.

"But we'll miss your fine motivational speeches and commentary."
Leigh leaned over and kissed them tenderly.

"I'll be cheering you on from a distance," Drew said.

"I'll listen out for you." Leigh straightened up and laid a hand on
their shoulder as she turned to go. "Seriously, no pressure, but it's fine
if you change your mind and wanna meet up later. Just let me know, so
I can tell you where we're to."

"Will do."

It was tempting to say they'd join her—they did want to, and it was a good compromise—but given they were only halfway through the assigned reading, it seemed unlikely they'd be done in time.

Leigh walked away but paused in the doorway and turned around again. "You like her, don't you."

"Who?"

"The host. Hannah, is it? You *like* like her." She said it as if it was more a fact she was checking than a question.

As if it was as clear and simple as whether she'd got her name right.

"That's not why I'm doing this." Drew wasn't about to deny it but was still figuring out what it meant. And if Hannah felt the same way.

"Nice dodge." Leigh smiled and tilted her head to the side, holding their gaze. "I look forward to hearing more at our next check in."

"We'll see if there's anything worth mentioning." Things weren't at a point where they would usually tell Leigh, but as she'd already picked up on the vibe, they relented. "Either way, we can talk about her then if you want."

"Okay. See you later, darling."

"Later. Love you!"

Leigh blew them a final kiss before properly leaving and closing the door behind her.

When was their next relationship check in? Drew put down the book to check the calendar on their phone. In a week's time. That didn't give them long to figure things out, but they didn't have to have everything figured by then. They just had to be able to give Leigh some idea of where they were at.

The monthly check ins had been a staple in their calendars ever since Drew and Leigh had seriously started to explore poly and found something was needed to ensure they talked things through without it taking over all their time together. Even though it turned out other romantic relationships weren't something Leigh wanted long-term, she hadn't tried to shut Drew's poly side down and still saw the benefits of having that time put aside. Despite living together, they had separate enough lives that it was easy to miss something, and Drew didn't want to be that guy who didn't remember even the most important things in their wife's life if it didn't directly involve them.

While Drew was checking their calendar, they couldn't help seeing their notifications. There were three messages from Hannah: two confirming logistics for the recording and one featuring her work dumpster cat—a clearly not-homeless moggy that hung around the back of the high street shops charming all the staff. Hannah had confessed to keeping a bag of treats by the back door for when it deigned to visit and that she suspected she wasn't the only one.

They tapped a thumbs-up on the info messages, then snapped a shot of Pebbles in return. He had wriggled his way onto their lap and tucked himself between them and the book. He stretched over the open page, hinting at where he thought their attention should really be.

Pebbles still reckons he's better off inside.

"I am going to get back to reading that, you know."

Pebbles gave them a sideways glance that confirmed he had other plans.

Can't blame him when there's the option to be curled up in your lap.

Hannah's response made them grin. Okay, surely there was no question that was flirting.

You'd be welcome to join him, there's plenty of space.

Though if she did, they would definitely not be getting any reading done. Which genuinely was why they'd stayed home. Hannah was just very…distracting.

Was that invitation for me or dumpster cat?

You. I doubt Pebbles would agree to opening up our relationship, so we will have to remain a one cat household.

Drew was more than a little curious to see how far Hannah would let this go. Their conversations had flirted with flirtatiousness but not so explicitly. Drew had been holding back, given Hannah was clear she didn't want a relationship.

I suppose a one pussy policy isn't as bad as a one penis policy.

Their laughter exploded out of them, making Pebbles jump and slide off them to find a more peaceful place to lie. The infamous One Penis Policy was not something Drew had ever had to deal with personally, not having dated any cishet men, who were usually the ones to demand they remain the sole provider. Funnily enough, they'd never come across a woman requesting limits on any body part, though that didn't mean it didn't happen. They couldn't imagine agreeing to either with any human, but their relationship with Pebbles was a lot more hierarchical.

It was very tempting to carry on the exchange, but they really should get on with the book if they were going to be prepared enough to not let Hannah down. They'd switched to audio for the older, denser text and managed to finish recapping it while at work. The twenty-first century book was an easier read—including emotionally—but they still had a good wedge to go. Their initial flip-through had only made it clear that they didn't remember enough to give an in-depth take, and that their view might well have changed since their first reading years before.

They reacted with the laugh-cry emoji before sending a sign-off text with a picture of the open book in their lap.

It's tempting to stay distracted by you, but I gotta get this finished if I'm going to keep up with Matilda tomorrow.

They wouldn't want to give the impression that they weren't enjoying the connection or wanted it to stop.

Hannah reacted with a heart immediately.

In that case I better let you go. I've heard she can be a strict mistress.

What could they say to that without wading into hotter water? It might be a joke but made them wonder about the allusion to kink. Was that something Hannah wanted or needed in her connections? It was common in the poly community, but it wasn't Drew's cup of tea. Power play wasn't something they enjoyed. Though the idea of being dominated by Hannah sent a not-unpleasant shiver through them.

It was a struggle to resist the urge to open Hannah's dating profile and check if there was anything on there to clue them in. Not everyone declared their kinky inclinations on the public forum, but if it was key to someone, there was usually some mention. They could look later if they finished the book before Leigh got home. It was seeming even less likely they'd be joining her and their friends. It was a good thing they hadn't promised anyone anything.

❖

"Is there anything else you'd like to talk about before we finish?"

Hannah was pretty sure they'd covered everything in her notes, but she hadn't checked much during the recording. The conversation had flowed naturally and hadn't needed much steering from her. Drew really was a great guest—bringing them back hadn't been a mistake. It helped that they'd spent a fair bit of time together, and texting, so she had an understanding of Drew's communication style. Though that didn't explain how well they'd got on the first time.

"I think we've covered everything for now. Plus I'm holding back some thoughts for later in the series so I don't run out."

Hannah laughed, instinctively moving back from the mic so she didn't sputter all over it. "Good plan. In case you hadn't heard, this isn't a one-off episode, and we're going to be making a miniseries for Pride, exploring LGBTQIA literature and how it's changed over recent decades. You can find out what other books we'll be covering by signing up to the *Beyond the Books* mailing list."

"And if you haven't heard enough from me already, follow me on all the socials. Or the ones I'm not too old for anyway," Drew added.

She'd given Drew permission to guide people their way. It might save her from having quite as much feedback to respond to if listeners could go directly to Drew, and they'd earned the boost to their follower numbers.

Hannah recited the rest of the usual sign-off, giving Drew a chance to say their goodbyes to the audience, though she often re-recorded the ending after editing. It allowed her to add in anything she realized had been missed only after shutting off the mics and to make sure it matched the mood of the final cut. But that could all wait for another day.

She gave a long cat-like stretch and rolled her shoulders. The movement and change in pressure were very pleasant after sitting in one spot for over two hours. Maybe she should've suggested a refreshment break, but she hadn't wanted them to lose their rhythm.

Drew smiled at her from the screen. "You're like Pebbles after he's woken from a nap. Speaking of which, I should go check what he's been up to while I've been shut in here. I suspect some further treats may be in order so he'll forgive me for not including him."

Hannah had the urge to ask them not to go, despite just spending that long with them, but swallowed it down. "Thanks for keeping him from interrupting. I hope he forgives you."

There were plenty of people who let their pets roam free and didn't worry if they showed up on a video call or recording, but she didn't like to risk the distraction or extra background noise.

"I'm sure I can bribe him to soon enough. What are you going to do now?"

Good question. She deliberately hadn't made any plans for the evening as she never knew how wiped out she'd be after a recording session, or how long it would take. Sometimes she needed to cocoon herself away for a while to re-regulate. But she didn't need or want to this time. "I don't know. How about you—once you've placated the cat?"

"I've got no plans." Drew tilted their head and smiled.

"Did you fancy coming over and celebrating getting it down? I'm not up to going out, but it would be nice to bask for a bit." Hannah looked at the top of the screen as she spoke, studying the fading blue streaks in Drew's hair, not wanting to read too much in their eyes.

"Sounds lush. When will you be ready for me?"

She glanced around the room, calculating how much needed sorting before she could have a guest round. It wasn't like Drew hadn't been there before. There weren't first impressions to worry about, and she didn't want to needlessly delay them or give herself time to regret the invitation. A warm glow was growing in her chest that was clearly not just relief at getting finished. "I'll be ready by the time you get here. Just let me know when you're setting off."

"I'll text you. See ya shortly." Drew threw a final beam her way before leaving the video call.

What had she done? She hadn't wanted the moment with them to end but had not planned on continuing in that fashion. No time to think about why or form any expectations for the night, which was probably for the best. A rush of adrenaline helped push her to her feet and straight into tidying mode.

By the time Drew messaged saying they were on their way, half an hour later, she had got everything in its place and managed to run the Hoover around. She didn't know exactly where Drew lived, but from their previous visits it must be fifteen to twenty-five minutes away. That meant she still had time to give the bathroom a quick wipe around, then put her recording equipment away while she listened out for them.

Except she found herself drawn to the bedroom first, checking for clean sheets, then stripping the bed. It was a job she could do while taking a clothes break. After rushing round cleaning up, she could use the opportunity to let her skin settle down: she didn't want to be uncomfortable in her body around Drew. Or untouchable. She tried to bury that last thought as she smoothed out the clean sheets, resisting the urge to lie down on them afterwards and enjoy the cool cotton under her naked body. She should definitely have clothes on when Drew got there, whatever direction the night might go.

As they were staying in, she did allow herself the compromise of not wearing a bra. She slipped on a loose long-sleeved blouse over a camisole that hopefully didn't reveal too much. And was Drew likely to complain if it did? The tone of their recent interactions implied she wasn't the only one questioning the nature of their connection, and the way Drew's eyes lingered on the exposed skin at her collarbone made it seem like they'd like to see more.

The intercom trilled, and her stomach fluttered in response. She buzzed them in, then paced her hallway as she waited near the front door, swinging her arms around her body to release some of the anticipatory energy.

When she opened the door, Drew stood armed with wine and chocolates. A casual jacket squared their shoulders and cut a line down their chest. Her eyes followed the cut down, then darted up when Drew spoke.

"I wasn't sure if you drank, but if not, I do know you like chocolate."

"Correct." She smiled and stood aside to let them come in, relieving them of their offerings. "And I do drink, sometimes, depending who I'm with and how I'm feeling."

"Good to know. And what do you feel like doing with me?" The quirk of their lips indicated they were aware of the potential double meaning. It wasn't just her.

Her eyes rested on their lips, and before she could process if it was the right thing to say, the truth popped out. "I want to kiss you."

Drew blinked for a moment, seeming caught off guard by her candour, then recovered and stepped towards her. They took their presents back from her and placed them on the hall table, then drew her into their arms. "Good, because I'm not sure I could resist you for much longer."

Hannah leaned in and kissed them deeply, not holding back as her body willed her to press closer, letting herself get caught up in them. They ran a hand round the back of her neck, holding her close, keeping the kiss going. She draped her arms around their strong shoulders, trusting them to keep her standing as her knees started to wobble.

Eventually Drew pulled back, but only an inch or two, and murmured, "Mind if I take my jacket and boots off?"

She giggled. "Sorry, I probably should've let you do that before jumping you."

"Do *not* apologize for that. It's good to know you want this as much as I do."

They kissed her briefly again before releasing her. She let her arms slide off their shoulders, but only so she could help them remove the unnecessary garment.

"Do you want a drink?" She mustn't forget her hostess duties entirely.

"Yeah. Why don't we open that bottle before we get too carried away."

Drew bent over to remove their boots, and she grabbed the bottle to help her resist reaching over to squeeze their butt.

The drink was a good idea. She needed to step back before she gave in to her instincts entirely. She led the way to the kitchen and heard them follow her. Drew leaned against the counter, their face flushed and their body emitting a warm glow that she wanted to step inside. She fumbled in the drawer for the corkscrew.

"The glasses are in the cupboard behind your head."

While their gaze was off her, she managed to focus long enough to find the right utensil.

"Allow me?"

Drew held out their hand for the corkscrew, and she relinquished it with relief. She didn't totally trust her coordination in the most controlled state, let alone when she was busy lusting over the person standing mere inches from her.

After expertly uncorking and decanting the red wine, Drew picked up both glasses and appeared to be waiting for directions. Hannah chewed her lip as her brain ran through the pros and cons of the possibilities.

"Shall I take them to the sofa?" they suggested.

Drew didn't seem annoyed by her lack of decisiveness, and she let out a breath of relief at the decision being made. She nodded and followed their lead this time.

Once seated, Drew held out their arms for her, and rather than taking the seat next to them she slid onto their lap. They welcomed her with a soft embrace.

"Comfy there?" They ran a hand up her arm, and she shivered.

"Yes." She leaned in to kiss them but pushed back after a long moment to grab her drink and allow them to breathe.

She studied Drew as they took a sip of their wine, keeping an arm threaded around her waist. She couldn't resist reaching over and running her hand through their short locks, releasing a sweet scent of hair gel.

Drew put down their glass and she copied, and they fell into another long, deep kiss. She squirmed on their lap, lifting her legs onto the sofa and letting their hand slip round to her butt to hold her in place. She didn't want to stop even to take a breath, but when they next pulled back to take a gasp, she took advantage of the space. She'd never asked about their relationship to their body, but now, she needed to know some things.

"I was wondering, how do you like to be touched?"

They chewed their lip at the question, and she had to resist pulling it into her mouth.

"I like a lot of things. Right now, everywhere, however you want, feels good. I'm weirdly more comfortable naked than in clothing, as long as there's no pressure and we can change things up if it doesn't feel right."

"Sounds good to me." She ran her hand up under their T-shirt and across their smooth belly. They shivered in the most delightful way. She hadn't planned to rush into anything, but it was seeming unlikely either of them would be keeping their clothes on for long. If they were really doing this, there was no point in forcing themselves to go slow.

"I also feel more comfortable naked—in my case for sensory reasons."

"Well then, maybe we should shed these pesky layers." Drew ran a thumb over her collarbone. "And how about you? How do you like to be touched?"

"I…" She stuttered as their hand moved downward and grazed her bare breast. "I like firm pressure, mostly, not light tickling touches."

"Mmm, like this?" They slid their hand round to fully cup her breast, squeezing and rubbing her nipple with their strong fingers.

"Yes." She gasped and kissed their wicked grin. "Oh, and just to warn you, my speech can fail me when I'm…worked up. But I can let you know what I want in other ways."

"I'll bet you can. I'll make sure to pay attention to everything." Drew slipped their other hand inside her trousers, squeezing her butt and moaning with her.

"And"—she pushed herself to continue while she could still speak—"as we've not talked about safety or shared test results yet, I like to use gloves."

"Ditto. Is that just for if I'm inside you, or…" Their other hand slipped from its hold on her butt to move to the clasp of her trousers.

She sucked in a breath involuntarily. Luckily she knew this script well. "Yes, just when you penetrate me."

"When?" Drew chuckled. "I'll take that as a request."

They tugged at the button of her trousers, and she let go of their hair to open it for them. Their fingers grazed the base of her panties, and she groaned, pushing into their hand.

"It's tempting to take you right here, but how about you show me to your bedroom and we get rid of all this clothing."

She smiled, glad this didn't require a verbal response, and rolled herself to her feet somehow, pulling Drew along behind her. Good thing she'd changed the bedsheets.

❖

When they made it to the bed, Hannah immediately flopped back onto it and pulled Drew on top of her. Drew obeyed and kissed her again, in a more leisurely way. Now that they had her there, they planned to take their time with her. She moaned and held them closer.

"Is this okay? I'm not—" They leaned their weight off her, resting on their elbow, suddenly mindful of how much smaller she was.

"Firm pressure, remember. I want you on me." She pulled them back over so their bodies fully connected.

Drew moaned at this and captured her lips again, their hands roaming down her body. The way she said exactly what she wanted was sexy as hell.

Hannah's hands crept under their shirt. "Can I touch your chest?"

"Please," they replied without hesitation, not wanting to break the spell by overthinking it.

She didn't make them wait and let her hands sweep round to their front, stroking their heaving chest.

"Mmm. And didn't we say something about it being better without clothes?" Drew kneeled back, straddling her hips, and started to unbutton their shirt.

Hannah watched them with an admiring gaze for a few seconds before sitting up and joining them, planting kisses along their collarbone as their body was slowly revealed. As soon as they pulled off their shirt, she slipped her fingers under the elastic of their sports bra. They took the hint and removed it too, and she caught the weight of their breasts in both hands as they were released. She kissed Drew as she teased their nipples, swallowing their moans.

"Do you want to suck them?" they asked, in case Hannah was waiting for permission.

She kissed her way down their chest until she captured a nipple, wrapping her arms around them as she sucked and flicked it with her tongue. They clasped her head against them, urging her on, and she raised her thigh to press against their aching centre. They rode her as she continued to tease their nipple but pulled back up when she moved to give her attention to the other one.

"Wait, you still have far too many clothes on."

"Then you better help me remove them." She nipped at their lip playfully.

Drew laughed but wasn't about to argue. They made short work of it, pulling her blouse and camisole off over her head in one go. Hannah shivered as her bare chest was exposed to the air, then lay back down, pulling them with her before they could properly take in the sight of her teardrop breasts. The glide of skin on skin made Drew squirm for more as she pressed her firm thigh against their crotch. They shifted to kiss her rosy nipples before they got too carried away, and she arched her back to meet them. When they stroked just under her waistband, she shifted her trousers down off her hips. She was definitely a woman who knew what she wanted.

They took the hint and slid down inside her panties, moaning with her as they found her swollen clit.

She pulled them up to kiss her, then murmured, "Let me get you some gloves."

"Please do." Drew rolled over to allow her some movement but didn't stop running their fingers over her.

She fumbled at the drawer in her bedside cabinet, and they chuckled as she seemed to struggle to maintain enough control to grab what she wanted.

"Need any help there?"

"No." She triumphantly flopped back with her prize. She held the packet up to them.

Drew pulled a pair of the sleek black gloves on. The sight seemed to make Hannah squirm even more. Clearly not wanting to wait, she pumped a little lube onto the smooth material, then took them by the wrist and guided them back to her centre, then seemed to remember she still had her trousers on. Drew stayed where she'd left them as she wriggled out of her remaining clothing, leaving herself completely naked at their fingertips. They kissed their way back down her body and stroked the downy hair coating her thighs.

"Please." Hannah pulled their head back up and kissed them fiercely. "I need you inside me."

"Whatever you need." They slid their gloved hand between her legs, then gave her what she'd asked for.

Hannah moaned loudly as they slipped inside her, bending her knees to invite them deeper. They started slowly but quickened to match the intensity of her thrusting against them and sneaked swift kisses between her gasps. When they finally took her over the edge, she hugged them tightly, clinging to their shoulders.

Drew ran their hands through Hannah's thick hair as the last shivers of her orgasm settled. The bands had come off at some point, and they finished unravelling the plaits with their fingers. Hannah sighed in a contented way and snuggled deeper into their chest. If they stayed like that for long, she looked set to fall asleep.

Which meant they should get moving. Not that they wanted to. Drew let their hands drop to Hannah's bare back and gave her a squeeze.

"Don't stop," she mumbled.

"I thought you were drifting off."

"No, I'm awake." Hannah opened one eye and peered up at them.

"Uh-huh." They leaned down and kissed her softly on the lips.

That seemed to wake her up, and she wriggled up their body to kiss them more thoroughly.

"Hi," they whispered between kisses.

"Hi." She smiled.

"*Sooo*, what just happened?"

Drew was pretty sure what page they were on, but it was best to check these things in case someone's imagination got carried away. In this case, it was likely them who was in danger of reading too much into the night of passion.

"We just had a wonderful time, indulging ourselves in celebration of a job well done." She traced a line around Drew's nipple as she spoke, and they had to grab hold of her hand to stop the distracting sensation.

"Good for us." They kissed her again, and as the kiss deepened they let her hand go and let their own roam the curves of her body.

"Oh, it was." Hannah rolled over onto her front so her whole body was pressed against theirs. "This wasn't a promise of anything else, though. I'm still not looking for a relationship."

Their heart sank slightly to hear it confirmed. But they tried to stay in the moment and not let whatever wouldn't happen next get in the way of both their pleasure. Hannah had been upfront about what she could offer from the start, and they had given in to the urge to check her dating profile again so it was clear in their mind. "I know."

Drew pressed their forehead to hers and closed their eyes. They didn't need their connection to be anything more, and they didn't want it to be anything less. It had definitely been worth indulging. They ran their hands back down Hannah's body and squeezed her butt. She giggled and squirmed against them, and they smiled with her.

"Given how good this feels, it would be a shame not to take advantage of the pleasure another time..." Hannah traced a finger down the flat centre of their chest to their stomach, where she rested her hand.

Their smile grew. "Just no soppy advances?"

"Exactly. Not getting into a romantic relationship doesn't mean we can't keep enjoying each other."

She crept her hand down lower as she spoke, and Drew quivered, making no effort to resist her. She paused over their crotch, and they couldn't help pushing into it.

"Can I take that as agreement?" She teased them with her fingers as well as her words.

"Yes," they gasped. "Who wouldn't want this?"

She laughed her agreement and kissed them deeply. "But for tonight, do you need to be getting home?"

Drew moaned again, this time in frustration. "What time is it?"

Hannah stilled and reached over with her other hand to grab something off the nightstand but came back empty. "I don't know where my phone is, and I don't want to get up to look."

They chuckled. "Ditto."

Not that the time really mattered. Leigh was out herself and wouldn't be wondering where they were. But rule number one of casual sex: *Do not sleep over and wake up with them.* It made it a lot harder to not catch fuzzy feelings.

"I should probably get going soon..."

"You don't want me to finish you first?" Her fingers started teasing them again.

"I said soon, not now." There was no need to deny themself that.

Hannah laughed. "If you want to take a shower before you head off, we could finish up in there."

"Ideal." They took a quick look at the twisted sheets, discarded gloves, and open bottle of lube they were tangled in. A shower was definitely a good idea.

"How about I go get it warmed up for us, and you can come join me in five minutes."

"Mm-hmm." But they couldn't bring themself to let go of her. "Or how about we stay here for now, and then you can go do that while I recover."

As nice as shower sex sounded, they weren't sure their legs were capable of holding them up. There'd been a well of sexual tension building between them, and now that the dam had finally cracked, there was no stopping it.

"That sounds like an even better idea." She withdrew her hand and met their hungry gaze. "And how would you feel if I put some gloves on, so I can feel you squeeze me while I make you come?"

"Lush." Drew felt themself pulse in anticipation and was pretty sure it was what they wanted. And if it wasn't, they were also pretty sure they could trust Hannah to understand.

"Excellent. Just tell me if it stops feeling right at any point." She kissed them gently. "I only want to make you feel good."

They moaned their appreciation and pulled her into a deeper kiss. Definitely no regrets.

They might not be planning to fall asleep in each other's arms, but they could still care for each other afterwards instead of Drew sneaking off in the night like they'd done something wrong. It would be a pleasure to wash away the excesses of the night together before they parted ways. It hadn't taken long for the benefits of Hannah's friendship to multiply, but that was hardly surprising given both their natures. Hannah might not be a romantic like them, but she was as passionate, if not more so, as shown in everything she did. As they'd said, who wouldn't want this? Who wouldn't want her?

CHAPTER ELEVEN

I had sex with Drew."

Min peered at Hannah over the tops of her reading glasses. Was that a look they taught them in therapist school? Sometimes Hannah wondered if she even needed the glasses.

"Okay."

"Last night. Here. Well, not here exactly"—Hannah waved at the soft furnishings they were sitting on—"in the bedroom."

"Well, that's alright then." Min chuckled, then gave a look over her shoulder towards said bedroom. "Are they still here?"

"No, no. They didn't stay over." It may have technically been the next day by the time they'd left, but that didn't count. They hadn't slept together in the literal sense.

"And how are you feeling about that?"

"Them not staying over or us having sex?"

It was Min's standard opening question, but this wasn't one simple thing to have feelings about. Plus her response bought a bit more time to figure out what she was feeling. It wasn't what she'd planned to bring to her therapist, but she couldn't think about anything else.

"Whichever you'd like to talk about."

"Umm." How to figure out where to start or what needed to be said? Her thoughts were entwined with the floaty afterglow from the night, which made it extra difficult to think straight.

"How about we start with what happened. No need for all the explicit details," Min warned, having learned to be specific about these things, "but give me some idea of how this came about. Who made the first move?"

Hannah trawled through her memories, trying not to get sucked in by the more intense moments. As Min said, she didn't need those details, and Hannah didn't want to share them. Those were just for her—and Drew—to enjoy replaying. *But later.* She squeezed the arms of her chair to bring herself back to the session. The faux leather was sweaty under her palms.

She located the moment and blushed. "I did, verbally. I told them I wanted to kiss them."

"And was that something you planned to say?"

That was Hannah's style, especially for significant moments like that, but she hadn't planned this time. Unless daydreaming counted. "No, not consciously. But they asked me what I wanted to do and…"

"You gave them the honest answer." Min smiled.

"Yep. I think that caught them off guard, but they got over it quickly." She smiled back. Drew might have seemed slightly surprised by her admission, but it clearly hadn't put them off.

"Perhaps they appreciated you putting it out there so you could both then decide whether to act on it."

"Maybe. They didn't seem to have any doubts about whether we should."

Things had moved quickly from there, and there probably wasn't much else she could say without making her therapist blush. Not that the sordid details would throw Min, who thankfully applied her non-judgemental approach to Hannah's sex life. Hannah had held off mentioning it when she'd first started indulging in hook-ups, but at her initial tentative revelation Min had only seemed glad she'd been open with her. Given it was her previous relationship that had landed her in therapy, the time spent with Min wouldn't have been much use if she couldn't talk about her sex life, but she'd had visions of being told her kinky pleasures were rooted in issues she should resolve. Having just started enjoying sex again, she hadn't wanted her therapist putting a dampener on things. Or even worse, given Min worked with the supported accommodation provider, telling the accommodation staff to prevent her from pursuing her desires.

"Did you have any doubts?"

Did she? Hannah sank back in her chair to consider this fully. Had she hesitated or not been certain at any point when she was with Drew? "No. I just wanted them. To be with them."

"And now what do you want?"

She sighed. She'd kind of been hoping Min would go easy on her and she could get away with not considering it too deeply. Had she forgotten who she was talking to? "I want…"

I want to be with them. I want to feel their skin glide over mine. To feel their heart beat against mine as we press together so tightly it's as if we're trying to fuse our bodies together. And for it to be more than physical closeness. But I want to be able to pull back apart afterwards. And I don't know how to make that sound logical or safe, even to me.

"You want…" Min prompted her to say it out loud.

"Sorry. Right now, I want to continue what we started last night."

"It sounds like there's a *but* on the end of that sentence."

Min flicked her pen between her fingers, and Hannah watched the metronome-like movement, getting sucked into the flickering until she lost track of anything else. Min stilled, and Hannah blinked herself back. She grabbed the plush dog off the arm of the sofa and squeezed it to her chest, cushioning her face in its silky fur. It wasn't as much comfort as a real dog, but she could squish it as hard as she liked without worrying about hurting it.

"But…?"

"But that might just be the afterglow talking."

Min chuckled. "That's a fair point. It's easy to get caught up in the nice feelings and not consider the bigger picture. But it's also important to let yourself enjoy pleasant moments and not think your way out of feeling good."

"Yeah. Part of me wants to just enjoy it, but another part of me worries what I'm getting into. Like, is it possible to keep it casual with Drew and not have it alter our relationship?"

"Would it necessarily be a bad thing if it did change? I know change and relationships can be scary, especially given your past, but might you be ready to explore something beyond a simple sexual connection?"

"No." Hannah said this with her mouth pressed against the dog's plush head so her voice came out muffled. "No. I'm not ready."

"Okay. I'm not going to push you to do anything you're not ready for. Perhaps we can explore why you don't feel ready and maybe think about what it would take to be ready, and how you'll know when you are. There is no pressure, but I know this is part of why you wanted to work with me."

"What if I'm never ready? What if I never want to put myself in that position again? I don't have to. It's possible to be happy without a romantic partner."

"It certainly is. That does partly depend on whether you want a romantic relationship and whether you have the option for one. It may be more difficult to be happy on your own if there's someone you want to be with. And who you could be with."

Hannah wanted to say that she didn't want to be with Drew. But it felt like a lie and so burned her throat. "There's more than one way to be with someone. Surely it doesn't have to be all or nothing."

Min paused at this, seeming to consider her next words carefully. Wasn't she the one always telling Hannah to be less black and white about things?

"You're right, there are many ways. So in what way do you want to be with Drew?"

Damn, she was not going to get around this. The downside of working consistently with the same professional was they got to know you too well for you to surreptitiously dodge their probing when they were on the right track.

"I want to explore our sexual connection more. It felt good with them, and comfortable. But not in a boring way. Better than with a random hook-up."

Min nodded but didn't say anything, leaving space for her to continue.

"And I want, I need, us to continue working together on the podcast and to not get distracted by our personal connection."

"Ah, so is that your concern? That it'll have a negative impact on your podcast?"

"Yes. I don't want it to impact our working relationship. If it carries on like this, it might seep into the recording and change the whole tone of it. And if it goes wrong, I could lose my cohost midway through the series and be left unprepared at late notice."

Talking about the podcast put her back on solid ground. It might not be her paid job, but it was as meaningful as a profession.

"That's understandable. I know it's an important part of your life.

Is your relationship with Drew something you want to consider more after the series finishes and that isn't a concern any more?"

Yes, it was important. And the series end was only two months away. That wasn't too long to wait, was it? Granted, she'd already failed to wait to get naked with Drew, but there was a chance she could stop things developing in any other way. If that was what she wanted. And it would give her time to figure out what she really did want in the meantime.

❖

Drew received the draft episode recording a week later, despite Hannah's plan to edit it quicker than usual so they could move on to the next one in the series. It didn't matter to Drew personally. They had already got through one of the books for the next episode and were actually on schedule for once. It was tempting to share that achievement, though they might not want to draw attention to their usual last-minute rush in case it made Hannah worry about future plans.

It was also tempting just to trust her and not bother reviewing the edit. They were pretty sure they'd not said anything they would end up regretting, and that Hannah wouldn't want to paint them in a bad light, though she was also someone who clearly took her work seriously and seemed unlikely to let her personal feelings about someone influence her product.

Whatever her feelings were. Since their steamy evening, Hannah had barely alluded to it and had just carried on her usual track, arranging the pod plus some friendly messages. Which made sense given that they were friends. Friends who had been incredibly physically intimate and held each other like they never wanted to let go. *Don't go there, Drew, you know what you're doing.*

They scrubbed the dining table maybe harder than was necessary. At least they weren't the only one sidetracked by what happened—when Hannah said the edits took longer due to being distracted by memories from that day, they'd had to smile. It seemed Hannah wasn't the only one who'd made an impression, and maybe her general messages didn't give the full picture of where her mind was at.

Out of the corner of their eye, they spotted Pebbles's fluffy tail as he bounded onto one of the dining chairs.

"Don't even think about it, buster."

He eyed the shining surface like it was a challenge.

"Down."

He eyed them like they were an insubordinate child attempting to order him around—amusing but still irritating.

Drew sighed and went over to pick him up. They needed to deposit him upstairs anyway to get ready for their check in with Leigh. If he was allowed to attend, he would try to ensure all the attention was on him, which didn't make deep conversations easy. In recent times he had been allowed to stroll in and out, as there hadn't been much to say. But Leigh's wish to hear about Hannah meant today would not be one of those days. They carried him through to the lounge, draped over their shoulder.

"Oh good, you found him. Do you want to put trouble up in the spare room for now?"

"Are you talking to him or me?" Drew chucked him under the chin, and his loud purring almost drowned out their own voice.

"You. If you've been causing trouble, we'll have to deal with that a different way."

Drew laughed, but not as easily as they normally would due to their chest tightening. What they had to say might not be what Leigh wanted to hear, and there might indeed be some unrest to deal with. They just had to remember that the chance to get close to Hannah was worth it. Wasn't it?

After depositing Pebbles in the spare bedroom and shutting the door quickly with an apology, they headed back downstairs.

"Are you ready for me?" they called over the banister as they descended back into the lounge.

"I'm ready if you are. Tea?"

A cuppa was definitely on the cards. "Of course."

Drew took a seat in one of the armchairs and made a few short notes on their phone while the kettle boiled. *Family = mom has a girlfriend!!* They hadn't been able to hold back that news, but it deserved recognition, and they could discuss how to introduce themselves. That was one trip Leigh would definitely want to be in on. *Work = ticking over. Podcast miniseries is going ahead.* Which wasn't officially work, but it was starting to feel like it. *Other partners = Rebecca missing Alex.* They should be giving her more attention to make up for it, but pod prep and Hannah had taken over. Which brought up *Hannah = added benefits*. How much more Leigh wanted or needed to know would soon become evident.

Leigh returned bearing two large mugs, and they jumped up to relieve her of theirs.

"Thanks, gorgeous." They took the opportunity to sneak a quick kiss before they sat down.

"You're most welcome." She gave them another kiss before heading for the chair opposite so she and Drew could comfortably look at each other and not rush into snuggles before they'd said what they needed to.

"So, where do you want to start. Little bits or big news for discussion?"

"Is there any big news?" Leigh peered over her cup at them.

"My mother just announced she's in a relationship, and not just any relationship—a queer one. How is that not big news!"

Leigh laughed. "Fair point. But I was thinking more poly-relationship-wise."

"Her partner was in an open marriage by the sounds of it, possibly poly."

Leigh shot them a look that said *You know that's not what I meant.*

Drew shifted in their seat. "You wanted to discuss Hannah, yeah." They tried to keep their tone casual and not picture the last time they'd seen her.

"I did think there might be something I should know about there. Has anything happened between you?"

"Yes."

There was no point trying to play it down, given they'd be spilling the beans in mere moments.

Leigh took a quick breath, and they could see her whole body tense, but then she let it out slowly and smiled. This wasn't the first time they'd been here. "Let's start there, then, otherwise I'll be wondering what and not taking in anything else."

"Fair dos." They paused to blow on their tea and take a sip, so they wouldn't blurt it all out insensitively. "Did I tell you already, she's not looking for any romantic relationships?"

"You did. Has that changed?"

"Nope. She brought it up again, after something happened between us."

Leigh gazed at them and seemed to be waiting for them to continue. So she did want to know more.

"She's not up for romance, but she is open to friends with benefits."

"Ah." Leigh nodded her understanding and appeared to relax in her seat.

"And it seems she wants that with me. Okay, she definitely wants that, and we've already crossed that line."

"I knew it." Leigh smirked.

"Hey, this was after that night when you asked me about her. I wasn't sure what she wanted then."

"I knew you wanted her, though, and how could she not want you?"

Drew smiled and felt themself flush. "Not everyone has your good taste."

Leigh laughed. "That's probably for the best. So, what are we talking here? Have you made any plans or agreements?"

"Not apart from to keep out of romantic relationship territory. And to use barriers during sex."

"That was going to be my next question."

"Don't worry, I wouldn't do anything to put you at risk."

They hadn't gone prepared to Hannah's as they hadn't believed sex was on the cards, but if Hannah hadn't brought it up, they would have done. At least they should have.

"So that's what she wants. What about you? I don't have a problem with that arrangement, but I know you, sweetie." She lessened the sting with a softer tone and a hand on their knee.

"I want to enjoy this connection without needing it to be anything more."

Hannah was right, they were too good together to not do it again. They could just have fun, right? Sex didn't have to be a big deal and come with big feelings.

"Good. I want you to enjoy yourself. I just don't want you to be left heartbroken if you fall for her and she doesn't reciprocate."

That was the risk, Drew knew it was, but it was one they were willing to take. They couldn't deny that if Hannah had been open to dating, they would've jumped at the opportunity, but that didn't mean they couldn't be happy with what she was offering.

"I know. I'll try to avoid that."

"Good. Because your heart is too precious to be messed with." Leigh rubbed their leg in a soothing caress.

She only wanted Drew to be happy. But if Drew cut off from Hannah now, that was the guarantee that they would get hurt. The bond between them had deepened quickly, and Hannah was someone Drew wanted in their life, in whatever form that took. No connection was ever guaranteed to last, and at least Hannah had been honest about her intentions all along. They could never ask any more of her than that, no matter how much they might find themself wanting to.

CHAPTER TWELVE

Hannah checked her notes as the video loaded, running her finger over the words even though the gel ink sat flat on the page. A notification popped up to say Drew was in the waiting room. She finished checking the series schedule she'd drafted before letting them in.

"Hey, you." Drew beamed at her from the screen.

Their hair glistened under the overhead light. It wasn't raining, so they must have just got out of the shower…which was not what she should be thinking about. The point of meeting online was that they wouldn't get distracted by the urge to get each other naked again.

"Hello." She kept her greeting more formal, though it was tempting to echo Drew's. It was a work call.

Drew seemed to pick up on the vibe, and their smile diminished but didn't go out altogether. "I'm guessing this isn't a social call. What do you want to talk about?"

Hannah breathed a sigh of relief at them getting straight to the point. It could be difficult to get through all the unnecessary social niceties required before you could get to the real purpose of any conversation, something she was pretty sure she'd already commented on to Drew. Maybe they'd remembered and adjusted their approach for her? The possibility gave her a warm feeling in her chest.

"I wanted to do a brief review of how the last episode went and discuss any changes we might want to make for next time. Plus I drafted a schedule for working on the rest of the series and want to run that by you."

It was her first time doing a series or covering two books in one show, so she was still trying to get the format clear and create a sensible plan.

"Sounds good to me." Drew tilted their head and ran a hand through their glistening hair. "Before we get down to it, though, I was wondering when we can get together again."

They delivered the line without any trace of innuendo, but she was guessing they weren't just imagining a friendly coffee. She certainly wasn't.

She brought up her calendar on her phone. "I could do Thursday?"

"Damn, I'm already booked then."

"How about after the recording on Saturday?"

Hopefully she would still have the energy to talk more afterwards, but that might not matter anyway given how quickly they'd got physical last time. And it could be the start of a nice routine—work hard on each episode, then get naked together as a reward.

"That works."

This time Drew's expression was definitely not professional, and she could guess what they were thinking. A pleasant shiver ran through her as she looked at their curved lips. It was definitely a good idea not to do the business meeting in person.

"Can we book it in and then sort what we want to do later?" she said.

"Fine by me. Sorry for taking us off track. Back to you."

They didn't look sorry, but commenting on that would not get things back on track.

"Shall we go over the schedule first, then discuss the recording?" It made sense to do the quantitative, clear part first, then see how much time they had to discuss the more fuzzy qualitative stuff.

"Go for it."

"Obviously it's up to you when you read the books, but I've included that in the schedule for my sake."

Drew shrugged. "It's good for me too. A deadline helps get me started."

"Great. So I'll finalize the edits, ready to publish on Monday morning—though I'll upload and schedule it on Sunday evening. Will you have time to review it before the weekend?"

"Sure, should do. And if not, I'm happy to trust your editing skills."

She smiled. Not having to wait on their response would help keep her on schedule.

Unless they didn't mean it, but hopefully they knew her well enough to not say that if they didn't want it to be taken literally. She deliberately didn't ask if they were sure. There was no need to play that game and risk ending up with a decision they both weren't happy with out of misguided politeness.

"Hey, I was thinking, did you record the video as well?"

"Yes. I keep the meeting recording as a backup in case either of our tracks failed to record properly."

"Great. Cos that could make a good bonus—other podcasts use it as a subscription perk—and it wouldn't mean any extra work for you."

By the strength of their smile, it seemed like they thought they'd just hit on a genius idea.

She sighed. "True. But you appear to be forgetting that I don't want people to know who I am. I value my privacy, and once the video's out there, it won't take long for people to find out my identity."

Including parts it might be best they didn't know for sure. Before she learned to stop looking herself up, she'd seen comments about her queerness and neurotype that were none of the business of strangers on the internet, and that could make her a target of various volatile subsections lurking online. She did not need their speculations to be given the boost of video evidence.

"It would only be for subscribers." They crinkled their eyes in a way she might have found adorable at another time. "If you were open to reconsidering that side of things…"

Hannah took a deep breath. "And you think subscribers wouldn't be the people invested in finding out more about me?"

"Fair point," Drew readily conceded, "but that doesn't mean they'd share their findings publicly—"

"*A*, that's not the point, and *b*, it seems unlikely none of them would. Even if the sleuthing starts on a private message board, it only takes one person to leak it to the wider world."

She was aware she was starting to sound paranoid, but it was true. She might not spend much time online any more, but she wasn't totally ignorant about the way people behaved in cyberspace—it was a big part of why she tried to stay out of it.

"Would that be such a bad thing?" Drew ventured in a gentle tone.

"It's not like people knowing would hurt your career or relationships. It wouldn't reflect badly on you or tell people around you anything they don't already know. Assuming it's not a secret you like books."

She smiled tightly at their attempt to lighten the tone with humour. "I do work in a bookshop."

"Exactly. It might even help your standing there. Not that I'm sure they don't already know how dedicated and brilliant you are."

She refused to acknowledge the compliment, given it seemed to be coming from a place of manipulation rather than honesty. It had already occurred to her Barnaby's probably wouldn't see her doing the podcast as a bad thing, as long as she was clear the company wasn't responsible for any of the opinions expressed. But that had never been the main issue that held her back.

"It's not just about people knowing my real name. It's about them knowing more personal details and expecting me to share more of myself in the show, especially in any bonus content."

"Again, would that be such a bad thing? I know you want to help folks see beyond stereotypes, so surely listeners knowing more about you and your life would only help with that. You've got this amazing platform and—"

She cut them off before they could get any more carried away. "And that's not what it's for. I didn't create this to share myself with the world. I know it's more common for podcasters to share personal stories and insert themselves into the narrative, but maybe my listeners like that I don't do that and take a more traditional media approach."

"Maybe. But you could be a role model for—"

"No!"

Just the thought of that level of social responsibility sent a violent chill through her. It wasn't what she wanted, and she wouldn't be pushed into being something she didn't want to be. She tried to summon the words to explain this to Drew in a way they would understand, but her internal connections were beginning to melt under the pressure.

And the connection between Drew and Georgia was seeming stronger, adding to the mess in her mind. Georgia had gradually taken control of every aspect of her life until Hannah had turned around one day and found it was no longer a life she wanted, the realization of which had spun her into even darker territory. Had she invited someone else in who would do the same?

Hannah's words failed her, but she grasped for some other way out and landed on her half-empty mug of tea.

She held the mug up to the camera.

"Tea break?" Drew looked like they wanted to ask more but thankfully resisted.

She nodded. The remaining tea was getting too cold to drink, and it would give her the chance to re-regulate.

"Hey, I'm sorry if I upset you and seemed pushy. I just admire—"

She held up her hand to stop them. She didn't need their apologies. She needed their understanding and for them not to add anything else for her to process. She clicked mute and turned her camera off, then realized they might need more information. When she didn't explain, people seemed to assume she wouldn't return. She might not be able to form mouth words, but she could type a simple sentence.

Can we take a ten minute break?

Of course. See you shortly.

She began to get up but saw Drew was typing something else. She waited for the push to explain or change her mind.

Sending calming squeezes.

It took her a moment to process the lack of argument and gesture of support. At least Drew understood and accepted some of her needs—in that way they were very different to Georgia. Hannah tried to highlight that point and save it as her overloaded brain slipped further out of her control. She managed to make it to the kitchen and put the kettle on before going to lie down in her bedroom, pulling the curtains tightly closed. She pulled her weighted blanket over her and grabbed a spinner. If she could rest and twirl through it, she might be able to bring herself back online in time to rejoin Drew. And if not, hopefully they would carry on understanding and prove she had no need to be afraid of their intentions.

The traffic came to a complete standstill, and Drew swore out loud. At least they weren't making anyone else late, and the others could start without them and knew Drew well enough to order for them if it came to it. Leigh had gone straight from work, knowing there was zero chance of her making it home and back in time in rush hour traffic.

That wasn't an option for Drew, though. They couldn't turn up to a restaurant in muddy overalls, and they definitely couldn't go to the theatre in them. They imagined the ushers politely turning their noses up and turning them away. Unless Phoebe was working and could sneak them in unvetted—they should've checked if she was on duty for that performance.

The radio news jingle signalled it had hit six o'clock, which was when their table was booked for. Drew sighed and gave in to the inevitable, shooting off a quick voice note to Leigh apologizing and asking her to order for them. At least they should be there in time for the food to arrive, though the way things were going it wasn't guaranteed. Their stomach grumbled, and they sat up straighter to stop the base of their binder digging into it.

They'd been running late and distracted all day, after a tense call with Hannah the day before. They hadn't been sure she'd come back after she'd seemed to lose the power of speech and left partway through, after another disagreement over expanding the podcast to connect more with its followers. When she did return, she was quieter and all business, in contrast to the enthusiastic host they were used to. Hopefully she would get her spark back before the next recording. Drew had only recently come on board, but they cared about the show too. And about Hannah.

Drew managed to glide through the traffic lights at the next change, leaving them with a fighting chance of getting a hot dinner, and a slight chance of a traffic ticket if the lights had reached red before they'd completely passed through. They would definitely be in time for the show. It was Rebecca's choice, of course, and the night out had started as a gift to cheer Rebecca up and make up for neglecting her while she was without Alex. But when Rebecca mentioned it to Ishani, she'd wanted to come too, and Leigh'd had the same response.

The benefit of their friendly arrangement was that they could all just go together, rather than having to go multiple times to keep everyone happy. It had taken a while for Leigh to get used to the idea that you could hang out with your partner's other partners and relax around each other. It helped that Rebecca was one of the most sensitive and empathetic people they'd ever met. Ishani's willingness to engage in double dates helped take the pressure off too, and from awkward beginnings they had formed an unlikely quartet, spending many enjoyable evenings together. It was the poly dream, though for some the fantasy would involve a kinky foursome, and that was definitely not on the cards, kinky or otherwise.

The multistorey car park by the theatre was emptying out of daytime workers and hadn't yet filled with the audience for the evening show, so Drew was able to find a space without any circuits or stalking of people brandishing keys. The ease with which they glided into a nice big space helped improve their mood. No squeezing between badly parked cars and having to force their body out while trying not to scrape themself or the other vehicles with the door.

There was a short queue winding out of the restaurant's door, and by the look of the fancier than average get-up, they were probably people heading the same direction after. Good thing they'd booked and some of their party had got there early. Drew apologized their way to the front of the line, then spotted Rebecca waving at them from across the bustling space. They waved back, ensuring everyone in the line was clear they weren't cutting, and motioned to the waiter before heading over with the waiter's blessing. Heaven forbid anyone think they didn't respect the great British queue.

Drinks had already arrived, and a rosy glass of wine was waiting for them by an empty chair. Ideal.

"Hey guys, sorry I'm late. Traffic was bad."

"No worries, darling. We ordered for you, so we won't be rushing." Leigh stood up to give them a quick squeeze.

"We may have had a wager on when you'd get here." Ishani spun her chair around to greet them as they passed.

Drew laughed. They couldn't be offended, given their established pattern of tardiness.

"Who won?"

"Me," Rebecca said and blushed. She squeezed their hand across the table as they sat down.

"Congrats." They lifted their glass and clicked it to hers.

"I wasn't working today, so I picked up Ishani from the uni, then headed straight here."

Which was Rebecca's polite way of saying everyone else had been on time.

"So, I hear you've recently landed yourself an extra gig as a podcast host." Ishani kindly changed the subject.

"I have indeed. Though it's only temporary, for a mini Pride series."

Drew didn't know what Rebecca had told her and hoped she'd not made it out to be anything more.

"You never know, if it goes as well as your first episode, maybe she'll keep you on or at least want you to do it again next year." Rebecca did indeed seem to have gotten a bit carried away with their prospects.

"Maybe, but it's doubtful. She doesn't seem keen to hear my thoughts on anything further."

They tried not to feel bitter about it. It was Hannah's show that she had built from scratch by herself.

"Oh really? Wasn't the series your idea?" Leigh leaned into their side, giving them a gentle nudge with her elbow.

"True." Drew smiled.

"Have you pitched any other ideas?" Ishani asked.

Which left Drew with no choice but to recount some of their recent argument, something they'd not been planning on getting into.

"It's a shame, as I reckon there'd be a good uptake and would mean she gets paid for at least some of the hours she puts in," they concluded.

"We have to remember it's not her job, though, and that's not why she's doing it," Rebecca countered.

"That's what she said," Drew muttered into their glass and took a healthy swig.

"Then it's probably best to drop it. I know you care about the podcast too, but if it's not what she wants or needs, then..." Leigh squeezed their thigh.

"I know." They laced their fingers though hers and squeezed back.

"Maybe you could start your own podcast if you're interested. I bet you're getting lots of useful experience," Ishani said.

It was a thought. Did they want that level of involvement and responsibility, though? It seemed like the podcast and everything surrounding it took up most, if not all, of Hannah's spare time. Ah. Maybe they should've been more understanding of her not wanting to take on anything more.

"I don't think I'm up for that. It would be a lot of work to start with and to build an audience. Hannah—" Crap, should they be using her real name? They'd resisted sharing it with Rebecca so far, along with other inside info, and they were in a public place. "She's already built a great platform. I just think she could make more use of it. It's not just about the money."

"Then what is it about?" Rebecca seemed genuinely lost.

"It's about, you know, using it to help challenge stereotypes and break down barriers."

"Isn't that what she's doing already with the way she approaches the subject matter?" Ishani clearly didn't get it either.

Drew took a deep breath and tried again. "Yes, but she's holding herself back. I just think if she shared her background and perspective, it would make it even more hard-hitting. She could be a real role model."

"And what does she think about that?" Leigh prompted, catching their eye and lifting an eyebrow.

"She doesn't want to put herself out there and prefers to remain anonymous," Drew admitted.

"God, I can't imagine anything worse than taking up that position online. I've gotta admit, I'm with her," Rebecca said.

"That may be a position you're confident taking, darling, but it's not for all of us. Some of us prefer to be able to live our lives away from public scrutiny," Leigh added.

It looked like Drew was outnumbered. "But you don't have her platform. It just seems a waste."

"It seems her show is doing its part by having nuanced discussions about creative content and seeking out people who aren't usually handed a microphone. That sounds like she's doing plenty." Ishani weighed in.

Shouldn't at least one of them take their side?

"I guess."

Leigh nudged them again.

"Okay, okay. She's doing a great job, and I shouldn't expect any more from her. Happy?"

Three hands reached across the table and bundled Drew's in a rush to comfort them in their defeat, preventing them from feeling too sorry for themself. Drew leaned onto Leigh's shoulder and accepted a reassuring kiss on the forehead. They might have been ganged up on, but at least their polycule weren't holding their apparent fuck-up against them.

Was that the core issue, that they were expecting too much? They'd always held themself to a high standard in order to combat the low expectations people had of the fat, queer kid, but they tried not to do the same to anyone else. Especially someone like Hannah who clearly hadn't glided through life. Maybe they did need to quit asking more of her and give her space to do what was right for her. Like Drew was doing in their personal connection, which they hopefully hadn't completely screwed up just when things had gotten exciting.

CHAPTER THIRTEEN

The lights went down, and Hannah breathed a sigh of relief at the still empty seats around her. As much as she liked going to the cinema alone, it held the risk of being packed in between potentially noisy neighbours. The whole point of going alone was so she could fully concentrate on the film, and antisocial strangers were even worse than talkative friends, who might listen when you asked them to be quiet. It never made sense that going to the cinema was considered a social activity—surely sitting in the dark somewhere you're supposed to not speak is the opposite of social.

Unless the person you were sitting in the dark with was someone you wanted to snuggle up with. That was one disadvantage of Hannah's current relationship status. One-night stands and casual encounters didn't tend to be interested in outside activities. An advantage of genuine friends-with-benefits was the cinema could be a mate-date or a date-date so could be undertaken with no pressure. It had crossed her mind to see if Drew was interested, but the film might not be their cup of tea, and she was still not entirely happy with them after their most recent disagreement over the podcast. It was a matter of waiting to see how the next recording went.

The screen filled with a bustling old London street and people dressed in what she had been assured was historically accurate clothing. Thankfully her earplugs took down the worst of the background noise, as well as the unnecessarily loud music, so she could relax into the film. She'd been looking forward to seeing it since it was announced with the promise of a more faithful adaptation of one of her favourite literary classics.

The previous attempt had been frustratingly simplified, and the mood was all wrong. Sure, they had to make some cuts to fit a whole book into a two hour screenplay, but the choices they made changed too much and lost the essence of its inspiration. From the interviews with the director leading up to this release, she'd felt the same way as Hannah and was determined to put it right. She'd stopped short of publicly shaming the first try, but that seemed to be more due to workplace politics than any positive feelings about it.

Hannah wiggled down in her seat and pulled her weighted lap pad from her satchel. The velvety soft cover meant it doubled as a mini blanket. She stroked it as the internal beads settled around her thighs. It would've been tricky to heave her full-size version there on the bus, and there was the risk of more than a raised eyebrow from the staff and other patrons. Plus even with the air con, she might get too warm under the heavy cover as in public she was expected to be fully clothed. Going out was full of compromises, but it wouldn't have been the same watching on a small screen at home.

From the first lines of dialogue, it was clear the director was telling the truth and had improved on the previous adaptation. Twenty minutes or more had gone by before she remembered the tub of sweets in her bag, and even then she was reluctant to take her eyes off the screen to get them.

It was a good thing she hadn't invited anyone who might accidentally, or deliberately, distract her. It seemed unlikely she and Drew would be able to fully behave in the dark, given the strength of their attraction when they'd finally both given in to it. It was very doubtful that wall could be rebuilt and stand firm again. It would be nice to have them to dissect the film with afterwards, though. Drew didn't always agree with her, but that didn't matter—they had interesting things to say and not only put up with listening to her in-depth takes but joined in with fervour. What would they think of it? Would they have read the book?

Somebody barked a laugh behind her and brought her back fully into the room. It made her jump, but she silently thanked them. She did not want to lose herself in thoughts of her new connection, like she had done so often recently, and miss something important. She shoved a spiky sweet in her mouth and let the sour tang pull her back into her body. Not having anyone to talk to in person about the film afterwards didn't mean she couldn't enjoy dissecting it. She could write it up for her blog, comparing it to the book, and see what her readers thought. She'd been so occupied with her podcast—and cohost—lately that she'd been neglecting the blog. She'd done the minimum of posting an article based on each podcast episode, but it'd been months since she wrote anything else. Maybe it was time she went back to her roots and explored things in the written word.

Blogging had always been her preferred format—there was more space for elaboration without leading a conversation off track, and time to find the right words. Not that she didn't enjoy the podcast. Maybe once her podcast miniseries was over, she could do a blog series about film adaptations. She'd have to decide whether to theme it any further. She popped another sour sweet in her mouth. Not now. The risk with her side project was that she could slip into treating every book, and now film, as something she needed to report on. With the blog, she could always just choose to write about it after if she felt like it and had something interesting to say. No advance commitment. Being able to create something when she wanted to instead of because she had to was a luxury she should take advantage of.

The two-hour film passed in what felt like a lot less, and she blinked fiercely as the lights came up at the end, shading her eyes too late. The other patrons started shifting and talking as soon as the credits started to roll, but Hannah waited until it was completely finished. She sat still, letting herself slowly readjust and waiting for the bustling line to the doors to disappear. There was no need to rush. She'd got the bus in but had planned to treat herself to a taxi home, as the switch from the large, airy, quiet, dark space of the cinema to the sensory onslaught of public transport would be too much. It was tempting to get cabs everywhere, but she couldn't afford it, and there was always the risk of an over-friendly driver. That evening if they decided to attempt a conversation, she could quite happily monologue about what she'd been to see, so it wouldn't be a problem.

When she got back to her flat, Hannah was disconcerted to see a small parcel left in front of her door. She hadn't ordered anything recently, and staff usually took delivery, then texted her to let her know to collect it from the office. They didn't just leave it there where any other resident or visitor could take it, especially not without notifying her. Or they shouldn't. Maybe she should complain, but that would take too many social spoons with likely zero positive outcome.

When she got closer, she noted there was no postage label on the box and only her first name, therefore it must have been hand-delivered by someone with access to the inside of the building. Was it something for the flat from the staff, or possibly a gift from a neighbour—Phoebe clearly enjoyed baking and regularly shared her creations. There were definitely worse neighbours to have, and Phoebe far outshone the previous tenant who frequently required intervention including from the emergency services and didn't always go willingly.

Hannah picked up the box before opening the door, noting the lack of smell or warmth to indicate freshly baked goods. Though it could have been there for hours. The door caught on an envelope that must've been pushed under it. So whoever left the parcel did seem to have attempted to tell her so. The envelope also had just her first name scrawled across it in the same handwriting. When she pulled out the card inside, she opened it straight away, and her eyes darted to the name at the bottom.

She hadn't been far off when she'd guessed it was from Phoebe. It was from a visitor of hers, which explained how it had gotten inside the building.

It was only a short note in which Drew explained they hadn't wanted to disturb her but wanted to apologize for pushing her and promise to stop, and they hoped it wouldn't put a dampener on Saturday. She smiled at the perhaps unnecessary gesture and the fact they'd known her well enough to not expect her to appreciate an unplanned visit.

When she flipped back to the card's cover, she laughed out loud. It was a standard picture of a waterfall, the kind you usually saw in a meme, but the cut-out letters pasted on top made it look more like a ransom note. The creepy text read: *We don't have to agree on everything, but we can agree to see the best in each other.*

The contents of the box also made her smile. She carefully removed the tape, then peeled back the lid to reveal a fluffy dog that immediately made her want to bury her face in its fur. It was like a travel sized version of the stuffed animal that sat on her sofa. She hugged it to her and found the fur was as strokably soft as it looked.

It had been a long time since anyone had sent her a gift, except at the mandated seasonal occasions. And it was a long time since anything she'd received from someone had made her feel that fuzzy inside. She squished the dog harder and tried not to think about what that might mean.

❖

The little plane icon appeared to be going around in circles. Was it supposed to do that?

Drew peered over Phoebe's shoulder to get a better look. The flight tracker seemed to have been working properly up until then. Phoebe had not stopped looking at it the whole drive over without reporting any glitches.

"Why is it going in circles?" Phoebe said, confirming that this was not what it usually did.

"It circles while it's waiting to land," Rebecca said, though she was also frowning as she stared at an identical image on her own phone.

"That makes sense. It can't exactly stop in midair to queue." Drew assumed Rebecca knew what she was talking about. She usually did. Unlike them, she thought before she spoke.

Drew was resisting getting out their own phone to watch the flight path. It was totally unnecessary given the other two were, and Drew would be distracted looking for a message from a certain someone. Plus they'd been lumped with the banner, which Phoebe had assured them would not happen, but here they were.

It was more of a placard than a banner, made of stiff recycled cardboard that until recently had been a moving box. Phoebe had painted *Welcome home* in red, orange, and pink letters, with Alex's and Willow's names underneath. She had also attempted to paint a portrait of Alex's cat, though the likeness was questionable. Not that Drew could do much better. They'd helped by providing the stencils for the letters, from which many placards had been written, and had added a few decorative touches around the edges until Phoebe told them to stop. Which was probably the right call.

Drew was just glad to have been included in the occasion. They hadn't been certain anyone would want them to tag along. Friends mattered as much as partners and family, but it didn't always play out like that in reality. Maybe they wouldn't have been included if they hadn't been needed to act as a chauffeur—Rebecca did drive, but not to places she didn't know. Though when Drew had floated the idea that they could just hang around in the car while the others went into the terminal to meet the flight, saving on the ridiculous parking charges, there had been an outcry that reassured Drew of their place in the welcome party.

If they were going to be waiting much longer, they were going to have to give in and purchase another overpriced coffee. A cluster of empty cups already stood at their feet. It had been a ridiculously early flight, but they couldn't blame Alex for opting for the cheaper antisocial option. Alongside the caffeine they'd been regularly topping up, they were buzzing with excitement of their own. They missed Alex, who had quickly become one of their closest friends over the past two years and their choice of sounding board. They couldn't talk to her about their relationship with Rebecca, a boundary Alex was keen on, but she'd probably have something to say about the Hannah situation. Not being married or living with a partner, Alex's background was more like Hannah's, and maybe she'd have some insight, including on starting dating again following a trauma break.

But it seemed unlikely Drew would get to see much of her for a good few weeks given the way Rebecca had been pining for her. Not to mention Phoebe, whose attachment to Alex was more than flesh-and-blood sisters. It was rare for Drew to have any hard feelings about being an only child these days, but the sisters' relationship did make them wonder what it would've been like having a fiercely loyal companion by their side from the start. As well as the backup, they wouldn't ever have been bored or lonely.

"Phoebe!" someone called from across the concourse.

Had they somehow missed the flight getting in, and the passengers had come in a different entrance? They'd been there staring at the arrivals board since long before it was due to land. The voice wasn't familiar, but they had never met the infamous Willow, who only dropped in on Alex when her touring allowed. Alex's decision to join her on her European stand-up tour meant they'd been together more in those few months that they had been in years.

Phoebe was still staring at her phone. Drew nudged her and peered around, trying to spot where the cry had come from. An unfamiliar older white couple were heading towards them with big smiles and no luggage.

"Phoebe!" the woman called again, and this time Phoebe did hear her.

Drew only just caught her phone as Phoebe shoved it into their hands and bounced over to embrace the couple. From the amount of fussing over her, it seemed they hadn't seen each other in a while.

"Do you know who they are?" Drew muttered to Rebecca.

"No, I don't think I've ever met them. Unless..." Rebecca's brow furrowed.

"Maybe it's Willow's parents?"

"Exactly."

Given that Willow and Alex had known each other since childhood, it made sense that Phoebe knew her parents too. Drew had never met Alex and Phoebe's parents, but from what they'd gathered the couple would definitely not be showing up to see their prodigal daughter return. Alex's lack of relationship with her parents made Drew extra grateful for their devoted mum—they didn't have a doting sibling, but she'd done her best to make up for that.

Rebecca clearly hadn't been expecting to meet her metamour's parents. She was twisting her hands in an anxious tell, and Drew reached over to offer their hand to clasp instead. She took it.

Was some of her anxiety related to being autistic? Rebecca wasn't diagnosed, but the more time Drew spent with Hannah, the more their suspicions were cemented. It would hardly be surprising given the number of neurodivergent people in queer and poly communities, especially when the two intersected. The fact Rebecca had never mentioned it made them wary of bringing it up—surely she would know herself and would say something if she wanted it known? Though as Hannah had pointed out, sometimes people in Rebecca's line of work didn't recognize autism because they were so used to seeing it only in combination with a learning disability. Maybe they should say something.

The initial cooing calmed down, and Phoebe led the couple over to join them.

"This is Keith and Emma. Willow's parents."

Bingo. Drew gave Rebecca's hand a subtle squeeze, and she squeezed back. To be fair, if they were unexpectedly faced with Ishani's parents, Drew would be shitting themself too.

"Hello, lovely to meet you." Emma smiled at them without an ounce of apparent discomfort.

Phoebe didn't seem to be planning on introducing their side, so Drew dived in.

"You too. I'm Drew." Should they try to explain their connection to Willow, or was it best to leave it there?

"Hi, Drew. Great to meet you. We hear you've been a terrific friend to Alex, helping her integrate after…everything." Mike reached out to shake their hand.

He clearly knew about Alex's past but thankfully resisted spelling it all out. Talking about the crash and her difficult rehabilitation was not the way to lower Rebecca's nerves.

"And let me guess, does that make you Rebecca?" Emma said.

"Hi." Rebecca gave a small wave and smile but continued to cling to Drew.

"We've heard a lot about you too," Mike said, then seemed to pick up on Rebecca's unease, "all good, of course. I suspect you've played a big part in helping our Alex look forward again too."

Rebecca smiled more naturally and blushed at this. "Thank you. And I've heard good things about you both. Alex and Phoebe were lucky to have you there for them growing up, and since then."

It was clear Rebecca was being sincere, she always was, and Emma's eyes welled up. Drew didn't know the full backstory, but it sounded like Willow's parents might have helped make up for Alex's parents' shortcomings. It was good to hear there had been someone responsible there for her when she was too young to completely fend for herself. Although Drew tried to give everyone a chance, they could never feel empathy for parents who disowned their queer kids. It was probably for the best Alex's parents weren't there, as then it would be Drew who struggled to stay calm.

"Now, now, let's save the tears for when we welcome our girls back," Mike said.

It was always going to be an emotional day, but he was right, there was no need to add anything more. Out of the corner of their eye, Drew saw Rebecca catch a stray tear on the back of her finger. They stroked their thumb over her hand they still held.

"I guess the only issue is, who gets the first hug?" Drew said. It wasn't like they were in the running, but it was something to say, and they suspected Rebecca was thinking it.

"I'll fight you for it." Phoebe held up curled fists.

Emma responded in kind, to Drew's surprise, shifting to match Phoebe's pose. "Oh, you think you're big enough now to take me?"

Phoebe dropped her fists in a fit of giggles.

"I didn't think so. How about I take Willow and you can take Alex."

"Deal!"

That was that, then. Drew figured Phoebe would push for priority and Rebecca would let her. It was Phoebe who had brought Rebecca and Alex together, after all, and she would always have the superior claim over all of them from loving Alex her whole life.

"Ooh." Rebecca dropped their hand suddenly. "It's coming down!"

She was staring at her phone again, and Drew leaned over to look, forgetting they were still holding Phoebe's until it was wrenched from their hand.

"Phoebe! Don't snatch," Emma said.

"It's my phone." Phoebe stared at it with the same intensity as Rebecca. "They're landing! They'll be here soon."

"Bear in mind we'll have to wait for them to collect their bags and go through passport control, so they'll still be a while," Emma cautioned.

"How about I get us some more drinks while we wait?" Drew offered. They weren't needed there, especially with Willow's mother taking Phoebe under her wing, but they could be of some use.

"I'll come with you." Rebecca seemed determined not to let go of them. Not until Alex had finally arrived anyway.

They were about to ask if she was sure, when they took in the fear still dancing in her eyes. Maybe it was more Rebecca didn't want to be stuck playing hanger-on with Phoebe and her metamour's parents.

It only took light persuasion to get Emma and Keith to let Drew buy the coffees. Likely they'd been up just as early.

The size of the kiosk queue made them wonder if it was a mistake, but they were back armed with steaming cups before anyone starting trickling through the arrival gate.

"Is this their flight? Quick, the banner!" Phoebe took charge when passengers eventually started filing through.

Drew picked it up from where they'd abandoned it leaning against an advertising column. Drew's arms were strong, but there'd been no need to keep it aloft for the hours of waiting, and even they would've sagged by then. "You want me to hold it or will you?"

"Me. No, you. I need my arms free to hug." Phoebe was bouncing on her heels with anticipation. Alex better brace for impact.

"What about you?" They offered it to Rebecca, but she didn't reach to take it either.

"I want the hugs too."

"I guess it's all down to me, then." Which they had guessed it would be all along. At least they had a clear role still in the expanded welcome party.

"Our hero," Rebecca said and gave them a quick kiss before facing back towards the entering throng.

Drew stood tall. They might not look like the typical comic book jacked-yet-slim superhero, but they had their moments. It was good to be of use to the people they loved.

When Alex finally appeared in view, hair highlighted by the sun and a tan bringing warmth to her tired face, both Rebecca and Phoebe couldn't wait for her to reach them and ran over, leaving Drew standing with Willow's parents, who had resisted the temptation to do the same. Drew itched to join in welcoming their buddy but hung back to give Rebecca space. Alex spotted them, though, and beamed and waved over Phoebe's shoulder.

Now that she was back, Drew wouldn't need to check on Phoebe any more. Which was kind of sad as they'd grown fond of Alex's emo sister, and it was unlikely she'd want Drew hanging around now that she didn't need them. That was usually the way—people were happy to have them around while they were of use but after that…Well, it often became clear that they hadn't been so much wanted, just needed. And not forever.

CHAPTER FOURTEEN

Hannah had never felt so unprepared for a recording. Her chest was tight, and her breaths were too fast and shallow. Part of her wanted to just cancel and go hide under a blanket until she could breathe properly again. But that wouldn't resolve anything, and it wouldn't only be her time she was wasting.

She logged on and tried to focus on the few notes she had made. She'd hoped to add to them before starting, but they kept swimming in front of her eyes in a way that made that difficult. *Get it together!* This was hardly her first time, and she'd dealt with recording issues before—she just usually wasn't the one who was underprepared. And she couldn't decide if it was better or worse that Drew would be there to witness her state.

They didn't seem to be having the same issue and were already waiting in the virtual lobby when she started the meeting. She didn't have to let them in straight away, but not doing so would just be delaying the inevitable.

"Hey!" Drew said as their picture appeared on her screen. They looked all smiles and bubbling confidence.

"Hey." Hannah tried to return their enthusiastic greeting but could see she'd failed in her own on-screen image and the sinking of Drew's smile.

"Is everything okay?" Drew didn't pretend not to notice but peered into the camera with a look of obvious concern. "Are you okay?"

Hannah knew the socially acceptable answer was *fine*, but she didn't want to lie, especially to them. "I was up late finishing the second book. I've been running a bit behind schedule."

"Ah, okay. Do you still want to record today? We could take a rain check or—"

"No! I mean, I'm okay to go ahead."

She had planned to spend the afternoon recording, and a last minute change in plans would add to her stress level, even if it was for her own sake. Rescheduling would also cause her more anxiety, not less, as that would throw off the structure of the rest of her week and possibly longer, depending when they could both next fit a recording in.

"No problem. I'm happy to go with whatever you want." Drew tilted their head, seeming unconvinced. "I gotta admit, I did struggle this time too. And I didn't have to do all the editing and shit."

Hannah let out a long breath. At least they didn't seem to be judging her and seemed to understand how much work it had been. "Yeah. I definitely won't be putting out episodes this often moving forward. Especially episodes requiring double the preparation."

"Yeah, we may have got overenthusiastic there."

Drew laughed and Hannah joined them, some of the weight lifting off her chest. That was the problem, wasn't it. Two passionate people were more likely to enable than rein each other in. But she didn't want to dampen either of their enthusiasm.

"It's a lesson learned. We may need to think a bit more about if we're being realistic next time."

"Next time? So it's not put you off working with me?" Drew grinned.

Hannah chewed her lip while she tried to get her thoughts into an order she could say without offending them.

"No, but I'm planning on going back to the original format once we've finished the miniseries."

Drew's smile froze but didn't disappear. That was always the plan, so they shouldn't be surprised.

"Are you okay to do the rest of the series? We could tailor the plan if it's putting too much pressure on you," they said.

She had been worried they'd be disappointed, but instead they seemed to be focused on her still for some reason. More weight lifted off her. Why had she ever thought Drew was like Georgia?

"Yes, I'm okay to do it. I want to do it."

Drew twisted in their seat. "Obviously it's up to you, but if it's too much studying two books and everything, how about we compare a book with its film adaptation instead? Just a thought. We could even watch the film together..."

The idea had occurred to Hannah too, especially after writing her latest blog post along those lines. Had Drew read it and been inspired?

"That would take the pressure off. I don't like to mess with the plan, but if the plan's not working...And we've not announced what we'll be covering next yet."

The explanation was for her more than Drew. Sometimes it helped to say things out loud to convince her logical self that it was okay.

"Exactly. No one has to know we've changed it. As long as you can manage that."

Hannah let out a little laugh. "Change isn't my favourite thing, but it can be okay when it's planned ahead, and sometimes it's definitely a good thing."

Especially change that sounded fun—like curling up in front of a movie with Drew instead of pushing herself to do too much. She'd been planning to ask them to meet up again before the next recording anyway, so she'd already put space and spoons aside in her schedule.

"It is." Drew smiled at her, like they were thinking of something else. "How about we take a bit of time to prep before we start recording today? That way we can both feel like we have a better idea what we're talking about."

"Good plan." Although she was feeling a lot more relaxed, she could still do with a chance to get her thoughts in order now that she was capable of doing so.

"And I don't have to come round later if you need downtime after." Drew paused, then added, "Not that I don't still want to."

"Good, because I still want you to. I might want your help releasing some tension and relaxing." An evening spent indulging in Drew seemed like a good reward at the end of a busy week. "Though I may not be up to talking much."

Drew smirked. "It wasn't talking I had in mind."

"Excellent. I might be talked out by then but wanting to connect in other ways."

"Whatever you want. I gotta admit, I haven't been able to stop thinking about the last time we were together and hoping it wasn't a one-off."

"Ditto." She cleared her throat. "But for now, we should focus on the recording. Afterwards, we can do whatever we want."

Thankfully she'd already prepared her flat for Drew's visit, so there would be no need to rush around after, and she could start relaxing and switching modes as soon as she switched off her mic. Some of the tightness in her chest was replaced by a fluttering excitement.

"Can I grab a cuppa, then meet you back here in five? I promise I will be focused on the books then." Drew winked.

It was a good idea and would give her the chance to focus too. Knowing she had their visit to look forward to boosted her enthusiasm, but she had to be careful not to let those plans lead her thoughts astray just yet. One thing at a time.

She never usually had a problem staying on task, quite the opposite, but Drew was more distracting than her usual guests, even without knowing she'd get the opportunity to act on her desire for them shortly after. And it wasn't just sexual chemistry. Drew's apparent concern and support were touching. They weren't just a random fuck buddy. They seemed to really care—about her work and about her. And she cared about them. They were fascinating, and she wanted to get to know every inch of their mind and body. She couldn't remember when the last time was that she'd connected with someone like that. Except she could remember, she just didn't want to. There had been no one since Georgia.

❖

Drew hadn't been sure what to expect from Hannah given her state earlier that day. They'd been trying not to harbour any expectations so they wouldn't be disappointed if it turned out she wasn't up to getting intimate in any way. They definitely hadn't expected her to answer the door naked.

Okay, so she wasn't completely nude, but it didn't look like there was any clothing under her fleece dressing gown. The fabric was a deep blue that brought out the sapphire of her eyes, and her long hair was loose for once, further blanketing her neck and shoulders.

"Come in," she said, her eyes darting to somewhere over their right shoulder.

They followed her gaze. Ah yes, the security camera. If that wasn't there, would she have even bothered with the robe?

Did it also mean the accommodation staff knew that Drew was there and why? They tried not to let that bother them. Surely they could trust Hannah not to share too much. Not that they had anything to be ashamed of. Hannah was clearly a consenting adult and no one—hopefully—should feel the need to come check up on them. Drew did as instructed and moved out of the hallway, and Hannah quickly closed the door.

"Hi," she said, twiddling the belt ends of her robe.

Drew realized they hadn't said a word yet. "Hey, you."

"Do you want to take off your jacket and shoes?"

Hannah was looking at them like she was trying to work out if they'd been abducted by aliens and replaced with a clueless clone.

"Sure, sorry. I was a bit distracted by your"—they gestured at her gown—"outfit? Or lack of."

This caused Hannah's cheeks to flush, and she looked down shyly. "I hope you don't mind. I just had a shower and couldn't bear the thought of getting dressed again. I wanted to be comfy."

Drew hung their coat up behind her, then held out their arms. "Definitely no complaints here."

Hannah didn't hesitate to step into their embrace, and they wrapped her in their arms, burying their face in the cushiony fabric. A hint of lemongrass reached Drew's nostrils, evidence of her freshly scrubbed skin. She let out a contented sigh.

"As much as I could happily stand here holding you all night, shall we go sit down?"

The hallway wasn't the most comfortable place for them to snuggle.

"*Okaaay.*" Hannah drew out the word with a show of reluctance. "But more holding then?"

"Absolutely." Drew unfolded their arms and took her hand instead, leading her into the lounge. It was tempting to head straight to the bedroom, but they didn't want to push Hannah especially given she seemed to be in a vulnerable state.

They landed on the couch together, and Hannah nuzzled into their side. She fiddled with their clasped hands.

"Just to be clear, I'm not up for talking lots, but I am up for other things."

"Good to know." They turned their head towards her, and she leaned into a long, sensual kiss.

"Mmm. Exactly what I need." Hannah swung her leg over Drew's lap and kissed them again, pressing their bodies closer.

Drew ran their hand up her thigh and up to her waist without meeting any resistance. They had been right about her having nothing on beneath the robe, and they pulsed with excitement. They pulled her completely onto their lap so she was straddling them. Hannah squirmed, and her tongue danced with Drew's as the kiss deepened.

Her hands left their neck and joined theirs at her waist, untying the robe. Drew leaned back for a moment to admire Hannah's unrestrained breasts as the robe swung open to display them.

"I want you," Hannah whispered in their ear.

It would be cruel to deny her, not that they wanted to. Drew slipped their hands inside the open robe, cupping one breast and using their other arm to pull her up so they could take her nipple in their mouth. Hannah moaned and grasped their head. They sucked hard, and her moan deepened. When they came up for air, she pushed them back against the sofa. Her hands spread on their flattened chest as she kissed them and brought a rush of euphoria.

"You want to keep this on?" Hannah ran her hands over their T-shirt.

It was tempting to risk it and say no, take it off, but it was one of those days when they could breathe better with their chest bound. "Yes. As long as you keep touching me like that."

"Like this?" She spread her fingers and pushed Drew into the back of the couch again, then trailed one hand down over their stomach to the top of their trousers.

"Yes," they whispered, as she brushed a finger under the waistband.

Drew edged their hands back over Hannah's bare thighs and this time curved inwards to her centre. She gasped in their mouth when Drew discovered her wetness. Unlike Drew, Hannah had not been holding back her anticipation. They ran their thumb over her swollen clit and captured each moan she gave in their mouth.

When they paused and drew their head back, she moaned with clear frustration. They couldn't help letting out a deep laugh at that.

"Would you like to ride me? I brought something with me." They indicated the satchel, which had been dropped forgotten on the other side of the couch, with their eyes.

Hannah bit her lip. "I would really, really like that." She grabbed the bag and pulled it over. "As long as I don't have to get up."

Drew laughed. "I can work with that."

"I'll help." She unbuttoned their trousers and pulled down the zip like she couldn't wait.

Their thighs clenched around their throbbing centre. It was a good thing they'd decided to put on their O-ring pants beforehand. They slipped the packer out of its pocket and replaced it with their favourite curved dildo.

Hannah helped herself to the lube and squirted it onto her hands, then started to stroke their cock. She kissed Drew again while continuing to stroke and press their cock down hard against them so they moaned.

"If you carry on like that, I'll come before I even enter you," they warned.

"Oh no," Hannah replied but didn't stop. Instead she lifted herself up on her knees and hovered over them as she rubbed them faster.

Drew took hold of Hannah's hips and guided her down onto them. She let her hand slip to her crotch, parting her lips so Drew easily slid inside her. She let out a loud moan as she took them fully inside.

Hannah started to ride them slowly, and Drew matched her pace, keeping hold of her hips. Soon they were thrusting wildly and her breast was at their mouth, begging them to suck it. Her moans grew even louder as they did, and she sounded close to the edge. They moved their hands to her butt and thrust deeper until she came to a shuddering climax.

"Mmm." Hannah sighed as she rolled off Drew, keeping one leg spread over their thighs. "Definitely what I needed."

"Glad to be of service."

"How about you?" She eyed them out of one half-open eye.

"I am good. That was something I've been daydreaming about for a while now."

"Good to know." She let out a soft laugh. "But was it all you need?" Her hand slipped back over to the shaft between their legs and pressed it against them. They let out an involuntary groan. "Sounds like you could use a little more." She worked it with one hand while pressing them back against the sofa with her other one.

"Maybe a little." Drew fumbled in their bag and retrieved a bullet vibrator. They'd both been too worked up to pause and position it before. "Mind if I…"

Hannah grinned and turned it on in reply. She paused her stroking for a moment as they got it into position but resumed as soon as they did.

Her robe was flung entirely open, so her body was on display before them, and her chest was flushed. Drew stroked her with their eyes and fingers as Hannah pressed them to climax. They let out a final gasp, then closed their eyes while they got their breath back. Hannah removed the vibe but kept her hand still grasping them.

"That was hot," she said.

"It was. I like a woman who knows what she wants."

Hannah's sexual confidence had been a very nice surprise. She might not like to put herself on display publicly, but she clearly had no issues in private.

"Interesting. So may I ask, does that extend to BDSM?" She trailed a hand up their arm, her nails scratching them gently but purposefully.

"I'm afraid I'm pretty vanilla."

Hannah withdrew her nails. It seemed to surprise people for some reason, but kink had never appealed to Drew. They didn't judge others who liked it, but the thought of hitting a woman sent cold dread through them, particularly since they'd realized they weren't a woman themself. They didn't want to be that guy.

"That's okay, I'm not judging." Hannah planted a very vanilla peck on their cheek.

"How about you? What's your flavour?" They might not be planning to play with her themself, but they couldn't help being curious.

"I enjoy sensory play mostly, including impact play. Firm pressure, you know."

"Ahh." Drew hadn't interpreted it that way when she first said it. Maybe that was them being naive. "So, it doesn't hurt you?"

"Not in a bad way. It can send me soaring. No drugs needed, my body's natural chemicals are enough." She floated her hand in the air.

"So you're a submissive?" Drew was intrigued. That did not seem the case from where they were sitting.

"I'm a switch. It's not so much about the dominant-submissive aspect for me, though I'll admit I get a thrill from being in control or giving it up sometimes. As I said, I'm in it for the floaty feelings, and I don't need role play to enjoy all the sensations."

She seemed to have perked up and regained her talkativeness, and Drew wanted to ask more. What she was describing wasn't how they tended to think of BDSM, though they still didn't imagine they'd ever want to deliver the impact. And the fact that Hannah wasn't bound to the submissive role was interesting. They couldn't deny how turned on they'd been when she'd taken control or the tingle left by her nails scraping against their skin. They were already out of their comfort zone, so maybe they should take the opportunity to explore more while they were.

But then there would be no question that they were getting completely out of their depth. And the further they went, the harder it would be to pretend it didn't matter when Hannah decided she'd had enough of them. She had made no promises to stay with them, after all, just the opposite.

CHAPTER FIFTEEN

It was a Thursday evening, and Hannah was going out. It was best not to think about how long it'd been since she did that, especially with a group—an advantage of dating apps was that you didn't need to head out to find company for a night. But it wasn't the same as having a real-world community to hang out in, and her confidence was gradually recovering enough to make her want that. Not that she'd ever been a big social butterfly, but she'd had a small network of friends she'd liked spending time with until Georgia had disconnected it piece by piece.

It was time to leave soon, but she still hadn't decided what to wear. She didn't want to overdo it and look like she was on the pull— the meetup clearly stated it wasn't a dating event—but it probably wouldn't give a great impression if she went in her comfy home clothes showing zero effort. If she was going to the local munch, her original idea, then she would know what to wear. She'd been to kink meetups in other towns, before things got serious with Georgia and she ruled them inappropriate, and was comfortable fitting in there. She'd only been to one poly meetup, that time with Georgia, and well, she hadn't gone back.

It wasn't that anyone had been unwelcoming or inappropriate, but that possessiveness and uncontrolled jealousy did not go down well. It turned out Georgia was much less okay with opening their relationship when it was Hannah getting attention. Maybe if she and Georgia had others to turn to who had been there, done that, they might not have made such a mess of things. Or Hannah might have realized she needed to get out sooner.

Which was why she'd accepted Drew's invitation to the local poly meet. It was her chance to start again and do things the right way this time—of course, Min would say there was no right way, but that wasn't the point. She wasn't going *with* Drew. She was determined to approach it by herself this time, but as the organizer Drew would be there to do introductions and support if needed. She had to admit, it did make the whole prospect less scary.

She settled on a sleeveless shirt, sized up to not swaddle her, and cotton shorts. She didn't need to be sweating or squirming in a not fun way, more than was inevitable in a new social situation anyway, as she met the group for the first time. If anyone was put off by her hairy legs being on display, it would be a sign they were not someone she would get on with.

"Here we go," she muttered to herself as she checked her bag for the umpteenth time to ensure she had everything. She added a pack of playing cards as a backup in case it was difficult to find something to talk about.

The meetup was due to start at seven. It was just after quarter past six when she got off the bus, and the pub was only a few minutes' walk. That was okay, though, as she planned to order food and get settled before anyone else arrived. She'd found the menu online and was satisfied there was something she could manage, and it saved trying to rush dinner at home. She hated leaving a mess and coming back to a smelly flat, but by the time she'd cleared up it would be way past the start. It was better to get there early, allowing for gradual introductions, and build up to a potentially busy social scene.

Service was quick, and she'd already finished her burger when the first couple of people arrived who looked like they might be attending the poly meet. They made their way through to a semi-separate back room, and then there was the scrape of tables and chairs being rearranged. She wiggled her earplugs to ensure maximum protection.

Should she join them and offer to help? But what if she was wrong? She still had a few chips left, so could safely pick at them and monitor the situation from a distance. She speared a chip and dunked it in mayo, keeping an eye on the doorway.

She heard the main door swing open behind her and one pair of feet enter, along with a familiar voice. A tingle went through her as it stirred pleasant memories. *Not now.* She needed to not think about getting naked with Drew if she was going to be able to relax and talk. She tried to zone in on the food in her mouth instead, but the grease was suddenly overwhelming.

"Hannah!"

Drew seemed less interested in playing it cool. There was a note of delight in their voice that she couldn't help feeling pleased by. She turned to see Drew was still by the door, holding it open for someone using a wheelchair.

"Shall I get the drinks in, and you can go say hello?" Their companion cocked a smile in Hannah's direction and rolled towards the bar.

Perhaps they had also picked up on the pleasure in Drew's greeting. At least it wasn't someone who seemed to take any issue with their interest in her. Drew had assured her that neither of their partners would be there, so she didn't need to worry about those awkward introductions. She didn't know what, if anything, Drew had said to them about her.

"Cheers, Ish," Drew said, then headed straight for Hannah.

"Hi," Hannah said, once Drew was within a couple of metres of her.

"Hi." Drew stopped short of her table and tilted their head to the side, hands in their pockets, like they were deliberately resisting the temptation to take hold of her. Or was that wishful thinking on her part? Their hair had grown out to the point where it was ruffled by the breeze. She itched to reach out and stroke it back in place. "You came."

"I did. I figured I'd get here early and grab some food to save rushing." She indicated her nearly empty plate.

"Good plan. I forgot to say, part of why we meet here is the food's pretty decent, and people often don't have a chance to eat beforehand."

That would've been helpful information to have, but she probably still would've gotten there early and eaten alone instead of attempting to eat in the potential overwhelm of a new social group.

"So, who did you come with?" She looked over to the bar where their companion, who looked to be a South Asian woman about their age with black hair tied back in a loose plait, was checking her phone while the bartender pulled pints.

"That's Ishani, Rebecca's nesting partner. Rebecca's occupied catching up with Alex now that she's back, so I said Ish could hang with me."

"Alex, is that Phoebe's sister?" Hannah was still getting the hang of all the people in Drew's life.

"Yep, she got back last week from her travels. Which also means I won't be dropping in on Phoebe so much."

She let that news sink in. From a selfish point of view, it meant Drew wouldn't be hanging around the flats any more, and she wouldn't have to worry about seeing them unless she wanted to. But they probably didn't need her to point that out.

"I bet Phoebe's glad to have her back too."

"You bet." They glanced back over their shoulder to see that Ishani was receiving their drinks order. "I better grab these. See you in there?"

"Sure."

Hannah made no move to get up and follow them. She didn't want to cling to them for the evening, as tempting as that was.

She also wanted to process what she'd just learned. Alex wasn't the only metamour Drew was friends with, which indicated it might be deliberate and not just a matter of happening to like her. Would dating Drew mean having to enter into relationships with their partners too? Not that it mattered—she *wasn't* dating Drew so didn't need to worry about those complications. Unless she did make that move further down the line. It was starting to get difficult to keep thinking of Drew as a friend when she was pretty sure they both wanted something else.

Hannah wanted to meet people in the poly community, but people of her own choosing. She wasn't sure she'd ever want to befriend anyone from a partner's wider network. If or when she was going to start dating again, it would be with other non-monogamous people even if not with Drew. Did everyone want metamour relationships? Cass did too, but that was mostly in the context of broadening their Dungeons & Dragons group.

Best wait for a few more people to filter in so she would have more of a choice of who to talk to. Drew's metamour was only one step away from their partner, after all.

As she gathered her things ten minutes later, finally ready to risk entering, another couple entered the pub and headed in that direction. She stood back to let them pass.

"After you." The guy gestured for her to come out.

"Um, it's okay, I'm going this way." She pointed to the back room. "Great."

He exchanged a look with his partner that made her wonder what their intentions were. Looking for a threesome and happy to meet a potential single bi woman? She smiled to herself. She didn't mind— they were both cute. The guy had closely cropped hair and light facial hair, the smooth stubble adding a few years to his fresh-faced look. She was tempted to reach out and stroke his chin to see if it was as soft as it looked, but that probably didn't count as a socially appropriate greeting among strangers. Or friends, for that matter.

"Us too," his partner added, unnecessarily. "I'm Olivia and this is Nick."

"Nice to meet you. I'm Hannah." She returned Olivia's warm smile.

"You weren't here last month, were you?" Nick added.

"No, it's my first time." She couldn't decide whether to put her jacket back on for the short walk to the other room and settled with draping it over her arm.

"It's only our second," Olivia confessed. "Do you know anyone here?"

"Only the organizer, I think." There was no need to mention how well she knew Drew. "Though you never know who you'll bump into at these things."

"True. I worry about bumping into someone from work and having to explain or becoming office gossip."

The thought had occurred to Hannah when she'd first started attending kink meetups, but she soon logicked her way out of it. "Except if they're here too, you know they're okay with it and may well not want to be the object of gossip either."

"That's what I said." Nick put his arm around Olivia's shoulders, and she leaned into him.

Definitely a couple. A ring glinted on Nick's finger where it lay on Olivia's shoulder, and a quick glance down confirmed Olivia sported a matching one. A married couple, who by Olivia's nerves seemed new to the lifestyle, not just that particular social group. Her first instinct might well have been correct.

"How about I get us some drinks, and you two can head in together?" Nick suggested. "Can I get you one too, Hannah?"

Accepting the offer would mean committing herself to hanging out with them, at least to start with. She looked at Olivia, who had started to twist her long wavy hair around her fingers. She wore a light coat of make-up, enough to accent her delicate features but not overpower them, and her cheeks seemed to gain more colour as Hannah gazed at her.

"Yes, thank you. Just a Coke, please."

Olivia's colour rose further, and she gave Hannah the cutest nervous half smile. It shouldn't be a chore to hang out with her.

"Shall we?" Hannah held out the elbow that didn't contain her coat and bag.

Olivia giggled before taking it and holding tight. "Let's go."

When they entered the back room, there were a half dozen people scattered around, and a few more entered behind them. Drew's gaze fixed on her, though, only flickering back and forth between her and the woman on her arm. Then they broke into a slightly delayed smile and came over to welcome everyone.

"Hello. Good to see you again, Olivia." If they were jealous, it wasn't enough to stop them fulfilling their hosting duties.

"You too." Olivia dropped Hannah's arm to give them a hello hug.

Olivia didn't seem immune to Drew's charms, and Hannah tasted a tinge of something bitter at how she looked at them. Maybe it wasn't Drew she needed to worry about getting possessive.

"Your husband not with you today?" Drew studied the small group that had come in behind them.

"He's just getting the drinks, so Hannah here kindly agreed to escort me in." She gave Hannah's arm a little squeeze, clearly in no rush to let her go despite the more attractive company.

"Lucky you." Drew grinned at Hannah. "Are you two happy if I leave you to carry on while I say hello to the others?"

"We're good," Hannah said. She had promised them, as well as herself, that she wouldn't get in the way of their general hosting duties.

She found an empty table with a seat where she could relax with her back to the wall and study everyone around her. As she got to know Olivia and Nick, who were indeed a married couple only just opening up their relationship, she could see Drew flitting between groups and welcoming latecomers. They oozed confidence but seemed approachable and down to earth too, a social butterfly, not a pariah. She enjoyed watching them in their element but felt no urge to join them. She was content hanging with the new couple who also appeared more than content to stick with her. The couple's backstory held no surprises. It certainly wasn't the case that every male-female couple looking to open up did so due to the woman wanting to explore her bisexuality, but it was a familiar tale. Although she'd not had the chance to explore her local community much when she'd opened up, she'd done plenty of reading and listening to podcasts. It was good to hear that reality matched her research.

It was also handy that Nick and Olivia were at the stage where they wanted to tell all and discuss it with other open people, so there wasn't much space to share her own story. She didn't want to get into the unhappy ending of her relationship, which was unlikely to reassure the couple and would put a dampener on their interaction. An interaction which could perhaps be classed as dancing with flirtation. Olivia's frequent gazing at her surely wasn't neutral, even for a neurotypical. Rather than move on when she'd finished the drink Nick had bought, Hannah offered to buy the next round.

Drew joined her as she waited for the bartender to be free. Or maybe they just happened to be getting a drink then too.

"Hey, how's your night going?" A note of tension to their tone made the question sound not just casual.

Hannah felt a shiver go down her spine, replacing the initial pleasant tingle from their close proximity. "Good, thanks. You?"

"Yeah, good. Glad you're enjoying it." They looked over at the bartender, who gestured that he'd be one minute.

"I am. I'm glad I came."

She had wondered if she'd regret accepting the invite, but so far it had been fun. As long as there was no drama brewing, that was—it had seemed fun last time until Georgia cornered her and made it clear she wasn't happy about how much she was enjoying herself.

"That couple aren't bothering you, are they? We have made it clear it's not a cruising ground, and I can talk to them if—"

"No. It's fine. I'm enjoying getting to know them. I would walk away if I wasn't."

"That's okay, then. Just be aware sometimes couples like that can be a bit preoccupied, you know, with finding a third." Drew rolled their eyes.

They probably think they're being helpful. Hannah tried to dispel the feeling she was being patronized and that her new friends were being judged. "I'm aware that can sometimes be the case."

"Good. Not that I'm judging, but you know where I am if it does start creeping that way."

Why did they assume she'd want them to intervene?

"If it does, I can handle it. Besides, they're both cute, so I wouldn't necessarily say no."

She wasn't going to pretend not to be interested. The couple were attractive, and it could be a good step moving from casual sex towards relationships again.

"Oh, okay." From the look on Drew's face, they definitely hadn't considered that possibility.

"I am, after all, a single bisexual woman."

She winked and slid her hand into their back pocket to gave their butt a squeeze, in an attempt to bring the smile back to their face and reassure them that the couple weren't the only ones she was interested in.

It worked, and Drew broke the atmosphere with a laugh. "You are indeed the elusive single, hot, bi babe. Have fun, gorgeous."

They bumped hips with Hannah, sending a jolt of a more pleasant variety through her to dissipate the icy feeling. It was clear their instinct had been to jump in and rescue her when she didn't even want or need it, though at least they'd backed straight off at her word. She enjoyed being with them, as a friend and in bed, but didn't want them thinking they now had a say in the rest of her personal life. Their interference in the podcast was enough, and they better not have the same instinct to try to guide her outside of it. Or she would have to put a stop to whatever was between them before someone got hurt.

She had made the mistake once of allowing someone to have a say over her other relationships, and she wasn't going to make that mistake again. It wasn't just her newer partner who'd been left broken-hearted when Hannah had ended things at Georgia's wish. She'd broken her own heart in the process, and it was only just starting to feel whole again.

❖

"How do I look?" Drew tugged at the loose boho top trying to get it to sit right.

In the mirror behind them, Leigh made a face like she was trying to figure out how to say nicely that they looked like crap.

"Not good?"

The pastel top had been a charity shop find—bought because it was the right size and a bargain more than anything.

"No, but…" Leigh chewed her lip. "Not like you."

Drew sighed and stopped trying to pull it into shape. She was right. If only they could fit into mainstream menswear like some of their slimmer AFAB friends, but a binder could only do so much, and accessing top surgery was a joke due to the ridiculous BMI limits, not to mention other medical gatekeeping. For some reason, doctors were only interested in making them smaller in ways that didn't help them feel better. Given the variation in how they felt in their body, it wasn't a hundred per cent certain surgery was the answer for them anyway. Would they be happier if they never had to worry about binding their chest or fitting into a shirt ever again? Quite possibly, but as that wasn't a real option, they'd decided to save themself the trauma of trying to convince the establishment of who they were. Sometimes being able to live with that choice felt like a privilege, sometimes not so much.

"I know you want to make a good first impression, but your mum wants to introduce you—not some model respectable offspring."

Leigh moved closer and put her arms around their waist, dropping a kiss on their shoulder.

"Are you saying I'm not respectable?" They raised an eyebrow at her in the mirror.

"And I wouldn't want you any other way."

She drew them into a long kiss that melted away some of the tension they hadn't realized they were carrying.

"In that case…" Drew pulled off the offending top and dropped it on the floor, then nudged Leigh so she fell backwards on the bed.

She didn't complain, instead pulling them down on top of her. "When did you say we'd get there?" she murmured.

Drew looked round at the clock. "By one, so we can have a proper sit-down lunch. Which means we need to leave in…"

"The next half hour. You don't need to dress up, but we should try to get there on time." Leigh rested her hands on their butt, not seeming in any rush to get up.

"Yeah." They sighed. "Though if you help me pick an outfit, it'll only take me a few minutes to get ready."

Drew leaned on their elbow and ran a hand down Leigh's side. They could think of something that would perk them up and have them feeling more confident for the big occasion.

"I can do that. If you help me with something in return," Leigh said.

She pulled them closer and made it clear what she wanted. She always knew how to bring them back to themself. Having been together so long, they both knew how to push each other's buttons in the best way.

By the time Drew was dressed again—this time in a casual short-sleeved shirt—they were less hung up on making anyone else like them.

Unfortunately, the almost three hour journey to the coast gave Drew plenty of time to get nervous again. They hadn't met a partner of their mum's since they were a child and risked slipping back into that desperate need for approval. This being their mum's first queer relationship, and the first one they'd known to turn her into a swoony teenager, it felt even more important that they hit it off.

"She's going to love you," Leigh assured them, not for the first time.

"Maybe. Hopefully she'll at least accept me. Or tolerate me."

Sometimes it was best to set the bar low. They weren't everyone's cup of tea, even without bringing their gender into it.

"I reckon you can aim higher than that. If she's anywhere near as infatuated with Fran as Fran is with her, she'll be viewing you through deeply rose-tinted glasses."

"True." They wrinkled their nose. "Are they gonna be all over each other? Cos I'm not sure how I feel about seeing my mum get felt up by a frisky lesbian."

"Why do you imagine your mum being the passive one in that scenario?"

"Good point. I don't know how I feel about my frisky mum touching up her lover in front of me."

Leigh laughed. "I'm sure they'll both be on their best behaviour too."

It was hard to imagine Fran getting carried away in public, but then again they'd never imagined seeing her blush about another woman. It turned out she could still surprise them at her age. It was kind of reassuring to think you didn't have to have everything figured out early on and could still be discovering new paths to happiness in your later years. But they mustn't mess up this chance for her.

When they pulled up outside the bungalow, there were already two cars in the drive—only one of which Drew recognized. The other was a shiny Honda that looked very well cared for. Hopefully that was a sign that Vivienne was a caring person, and not that she was more in love with her car than her partner. Drew tried to push back their defensive instincts. Fran was a grown woman and knew what she was getting into better than them. They'd already made a fool of themself the other night with Hannah, assuming she wasn't interested in the new couple who seemed very keen to get to know her and, even worse, that she was naive to their intentions. Hannah was another woman who clearly knew what she wanted.

The car door slammed and brought Drew back into the moment. They shouldn't be thinking about Hannah—they should be thinking about how not to make a fool of themself again.

They edged their way past the cars, trying not to get caught on the overgrown rose bushes lining the drive. Fran had always been a keen gardener, it was where they'd got it from, but must've been occupied elsewhere lately. No need to imagine how.

"Hello, my loves." Fran opened the front door before they reached it and came rushing out to meet them. She enveloped Drew in an affectionate hug, then reached for Leigh. "It's been too long! You're looking lovely. Let me look at you."

Leigh gave her a kiss on the cheek, then stepped back as instructed. She'd first met Fran before transitioning, and Fran had marvelled—sometimes embarrassing so—as each time she saw her she grew more into herself. Those changes had finished years ago, but Fran's open adoration hadn't faded.

"That dress is gorgeous on you. Where did you get it?"

Drew shifted impatiently at the small talk they couldn't really take part in. Fran didn't tend to be complimentary about their appearance, though she was proud of them in other ways, and did stick to the agreement not to negatively allude to their weight or try to persuade them to dress up in something pretty.

"Shall we head in?" Drew eventually prompted.

"Of course." Fran looped her arm through Leigh's and led her back towards the front door. "Viv's already here and dying to meet you."

"Great. We've been looking forward to meeting her too," Leigh replied and shot Drew a look reminding them to act like it.

"Yep," Drew said, their nerves getting in the way of saying anything more.

"She's gonna love you." Fran paused to reach over and squeeze their arm.

Just then, a Black woman with vibrant grey hair cropped short into tight curls entered the other end of the corridor. She looked to be an inch or two shorter than Drew, but around their size. Her turquoise dress fit so perfectly that they suspected she'd made it herself. It was one solution to the clothes issue that they'd not tried but probably should one day.

"Hello. You must be the love of Fran's life. I'm Vivienne."

Vivienne strode towards Drew, arms stretched out for a hug, but paused before embracing them as if to make out they had a choice in the matter.

Viv's warm welcome immediately disarmed Drew, and they stepped into the hug. "Hello. You must be the woman who's put a spring in her step."

"Guilty."

Vivienne chuckled and stepped back from their embrace to shoot Fran a look of longing that left Drew tempted to tell them to get a room. They bit their tongue. Fran might want to introduce the real them, but she'd not appreciate too much cheek.

"And this must be your wonderful wife." Vivienne moved towards Leigh.

"Guilty," Leigh echoed and gave her a full-bodied hug.

Fran looked so happy Drew was afraid she might burst into tears. Her voice subtly cracked as she ushered them through to the dining table.

The table was already set with decorative placemats sporting rural scenes of Somerset that her mum only brought out for special occasions. Someone had even folded the napkins into elegant birds.

"Have you taken up origami?" Drew asked, picking up one of the delicately folded pieces with care.

"Not me. Those are Viv's work. She's very crafty."

"I bet she is," Drew said before realizing what they could be implying. *Oops.*

Leigh shot them another look from across the table as she settled into the seat opposite them.

"They're really good. I might have to get you to teach me." They gave Viv an encouraging smile, which hopefully made up for their first remark.

Fran disappeared to fetch the food, trusting Drew for a couple of minutes at least, leaving them all sitting staring at each other.

Drew was about to ask if Viv's creativity did include making her own clothes, something they would be genuinely happy to discuss, but Viv got in first and changed the subject.

"So, I couldn't believe you are on my favourite podcast. Fran was so proud when she told our book group. We all listen."

"I couldn't believe it either. It's been a great opportunity," Drew said. *And should be a fairly safe topic.*

"I'll bet," Viv said. "So, tell me, what's she like, the host? Is she as interesting off mic? Are the rumours true that she's one of us?"

Leigh must've taken a gulp of wine at the wrong moment, as she spluttered and covered her mouth with a swan. Her eyes danced behind the napkin.

"Am I missing something?" Viv looked between the two of them with a curious smile, clearly not missing a thing.

"We've actually gotten rather close."

Drew didn't try to hide their smile. It wasn't like they could talk about Hannah easily without giving the game away, so they might as well take the chance to lay their cards on the table in the privacy of their mum's home. Especially as Leigh's reaction meant she had to take some of the responsibility for the topic.

"Seriously?" Viv raised an eyebrow, then looked at Leigh for confirmation.

"Indeed." Leigh grinned and picked her wine glass back up.

"Nice!"

Viv offered Drew a fist bump over the table, and they returned it just as Fran rejoined them.

Fran held a big Crockpot balanced between gloved hands. "Looks like you're all getting along. I hope I'm not missing anything exciting."

This time Viv joined in with the knowing look, and they all burst out in laughter.

"What? What did I miss?" Fran looked to Drew to fill her in.

They hadn't been planning on announcing their involvement with Hannah, but it would be unfair to leave Fran out. And what could have been an awkward conversation with her new girlfriend present turned out to be the icebreaker they all needed. Viv's own history of consensual non-monogamy probably helped, though the more they chatted, the more it seemed she was just an open person. It warmed Drew's heart to see how their mum lit up in Viv's warm presence, and their concerns disappeared completely. It was wonderful that Fran had discovered the joy of queer love and seemed happy in her new life. She deserved to. They could see what she saw in her charismatic new partner, who in turn seemed to see what Drew saw in Hannah. They just had to try to stop everyone getting too carried away. Hannah was clear she wasn't looking for a happily ever after. At least not yet, or with them.

CHAPTER SIXTEEN

"Do you want to watch the original first, or the modern one?" Drew held up the two DVD cases.

"What kind of a silly question is that?" Hannah reached out for the box with the distinctly eighties cover.

Drew laughed. "Fair enough."

They had disagreed about which to watch in preparation for the next podcast recording so had settled on watching both. After a busy week doing the edits for the last episode, Hannah was happy to flop in front of a film or two. She would miss working with Drew but would be glad when the series was over. And not working with them opened up possibilities to follow their connection in a different direction.

"I'll let you put it on. I don't know when I last worked a DVD player." Drew sank onto the sofa next to her.

Drew had initially teased her about her lack of modern tech—she had no need to pay for streaming services when she watched so little TV—but had then purchased both of the DVDs. As they claimed to not even have a TV that played DVDs, it had cemented the plan for them to watch the films together at her place. Not that she was complaining about that.

"How much do I owe you for these? Assuming you're not converted and want to keep them."

"You keep them, but you don't owe me anything. Call it a reward for all your hard work—I know it's been a lot."

"Thank you."

It was nice to have someone see and appreciate everything she did, unlike many spectators who felt entitled to demand more for nothing. Yet another reason she didn't engage online, or have sponsors for the show. To be fair, she tried not to resent it when content creators interrupted her listening to earn ad revenue, but it was hard not to want to switch off. She supposed ads made sense if the podcast was a business and revenue had to come from ads or subscribers—someone had to pay—but her podcast wasn't a business. So it would feel more like blackmail to inundate her listeners with annoying ads unless they started giving her money to make them stop.

Plus she might end up having to promote businesses she'd prefer not to. She didn't want to direct people to buy from the massive online corporations most likely to pay her. She preferred to direct them to the actual bookshops that those corporations risked putting out of business. She wasn't naive enough to think her influence would be enough to save those endangered spaces, but she at least didn't want to be part of the problem.

It was tempting to offer to pay Drew back in a non-capitalist way, but she was determined to properly watch the film and had even texted them beforehand confirming it was a clothes-on work date. They'd replied with a crying-laughing smiley and *Got it.*

Now that they were there within touching distance of her, she was starting to regret that boundary, but it was good to establish that sex wasn't always on the cards when she invited them round. Even if she wanted it to be. She picked up a notepad off the coffee table and sat poised to be inspired.

"Should I be taking notes?" Drew gave the pad a suspicious look.

"Only if you need to. I write it down so I remember and cos I'm not good at thinking about more than one thing."

"Oh really," Drew replied with a smirk and reached for her thigh.

"Not that." She batted them away lightly with the notepad. Though it was closer to the truth than they maybe realized. The notepad was a concrete reminder of what she should be thinking about, not the warm body next to hers.

The original film wasn't one either of them had seen, which was strange given they'd both sought out queer content and had seen most classics. It slowly became apparent why. The queerness had been played down and edited out to the point where it was practically non-existent. If she hadn't read the book already, she might not have known it was ever supposed to be anything but your usual heteronormative tale. As much as she usually disliked talking during movies, she couldn't help joining in with Drew's grumbling and was glad to have someone there to share the frustration. Otherwise she might've been tempted to reactivate her social media, just to have someone to scream about it with. If she hadn't known what the film was based on, maybe she would've enjoyed it for what it was, but the book was too fresh in her mind for her to forgive the film's trespasses.

"Well, now we know why they remade it. I'm glad we got both." She couldn't think of anything better to say after it finished.

"Yep, and that we started with this one, so we're not finishing on a downer."

Drew stretched out their limbs, unfolding themself from their position squashed up with her on the sofa. She hadn't managed to stay away for the entire film—Drew's cuddles were too good to pass up—but its bad vibe had temporarily dampened any sexual sparks.

"We don't know how the other one ends," Hannah said.

"I do. Well, I don't remember it all exactly, but I remember enough to know it was at least very, very queer." Drew winked at her.

Hannah laughed. "I guess it had a lot to make up for. Shall we pause for dinner before we start it?"

Not that she was planning to cook. Takeaway would have to do again if they were going to have time to watch two full-length films.

"Yes, let's order. What do you fancy?" Drew spread their arm along the back of the sofa and turned fully towards her.

She bit back the cheesy line—*you*. That wasn't what Drew was asking, but it was a fight not to dive back into their arms and let them help her forget the disappointing start to the evening.

"What?" Drew took in her silent study of them. "What are you thinking?"

She should say *nothing* despite it being untrue. It was *always* untrue—why did anyone ever say that as if it was an innocent answer? "Not about food."

Drew grinned. "Ditto, but I'm under strict instructions to keep it PG."

She leaned in and kissed them lightly. "I'm pretty sure that's still PG. Nowadays anyway."

"Yep, thankfully we're past the days of having to fade to black."

"I should look that up actually, and check the dates in terms of what was officially and unofficially not allowed when the first version was made. It may not have been the filmmakers' decision to cut out all the queerness."

"Good idea." Drew pulled their arm back with obvious reluctance.

Hannah excused herself to get the takeaway menus, swerving the urge to lean back in for another less PG kiss. Maybe it really was useless to try to quash her growing attraction and feelings for Drew. She had theorized that having sex with them would snuff it out—getting it out of both their systems so they could focus on other things—but instead it had only made her want more of them, and not just physically.

"How did you find the poly meet, by the way?" Drew asked when she returned.

It was off-topic, but they were on dinner break so she shouldn't complain. She sat back down next to them and handed over the menus.

"Good. It was nice to be around open people. It helped confirm for me that, when I'm ready, that's the way I want to go."

"*Go* as in…?"

"As in, build relationships. It's hard to pull apart how things went with my ex and what it's like to be poly, but I do think it's right for me." She hadn't been planning on discussing it with Drew, at least not yet, but it made no sense to hold back.

"I'm glad your ex hasn't ruined it for you." Drew gave them a smile and a shoulder nudge. "So, was there anyone there you want to see again?"

"You mean apart from you?"

"Yes. I know it's not a dating event, but sometimes people want to get to know each other more after."

Hannah couldn't help feeling it was a trap but reminded herself who she was talking to. "I got on well with Olivia and Nick, but I've not made any plans. And I'm not sure I'm what they're looking for."

"Oh yeah? I hope they didn't make it weird in the end." Drew seemed to bite back something else, possibly what they'd already said at the time. At least they were learning.

"No, just they're looking for a deeper long-term connection than I'm interested in. At least with a couple—that's probably not the easiest place to start back in."

"Good call." They paused and looked her in the eye. "So, where would you like to start?"

With you, obviously. But she held back, not knowing what that would mean still.

"I guess I need to figure out what I do want. And what it really means to be with someone where there's no prospect of marriage, mortgage, and all those standard commitments."

Things had blown up with her ex before she'd had the chance to properly figure that out last time. Next time, she was hoping to find out how it could work.

Initially, the fact Drew was already married and happy living with their wife felt protective because it meant they weren't expecting that from her. But if they did get into a romantic relationship, what would it be without those tangible markers? She didn't want to push Leigh out or take her place; she wanted to find her own.

"It is confusing to start with. Like, we're taught that's what a committed relationship looks like. But you can be committed to someone you love without stepping on that relationship escalator. You show commitment how you want to, and pledge what you want to instead."

"I like that idea."

Hannah let herself relax into the couch and the comfort of Drew's soft body next to her. Sure, the uncertainty was scary, but what was truly certain anyway? Drew wasn't saying they couldn't commit to each other—they were saying they could do it on their own terms. Which was better, surely, especially given most of society's rules didn't make logical sense.

"So, you and Rebecca, you love each other and are committed? Like, if Leigh told you she didn't want you to be poly any more or she found your relationship threatening for some reason, you wouldn't just drop her?"

"No, of course not. Leigh wouldn't do that, and if she suddenly did, then the issue would be in our relationship, and that's what we'd have to work out."

"Okay."

Hannah's vision got cloudy, and she pretended to look down at the menu in her hand. A stabbing pain in her chest reminded her that she hadn't made the same call, so who was she to expect it of someone else.

"Hey, what's wrong?"

It was too much to hope Drew wouldn't notice the tears in her eyes.

"Nothing." She sniffed back the tears and the lie.

"Obviously."

"Just…" What would they think of her once they knew what she'd done? It was time to find out. She took a deep breath. "When that happened with my ex, when she told me to…"

She couldn't hold the tears back any longer, and they started to spill down her cheeks. Drew reached out to hug her, but she couldn't let them, not until they knew what she'd done.

"When she told me to end it, or that she'd leave if I didn't, I did it. I dumped my new love like she meant nothing." She looked down and let the tears cool her cheeks, which burned with shame. "I wouldn't do it again, and it was the beginning of the end for us anyway. But I did do it. I threw her away like she didn't matter to me, but she did matter. She really did."

Drew shifted towards her, and she couldn't read their facial expression when she finally dared look at them. At least it didn't look like outright disgust. They held out their arms again, and this time she let herself collapse into them. They stroked her hair, and her tears subsided.

"Of course she mattered. We all make mistakes and have to learn lessons, sometimes in the hardest way."

She pulled back and looked at them again, to be sure. "So you don't hate me now?"

"No, I don't hate you. Not one bit."

Then they kissed her, and she didn't even try to pretend it meant nothing. The love she'd turned her back on had mattered, and Drew mattered too. She wouldn't make the same mistake again.

❖

It was good to march, boots on the ground, wrapped up in a crowd brought together by anger and injustice and the desire to do something about it. Drew joined the chants against the destruction of the welfare state and villainization of those on benefits as the words rippled along the mass snaking its way through the city.

"People are worth more than pounds. Survival is not a privilege."

The passion of those surrounding Drew fanned a spark inside them, and in that moment it truly felt like they could change the world.

The speeches once they reached their final destination—a massive city park, overtaken by the placard-clutching mass and a temporarily erected big stage—stoked their emotions further, alternating between grief and fear and rage and hope, uniting them all as the speakers guided them though the waves. You could forget how many times you'd stood there, inspired and believing together you could change the world, only for nothing good to come of it. In that moment it felt impossible for nothing good to come.

Drew stood tall in the crowd, penned in on all sides by too many people to count. They'd travelled down with a gang of friends and acquaintances but had lost the rest of the group when the others had gone off in search of lunch. Being experienced in the field, Drew had come prepared to spend hours on their feet without access to facilities. Their trusty rucksack was packed with snacks and drinks, and a little device that meant they didn't have to worry about finding decent enough public toilets to sit down. They had offered to share their food, of course, but their companions fancied a sit-down lunch—who knew how far afield they'd had to go to find somewhere with a free table. It could be tricky in central London even when tens of thousands of people hadn't descended to raise their voices together near the seat of power. It didn't matter, though. It wasn't like Drew was alone.

The speeches were followed by a musical celebration, and the crowd started to thin and spread out. Drew found a free patch of grass and pulled the picnic rug out of their bag to claim it. As soon as they sat down, they became aware of the ache in their feet—they were used to being active, but not standing or walking slowly for hours. At least they'd remembered to wear sturdy boots, thoroughly worn-in over the years and still decent enough to keep them going for however long they needed to be on their feet. It was questionable whether the boots were still waterproof, but thankfully they'd not been put to the test that day. Drew looked up to confirm the sky was still unusually clear. Nature was on their side.

The boots were good but could come off for a bit. Drew peeled them off with a sigh and left them lying next to their feet, ready to pull back on quickly if needed. It was unlikely the police would burst in to clear them out, given the large crowd and celebrity-endorsed stage, but better safe than sorry. In smaller protests without official permission, they'd learned to never remove their boots even though the cops generally preferred to pen them in than clear them out. They had spotted the vans, which held the riot gear that was not put on show for family-friendly events, parked around the edge of the public space. Kids ran around freely among small groups who had joined Drew in taking the weight off their feet for a bit. And by the looks of it, white, middle-class kids. There was unlikely to be much trouble from the authorities.

Which meant they could safely check in on the response online. The big news outlets might not have posted their stories yet, but social media was popping off. They scrolled through streams of photos of the marching masses and close-ups of amusing placards. Drew had snapped a few shots of their favourites themself, including more than one rainbow-strewn person declaring themselves *Proud to be not for profit*. Drew would wait until they got home to post, though, otherwise they'd be distracted looking for responses for the rest of the afternoon.

While they were there, they did their usual check for feedback on the pod. No one seemed to have minded so far about the tweaked format—many had actually appreciated the book-film mash up—but they were ready for backlash if it came. What they were not ready for was a thread, started by someone whose pic they recognized, giving too much away about the host.

The original post was not too worrying, though they hadn't predicted Viv would post before they had the chance to talk to Hannah. At least Hannah was unlikely to read it.

Can't believe I might get to meet the woman behind the #BeyondTheBooks podcast.

They clicked on the profile to be sure. Yep, there was their mum's new lover, with her arm around Fran as final confirmation. Drew might have gotten a bit carried away on their visit. Viv had seemed genuinely impressed by their involvement in the pod and thrilled by their involvement with the host. They hadn't said she could definitely meet Hannah, just that they might be able to arrange something. They'd been planning to slip it into conversation when they were with Hannah, so it wouldn't seem too big a deal, but after her tearful confession about her relationship history, it had not seemed the right time.

And her confession had thrown them—they were trying damn hard not to be judgy, but they'd never imagined Hannah could treat a lover like that. She'd always come across as honest and reliable, not the sort you'd expect to ditch someone on another partner's whim. Sure, she'd said she'd learned her lesson and she wasn't with that partner any more, but still…They couldn't make it sit right with them. Just when Hannah was getting set to open up more, Drew had to question if she could be trusted.

And if she saw Viv's posts, Hannah might be thinking the same of them. A cold fear crept down their spine as they scrolled down through the comments. This was on them, surely. Had they told Viv not to give away Hannah's identity? Maybe they hadn't while caught up in the moment and the relief of finding Viv was someone they could get on with. But it was common sense, wasn't it? Yet as soon as her one of followers had asked, Viv had spilled Hannah's name and, possibly even worse, her personal connection to Drew. It wasn't explicit, but it would be easy to interpret as meaning Hannah and Drew were together and insinuate that Drew's presence on the show was not earned the usual way. They groaned. Who knew their mum's partner would turn out to be a gossip.

Which put them in a tricky position. They didn't have Viv's number so could only call her through their mum. And what would Fran think of them calling to tell her partner off? No, that would be a bad move and could undo their good start. Viv might well not appreciate being called out in front of Fran either. They would have to contact her directly and ask her to delete the post, nicely. They could take at least part of the blame.

Thankfully Viv had not changed her settings to stop anyone she didn't know messaging her, so they didn't have to do it publicly. There was no guarantee she would see their message straight away, but what else could they do? They could hardly report it. There was nothing that went against community guidelines, and even if there had been, the moderators were unlikely to do anything about it. From the number of times they'd pointlessly reported vicious, openly anti-trans content, they knew the internet overlords wouldn't bother.

Somebody tripped over Drew's boot and nearly landed on top of them but was caught by their companion.

"Shit, sorry. Hey, cool boots!"

They looked up to see a Pride-clad couple, around their age or a tad younger, inspecting their boots. The shorter of the two had picked one up, having kicked it away when they tripped. The boots were vibrant purple Doc Martens with non-binary laces that tended to attract their people.

"Thanks. And no worries, I shouldn't have spread myself."

"Nah, I should've looked where I was going." The stranger looked at their companion, who gave them a discreet nod. "Hey, I don't suppose we can be cheeky and join you. It's gotten pretty rammed out here, and we didn't come prepared."

They all looked down at Drew's picnic blanket, which clearly had space for two more.

"Go for it."

Drew smiled and tidied up their possessions to make more room. After being abandoned by their travelling group, it was nice to have some company.

The couple started removing their bags and jackets, and Drew took the opportunity to shoot off a quick message to Viv before introducing themself properly to their new companions. Hopefully she'd see it before her public post got picked up beyond her immediate friendship group, and there would be no harm done. It wasn't like she'd given Hannah's full name or anything else someone could track her down with. It was no big deal—even if the feeling in the pit of Drew's stomach disagreed. They would figure out later whether to mention it to Hannah. It wasn't like she would find it herself, and there was no need to freak her out over nothing. Or damage her trust in them over nothing. And Drew still had some processing to do before they could face, and trust, Hannah again.

CHAPTER SEVENTEEN

H appy birthday to you, happy birthday to you…"
Hannah tried her best not to flinch at her family's terrible singing as they brought over the candlelit cake. Her mother placed it carefully on the small patio table in front of her. She took a deep breath, gathered her thoughts, and blew out the candles as the song ended.

"Did you make a wish?" her mother asked.

"Yes."

It was a silly tradition, but she couldn't say no to a good ritual. She kept a note of her wishes, and they were interesting to look back on. The list gave an idea of who she'd been and who she wanted to be in future. The last few years had gotten more sombre in tone, but she was ready to dream bigger again.

"And?"

"And if I tell you, it won't come true." She held up a hand and shrugged as her mother started to protest. "I didn't make the rules."

Not that she would have wanted to tell her anyway. There were bound to be more questions if she confessed her sincere wish: to be able to fall in love again without fear. Plus it sounded corny even to her, and she couldn't take them laughing at her delicate desire.

"True. Right, I better get back to the barbecue so we have some real food to wash down that cake," her father said and wandered back over to the smoking barbecue.

He'd been keen to take advantage of the sunshine, which was fair enough given how you couldn't count on the weather staying that nice for long, and Hannah had managed to position herself safely upwind from the stench. A standing fan helped ensure it stayed that way and took the edge off the unusually hot day.

"And I'll go cut this up. The real food will be a while, so I'm sure we can manage a small slice in the meantime." Her mother headed in the opposite direction, back into the house.

For some reason, society dictated that the kitchen was her territory, but when the cooking was done outside suddenly it was a man's job. Her parents had always seemed content in their gendered roles, but Hannah couldn't see the logic in it. People seemed to assume when she didn't follow social norms that it was because she hadn't picked up on the unwritten rules, when in reality sometimes she chose to ignore them because they just didn't make sense. Her parents weren't fond of her questioning the rules, and the same went for many of her teachers, so ignoring them seemed the best option. She did things her way and let them do things theirs, even when it was illogical.

Josh sat down next to her and his presence brought her back out of her thoughts.

"So, how's things?"

He stretched out in the deckchair and turned his face up towards the sun. His eyes were shielded by rectangular sunglasses that looked like a well-known brand but for the telltale lack of logo.

Hannah continued to look at him without even attempting an answer. It was too vague a question to know where to start, and it wasn't clear what he wanted to know, if anything—he could just have been asking to pass the time until the food was served.

"How's the pod? Are you doing that series you were talking about?" He half turned his head towards her.

Okay, so there was something specific he wanted to know. "Yes, we're doing it. We've been comparing a couple of books each time, or a book and a film, and putting out an episode every two weeks."

"Sounds like a lot of work. Hope you're not overdoing it. You know, there is such a thing as leisure time." He turned back to the sun.

"I like to stay busy." Unstructured time made her feel lost and in recent times risked her slipping off into memories she'd rather forget. "And it's not *work*-work."

Though it had been feeling like it at times lately. It was definitely a good thing it was a limited series, and she could slow the pace back down soon.

"Whatever you say," he said, in a tone that suggested he did not agree but couldn't be bothered to argue. "So when you say *we*...?"

"I ended up getting Drew back as cohost. It made most sense."

"I'm sure it did. And how are you getting on with them?" It was hard to tell his expression behind the sunglasses, but she suspected this was delivered with a wink.

"Good." She let herself stretch out and lie back too. "Really good."

If things went the way she might want them to, she would be bound to let slip to her family at some point. Her brother was probably the best place to start. He'd been less judgemental about her opening her marriage and had backed her up at times by pointing out Georgia had consented to her "affair" and had her own extramarital relations too, so Hannah hadn't been cheating. He hadn't managed to convince their parents of this, but it was still good to know he got it at least.

"Oh yeah?" He rolled over so he was facing her fully.

Hannah resolutely stayed facing the sky. It was easier to talk without looking at him anyway.

"Yeah. You were right—they are hot."

"I knew it!"

"But not just that. They're also interesting and passionate and caring, and so easy to be myself with."

"Sounds like a keeper. So have you made a move?" He spoke in a lowered tone. "I won't tell Mum."

She laughed. "Probably best not, at least not until I know if it's going to turn into anything long-term. You know how they were before, and...Drew is poly."

"Ah. Glad to hear you've not let what happened with Georgia put you off. That wasn't your bad, you know."

Hannah felt tears prick her eyes. "I know," she said in a shaky voice. She did, mostly.

Josh reached over and held out his hand. She took hold of his wrist in that way she had as a child, and he curled his fingers around her wrist with a firm grip in return. Whatever tough face he might put on in front of others, her brother had embraced her quirks and been the person who most got her at home. Even from a young age, he was the one who'd understood how to hold her.

"You didn't answer my question. Have you made a move?"

He curled his fingers to tickle her wrist but stopped when she started to pull away. He was also an annoying little brother.

"Yes," she whispered.

Josh returned her grin.

"But not romantically. I'm still figuring out if I'm ready for that."

"And how long are you gonna wait? No offense, but if you wait until you're completely over everything that went down with Georgia, are you ever gonna be ready?" He massaged her wrist with his thumb. "Sounds like this Drew is someone special. Make sure you don't let her ruin that for you too. She's done enough damage."

Tears filled her eyes again, and this time there were too many to contain. When did her brother get so wise?

"Seriously, Han. You deserve some happiness."

"Thank you." If they both weren't so comfy on the deckchairs, she would have been tempted to hug him.

"You're welcome. Happy birthday, sis."

It was the best birthday present she could hope for from him. Josh was not known for his taste in gifts, and it was always awkward trying to fake gratitude when someone gave you something you didn't want or need. But the tears escaping Hannah's eyes indicated that she had needed his words. She wanted to believe that she deserved a chance at love again and that it was worth the risk, but it was hard based on past evidence. Josh wasn't the type to say something tender unless he meant it, so maybe it was true. Maybe she was ready for and deserving of a little romance. Maybe even a big romance that would renew her belief in that kind of love.

The balloons outside the house made it look like a kid's birthday party. Thankfully there wouldn't be any children present as far as Drew was aware. They hadn't been privy to the guest list. By the unusual number of cars lining the street it seemed plenty of people had got there before them. They ended up having to squeeze in a space a street over, making them even more late. Parallel parking was not something that should be rushed, and a lamp post almost got injured in their haste. At least it wasn't a pedestrian.

Drew could hear nineties pop music before they reached the front door of the bungalow. It seemed unlikely anyone would hear them knock, but at least they'd remembered their key. If they slipped in quietly, maybe they could pretend they'd been there a while.

"Drew!"

So that wasn't going to happen. Drew hadn't even removed their boots when Phoebe came rushing to greet them. They straightened back up and held out their arms to receive her hug.

"Hey. It's good to see you. Feels like it's been ages," they said as she bundled into their arms.

It must've been since they picked Alex up at the airport, which was, what, three weeks ago? So not that long, but Drew had got used to popping in on her regularly.

"Yeah." Phoebe seemed reluctant to end their hug. Maybe she'd missed them too.

"Where's the guest of honour?"

It was unlikely Phoebe had strayed far from Alex's side, now she'd got her back. Apparently Alex had been reluctant to have a big welcome home party, and it had been Phoebe who'd talked her around. She would likely be keeping close watch on her older sister to ensure she didn't make an escape. Unlike Phoebe, Alex wasn't someone who enjoyed being the centre of attention.

"She's in the garden. She wants to help with the barbecue, but Ishani won't let her."

"Sounds about right."

The barbecue was Ishani's pride and joy, and she took her hosting duties seriously. It had been modded to make it the right height for her and so her wheelchair fit under—a project both Drew and Alex had a hand in. Mostly Alex. Ishani had made do with disposable versions she could put on a table before, but now that she had a proper fancy set-up, she was keen to use it whenever the British weather allowed. Drew was often invited to join whenever she had it in action, and they had no objections whatsoever. Not everyone got as lucky as them with metamours. Hannah's confession came to mind again, and once again they tried to brush it aside. This was Alex's day, and she didn't need them brooding.

The weather gods had been kind to them for the party. The sky was a lush blue with only thin streaks of wispy cloud that looked like candyfloss. Drew followed Phoebe out to the garden, where Alex was indeed hovering near Ishani's side. Garlands had been hung along a washing line to give a street party atmosphere, and the garden was full of deckchairs and clusters of people enjoying the sunshine. Phoebe saved them from getting distracted saying hello to everyone by pulling them over to the barbecue corner.

Alex might have been hanging there to avoid the throng. She was leaning against the fence post with a beer bottle in hand, silently watching the crowd.

"Look who I found!"

Alex looked their way at Phoebe's announcement and broke into a smile.

"Good work. Now the party can get started." She strolled over and gave Drew a shorter but no less enthusiastic hug.

"Sorry I'm late."

"Nah, I was kidding. There's no schedule, unless Becca's been making plans I don't know about."

Alex looked doubtful after saying this, as if suddenly fearing there could be something shady underway.

"Not as far as I know either. We agreed to let you off making a big speech, and the presentation has been whittled down to an hour, tops."

Alex snorted a laugh. "Long as I don't have to stand up in front of everyone, you can take as long as you like."

"What presentation?" Phoebe said.

"It was a joke. We're just going to relax and have fun."

"Okay. Me and Becca have planned some games."

Alex looked like she was biting back a groan.

"Cool. I'm gonna grab a drink, does anyone want one?" Drew said before Alex found the words to argue against the game plan.

"I'll come with," Alex offered. "Do you want a top-up, Ish?"

"Yes please." Ishani held out her glass. "Hi, Drew. Excuse me not coming out to hug you."

"No worries. I can see you're busy."

"Phoebe, are you okay to stay here to help while we get the drinks in?" Alex said.

It looked like Ishani had everything under control, but it would give Drew a moment with Alex to chat one-to-one. The two of them headed to the kitchen before anyone could object.

"So, how's things?" Alex asked.

She pulled another bottle of beer from the fridge, then leaned against the kitchen side as if in no hurry to head back out there.

The kitchen was empty—of people, anyway. Every surface was spread with bottles and plates of nibbles, plus cake boxes that looked sure to house some of Phoebe's creations. Drew felt bad for not contributing anything, but there clearly wasn't any need for them to add to the banquet.

"Good. Busy, with the podcast series as well as the usual. We're recording the last episode soon, and I must admit it'll be nice to have some spare time back."

"Fair dos. Which brings me onto…how's Hannah?" Alex gave a suggestive smile.

Drew checked to see that no one else had come in behind them. They hadn't discussed the latest events with Rebecca yet but would need to soon. If they still wanted to take things further with Hannah.

"Good." They attempted a smile back.

"Why doesn't that sound totally convincing?" Alex moved closer and dropped her voice.

"No, things are good between us. She just dropped a bombshell the other day that made me a bit…less certain."

It was always a risk getting with someone who wasn't very experienced in poly as you didn't know how they would handle it. And in Hannah's case, what Drew did know wasn't good. In fact it was one of the biggest red flags out there: someone who dumped a partner on another partner's whim. Drew needed to somehow make peace with that if they were ever going to truly trust her.

Or expect their polycule to. They'd not told Leigh that part of Hannah's history for obvious reasons and because they had no doubt what they would do if Hannah tried to pressure them into ending another relationship. They weren't going to pretend it wouldn't hurt to let Hannah go, but it wouldn't be a hard choice. Even in the early days when there'd been more explicit hierarchy in their relationships, Drew had still drawn the line there—Leigh had never had a choice in who they got with and she never would, something Leigh thankfully agreed was as it should be.

"That explains it. So, what was it?"

Drew sighed. It would be good to tell someone, and Alex wasn't the type to spread private information. "She carried out a veto in her previous relationship."

"Shit."

"It wasn't her idea—her ex pushed her to dump a newer partner, and she did it. And she seems to regret it now."

It clearly hadn't been an easy decision for Hannah, and years later she still seemed cut up about it. That was a good sign, wasn't it? Surely she wouldn't do something again that had felt that wrong.

Alex took a moment before responding, "Ex? Well, at least you shouldn't need to worry about them."

"True." That was what they kept telling themself.

"Do you think she'd—"

"Hey, I didn't realize you'd got here!" Rebecca came bustling into the kitchen with two hands full of empties.

She gave Drew a quick kiss on the cheek, then looked around for a place to deposit the glasses. Drew started to clear space for her.

That would have to be the end of the talk about Hannah. Which was probably for the best. Maybe they were overthinking the whole thing and just needed to let Hannah leave her past behind her. Everyone made mistakes. Why should they expect her to be any different? And she seemed to have learned from it, which was the main thing. As Alex was quick to point out, her ex who'd initiated the mess was out of the picture. Drew didn't know too much about them, but from what Hannah had said, it had not been a healthy relationship in more ways than that. She wanted to move on, and Drew wanted to encourage that, whether it was with them or not. That's what a good friend would do, and they should be that to Hannah, whatever else they might be.

CHAPTER EIGHTEEN

There were only forty-seven minutes to go until Hannah finished and could head home to get ready. She didn't usually find herself counting down the minutes until she could leave work, but she didn't usually have a date.

Was it a date? Drew had offered to cook for her before they snuggled up in front of another movie together, which was difficult not to characterize that way. It was for the podcast, after the success and ease of the last episode, but it was difficult to think of it as work. Especially since if the film was anywhere near as spicy as the book, it was going to be very hard to keep their interactions PG.

Being at Drew's house might help—they'd assured her their wife was out for the evening and wouldn't be back until late, or with advance notice, but Hannah imagined she'd be watching out for her return. Hannah might not be interested in befriending Drew's other partners, but she didn't want to get in Leigh's bad books by having her walk in on them fucking on the couch. Especially as it would be the first time they met.

She didn't plan on meeting Leigh at all, at least not that evening. If things went further with her and Drew, then meeting would become inevitable eventually. It was something that brought a spike of anxiety, a new social situation that she had no script for. It would be fine. Wouldn't it? Hannah might not have been there before, but Leigh was clearly experienced at the whole metamour thing.

The term gave good vibes at least—it brought to mind some kind of comic book character and felt satisfying on your lips.

"Metamour, metamour, metamour." She repeated it out loud, enjoying the flick and purr of the sounds, which helped settle her mind.

"Did you say something?"

Hannah jumped at the sound of her supervisor's voice. She hadn't heard her come into the stockroom. She felt her face heat and pinched her lips to stop any more echoes escaping, then realized she should reply. "Just talking to myself."

Should've said no. But she didn't want to gaslight the woman when she had obviously heard something. Talking to yourself wasn't that unusual or socially unacceptable, was it? Even if most people didn't do it in quite the same way.

Tracy laughed, but not unkindly. "Fair enough. We'll be getting ready to close up soon. Have you got any plans for tonight?"

"Just heading to a friend's to watch a movie."

It tasted a little sour on her tongue—the taint of a lie—but it was true. Drew was still her friend.

"That sounds nice. I do enjoy crashing in front of a movie after work. And there's this great movie podcast I listen to. Do you like podcasts?"

Hannah's chest clenched, and she turned to find Tracy studying her. It was just a casual question, wasn't it? But there was something in Tracy's stance that was not quite casual, though Hannah couldn't say what it was.

"I listen to some." She deliberately kept her answer non-committal, adding a shrug for good measure to indicate it wasn't a topic she was interested in pursuing.

"Cool. Know any good book ones? I'm always looking for more if you've got any recommendations."

Again, Hannah could just be paranoid, but there was something in Tracy's tone that sounded as if there was some subtext there. But she couldn't be sure, so she once again kept her response carefully vague. "I can have a look."

"No need to on my account. Just if you think of anything and want to let me know…"

Hannah stiffened. "Okay."

The invitation seemed like more than an openness to share recommendations, but she couldn't be certain what Tracy did want to know, and she didn't want to make it more awkward by asking.

Because if her instincts were right and Tracy was asking about her own involvement in podcasting, she would prefer to have the option to not tell all.

The bus was warm with too many bodies and too long idling in rush hour traffic, and her clothes felt sticky and uncomfortable when she got back. She stripped them off straight away and wandered nude through the flat. A joy of living alone. She didn't know how Cass coped with their platonic housemates who would probably find nudity awkward. She would shower soon but didn't want to right away. She needed to settle first from the overstimulation of the crowded bus.

She flopped naked on her bed, appreciating the cool cotton sheets, then pulled the notepad from her bedside table. It was open to a pros and cons chart, which she had been gradually filling over the past week. Min had suggested doing the chart on opening herself up to romantic relationships again, following some tentative discussion in her last therapy session, but she'd decided to make it more specific. There were too many unknowns and variations when she looked at relationships as a general concept, and besides, she wasn't interested in a relationship in general. She was interested in a relationship with Drew.

When written out in black and white, it was increasingly clear how comparisons with and fears of repeating her mistakes with her ex dominated the cons. Were there even any real concerns to do with Drew? Their relationships with their metamours seemed a lot closer than Hannah would want, but there were no signs that they were mandatory, and it might just be Drew being a more sociable person. It didn't make sense to hold Drew's being on good terms with the rest of their polycule against them.

She wasn't oblivious to the potential complications or in denial over her past mistakes so wasn't likely to fall into the trap of repeating them mindlessly. She'd told Drew she would never make the same choices again, and she really couldn't imagine she ever would. She'd proved herself able to say no to Drew when she needed to, and they'd stepped back and apologized, recognizing when they'd pushed her. Both of them had proved they were different, even if Drew did appear to have a bit of a hero complex.

And couldn't that be a pro in some ways? Someone who genuinely wanted her to be safe and happy—shouldn't that be what she should look for in a partner, though Min was likely to interrogate all the *should*s in that. It wasn't like that was all Drew had going for them. They were passionate and interesting—she could happily talk with them for hours—and funny and down to earth. Plus they were hot and good in bed, attentive in the best way. Sexual compatibility wasn't everything, but she wasn't going to pretend it was nothing. They were straight-talking but kind, perceptive but open-minded...Making the list made it clear just how big a crush she had on Drew. Who was she kidding when she tried to pretend they were just a fuck buddy? She had vowed not to repeat her mistakes, and if she didn't pursue her chance with Drew, she could be at risk of breaking her own heart again.

A night in at theirs might be the perfect time to put herself out there. If it all went wrong, she had the option to walk away with no witnesses to make it awkward for either of them. She'd never found public proposals romantic. Surely they were just coercive, as it must be harder to say no in front of everyone—even she would struggle with humiliating someone she loved like that despite her usual honesty. How many marriages also wouldn't go ahead if no one else was in on it? It would be interesting to see the stats on how many fell through when a big wedding party wasn't planned, though other variables would have to be taken into account, such as why they were planning a quick and quiet ceremony in the first place. There was a difference between the legal and social contracts of marriage, though it was difficult to fully untangle the two—she still wasn't sure how much of each had been involved in her own decision to wed. It was a decision that hadn't been as thought through as her choices usually were, due to the rush of emotions that interfered with her rationality when Georgia proposed, and it was a decision she had come to regret.

Not that she was planning on proposing to Drew or anything else so concrete. Marriage wasn't something she was ever likely to want again, so she was kind of glad they'd already ticked that box with someone else. There was no pressure to hit any relationship targets that didn't sit right with her. Drew's style of relationships meant setting your own standards rather than going along with those already set by society. And as much as Hannah liked knowing what to expect, that suited her too.

Her phone buzzed, and she picked it up to see a text from Drew, asking when she'd be ready to come round. She glanced down at her naked body and sighed.

Soon, if I can persuade myself to get redressed.

Drew might appreciate her current state, but she still had to get there.

They replied with a hug emoji. *I promise you won't have to stay that way if you don't want to.*

Good x

It was an obvious change to her message last time asking to keep things PG. She might not be great with hints, but the meaning should be clear enough to not need any more words. There was only one film to get through this time, so there would be plenty of time to enjoy other pursuits as well. And have the conversation which she had been putting off long enough.

❖

Drew rushed upstairs to the spare room. They had been busy prepping dinner and tidying downstairs, but on receiving Hannah's texts their priorities changed. The guest bedroom doubled as a home office and was generally used for the latter so might not be ready for visitors. They opened the door with bated breath, then groaned. The desk was strewn with books and paperwork, as was the bed. It was unclear why Leigh always left a paper trail—surely everything was done digitally these days—but somehow it quickly took over the room between guests.

It's okay, there's still time. The coffee mugs and overflowing bin were the obvious place to start. The bin ended up in their bedroom, which they thankfully did not need to sort. The agreement was to use the guest bed if taking anyone else upstairs, which meant they didn't need to worry about leaving the bed smelling of sex that Leigh hadn't got to be a part of, and it also meant there was no need to tame the clothing jungle that had become overgrown in the main bedroom.

It was a good thing they'd started with the mugs as when they stepped back into the kitchen to deposit them, the pan on the hob was making overly excited noises. They reached it just in time to prevent the pot boiling over, lifting it up briefly and allowing the contents to settle before replacing it on a lower heat. It was a simple meal, but they'd started the pasta sauce early to give it a chance to reduce before they added everything else nearer the time. On second thoughts, they turned the hob off altogether and gave the sauce a quick stir before adding the lid. If Hannah was in the mood to get naked as soon as she arrived, dinner would have to wait.

As would serious conversations. Drew still hadn't totally decided whether to tell Hannah about Viv's social media slip-up. She'd picked up their message and deleted the thread without hesitation, so it didn't seem like there was any harm done. *What you don't know can't hurt you* wasn't generally a motto Drew lived by, but in this case, was there really any need to piss Hannah off?

Their phone buzzed again, this time letting them know Hannah was on her way and reminding them what they were doing. They charged back upstairs to finish clearing the room and get dressed. As they weren't planning on staying dressed for long, they decided to forgo a binder. A tight sports bra would do until Hannah hopefully relieved them of their clothes, and they buttoned a clean short-sleeve shirt over it, sized up to avoid straining over and drawing attention to their chest. Though they didn't object to Hannah attending to it. They'd learned a while ago not to question the contradictions in how they felt about their body and to focus on what felt right. Hannah running her eyes and hands over them definitely felt right.

The doorbell rang as they did up the final button. They rushed to answer the door but slowed down halfway so it wouldn't be obvious they'd run there—and so they didn't fall down the stairs. An evening in A&E was not what they had in mind.

When Drew opened the door, they found Hannah in a dark flowing jumpsuit holding a bouquet of roses. She held the flowers out to them, and they hesitated for a moment, not used to being on the receiving end. Plus roses were not what you usually brought for a friend, surely? A look of panic streaked across Hannah's face, as if suddenly doubting she'd made the right move, prompting Drew to reach out.

"Thank you. Sorry, it threw me for a moment. No one brings me flowers."

Whether people worried Drew would experience it as a gendered thing or it just didn't occur to them, Drew didn't know. They buried their nose in the bouquet, breathing in the sweet and spicy scent.

"I hope you don't mind—"

"Of course not. I love them."

They had to bite back an *and you*. It was definitely too early for even thinking about saying that. Hannah's romantic gesture was likely a big enough step for her. They moved back to let her in the house.

"So, what do you want to do first? I've started dinner, but it can wait—"

They didn't get any further as Hannah finished their sentence for them with a kiss. The initial light touch turned into a passionate kiss that had them pinned against the wall, with the bouquet hastily dropped on the cabinet next to them.

"I want to do you," Hannah whispered with a mischievous smile between kisses.

"In that case, may I suggest I show you the upstairs first."

Hannah chuckled. "Excellent plan. Though we should probably put those in water." She pointed at the abandoned bouquet.

"Okay." Drew grabbed it and headed to the kitchen, then propped it up in the first receptacle they could get their hands on. They could trim and arrange the flowers while dinner was cooking.

Hannah had taken the opportunity to remove her jacket and shoes, though she remained by the coat rack as if waiting for them to invite her in further. Drew took her hand and led her through the lounge to the stairs.

They had only taken the first step up when a flash of fur interrupted them. Pebbles was not going to let Drew get away with not introducing him. He placed himself between the two of them, winding around Hannah's legs in a figure-of-eight greeting.

It had been worth a try. Drew gave in to the inevitable. "This is Pebbles, the lord of the manor."

"Good evening, sire." Hannah crouched down to say hello properly, and he turned up the purring to full volume as she fussed him.

As much as Drew was glad to know Hannah got his approval and vice versa, they would prefer her hands were on them.

"How about you give him a treat as your entry fee, and then we can run upstairs while he's distracted."

"Good plan. But I will see you later," she crooned to the cat as she gave him some final scratches behind the ears.

It was lucky Pebbles was easily distracted by his stomach. Hopefully he wouldn't race to find them straight after. Drew put out his dinner just in case, to buy them more time.

On their second attempt, they made it upstairs and went straight to the guest bedroom. Hannah didn't hesitate to push Drew back on the bed and climb on top of them. They laughed in surprise but made no objection and pulled her into a deep kiss.

Hannah sat up abruptly, and before they could ask what was wrong, she undid the tie at the back of her neck and shimmied the top of her outfit down. This revealed a satin bra that was made to be touched. They reached for her and ran their thumbs over the buttery soft material, then pushed her outfit down further until she kicked it off entirely. They reached down and teased at her panties, which were already damp with her desire.

Hannah rolled on her side and tugged at Drew's shirt, her eyes seeking theirs for permission.

"You can take it all off."

She didn't hesitate to take them at their word. Soon they were pressed together on top of the sheets, skin on skin. Their closeness felt more than physical this time, and Drew wanted to slow down to savour it.

"Before I get you to take me, I want to taste you," Hannah murmured. She ran her hand down their body and pushed at the waistband of their boxers.

Drew moaned in anticipation before remembering there was an issue with that idea.

"I got tested this week and everything was negative," Hannah said. "And I haven't been with anyone else since…" A different kind of flush reached Hannah's cheeks, and she bit her lip. "Honestly, since we first had sex."

"Good to know."

Actually, what did that mean? Aside from not worrying about using barriers. Had she decided she only wanted to be with them? Which was her choice…as long as she didn't suddenly expect them to also become monogamous.

"I've not been with anyone else new since last testing at the start of this year."

"*Sooo*, may I?" Hannah cupped their crotch.

They could feel their own warmth and wetness against her hand, but what if she was asking for more than they could offer?

She saw their hesitation and stilled. "You know, I'm not saying I won't get with anyone else in future. I meant it that poly is what I want for myself too. But right now, I'm all caught up in NRE and can't stop thinking about when I can next be with you."

"Hang on, let's be clear here. You're talking about New Relationship Energy? But doesn't that mean…" Drew smiled and trailed a teasing hand down her side. They didn't want to put words in her mouth, but it wasn't how you spoke about a hook-up.

"It means I'm not pretending that's not what I want any more. I'm still nervous, but I want to be with you and not let the chance for whatever we can be slip away." She curled around them and tucked her head into their neck. "If you'll have me."

Drew wrapped their arm tight around her and cupped her face with their other hand, drawing her into a long kiss that was less rushed than their earlier kisses but no less intense.

"I want that too. I think we can be something special," they said, with a giddiness at not having to pull back their feelings any more.

"Agreed." She kissed them tenderly, then with more force, eliciting an involuntary moan. "Now, where was I?"

Hannah lifted herself onto all fours and edged backwards down their body. Drew let themself sink back into the bed and open to her. Yes, this felt right. If neither of them was holding back, they could finally find out what the spark between them could grow into. They would need to talk more about what exactly being in a relationship meant for them, but there would be time for that later. There was a balance to be found between talking and doing, and it was best take advantage while they had the house to themselves.

It was done. Hannah breathed out a massive sigh of relief and sank back into the cushions. Eyes closed, she felt her whole body soften as if it had been waiting a long time for this moment to relax.

"You alright there? Shall I go?"

She opened her eyes again to see Drew staring at her from the screen. Oh yeah—she'd stopped the recording but hadn't closed the call.

"Yes. Just relieved to be finished."

"It has been a busy couple of months. Not all bad, though." They raised an eyebrow. Was that comment flirtatious or seeking reassurance? Or both?

"Definitely not all bad." She wouldn't agree to do it again, unless she had a lot more time on her hands, but she'd survived, and it had brought them together. "I am glad to have six weeks before the next one."

The way the extra episodes had fallen meant she would either have to rush into another, change the schedule, or take a break. Having learned her lesson, she'd opted for the break. She would need to start preparing in a few weeks, but the gap should still be enough to allow her to relax and focus on other things properly. Like how she'd finally taken the plunge into relationship territory and needed to revise how to navigate that. Or throw out everything she'd learned previously and start again.

Starting from scratch with no expectations was a freeing idea, if a little terrifying. It was a good thing she'd kept all her books on polyamory from before. It was time to reopen those texts.

"Have you got any plans for how you're going to spend it?"

She kept forgetting Drew was still there. She really did need the break.

"I've got some non-podcast related reading to do. And it would be nice to spend some time with you without having to focus on work."

"I was thinking the same thing. Well, the you part. Forgive me if I don't pick up another book for a while." Drew chuckled, and there was no way she could hold it against them.

Not that she needed her partners to share her passions anyway. In fact, it was better to keep some things just for herself, as long as they were happy for her to pursue her own interests and monologue on them from time to time.

"What would you like to do?"

Drew raised an eyebrow in response.

She laughed. "Aside from that."

While everything had been structured around the podcast recordings, they hadn't had much choice in how they spent their time together when fully clothed. Now they could do whatever they wanted, hopefully they had enough in common to keep things interesting.

"I was wondering if you fancied a trip to the seaside. It's a good time for it, while it's warm out and the schools have gone back, so it should be pretty quiet. We could even make it a minibreak if you fancied going away for a few days."

Hannah took a moment to consider this. She'd never been a big traveller, preferring to travel in her head via stories than in the real world, which was always more stressful than in fantasy, but a British seaside holiday was something she could appreciate. Especially when not full of screaming kids. She hadn't used any of her annual leave yet that year so could even book time off work, rather than squeezing it between shifts, and have a decent break with time to prepare and readjust to everyday life after.

"What are you thinking?"

"That it sounds nice, if I can book the time off work so there's no rushing around. I can check when I'm there tomorrow."

She would usually give much more notice, but as long as no one else was already booked off, Tracy should be able to find cover for the odd shift or do without her. A bit of spontaneity wouldn't do her any harm, within reason.

Drew beamed. "Lush. Let me know when works for you, and I'll make sure to keep the days free. If we head to where my mum lives, I can vouch for a couple of places we booked while she was house-hunting."

"Somewhere you've been before would be good."

That way there should be no nasty surprises. You never could trust the carefully shot photos and glowing descriptions that made everywhere sound like a five-star resort. If she knew what it would really be like, it would take away some of the stress of going somewhere new.

"We could even drop in on her while we're in the area. Her girlfriend is a big fan and dying to meet you."

Wait, did she just accidentally agree to meet Drew's mother? Hannah watched her own eyes widen in a horrified expression on the screen.

"No pressure though." Drew held out their hand as if they wished they could snatch the words back. "I know it's a big step—meeting the parent—but I didn't mean it like that."

"Okay."

Hannah didn't know what else to say or if it really was okay. It was a big step, however you looked at it. And besides the part of her that was freaking out, there was another part that was flattered that Drew thought she was worthy of introducing.

"I'll think about it."

"Is that a polite no, or do you genuinely need to think it through?"

Hannah smiled. Drew's directness was part of what made them a good match.

"I genuinely need to consider it. Especially having just finished up here. My brain needs a rest first."

"Of course. There was something else I wanted to talk to you about…" They paused and seemed to study her through the screen. "But it can wait. And it's nothing to worry about."

"If you're sure." Though now Hannah was of course worrying about what it could be.

"I'm sure. And seriously, no need to worry about it, everything's okay."

"Okay."

"In fact, everything's better than okay, cos we're going on our first minibreak." Drew raised a glass to the screen as if toasting to it.

"If I can get the time off work," she had to remind them. "Though if not, we could still take a day trip when I've got a weekday scheduled off anyway."

"Excellent idea. Just keep me updated, and I'll try not to get carried away in the meantime." They winked.

She got the feeling they'd be looking at holiday lets as soon as she ended the call, but there was no need to stop them. It was a situation where she was happy to follow their lead. She didn't have the brain space to plan a holiday, but if Drew did, then great. Sometimes it did make sense to let someone else help. It didn't mean you were helpless, and it wasn't always about control. Or that's what she tried to tell herself.

"So, want me to come round as usual tonight? I can bring pizza."

It had become their post-recording routine, and it was something Hannah would miss. Maybe they could continue, but it wouldn't be the same after recording with someone else, and Drew might well want to hear all about it rather than flop, like her.

"Of course. Long as you don't mind me switching my brain off."

"As much as your brain interests me, I'm happy to focus on other parts tonight."

"Excellent." She returned their grin.

It was amazing to have found someone who understood her so easily and didn't question it when she still wanted to be around them but wasn't talkative. Cass got it, and they often engaged in parallel play activities, content in each other's gentle company. Though that wasn't what she wanted from Drew—she wanted to connect with them intimately, through senses that didn't need words. She wanted to feel their soft welcoming body and the weight of them pressed against her. She wanted to hear their moans and see how their breath hitched when she touched them in a sensitive place. She wanted to breathe in the subtle scent and warmth of their presence.

And she wanted them to stay with her after and to wake up with them, not having to fear what it could mean. That part could wait until they went away together. It would be their chance to laze around in bed, or at least undressed, together most of the time. A minibreak did sound like exactly what she wanted and needed. She hadn't told them about her birthday to save any fuss and confusion over their role in her life, given that wasn't all figured out yet, but she could think of it as a birthday treat. And if she had to endure a little visit to see Drew's supportive family, she could manage that for them. And they could make it up to her after.

Chapter Nineteen

Drew wrestled the suitcases out of the car boot. The cases had been crammed in alongside various other bags of supplies despite their only going away for a few days. It was a good thing they'd driven and had the luxury of a private car to pack it all into—they would not have wanted to wrangle it all on public transport. The plus side was they wouldn't need to worry about finding a shop on a Sunday afternoon, as Hannah appeared to have packed the contents of her kitchen.

The cottage was just as Drew remembered. It sat on the edge of a farm, away from the main house and working areas, surrounded by fields. Hedges blocked out the view of the road, making it feel even more remote, and looked to be ripe with blackberries. They would have to check if picking them was permitted, though it would be tempting to grab some to snack on anyways—surely a few wild berries wouldn't be missed. Their immediate neighbours were a small herd of cows, with their not-yet weaned calves sticking close to their sides, munching lazily in a neighbouring field.

Apple trees formed a barrier between the cottage and the farm. From a distance those fruits also looked ready for the picking, though they'd have to take a closer look. The grass around the cottage had been allowed to grow wild and was dotted with daisies. The tiny flowers always reminded Drew of school playtimes in September, when they would lie in the grass making daisy chains with their friends. It wasn't a traumatic association. No one had questioned too fiercely Drew's desire to not wear any of the flower jewellery themself, and their creations were joyfully accepted by the girls they gifted them to. Simpler times.

The cottage itself was pebbled with various shades of grey but didn't have all its original features—the thatched roof having been replaced by tiles, and the chimney now for decorative purposes only thanks to the installation of central heating. It was a bit of a shame as they fancied the idea of curling up in front of an open fireplace with Hannah, naked apart from the blankets they lay wrapped up in.

Hannah had got out and was gazing at the cottage with a big smile on her face. Drew's own smile widened at her look of approval. She'd pretty much left it up to them to choose the place, only weighing in once they'd narrowed it down to a few suitable options. Not that they were complaining—it was good to have some way to help now that their role on the podcast had ended. They'd kind of hoped Hannah would come up with a way to keep them involved in some capacity, but she didn't want to talk about it whenever they raised the subject of the pod. To be fair, Hannah had earned a total break from it, which was a big part of why they were there.

The key was stowed in a locked box, which was opened by a code they'd been emailed. Drew scrambled in the vines of yellow-edged ivy crawling up the wall to locate its hiding place. Inside was an envelope containing two sets of keys and the all-important Wi-Fi code. The idea of a digital detox was appealing in theory—at least to Hannah—but in reality, Drew needed to be plugged into the virtual world where everything was organized. Plus the phone signal was rubbish out in the sticks, so they at least needed the internet to relay messages, including making plans with their mum.

They presented a set of keys to Hannah, and she seized them and headed straight to the front door. The luggage could wait. It wasn't like they had to worry about anyone poking around their car unnoticed. There were some benefits to being away from the rest of humanity. Hannah let out an *oooh* that coming from anyone else they might have suspected was sarcasm. She held the door open as they shuffled in behind her, gazing around the living room that they'd stepped straight into. Dark wood panelling mixed with embossed wallpaper to give it a modern but timeless look. Large well-stuffed armchairs and a small sofa centred around the replacement electric fireplace, which had a widescreen TV fixed on the wall above it. It wasn't the roaring open fire of Drew's fantasies, but Hannah still seemed impressed.

"Why don't you take a look around while I bring in the rest of the stuff from the car."

Drew already knew what the rest of it was like. Though it was tempting to follow her to witness her awe, that could be seen as a bit creepy.

But Hannah held out her hand. "That can wait. Come with me."

They turned back and walked to her, then couldn't resist planting a kiss on her smiling lips. She kissed them back, unhurried but deep, burrowing into their arms. The luggage could definitely wait.

"We could go check out the bedrooms together..." Drew murmured.

Hannah laughed. "I need to take a shower first. I feel all sweaty and gross from hours in the car."

"You still feel good to me." They kissed her again and felt her melting in their arms.

"Good. Of course, I don't like getting dressed straight after..."

"I'll be waiting."

There was no rush of course, with three days together to spend however they pleased, but now that Drew had her there, they only had one thing on their mind.

Hannah pulled back and took their hand again, leading them through to the rest of the house. "Let's get acquainted with this place first."

Drew allowed themself to be led by her, only parting ways once they had explored each room and ended up in the main bedroom. Hannah took her case into the smaller bedroom, which she assured them she didn't plan to sleep in, but appreciated as a space to retreat to when she needed time to herself. Drew tried not to take this personally. Hannah had always been clear her regular need for solitude was no direct reflection on their company.

While she sorted herself out and took her shower, Drew fired off texts to Leigh and Fran letting them know they'd arrived safely. They'd not arranged exactly when to meet up with Fran and Viv, but Hannah had agreed to it, which meant they really did need to get it over with and tell her about Viv's screw-up.

They could just ask Viv not to mention it and Hannah still might never know, but hiding stuff from Hannah that clearly was her business would not be a good start to their relationship. And although Drew maybe could convince themself that Hannah didn't need to know, they could not believe that she wouldn't want to know. They didn't want to imagine the trust they would lose if someone else told her first. It might not make them look perfect as it was, given they had clearly been the one to tell Viv in the first place, but someone else telling her would make it far worse. *Just get it over with.*

Hannah returned wrapped in a fluffy white towel. Her body was glistening, but her hair looked dry under a see-through shower cap. She pulled off the cap and placed it on the windowsill, and her wavy hair tumbled instantly over her shoulders. Drew reached out to her from their position propped up on the bed. Hannah took the cue and climbed up to join them. As they kissed, her towel slipped down, and their hands stroked bare skin. Drew managed to pull back before they got completely distracted from their mission.

"You okay?" Hannah rested on her side next to them.

It was unusual for them to pull back from a beautiful naked woman who somehow wanted them too.

"Yes, just…"

They hadn't been planning to raise it like this, but given Hannah was most comfortable undressed, maybe it was for the best?

"Tell me." She poked them playfully in the ribs.

"There's something I wanted to let you know, before we go see Fran and Viv. It may not come up, but I thought I should tell you anyway."

They felt Hannah stiffen next to them.

"What is it?" All playfulness had left her voice.

"It's not a big deal, I spotted and sorted it straight away, but Viv slipped up on social media. She was stoked about possibly geting to meet you, and when someone asked for more details she…used your real name. And hinted at our relationship."

Hannah groaned and rolled over onto her back, resting an arm over her face. "When was this?"

Drew bit their lip. "A few weeks ago."

"Weeks?" Hannah gave them a sharp side-eye. The *and you're only telling me now* part was implicit in her tone.

"It wasn't a big deal. I spotted it and messaged her, and she took it down straight away. It's not like she's got tonnes of followers, at most it was probably only a few of her friends who saw it."

Hannah stared up at the ceiling as if trying to bore a hole through it with the power of her pseudonym's namesake. "That's not the point. You should have told me."

"I know, I should've told you sooner, and I was going to, but other things kept coming up and there never seemed a good time—"

"You should've told me straight away." Hannah emphasized the last two words through gritted teeth. "It wasn't up to you how to respond. You should've given me the choice before you swooped in."

"Would you have wanted anything different? I thought it was best to act quickly before it spread—"

"But it's not just about what you thought! Did you even try to contact me? It's my show, my years of work, my identity." Her voice cracked as if sobs were trying to spill through.

"You're right, I'm sorry. I was just trying to help." They reached out for her, but she jerked away.

"I know. You always are. But sometimes people don't need you to help. We need you to stop and listen."

The harsh truth of her words made them clam up. She was right. They'd swooped in assuming they knew best and that it was their call to make. But neither of those things was true. Had they known that, deep down, and that's why they'd put off telling her what they'd done?

"I need to process and get dressed. I'll see you in a bit."

Hannah rolled off the bed without looking back at them, pulling her towel tight around her and disappearing out of the room. They heard the other bedroom door open and click shut.

Well, that was definitely not how they'd pictured the start of their break. They were supposed to be helping Hannah relax, but now... Drew groaned. Hopefully Hannah would forgive them before long. At least she hadn't threatened to head back home. Drew really had just been trying to help, but somehow they had made it worse. Maybe they did need to learn to stay in their lane, no matter how much it went against their nature and what they saw coming at those they cared about.

❖

Hannah dug through her suitcase for something to wear. Her nudity, which was usually freeing, felt suddenly vulnerable. She found a soft lounge hoodie that she was used to wearing with nothing underneath, for those times when she didn't want to get fully dressed but needed something to warm her up.

Not that she was cold in the physical sense. Their hosts must have put on the heating to take any chill away from the stone building in anticipation of their arrival, and when she touched the radiator there was still a trace of warmth. She turned the knob down in case it came on again. She didn't want to be clammy when she got fully dressed later.

At least they didn't have any strict plans that would mean having to rush to make up and head out. Why Drew had left it until then to make their confession was beyond her. If they were always going to tell her, why risk ruining the holiday? Unless they were scared she'd cancel so waited until they'd already got her there and she no longer had that choice. A familiar cold dread crept over her, and she burrowed deeper into her hoodie. There were no direct trains or coaches, and she was reliant on Drew to drive her back. There was no easy way to head home. *No way out.*

She took a deep breath and tried not to follow that line of thought, uncurling her hands to stroke the smooth sheets beneath her. She wasn't stuck with Georgia. She was safe. She had gotten out, and now she was where she wanted to be. She might not be able to head home easily, but she didn't need Drew to taxi her around everywhere. This was her well-earned break, and she was going to make the most of it, whether with them or not. The cottage was walking distance from the nearest village, and she could probably find somewhere nice to hang out there or get a bus to somewhere bigger. There was a folder full of leaflets for local attractions on the coffee table in the lounge. It was tempting to go and grab that to cheer herself up and calm herself down with planning, but she didn't want to risk bumping into Drew just yet.

Why did Drew have to treat her like she needed them to come to her rescue, instead of trusting she was a responsible adult who could make her own decisions? They wouldn't be the first person to take that stance. Yes, she benefited from support sometimes, and she wasn't going to pretend everything was easy for her. But that didn't mean she needed their protection. Wasn't part of the point of a relationship that you dealt with things together and supported each other through life's twists and turns? Could Drew ever be trusted to do that instead of assuming control at the slightest whiff of danger? She didn't want a hero looking down on her. She wanted a partner.

She wasn't one hundred per cent clear on what exactly that meant in the poly realm, but she wanted them to be equals. Except on occasion in the bedroom if Drew was up for that—maybe their tendencies could be channelled into fun role play where there would be no real harm. They had said they didn't get BDSM, but it seemed like this wasn't an informed or outright rejection, and frankly, the way they responded to her didn't seem vanilla. There were hints that instead of needing the chance to take control, they needed the safety to submit. It was something she could tease out…if their relationship lasted that long.

There was a creak outside her door and then the sound of footsteps on the staircase. Good thing she hadn't gone down. The tension and cold were starting to seep out of her, the thought of teasing a submissive Drew helping, but she couldn't let her sexual desires and their chemistry make her overlook the issues. It would be okay if Drew was just an occasional hook-up who she only connected with for sex. Maybe she should've left things that way. Except it had never been just sex with Drew, no matter how much she'd tried to ignore her blossoming feelings. A part of her that she'd locked away had slipped out the first time they'd spoken, the part of her that still believed in kind-hearted people and happy endings.

The footsteps creaked back up the wooden staircase, this time stopping outside her door. She braced herself for a knock and tried to pull together something to say. It wasn't okay, but it wasn't beyond redemption either. But there was no knock. Instead, a folded sheet of paper slid under the door, and the footsteps moved on. She stared at it for a moment as if she could somehow read the message it contained from across the room. Except of course she couldn't.

The fact that she didn't have to take it from Drew's hand or read it in front of them helped. Writing was easier to process, but when someone was watching you read their outpouring, it was like opening a present publicly. You had to pray it was something you liked, so you didn't have to school your face and voice in a lie to not hurt anyone's feelings. She needed to be able to process without worrying about what her face was giving away without her permission. Hannah pushed herself off the bed but paused to grab some PJ trousers before picking up the note. Her legs were shaky, and the lack of covering could be part of the issue.

It was a longer letter than the note she'd found with the parcel outside her flat door that day, and it was printed carefully as if each word had been as carefully thought through.

> *So, I fucked up and I'm sorry.*
>
> *I want to say that up front, so you know this isn't gonna be a load of excuses and trying to pass the blame. I get it—I should have told you straight away. Deep down, maybe the reason I kept putting it off was because I knew that, rather than it just being about waiting for a good time. By the time I admitted to myself that I had to tell you, it was already too late.*
>
> *I don't really know why I didn't. I think part of me knew I'd fucked up already by not briefing Viv properly, and that you were gonna be upset whatever I did to try to fix it. In that moment it felt like if I could just get her to delete it, it would be like it never happened. Naive, I know, but I wanted to try because I couldn't bear the thought of upsetting you…again!*
>
> *I know I've got the tendency to speak/act before I think things through fully, and that can get me in all kinds of trouble—except that makes it sound like the trouble isn't caused by me. It can cause trouble. I can cause trouble. I am trying to work on that, though I doubt I'll be able to ever fully shake off my impulses. I can prod myself to talk to you first when it's anything to do with you. And listen before I charge off trying to be a hero—yes, I'm also aware I have a bit of a hero complex. I don't want to take away your agency, and I have no doubt that you are very capable of figuring out what needs to be done yourself. I will try to wait for orders next time.*
>
> *So no excuses, but that partly explains where I was coming from. I do want to tell you what happened as I figure you'd like to know all the facts. Here they are…*

Drew had bullet-pointed out exactly what happened and copied out the exact words from the social media posts, which meant she could see it all clearly and replace the worst-case-scenario stories taking shape in her mind. Maybe it wasn't that big a slip and her identity was still safe. She couldn't help but smile at Drew's description of needing to battle their hero complex. The fact that they also recognized that meant something. Georgia had never acknowledged or taken responsibility for her own issues, except in moments of self-pitying tears that lacked meaning except to manipulate Hannah into staying. Hannah tried to allow herself to believe this wasn't the same.

There was a complimentary notepad and pen on the bureau, so before her walls could close her back in she started to write a reply. She told them just what and why their response was an issue for her, not details they didn't want or need to know, just enough for them to understand. Because as Min would say, it was best not to rely on anyone's ability to mind-read. It had always struck her as ridiculous how people say autistic people can't mind-read, as if everyone else can. Was she seriously supposed to believe everyone else was telepathic? No, which was why you had to make the unspoken spoken. Or written.

Drew's note had been delivered with a cup of tea, left outside the door, and she took breaks to hold the warm mug and inhale the steam between paragraphs. It wasn't until she'd finished her response that she took her first decent slurp. It was still warm enough, just. The sting had gone out of the heat, and she glugged it back in hefty mouthfuls. She waited until she'd finished it before taking her note back to the door, having not changed her mind during her tea break. If she wanted this to work, they both needed to start communicating better.

She slipped it partway under her own door, then paused. If Drew saw it, would they realize it was for them from Hannah and not their own note? Maybe she needed to push it under Drew's door instead. Yes, that would be the logical thing to do. But before she could bend to retrieve it, she heard footsteps heading her way. The paper disappeared fully under the door, and the footsteps faded back away.

She should've held back at least some of the tea to drink while she waited for their response. She couldn't just sit there. At least she had her suitcase with her, and inside it she had stowed the little grey dog Drew had gifted her. She retrieved it and went back to the bed, holding it in her lap and stroking its velvety ears. "What do you think, should we forgive them?"

The dog looked up at her with glassy yet soulful eyes.

"You're biased," she pointed out. But so was she. If someone else had made the same bad call as Drew, she'd be inclined to shut them out. She was in too deep to leave Drew behind, though, without both of them getting hurt.

Drew's next note appeared in the same manner as the first, except this time she was watching out for it, and she scrambled up as soon as she saw it start to poke through. It was shorter this time, but sufficient. They got it or at least claimed to.

Hannah picked the notepad back up to reply but decided that was enough. She didn't want to spend their whole holiday passing notes under doors to each other. She would much prefer to take advantage of the lack of neighbours to enjoy themselves at full volume. As she padded to the door, she removed the trousers. The hoodie hung just low enough to prevent indecent exposure if someone spotted her through a window.

She found Drew sitting on the floor in the main bedroom, leaning against the foot of the bed where they would be able to keep an eye on Hannah's door. When she stepped towards them, they made to get up, but she held up a hand.

"You can stay down there."

A flicker of confusion crossed Drew's face, but they obeyed without question. And with a half smile. There was definitely a submissive streak in them, and Hannah was in the mood to make use of it.

"We've said all we need to for now, don't you agree?"

They nodded, as if unsure whether they had permission to speak. *Interesting.*

"Good. Because the advantage of having an argument is the make-up sex after."

Drew's smile widened into a full grin. "How do you want me to make it up to you?"

Hannah strolled over, deliberately taking her time, and sat on the edge of the bed. She parted her legs. Drew didn't move, seeming to wait for permission. She almost laughed in delight. Seriously, how had no one noticed or pointed it out to them before?

"Get on your knees and get over here."

She could swear a little moan slipped out of their mouth when she gave the order. *Very interesting.*

Drew shifted onto their knees and crawled the few steps to position themself between her legs. They started with gentle kisses along the inside of her thighs. Hannah sighed and let her eyes close, then gasped as they reached her centre. She placed her hands on their head, keeping them where she wanted them, and this only seemed to increase their enthusiasm. She flopped back on the bed and wrapped her legs around them instead, and they stayed on their knees until she came. They stayed there even after while she recovered her breath. When she relaxed, they gently lifted her legs off their shoulders.

"You enjoyed that?" She lifted her head briefly to look at them.

"Very much." Drew stretched forward and took her hands in theirs but remained on their knees.

Were they waiting for permission to move?

"Good." How far could she guide them before they slipped into territory that required more advance negotiation? "How about you get up here and show me how much."

Drew rose and climbed onto the bed, sliding their body over hers.

Hannah quickly undid the button of their trousers and slid down the zip. They rolled off her and stood up to pull them off completely, then went to move back on top of her.

"No. Show me."

Drew blinked a few times and tilted their head, before lazily sliding their hand into their boxers. They let out a gasp at their own arousal. "Like this?"

"Exactly."

Hannah pushed up on her elbows so she could watch the show. Watching actors touch themselves had never done much for her, but this was different. Drew didn't appear fazed by her request, and by the moans they let out as they stroked themself she suspected they were enjoying the audience. And doing it under orders.

There were definitely more discussions to be had. But right then, there were more urgent things to take care of. When it looked like Drew couldn't stay standing much longer, Hannah shifted forward and helped them onto the bed and out of their remaining clothing.

"Don't stop," she whispered as she kissed each part of their body as she revealed it. She laid them back on the pillows and guided their hand back between their legs. They didn't need any further guidance, but she kept murmuring words of encouragement, delighting in the way it made them moan louder. She squeezed and stroked all the beautiful curves of their body as they lay spread before her. She wanted to explore every hill and hidden valley. She would need more from them as soon as they brought themself to climax. There was no rush, though, apart from the pulsing between her legs. She and Drew could spend all evening like this if they wanted. And she might demand they do just that to make up for the holiday's false start.

❖

"You sure you want to do this?" Drew asked, not for the first time. They didn't want to push Hannah into anything, especially after already messing up once that holiday.

Drew walked hand in hand with Hannah along the sandy beach, their sandals dangling from their other hand. The warm sand sank between their toes as they enjoyed the stroll in the sunshine. Hannah paused and crouched frequently to examine a potentially interesting shell, running her fingers over the surface as if reading its history there and removing any sticking sand with a squirt from her water bottle before deciding whether to keep it. She had come prepared with a small pot, in which she carefully placed any chosen shells before slipping it back in her beach bag.

Drew didn't feel the need to join her but was content with the unhurried pace. While Hannah examined potential bounty, they gazed out over the water and around the seafront. They'd never spent much time just admiring it on their previous visits as they'd always been focused on catching up with their mum, or originally helping her house-hunt. It was a nice change to treat it as a holiday destination rather than a quick day trip with the pressure of several hours' driving. The waterfront stores were starting to shut down after the end of the school holidays, but there were still the year-round facilities to keep them fed and entertained.

"Do what?"

Drew bit back *You know what I mean* because maybe she didn't without clarification. They supposed *this* could refer to any number of things—something Hannah had pointed out on other occasions. They were learning that where someone else might just be attempting to dodge or delay answering, she meant it. Though she also could have the typical motives, given the subject.

"Are you sure you want to meet up with Viv and Fran?"

They had arranged to meet at their usual spot for chips on the beach, to keep it more casual than a formal dinner and less overstimulating in the open air.

"Yes, best get it over with," Hannah replied while crouched examining another shell, and she seemed to realize what she'd implied moments later. "I mean, I'd like to do it now, so I've not got the nerves for the rest of our holiday."

"Nice save." They laughed and accepted her kiss when she stood back up.

Hannah turned and looped her arms around their neck to give them a more thorough kiss, and for a moment Drew forgot they were on a public beach.

"I know this is important to you, so I want to do it. Okay? If I change my mind, I'll tell you. Promise." Hannah gave this reassurance with her forehead pressed to theirs, followed by another long kiss that made them glad the beach was mostly deserted.

When Drew pulled back and opened their eyes, they spotted two figures walking towards them. Now they were the one engaging in intense PDAs in front of Fran. At least Fran already knew about their relationship with Hannah, so it wouldn't be too shocking. "Good, because they are coming towards us now."

"Ah. So they saw that."

"Yep."

"So I should probably step back now." Hannah's arms were still around their neck, and she seemed reluctant to move.

"Afraid so. But I promise we can pick up where we left off later." They ran a finger along her collarbone and watched her shiver, then shuffled round to stand by her side.

"Hello, my love," Fran called over to them as she and Viv approached.

Drew took a few steps forward to meet her and secured a big hug, while Hannah and Viv hung back.

"I wasn't sure if we should interrupt," Fran whispered in their ear with a teasing lilt.

"Yeah, sorry about that, we got a bit carried away in the beautiful setting."

"No need to apologize. I must admit, me and Viv have been the same on occasion out here when it's quiet."

Drew wrinkled their nose but held in the *eww*. Seeing their mother with a new partner seemed to be regressing them to childhood, but they were both adults now and should accept each other's adult desires.

Viv had moved forward during their exchange and advanced towards Hannah with her hand out.

"Hi, I'm Viv. You must be Hannah. It's great to meet you. I'm a big fan." She delivered this last part in a whisper, as if to keep it from the ears of any passersby.

Hannah took her hand and shook it. "I am. Hi, it's nice to meet you too."

"And I'm Fran. It is lovely to meet you." Fran offered a handshake too, rather than her usual hug, but then seemed to change her mind and held out her arms. "Do you do hugs?"

"Yes." Hannah smiled and stepped into her arms.

"Well in that case…" Viv grabbed a hug after, then moved over to give Drew one. "I was just trying to play it cool."

"You nailed it." They laughed.

"Are you two hungry? Shall we go get food?" Fran asked.

"I'm ready to eat." Drew patted their stomach. It had been an active holiday so far, even if mostly in the bedroom, and they needed to refuel. "Hannah?"

"Yes, I can eat." Hannah moved back to Drew's side and slipped her arm though theirs. The press of her body against them was distracting but at least outwardly respectable. They could handle it. And they would have her in private again soon.

"Do you remember the elaborate sandcastles we used to build?" Fran gestured towards an abandoned fortress.

"Of course. We used to spend hours on them," they informed Hannah. "I'd say we were right experts."

Hannah smiled. "I'd like to see that."

"I reckon I could give you a run for your money. I was quite the expert myself despite the lack of kids to give me the excuse." Viv winked at Drew.

"You don't need kids to build sandcastles," Hannah agreed. "We could test your skills now."

"I don't know," Drew said. Sure, you didn't need children to do it, but it would look a bit suspect to just have a group of adults playing in the sand.

"Scared I'll beat you?" Viv was starting to show a competitive streak, though it all seemed in jest. For now.

"It could be fun," Hannah said. "I've not made sandcastles in years. Why should we stop enjoying things just because we're grown-ups?"

Hannah was very persuasive. And it wasn't like they'd be in anyone's way.

"Go on then." Drew turned to Fran. "Let's see if we've still got it."

Fran laughed, seeming genuinely delighted with the idea. "Sounds wonderful."

"I can go buy some buckets and spades while you get lunch. I saw a shop back there with them out front that looked open." Hannah pointed back along the beach.

"Excellent. I'll come with you, if you don't mind us leaving you two to get the food," Viv said.

"Or did you want some alone time?" Drew quickly added.

They didn't want Hannah to feel forced to hang with Viv if she needed time out. She hadn't had much time alone since departing from home. Viv might be planning to take the opportunity to apologize, though, without dragging Fran into it, which hopefully wouldn't be too awkward for Hannah. Thank God Drew had already told her and talked it out.

"No, it's fine. I'll go with Viv." Hannah slipped her arm out of their grasp. "Just avoiding the smelly chip shop."

"Ah, you should've said. We could go somewhere else—"

"No, I'm good with chips. I was just gonna wait outside and get you to pick mine up."

Drew chuckled. "Happy to serve."

"Mm-hmm." Hannah looked like she was biting back another response.

Possibly she was recalling how things had turned out yesterday. Drew needed to not think of that now. They were with their mother. The sandcastles might be a good plan after all. What could be more PG than that, and hopefully the competition with Viv would be distracting enough to keep their mind off what might happen when they got home later. It turned out there were still sides of their own sexuality left to discover, and now that they were aware of that, it was hard not to wonder what other pleasures Hannah might introduce them to that they had never considered. And a remote cottage where they didn't have to worry about anyone overhearing, apart from their bovine neighbours who made enough racket themselves, was a good place to find out.

CHAPTER TWENTY

Going back to work after a holiday, however short, was always difficult, and Hannah was really feeling it. She daydreamed her way through her first morning back, managing basic repetitive conversations with customers before slipping back into imagining she was still at the beach, curling her toes into the sand and watching Drew sculpt fairy-tale castles, which she decorated with washed up shells. It didn't help that she was tasked with dismantling the summer display of beach reads. Even though most weren't set at a literal beach, the bright colours and smiling figures did promote a holiday vibe.

"Earth to Hannah."

Hannah turned to see Tracy walking towards her.

"Did you not hear the bell? They need you on the till."

Oops. She looked over to find a queue had sprung up, and her one colleague on the till caught her eye with a pleading look.

"Sorry, I'll go now." She tried to find somewhere to place the stack of books she was holding, until she heard a sigh and noted Tracy's outstretched hands.

"Leave those with me. And once you're done on the till, management would like to speak with you."

Hannah froze with her arms still out. Why did they need to see her? Sure, she'd been a bit out of it that day, but surely that didn't constitute a disciplinary offence. And even then, it would only be dealt with by senior management if Tracy decided it needed escalating.

There was one obvious explanation—even Hannah had heard the rumours of upcoming redundancies and possible store closures. Despite their own online presence, Barnaby's struggled to compete with businesses that didn't have the overhead of a physical shop. What would she do without this job? She hadn't finished her university degree and had no professional qualifications. Her very narrow experience wouldn't make her a prize catch for any other business. But if that was what was happening, better she find out sooner rather than later and start coming up with an alternative career path. Maybe she would have no choice but to try monetizing the podcast. She should've gone for promotion all those times she was nudged to, instead of staying in the role she was comfortable in, so she would at least have some management experience to put on her CV.

Her hands felt numb as she scanned the customers' purchases and pressed the buttons on the till. Just when her life seemed to be moving forward finally, it might all fall apart. She kept her eyes down, not daring to make contact with anyone else's in case she read something in them that would send her building anxiety spilling over.

Once the queue had dissipated, Tracy came over, as if she needed reminding of her fate.

"If you can pop up now while it's quietened down, they're in the meeting room."

There was only one meeting room, the one room with a big enough table and enough seats to fit the whole team. Why they were seeing her there rather than in the management office, she didn't know, but it didn't matter enough to ask, and she didn't want Tracy thinking she was procrastinating to avoid the inevitable.

When she knocked on the door and followed the command to come in, she realized why. It wasn't just her store manager there, but the regional manager too and two other people she didn't recognize. Her stomach clenched further. This was big. Was the store closing, and were they about to offer her options for what she could do? She should've grabbed a notebook and pen on her way. At least there was likely to be paperwork to review and ensure she understood if this was heading where she thought it was.

"Hannah, thank you for joining us. Do take a seat." David, their branch manager, was the first to speak. He waited for her to pull out a chair and slide into it before continuing. "I realize this is short notice, but we didn't know you were on annual leave when we called this meeting, so apologies for putting you on the spot."

Did that mean they'd tried to notify her at work but she was away, or had everyone else already been called in? Again, it probably didn't matter now as this was a situation that couldn't be helped by preparation.

"I believe you've met Michael, our regional manager, but I don't believe you're familiar with our colleagues who've joined us from the national team today."

"No," Hannah said, then realized that might sound too blunt. "I have met Michael, yes, but not anyone else, so would appreciate introductions."

Hopefully that would make up for any perceived rudeness, though if they were about to fire her anyway, it hardly mattered what they thought of her.

"Of course. May I introduce Anita, HR consultant with the national office, and Gary from the publicity department."

Gary from publicity beamed at her as if he was genuinely excited at the chance to spin whatever was about to happen into something the public could sympathize with.

"Hello," Hannah said and attempted to smile back, minus Gary's manic energy.

"Hi, Hannah, it's great to finally meet you. I'm a big fan."

Gary's words made her blink a few times. He was a fan of her book displays? No, that didn't make sense. She might be in the bookshop, but it seemed that wasn't what they'd come to talk about. *This must be about the podcast.* She'd managed to convince herself that Drew was right and it was no big deal that Viv had exposed her identity, but she should've known better.

"We all are," Anita added, though who she was including in *we all* was unclear.

"I can't believe we didn't realize we had a star stocking shelves in our store." David chuckled, seeming to think this was a compliment.

Did he think that was all she did there, or that there was something lowly about it? Hannah squeezed her lips tight to prevent a correction slipping out. This might not be a redundancy meeting, but that meant she still had a job to keep.

"We were shocked to discover the person behind one of the biggest book podcasts was part of our team without our knowledge," David continued.

How exactly had they discovered that? Viv hadn't said enough for them to be certain, unless Drew had played it down. There must have been some sleuthing even if someone had guessed based on Viv's post. She probably didn't want to know how much, though if they'd done some dodgy snooping, she might be able to use that in her defence if things turned unpleasant.

"I prefer not to disclose my identity, so as to stop it interfering with other aspects of my life."

She tried to state this in a cool, professional manner that made it clear she didn't let the show get in the way of her day job.

"Of course. It can be a battleground out there on social media, can't it? I wouldn't put myself out there either," Michael said.

It was tempting to point out that a—probably—straight white man like him was likely to get little trouble in comparison to her, but this was not the time. At least he was attempting to empathize with her situation, and she might need his backup.

"It is a tough choice to make. But now that the cat's out of the bag, we need to think about where to go from here," Gary piped up.

Were they about to offer an ultimatum or push her into agreeing to something in the corporation's best interest? If only she had someone with her, or at least some notice to get her head in a place where she could better take what they were saying on board.

"We'd like to discuss a proposal with you. If you'd like to have someone else present—"

"Yes," Hannah broke in before Anita could retract what might have been a superficial offer. "I'd like someone with me."

The management team stared at her as one. *Damn, not a genuine offer.*

"Shall I call Tracy up…?" David asked the panel.

"And time to prepare a little. Sorry, I've just got back from holiday, and my head's still adjusting." Now that she'd put her foot in it, she might as well carry on asking for what she wanted.

"We all know that feeling," Gary said.

"And…" Was this the right time to bring it up? If she was going to, it was probably best do so now before things ran completely away from her control. "I'm autistic, I don't know if you've been told, so I need extra time as a reasonable adjustment."

The use of the legal term made Anita sit up straighter.

"Thank you for informing us." Anita shot David a look that

indicated he hadn't informed her beforehand but should have. "We can reconvene in a few days if you prefer. And you're welcome to have a supporter with you and any other reasonable adjustments you need."

It might be a good thing someone from HR was there. *Reasonable adjustments* was an incredibly vague legal term, and of course it was open to interpretation what was *reasonable*.

"Thank you." Hannah focused on Anita. "I shouldn't need too long, though, tomorrow should be fine. I think. I'll need to see if my... supporter...is free."

It made it sound like she had someone officially in that position. She could call on a support worker from her accommodation, but that would mean having to explain everything to them first. And there was someone else that came to mind, someone who was always keen to support her, and who had landed her in this mess in the first place. There was no one else who knew as much about the podcast and her. Plus she was pretty sure Drew had trained in employment legislation to be an advisor for a helpline. It was time to let them take on that supporting role and prove her trust in them wasn't misplaced.

Pebbles stretched out all four limbs as if about to make a move, then settled back in Drew's lap. He appeared to be making up for lost lap time after they had abandoned him for four days.

"I am going to have to get up sometime, you know."

Pebbles rolled his head back and gave them an upside-down glance, then headbutted their hand to encourage a pet.

"Don't even think about it." Leigh voiced his thoughts. "You abandoned me and now you must pay."

"You're right, I'm sorry. I am here to serve and make it up to you." Drew scratched his head and was rewarded with a deep purr.

"Quite right."

Pebbles let his head flop back onto their belly. As far as he was concerned, their body was one big cushion for him to enjoy. There were worse roles to have. Though after being entwined with Hannah for so much of the past week, they were missing the feel of her body against theirs and wishing it was still her curled up in their lap. Not that they would voice that to his majesty or their wife.

"You're missing her, aren't you?"

Unfortunately, Leigh could read them like a book.

"Maybe."

"You got it *baaad*."

She sounded amused by this. At least there was no trace of insecurity in her tone or smile. Leigh also knew them well enough to know this wasn't a threat to their relationship and that she might also benefit from the NRE flying around.

"Maybe."

Pebbles shifted slightly to give them a vicious side-eye. Was it really so obvious that even the cat could call them out?

"It's always hard coming back from a holiday. But at least I've got you two to look forward to seeing and to make up for the end of it."

Pebbles seemed satisfied with this and gave their thigh a claws-in knead.

Leigh came over to join them on the sofa, where they were clearly stuck for the foreseeable. She gave Drew a kiss. "Happy to help. We missed you."

Drew twisted to lean in and return her kiss. They had been focused on Hannah while they were away, but that didn't mean their heart didn't notice Leigh's absence. Would Hannah be up for a polycule holiday ever? It was the fantasy to not have to leave anyone behind, one that might well never become a reality.

"I still have it bad for you too."

"Glad to hear it." Leigh made herself comfy by their side. "So you admit, you're falling for her?"

"Looks like it." There was no point denying it.

"I know what it looks like, but what does it feel like?" Leigh gave them a gentle poke in the ribs.

"It feels like…this could become an important relationship. Longer term. I've not felt this way about anyone new since, well, Becca."

They had dated other people since meeting Rebecca, but no one else had got that close or stuck around for long. Not that there was any guarantee Hannah would stay. They hadn't got around to doing much talking while on their minibreak, and it was too early to be sure how their relationship would work. But Drew was sure they wanted it to continue growing.

"I guessed by the fact you introduced her to your mum."

"That wasn't because of how I feel about her. Viv wanted to meet her because of the pod."

It was true that no one else had met Fran, but if there hadn't been the podcast as a catalyst to prompt her meeting Hannah, they probably wouldn't have taken that step yet.

"I know, darling. I was partly teasing." Leigh linked her fingers through theirs and squeezed. "It's cute, seeing you all giddy and gay."

"I'm not *cute*." Drew scrunched up their face. Something about the word made them think of the girl they weren't, even though it wasn't a totally gendered term.

"I didn't say you were cute. I said you were gay and all giddy over your new woman. And I'm sorry, but it is adorable. I just love seeing you happy, and you know, I'm not averse to taking advantage of your excess energy."

Leigh squeezed their thigh, then quickly pulled back as Pebbles took a swipe at her. She might not be struggling with jealousy, but he was more prey to unruly emotions.

"Please do. Though looks like that will have to wait until a certain someone else has had enough attention first."

"He is your primary, and I know my place."

They had adopted Pebbles together, but he had latched on to Drew early on and quickly established his position as head of the household. He loved Leigh too—she said he tolerated her, but Drew had caught the two of them snuggled up together too many times to believe there wasn't a strong bond there. Everyone knew cats were polyamorous, at least in the sense that they liked to have multiple human worshippers to fall back on. Which wasn't how Drew saw Leigh, of course. Their love was sure and steady, but not dull, and still strong enough to shine through the fog of any new attraction. Even if they ended up settling down with just her, it wouldn't be settling.

"So when do I get to meet the woman who's got you in this state? Given she's already met your mum…"

It was hard to argue it wasn't time yet, but Drew was still wary of pushing Hannah especially given her history with poly. What if she couldn't handle being around Leigh or just never wanted to hang with her? She hadn't shown any interest in meeting Leigh so far, quite the opposite—she would check Leigh wasn't around before coming over. Which could just be about wanting privacy so they could be as intimate as they wanted with each other—as open as Leigh was, Drew did scale it back in her company—but what if it was more than that? Could they be happy with someone who didn't embrace being part of their little chosen family?

"I'll ask her."

There was no point putting it off. If it was going to be an issue, better face it sooner rather than later and hopefully find a compromise. Maybe Hannah would never be a fan of family barbecues, but she could be part of the family in other ways. And they needed to stop making assumptions and just ask her what she wanted—weren't they supposed to have learned that lesson? Maybe she would want everything they had to offer.

Their phone rang, and they worked to get it out of their pocket without disturbing Pebbles. He didn't seem convinced that was possible, and sharp claws dug into their thigh. "Ow!"

"Come here, mister." Leigh gently extracted him and his claws.

The surprise at Hannah calling them made them pause before answering.

"Everything okay?" Leigh said.

"Hopefully. I better get this."

Drew took advantage of Pebbles's removal to step outside to take the call. It must be something important for Hannah to ring, given her aversion to phone calls, and might not be something she'd want sharing with their wife. Or maybe she was just missing them too and needed to hear their voice. They really did have it bad.

Chapter Twenty-one

Hannah checked over her notes one last time before putting the folder of printouts in her work satchel. It had seemed sensible to put something together in case she lost her voice in the moment, and the preparation helped her feel less anxious about her upcoming meeting. Of course, as they hadn't got as far as any concrete proposals when she'd been called in to see management the day before, it was unclear if her notes would be relevant. But they were some comfort.

She'd spent the evening putting together an outline of how the podcast came to be—how, when, and why she started it—and how it worked, meticulously showing how it had not impacted on her job or the reputation of the business. The most you could argue in terms of a link was that the knowledge she'd built to do her job came in handy, but it didn't redirect her focus at work from her bookseller role. She still read and reviewed books that she didn't cover on the pod, and she included examples from the last two years to evidence this. She did use her employee discount to purchase the books she discussed on the show, but that wasn't against any rules, and she was pretty sure they'd prefer she buy them from there than from a competitor.

Her phone buzzed to let her know Drew was outside. They'd offered to give her a lift so she didn't need to worry about the buses being unreliable, and it would give them both a bit of time to prep together. She had rung them after work but hadn't wanted to spend too long talking instead of preparing herself. Drew had said they'd do their part by brushing up on employment law, just in case. The managers had seemed friendly and positive in the initial meeting, but that didn't mean they weren't planning to hit her with something disagreeable. People had the annoying habit of sandwiching bad news between pleasantries so you couldn't feel it coming or process it. As Drew had pointed out, there wasn't anyone from their legal team present, which indicated a lack of serious legal concerns. But you never knew. People were unpredictable and often illogical, in her experience, even when it came to business. It was part of why she preferred to keep her head down and stay out of office politics.

"Morning!" Drew reached over and opened the car door for her with a smile.

"Morning." She slid in and put her seat belt on, then checked her watch and tried to blank out the itch of the strap against her wrist.

She should get there in plenty of time even with the worst rush hour traffic. The meeting wasn't scheduled until noon, to allow the national team to travel in, but she'd be working as usual until then, and Drew had errands to run in town. It was probably for the best as she should have plenty to distract her—hopefully one of her regulars would come in for a long book chat. It was their chance to have some interaction and Tracy recognized the worth of giving time and attention to those lonely customers, not only in terms of their regular spending but also serving the local community. If that wasn't appreciated, Hannah might not have lasted in her job so long.

Possibly not much longer. Though that was probably overdramatic. Surely they couldn't fire her because of the podcast, and she couldn't see any reason they'd want to. She took care to be fair to the authors and not overly critical and couldn't imagine that even if the podcast was publicly linked that it would drive business away. The podcast wasn't in direct competition with Barnaby's—she didn't sell or even have affiliate links to buy the books she discussed, despite this being one of the things Drew had recommended from a business perspective, which she was extra glad she'd not agreed to, and the links she did share for those interested in getting a copy were for Barnaby's alongside independent bookshops and library apps. If she considered it logically, they had nothing to wield against her. But as management hadn't told her their intentions, it was hard to stop her imagination filling in the gaps.

"You all set?"

It might not have been the first time Drew asked this—she was having trouble getting out of her head.

"I think so. It's hard to know if I'm prepared as I don't know what they plan to propose."

"I'm sure it'll be fine. They must know what an asset you are, even more now. And I'll be there if anything starts going into dodgy territory."

"Thank you." She resisted the temptation to touch them while they were driving. "I really do appreciate you agreeing to help at such short notice."

"Hey, no problem. I'm here for you."

Although she'd struggle with Drew's irregular hours and their work herself, it was handy that Drew had the flexibility to be more available than most people in employment.

Hannah smiled and leaned back, closing her eyes. She was caught between wanting to discuss her predicament and wanting to save her brainpower for the big meeting and not encourage her imagination any more. Neither of them knew what was going on, so was there any point talking about it?

"Mind if I put some music on?" Drew broke what had turned into a long silence.

She nodded, then realized they probably couldn't and shouldn't see that while driving. "That's fine."

"There's a case of CDs in the glovebox if you wanna pick something."

"Wait, so CDs are okay, but not DVDs?"

"Long as there's a CD player built in here, they're still in operation."

"There's also a connector so you can plug in an MP3 player."

She didn't have really strong feelings either way, except in questioning the contradiction, but Hannah was glad of the lighter topic. The ensuing debate helped pass the journey, and she ended up plugging in her own music to keep her in the right mood.

Drew managed to pull up right outside the bookshop, though not in a legal parking space, so she gave them a quick kiss before stepping out. Despite its brevity, that also helped her mood. Would the buzz she got whenever they kissed fade with time? And even if it did, would it be replaced with something deeper that would be worth the loss? She had got used to the thrill of new dalliances, but she was ready to find out what else was possible. And there was the bonus that Drew didn't expect her to never get with anyone new again. Her love life was one area where she was happy exploring different sensations and possibilities, within the confines of pleasure and explicit consent.

Which was not what she should be thinking about at work, but it helped her get through the morning. The shop was also pleasantly busy, and she made it through to the designated time without too much anxiety building. At quarter to, Drew came strolling in and stood waiting for her while she finished serving customers on the till. That day was the first time she'd known them to be early, or even on time, for anything, and it gave her an extra boost to think they must have made a special effort for her.

She hadn't noticed what they were wearing in the car as she'd been too in her own head and they hadn't stepped out, but now she could see they'd made an effort there too. They were wearing smart black trousers and a short-sleeved button-down shirt that showed off their broad shoulders. It was tempting to reach over and squeeze the exposed flesh under their upper arms. Maybe she should have considered the potential distraction of inviting them into her workplace. There should be no squeezing at work.

It took five minutes to clear the queue for her till, and she needed to find someone to take over from her. Tracy strolled over before she could decide whether to ring the bell or risk leaving the checkout empty while she went to find someone.

"Are you all ready for your meeting? If you want to go now so you can pop to the bathroom and get a drink first, I'll cover here. The managers are getting settled, and I've made their teas but haven't done one for you or your...friend."

She said the last word with the inflection of a question. In other circumstances, Hannah might have explained, but now wasn't the time. And she didn't know what term to use to describe Drew's relationship with her, something she needed to discuss with them soon if they were going to get into the habit of introducing each other to people in their lives. But that was something to consider another day.

"Thanks. I will do."

Hannah made a quick exit before a queue reappeared and collected Drew on her way into the back rooms. She left them in charge of tea making while she went for an anxiety pee.

"You ready?" Drew asked when she returned.

"Just about."

She removed her folder of notes from her locker and quickly scanned them to remind herself of her script.

"Lead the way when you are." Drew picked up both mugs and stood waiting for her signal.

"Let's go." She wished she could lean into them for a reassuring hug and another good luck kiss, but that would not look professional if someone walked in.

It was a relief when she entered the meeting room to see the same four faces smiling at her as before. They all introduced themselves again for Drew's sake, but she appreciated the reminder of their names too. She'd remembered their job roles, which seemed most relevant, but not how she should address them if needed.

"Shall we get straight down to business?" Anita took the lead this time. "We appreciate you taking the time to meet with us again and don't want to distract you with small talk when I'm sure you'd like to know what exactly we're proposing."

Hannah smiled. Whether it was because they'd taken her autism on board, or they were just busy people who didn't have time to waste, she appreciated the directness.

"Thank you. Yes, it would be good to hear what you're thinking, unless you want me to talk you through the background to the podcast first."

"That would be interesting to hear, but let's see how much time we have today. It might be we talk about that in more depth without everyone else."

That seemed to be a polite no, so she left the folder closed in her lap. If it started to seem relevant, she could bring up parts as they came up. Unless Anita was saying no to the topic altogether.

"In essence, we want to propose supporting you with the podcast as a corporate sponsor. That could cover a range of things, of course, but basically we'd like to see if we can formally attach it to Barnaby's in some way," Gary explained.

Hannah sneaked a glance over at Drew. They seemed to let their shoulders relax at the mention of a potential deal instead of disciplinary matters. Because it was a good thing, wasn't it?

"We believe it could be a mutually beneficial arrangement: We provide funding and business support, and you help direct your listeners our way and help us to stay relevant." Gary continued with his publicity spiel. "We'll need to work out the details, but we're sure we can work something out that makes everyone happy."

Did she have a choice? It wasn't just a matter of what the deal was, but whether there was any deal to make. At least in her mind.

"That sounds like a great opportunity," Drew said.

Hannah wasn't sure whether to be annoyed with them or if they'd just had to say something as she had taken too long to respond.

"It could be," she added, "although I've always been clear that the podcast isn't a moneymaking business and not something I'm looking to be paid for."

It was best to lay out her position from the start before anyone got too carried away. She wasn't seeking anything from them, though the idea was less off-putting than linking with an ad company or online store.

"But what if you *could* be paid for it? You clearly put in a lot of work—is it right that you arrange and put it all together yourself?" Anita leaned forward. It wasn't clear if she was speaking with concern or admiration.

"Yes, I do it all myself, but I like doing it." Hannah tried not to sound defensive, but it seemed she might be in danger of losing control.

"Of course. We can tell it's a passion project. And we wouldn't ask you to give anything up you don't want to, but we can support with anything you would like, that maybe you don't have the capacity for at the moment," Gary reassured her.

"The last series was a lot of work for Hannah, and it would be too much to do more often without bringing anyone else on board," Drew said.

"It's the time as much as anything, but I've not been looking for a partner," Hannah added, in case they got the impression that she had. She shot Drew a look to try to indicate they were not helping.

"Of course. And that's something we could discuss, allowing you to use some of your contracted hours on the podcast, so that you don't risk burning yourself out," Anita offered.

Hannah considered this new possibility and started to warm to the proposal. She didn't want to leave her job or take on anything extra, but if she could swap out some of her hours it would take the pressure off. "That could be helpful."

"Yes, we don't want you feeling pressure to do too much. Especially given your...neurodiversity." Gary's confident tone wavered on this last word, as if not sure he'd got it quite right. He hadn't, but his point was still clear.

"It is important that we support our employees' well-being as well as the business," Anita added.

"That's good to hear," Drew said.

"It's also important to keep you at the centre. And in this field, people do have a real interest in the individuals involved, including shared identities. Your recent miniseries showed that. Have you had a chance to look at the figures?" Gary said.

"Only briefly." She'd noted an upswing but didn't want to discuss that in case it shifted to considering taking her and Drew as a team. Bringing them in to the meeting probably didn't help, giving the impression that they were still professionally involved. Maybe she should've considered that before inviting them.

"We've had positive feedback on social media," Drew said.

"Yes, we can see that. It would be interesting to see how people would engage with other topics relating to identity. I know you don't usually talk about yourself, but if it's no longer anonymous, that could open doors to connecting even more with your audience."

Wait, when did they discuss changing that? Bringing in a sponsor she already knew was one thing, but bringing in her identity was quite another.

"It could well work to focus on other communities in the same way, which she does already do to some extent." Drew seemed to be getting caught up in the idea too, and though Drew was bigging her up, she wished they would stop.

She wished they would all stop and give her time to think it through properly before they rushed ahead.

"Indeed. But maybe with even more of a personal touch," Gary said.

"That's something to consider. What do you think, Hannah?" Drew finally handed the floor to her.

"That's never been where I want to go with it. But I am open to considering how we could work together in keeping with the original approach."

Hopefully that didn't sound like a total no because it wasn't one. She just needed to drag the discussion back to what she actually did.

"Of course. It clearly works well and draws a big audience as it is, so there's no rush to change anything," Gary said.

As if there being no rush was the same as there being no need to change.

"And you wouldn't have to change anything you don't want to. You're the host, so you need to be comfortable and confident in what you're doing." Anita seemed more on her page.

"Yes," Hannah said, letting out a big breath. She wanted to say more but could feel the connections in her brain start to wobble under the weight of the possibilities, and she wasn't sure how much more she could say. "I need to think about what I want to do."

"It is a big decision, so don't feel you have to agree to anything now," David said, piping up for the first time. She had forgotten her manager was there.

"How about we all write some suggestions of how it could work, and then we could meet again to discuss specifics. We could send everything in writing beforehand for us all to consider before we talk it through," Anita suggested.

"Okay," Hannah said before anyone came up with a worse alternative. Being able to process alone with visual information would be a lot easier.

"Great."

Anita seemed to sense she had had enough for one day and started to wrap things up. Hannah wasn't required to say much else and sat back as the others rounded it off with pleasantries and promises to stay in touch. She seemed to have got away without handing the podcast over but would have to be careful it didn't slip away from her. And that no one else agreed to anything she didn't want on her behalf.

❖

Drew tucked into the warm panini and let out a little groan of approval. They'd decided not to wait for Hannah to eat lunch—given how she could be around food sensory-wise, it was probably best to finish it without her, and they were more than ready for lunch after their early start. They'd managed to get all their bits from town before Hannah's work meeting and had stashed them in the car, so there was nothing else they needed to do while they waited for her.

They were also trying not to get carried away with ideas for how to use the sponsorship deal until they heard Hannah's view. She hadn't seemed sure of it, but as far as they could see, there was no big downside. Yes, it wasn't ideal that it was a big national chain of shops instead of a local business, but it wasn't like there was an independent bookshop nearby. And even if there was, it was unlikely they could afford to sponsor her. Plus promoting a local business could make it obvious where Hannah lived, and that part of her personal info was definitely best kept off record. Other aspects, though…the publicity guy was right that it could help for her to connect more with her listeners on a personal level. It was what Drew had been trying to say too. Maybe Hannah would be more likely to take it on board from the higher ups at her work. Though her initial response suggested not.

At least she hadn't blown off the deal entirely, and the Barnaby's people seemed open to negotiate. Drew could just start writing a few little ideas down while they waited, which they'd leave up to Hannah whether to include in her email wish list.

She walked in just after they'd finished their last bite. Hannah peered around the cafe until she located them, then headed over with her eyes down and no smile of greeting. *Crap.* She should be celebrating, but it didn't look like she was seeing the proposal as such good news.

"Hi." Hannah took the seat opposite, not giving them the chance to get up for a hug.

"Hey, you." Drew kept their tone bright and light, hoping to buoy her up. Maybe it was just the stress of preparing for what could have been trouble that had left her sagging. "So that was a relief, huh? They want to offer you more money, not shut you down."

"Yeah. I guess." Hannah twisted the spare napkin from their tray.

"You guess? It seemed clear they want to make a deal, and if anything have you do more for the pod."

"True. But that doesn't mean I want to make a deal. It didn't feel like I have much choice in the matter, though." Hannah started to shred the strangled napkin.

"Is that what's bothering you?" They hadn't taken note at the time, but she did have a point. "You're right, it should be your choice whether you accept any deal. They can't make you sign anything, and if they try, I'm here to defend your rights."

They reached over to take her hand, but she pulled away.

"Your hands are greasy."

Hannah eyed their outstretched hand suspiciously until they withdrew it.

"I'll go wash them." They stood up to head for the bathroom.

"No need on my account." Hannah motioned them back down. "I'm not planning on staying anyway. I want to go somewhere quiet to clear my head."

"Fair enough."

Drew obeyed and took their place back at the table. Was Hannah happy for the excuse not to touch them in public? She hadn't corrected her colleague when they'd called Drew her *friend*. They tried not to take it personally. Hannah was overstimulated and needed to rest. It wasn't a rejection of them, was it?

"And…it didn't seem like you were set to defend me. You seemed happy to agree with them, even when you knew it wasn't what I wanted," Hannah blurted out.

"Hey, that wasn't what I was doing. I was just encouraging the positive direction it was going in."

Had they agreed to anything? Okay, they thought the PR guy was right, but they'd been careful to put it back to Hannah so she could make the call.

"That's not what it seemed like to me. You've been clear you think I should turn it into a business and put more of myself out there, so why wouldn't you agree to prop up their plans."

"What, you think I'm on their side instead of yours? That I'm conspiring against you somehow?" They were aware their voice was rising in pitch and volume, but they couldn't control it in that moment. What exactly was she accusing them of?

"Not in a conspiracy theory way," Hannah muttered. "But you seemed to conveniently forget what I'd told you I didn't want when an offer you liked was on the table."

"That wasn't what I was doing! I didn't make any calls, I was just being encouraging—"

"Encouraging of what? What I wanted?" Hannah made eye contact briefly, giving them a flash of the anger and resentment in her eyes.

"Encouraging of sharing ideas and finding out what was actually on offer. That's what you wanted from the meeting, wasn't it?" They wouldn't have gotten anywhere good if Drew had said she wasn't interested without even hearing them out. "And this wasn't an option we'd discussed. As far as I know it wasn't even on your radar before."

Maybe they should've guessed that was what Barnaby's was angling for so Hannah could have prepped a response, but they hadn't and it was too late now.

"Which is why I needed time to think before agreeing to anything."

"Which you've now got, so what's your problem?" Drew bit their lip. That was maybe too direct, even for Hannah.

"You don't get it." Hannah shoved away from the table, leaning so far back in her chair Drew worried it might tip over.

"No, I don't. Why did you even want me there if you didn't want me to say anything?"

"To support me, not act like it's your project and you have a say in it."

"I'm very aware I don't have a say. You've made that perfectly clear."

Hannah had seemed to like having them involved, but not in the decision-making or as an equal in any way. They were just supposed to do what she wanted and keep their mouth shut otherwise. But that wasn't who they were—at least outside of the bedroom.

Hannah stayed pushed back and glaring at the table edge she was holding on to.

"If you don't want me involved, then don't involve me. You're the one who asked me to come to the meeting."

"Maybe I shouldn't have."

"Maybe." Drew noted their arms were folded and deliberately let them fall back down onto the table, closing a little of the distance between them and Hannah. "I want to support you, Hannah. That's part of being in a relationship, being there for each other, but I don't understand what you want from me."

"I want you to back off." There was a bite to Hannah's words that went beyond her usual directness.

And it hurt. Drew was trying to do and be what she wanted, but it seemed that still wasn't good enough. Maybe Hannah was like all the other people who only wanted them around when it was convenient and Drew was helping where needed. Maybe they were no longer useful to her. And maybe they deserved better than that.

"Fine. I'm not going to be where I'm not wanted. I'm doing my best here, but if I'm not what you want or need, then feel free to walk away."

That came out more dramatic and final than Drew intended. But they needed her to assure them that she did *want* them, even if she didn't *need* them. A voice in their head was vindicated when Hannah stood up to go because they had known that wasn't the case.

"I think…I think I still don't know what I want exactly. But I know I don't want this."

Hannah didn't look at them. She tucked her chair back under the table and left.

Drew fought the urge to call her back. How had things escalated to this? Hadn't they just had a wonderful time together on their first getaway? She'd met their mother, and been a hit with her and her girlfriend, for fuck's sake! Hadn't they gotten too close for Hannah to walk away so quickly and with such apparent ease?

But Hannah was walking away as if forever, and they couldn't stop her. And they weren't sure if they wanted to. They loved being with her, but it seemed she still wasn't ready for a relationship. That had always been the risk, but knowing that hadn't prevented Drew getting attached and didn't stop it hurting deep inside their chest to see her turn her back on them.

CHAPTER TWENTY-TWO

It was two weeks since Hannah's big meetings with management, and the proposal was coming together. It was tempting to argue that she didn't need Barnaby's help and wanted to carry on as she was— by herself. But the benefits of a deal became more apparent once the emails started rolling in, and once she'd had time to let the potential big change settle in her mind.

Some suggestions she dismissed as too intrusive, but some, well, she had to admit would make it easier on her. She didn't want to give up what she was already doing, and being able to do it during paid work hours would make the biggest difference. She'd have to figure out what to do with all the free time she'd suddenly have, a part terrifying and part exhilarating thought. She could put that time back into her blog. Or she could put herself back out there socially, even romantically.

Except it had also been two weeks since she'd spoken to Drew. She'd expected at least an apology message following their argument, but she received nothing. Maybe she should've sent one herself once she'd calmed down and processed and realized she might have overreacted a little. Drew hadn't exactly pushed her or committed her to something she didn't want. They had just failed to advocate for what she did. Min said that one big argument didn't mean the end of their relationship, but it felt like it was. Or maybe they were both just too stubborn to be the one to reach out, and the socially acceptable time in which to do so had passed.

It also would've been good to talk through her final thoughts with Drew before she headed back in to face management again. Alone. She could've invited someone else, but there was no one else she really wanted there. Drew was the one who shared her passion and, or so she had thought, got what she was doing. And who she'd assumed would take her side, not the business's, something she couldn't rely on her support workers to do—they didn't always agree with her about what was in *her* best interests. She'd felt abandoned and lost even with Drew present. It was better she go alone and find her own way.

Her phone buzzed, potentially with a good luck message from someone for the negotiations. That day's meeting had been scheduled ahead of time and on a day she wasn't working. Which meant she hadn't had to rush out first thing in the morning and battle busy buses, but it also meant she didn't have work as a distraction. To save herself from overthinking and worrying, and to stick with part of her usual routine, she'd delved into the podcast correspondence. The first post-miniseries episode had gone live two days ago, and feedback was trickling in. Clearly less than from Drew's episodes, but the subject matter wasn't something she expected lots of people to be passionate about. Her cohost had been an interesting man, but it had felt flat compared to her chats with Drew. It would just take some adjustment to get used to the original set-up again.

And she needed to find a new post-show routine. She'd not had a consistent one before, as it depended how tired she was after, but she'd quickly become reliant on her ritual visit from Drew to decompress. There were other ways to do that. Less fun ways, but she didn't need Drew.

She missed them, though. And not just in terms of the podcast. She missed the way their eyes lit up and their hands danced as they passionately engaged in deep conversations that skipped over pointless small talk. She missed the warmth of their presence and how they'd finally made sense of that saying about somebody lighting up a room. She missed getting wrapped up in their soft body and strong arms. And she missed the connection between them that made casual sex seem boring and pointless in comparison. She missed the good kind of fluttering in her chest.

Alongside the list she'd been making of support she'd like for the podcast, she'd been writing one for what she wanted from a relationship. She'd been so focused on what she didn't want that she hadn't clearly thought through what she did. This list had actually been going longer, since she'd first confessed to Drew that she wanted to let their connection grow, and it had slowly helped her get things in perspective. Except maybe it had made things worse as her wishes morphed into expectations. She'd never gotten round to sharing the list with Drew, but in her mind had she already signed a contract for them?

When she'd finally looked at it again after *that* day, having avoided the pain of her shattered hopes as long as she could, she realized she'd written a list of what she wanted from someone else, but not what she could offer them. Given she wanted to avoid another unbalanced relationship, she had started to rectify that immediately, with Min's help. More than once she'd considered sending it to Drew, to assure them that she could be a good partner, but knew they'd need her to show it, not just say it.

She closed her laptop, then went to double-check her notes had crossed over properly to her phone. Sitting behind her laptop might come across as distant—no one else had one at the previous meetings—so she'd decided against taking it. Plus she preferred silently taking notes—no clicking of keys to distract everyone—and having a pen to grip.

It turned out the earlier buzz hadn't been a good luck text. It might have been, if she'd spoken to Drew and they'd known where she was heading. Instead it was a vague compliment from them about the latest episode. Which was nice, but not what she was looking for after two weeks of silence.

What was it supposed to mean? Sure, if they didn't share any intense history, then it could be a straightforward compliment. But was that really all Drew had to say to her? Part of her hoped it meant more, while another part hoped they knew her better than to expect her to read between the lines.

And what was she supposed to reply? She could tell them where she was going, but that might invite some kind of input, and she didn't want a repeat of last time. She didn't want them to be part of the podcast, but she did want them to be part of her life. She didn't have the time or brain space to figure out her response. She had a bus to catch.

This was why she shouldn't have gone there. As soon as she'd opened the door to Drew, literally and figuratively, she was ensnared by whatever irrepressible force pulled them together. It wasn't logical,

KIT MEREDITH

either in a pros and cons or hormonal sense, which meant she couldn't logic her way back out of it. Going cold turkey clearly wasn't working either.

❖

When Hannah got to work, she froze due to being unsure which door to go through. If she was arriving for a shift, she went in the back staff entrance. Thankfully Tracy spotted her and headed over.

"They're already waiting for you upstairs." Tracy stood by the front door acting as if she was holding it open for Hannah. She wasn't—it was propped open already—but it was a clear signal she should come in that way.

"Am I late?" She had left in plenty of time, hadn't she, despite the momentary distraction of hearing from Drew.

"No, no, don't worry. I expect they wanted the chance to get together before you arrived."

Hannah wasn't sure whether it was comforting to have them talking about her without her, but it wasn't like she had a say in the matter. "Shall I go straight up?"

"Yes. I've put a jug of ice water out, and I took the liberty of making your tea."

"Thanks." That might mean it wasn't how she liked it, but its main purpose was as a prop to hold on to. Hannah walked past her towards the nearest *Staff Only* door.

"And Hannah?" Tracy waited until Hannah stopped and turned to face her. "Good luck. Don't be afraid to drive a hard bargain."

"Thanks."

She wasn't sure what else to say to that, so she turned away again. It wasn't the same as the affectionate good wishes and cheerleading she'd had from Drew last time, but it was something.

The team were indeed ready and waiting and didn't waste time with long introductions.

"How about we start with you, Hannah, and the offers you're interested in. Then if there's anything else left uncovered, we can raise it afterwards." Anita was on agenda and note taking duty, sitting behind a glossy laptop that made Hannah think maybe she should've brought her own.

"Okay," Hannah said.

"Great, where would you like to start?" Gary clapped his hands together with more enthusiasm than was necessary or possibly genuine.

Hannah looked down at her notes. "Time would make sense. As in, how many contracted hours I can have to work on the podcast, as that will impact other decisions. Not that I'll only do it during work hours."

"I don't see anything wrong with you doing it all in work time if we are sponsoring it. Within limits of course—we're not going to pay you just to sit around reading." David laughed after the last statement, prompting a chuckle from everyone else. He was the only manager present this time. The regional manager must have decided he wasn't needed.

Hannah bit back the urge to point out she would never take advantage like that—he wasn't making a serious point. Instead she matched the laughter with her own.

"I've spoken with Tracy, and we can spare you, say, one day a week?" David continued.

"So what are we thinking, one week to record and the next to edit? So would that make it possible to put out an episode every fortnight?" Anita asked.

"Potentially. As long as I had time to organize the guests."

"So would you ideally want more than that?"

If she was honest, she hadn't even expected that much so was still planning on a monthly schedule. "No, I just want to ensure it's realistic. The recording doesn't take a whole day, so I can use some of that time to do admin."

"This does bring us to the subject of staff support. Have you considered having someone help with admin?" David said.

It was an idea that had been floated already, but handing over that responsibility would be too much. She didn't want to become the host just in a mouthpiece sense. She wanted to choose the guests and books too.

But there was one area she'd give them if they wanted it. "I'd prefer to keep a handle on the organization, but if someone could take on the publicity and social media side of things, that would allow me to focus on the content."

"Excellent idea." Gary was nearly bouncing in his seat, ready for his time to shine. "Did you have someone in mind to do the socials, or are we looking at hiring someone?"

"If you wanted to use, say, your cohost from the previous series, we could look at contracting them," Anita suggested.

"Yes, they did take on quite a bit in that area. And am I correct that this was the same Drew who came with you last meeting?" Gary said.

Great. She had been hoping to avoid mention of Drew, but at least they hadn't offered a role to them directly. If Drew had been there and responded enthusiastically to the idea, it would've been much harder to say no.

"That was the same person, yes, but they're no longer involved in the podcast." Before anyone could question this further she moved on. "I don't have anyone particular in mind, but I would want it to be another autistic person if they're posting on my behalf. Another queer autistic person."

It was a compromise she'd come to with herself but had no clue how they'd respond. She still didn't want to put herself out there too much personally, but that didn't mean she didn't want to improve visibility. Anita paused typing and appeared conflicted, hopefully just over whether to write the *Q* word rather than whether to agree to it.

"Excellent idea. There's definitely a good argument to be made for deliberately platforming marginalized voices, particularly where the central person is part of those communities." Gary didn't seem thrown at least.

"Exactly. I don't want to do it myself, but I'm sure there's someone else like me that would be grateful for the opportunity." As much as she steered clear of social media, there were plenty of other autistic people who thrived online and seemed to find it easier to navigate than the tangible world.

"Yes, we would have to be careful how we worded the job description, but that does make sense. Are you thinking you would directly hire and supervise this person, or want us to?" Anita sounded like she might prefer not to have to draw up that advert.

"I'd like to do it."

That way she would still have direct control rather than having to go through corporate hoops to try to address any content she didn't agree with. Hopefully they could avoid office politics and communicate directly with each other. It was another advantage of hiring a fellow autistic—their communication styles were more likely to match, and she shouldn't have to mask too much.

"That would likely be simplest." Anita definitely sounded relieved.

Hiring someone directly was a scary prospect, but hopefully she'd only have to go through it once, and it would be worth it to get the right person. Plus she could try to make the recruitment process much more accessible that usual. If she knew where to start.

"I may need support to go about finding someone, though. I've never hired anyone," she admitted.

"Of course. We can give you all the support you need to set up. To start with, we may want to use some of your allocated days and keep the podcast monthly. We can make a more detailed plan later."

Hannah tried to hold back a sigh of relief. The aim was to end up less busy, but it could tip the other way, especially while she set everything up, if she wasn't careful. She had been adamant she didn't want to make the podcast a job, but she hadn't considered the possibility someone would pay her and give her days off her day job to do it. It wouldn't be her main source of income, and when it eventually folded, she'd still have her work as a bookseller to keep her going.

There was no logical reason to say no, and though unplanned change was disruptive—and anxiety-provoking and overwhelming, with all the extra things to think about and do—this might be the chance she needed to move on with her life. She no longer wanted or needed to be completely engrossed in the podcast. Even if the person she most wanted to spend her reclaimed life with stayed away, like she'd told them to in a moment she wished she could edit out. As much as she prided herself on her directness and honesty, it turned out even she could say something in the heat of the moment that she didn't really mean.

Drew was early. If they carried on like this, it could become a habit and leave them too much thinking time while they sat waiting at their destination. They picked at the label on their beer bottle absentmindedly and tried to resist checking their phone. They'd finally reached out to Hannah by text and…no response. Well, except a simple *thanks* that might as well have been nothing. Maybe she was still mad at them.

Maybe they'd left it too late and she'd already moved on. Maybe it didn't matter why.

Needing a distraction from thinking about Hannah, they picked up their phone and, after only checking for missed messages once, started doomscrolling. They could count on there being no sign of Hannah on social media, but it failed to lift their mood. The adverts didn't help either—the algorithm might be right in targeting Drew as a queer consumer, but the clothing that was supposedly made especially for trans AFAB people would never work for them. Even the real people models were all at least half their size and didn't look like they needed any help to feel euphoric.

Surely Drew wasn't the only one that felt that way? It was alright for those slim, androgynous folk who fitted that picture and passed as non-binary. They tapped out a short post pointing out the lack of inclusivity, with possibly a bit more bitterness than usual.

> *Don't you wish that for once we could be represented by someone other than a skinny white person who could pass for a thirteen-year-old boy? I wasn't that small or supposedly innocent-looking even when I was a teen, and why should I want or need to look that way now.*

It was the kind of statement that they should definitely let cool before making public, but they'd explained it nicely in their first podcast interview, and who knew if that had made any difference, other than landing them in their current romantic mess. They hesitated for a few seconds before skipping the draft stage. Who were they kidding—they didn't have enough power for it to matter what they said. They hit post and were rewarded by a brief rush of adrenaline.

A familiar voice drifted across the pub, and they looked up to see Alex at the bar ordering her drink. She clearly hadn't been expecting Drew to beat her there, as she visibly startled when she glanced over and spotted them, before quickly recovering and giving a wave. She followed this with a *drink?* mime and raised eyebrows. Drew lifted their mostly full glass and shook their head. Given their current disposition, it was best they paced themself.

Alex made her way over to them with a big smile, and they tried to clear up the mess they'd made with the bottle label. And the beer mat that they'd stripped of its neon advertisement as if the bright colours clashed with their mood.

"Hey. Wasn't expecting you to be here yet, sorry. Am I late?"

Maybe it would be good to make this a habit rather than being that guy who kept everyone waiting. Everyone else might not appreciate so much time with their thoughts either. At least those close to them knew to be prepared—like Hannah, who would be engrossed in a book.

"Nah, I'm early. It's good to see you." Drew interrupted their own thoughts and stood up to give Alex a firm hug. They had seen her a few times since she'd got back from her travels, but it was the first time they'd got her to themself for more than a few minutes.

"You too." Alex squeezed back before withdrawing and settling into the armchair opposite them.

She looked good. More relaxed and confident with an easy smile that lacked that hint of guardedness they'd been used to from her. Her tan had faded significantly since her return—you didn't get so much sun in a warehouse in England—but her natural highlights still shone.

"How are you settling back in?"

"It's an adjustment, but it's nice to be back with everyone and the comfort of my own bed. I love the camper van, but it's not somewhere I'd wanna live long-term."

Drew laughed. "So you're not about to abandon us for a nomad lifestyle."

"Nope. But it's nice to have the option, and I might join Willow on shorter tours sometimes."

"You two didn't fall out being stuck in close quarters for so long then?"

Alex laughed at that. "I did wonder if we would, but we were fine. We're both happy doing our own thing so didn't get under each other's feet too much. It was nice to spend that much time with her. We haven't seen each other that often since I moved here. Gotta be honest, I miss her now."

Hopefully that didn't mean she was regretting her decision to stay in their little hamlet. They didn't want to be selfish, but Alex deciding to up sticks was not what they needed to hear right now. They'd only just got her back. It must be tough, though, after such an extended holiday. They'd struggled with not being around the person they should not still be thinking about after just a minibreak.

"That figures. When will you see her again?"

"She's promised to come stay with me next month."

"I'm sure Becca can help distract you in the meantime." And remind her of why she'd chosen to put down roots there.

Alex's face flushed, and she looked down with a smile. "I did miss her when I was away and we're…happy to be back together."

If Drew wasn't Rebecca's partner too, maybe Alex would say more. The boundary made sense, but Drew wouldn't have minded. The way Becca had been moping around, Ishani and Drew had been counting down the days to Alex's return on her behalf.

"Salem seems happy I'm back too. I was worried he'd want to stay with Phoebe as I'm sure she'd been spoiling him, but he didn't seem to have forgotten me."

"I'm sure he hadn't. She did a good job looking after him, but I'll bet he's glad to be back in his home territory."

"He's taken to sleeping in my suitcase. Whether he's just claimed it as a nice bed or he's saying I should take him with me next time, or he's trying to stop me packing and taking off again, I don't know."

Drew laughed. They imagined it was a combination of the three. They couldn't imagine Pebbles's response if they dared abandon him for that long.

"Phoebe is missing him terribly, though. She's managed to convince her supported accommodation that she can get her own cat, now she's proved she can be a responsible pet owner."

"That doesn't surprise me." Drew suspected that had always been her plan.

"While I remember, she asked if you want to come with us cat shopping. We're gonna go to the rescue centre. She's got her eye on a couple from their website, but we wanna see what they're like in real life."

"That could be fun." They had missed hanging out with Alex's sister.

"No pressure. I'm taking her, so she doesn't need your help, but she thought you'd like to come and meet all the moggies."

Drew found themself suddenly choked up. Maybe Phoebe actually missed hanging out with them too, and not just their support. "Count me in."

"Hey, what's up?" Alex leaned towards them with a furrowed brow.

"Just, it's nice to be wanted and not just needed, you know?" They shrugged and blinked back tears.

"It is. I'm guessing this isn't just about Phoebe, though. Wanna talk about it?"

Alex reached over and laid her hand on theirs, which was once again worrying at the beer label.

Drew nodded, not trusting themself to speak for a moment. The pub wasn't busy, but they still didn't want to make a scene by bawling.

"How about I get you another drink, then you tell me all about it. I'm in no rush." Alex stood and headed to the bar, giving them a moment to pull themself together, not waiting for their answer.

It would be good to talk to someone about Hannah and let it all out, but where to start? They'd not said much to Alex about her, partly because it seemed to be over so soon after it had begun in the romantic relationship sense. If they'd kept it at a friends-with-benefits level, would they still be enjoying themself with Hannah? Maybe they'd nudged her towards something she didn't even want. Maybe they just weren't capable of staying casual and not diving right in—they shouldn't have let their hormones make them forget who they were and what they really wanted at the start.

Their second bottle was almost finished by the time Drew had given Alex the whole story, and they got up to get her another pint while she digested the whole mess.

She took a long drag as soon as they passed it to her. "So, how are you feeling about it now?"

"Shit, obviously. It feels like she tossed me aside so quickly when I wasn't useful any more. She doesn't want me involved in her life decisions, and I can't help feeling I don't matter."

"You matter." Alex gave their hand another squeeze. "Not wanting you involved in her work doesn't mean she doesn't want you involved at all in her life. I gotta admit, I'm not one to give up my independence when it comes to decision-making either, no matter how much I care about someone."

This was why they wanted to talk to Alex. She got more where Hannah was coming from, and it was clear that she cared deeply about her partners despite her independent stance. So maybe Hannah cared in her own way too.

"I get that. I know I maybe took it a bit too personally."

"Hey, I'm not saying she's been completely reasonable. I don't get why she asked for your support only to tell you to back off." Alex rolled her eyes.

"It makes a bit more sense when you know her past. She's got trauma she's been working through, and that's at least part of why she wasn't sure about getting into a relationship."

"Ah. Now that I can understand. You know what I was like when I met Rebecca, but once we finally got together, I knew it was right. That doesn't mean it all went completely smoothly even then. You can't just shrug off your past no matter how much you want to."

Drew did remember, despite Alex's attempts to keep them out of it. They hadn't been sure if it was going to work out between Alex and Rebecca at first, but they'd recognized that the couple needed to give it a shot.

"True, but…I don't know. Maybe we're just not compatible."

Did they really want to pursue someone who might not be ready to be in a relationship for that reason? They didn't want to be that guy who thought their love was a magic cure that meant someone should just get over everything once they were together. That wasn't how people worked outside of the movies.

"Maybe. But do you really want to give up already, or do you want to find out for sure?" Alex gave them a serious look. "Hey, I'm not trying to push you either way. It's up to you if you think she might be worth the trouble. But I know I questioned if me and Rebecca were, and I'm glad I still gave us a chance."

"It's not just up to me, anyway. Nothing can happen if she won't talk to me."

"You sent her one text, dude. And not even a personal one."

"Okay, you got me." Drew laughed.

Damn, it was good to be able to laugh about it, and their chest already felt lighter.

"That's enough of my whining for now. I want to hear all about your adventures, and not just the PG version you shared when we were in front of Becca."

That got Alex spluttering a laugh too. She looked like she might refuse but agreed they needed cheering up with some lighter tales.

"So you wanna hear about the Swedish sauna?" She quirked a smile that told them what type of sauna she was referring to.

"Exactly what I need to take my mind off my tragic failed relationship."

Alex reached over and gave them a pat again at that, then rested back to regale them with her more sordid stories. Drew could see their phone lighting up with notifications, but it surely wasn't anything important, and someone would call them if it was. They slipped it back in their jacket pocket so they could focus on their friend—Alex was what they really needed to make them smile. They had been too busy worrying about Rebecca's pining to realize that they'd missed Alex like hell too.

By the time they'd finished that round, Drew hadn't decided what to do about the whole Hannah situation but did feel less rejected and depressed about it. Alex was right—they'd hardly made a big effort to reach out and fix things. But it would be nice if, for once, someone else would make the first move and come to comfort them. Being with Alex reminded them that they didn't always want or need to be in a support role. Maybe they could even become a person who other people were drawn towards effortlessly like her.

Except they didn't look like a romantic lead any more than they looked like a superhero. They weren't someone people fought for. They were the dedicated doormat who didn't matter in the end. The movies seemed to get that part right.

CHAPTER TWENTY-THREE

"Congratulations!" Cass beamed at Hannah and held out a colourful bouquet. "I hope you like them. I checked that they're not too smelly."

"Thanks." Hannah smiled at the thoughtfulness and the statement. "Come in."

She stood aside to let Cass in and took a gentle sniff of the flowers. Cass was right—they weren't overly pungent but had a pleasing fresh scent. Cass hadn't said what they were for, but didn't need to. Hannah had finally signed the deal for the podcast, and it was time to celebrate. She tried not to resent that there wasn't a certain someone else there with her bestie for this big moment. Cass was a great friend who had been by her side through all her recent trauma and transformations. Why would she need anyone else?

Logic still wasn't working on her Drew feelings, but time hopefully would. It had been tempting to contact them after everything was agreed, but that might make them resentful at being so obviously left out. Which meant her last message was still just a *thanks* in reply to their polite feedback. Was it possible for them to go back to being friendly strangers who had just worked together once?

"You're thinking about them again, aren't you?" Cass interrupted her thoughts.

"I don't know who you mean." She gave the fake line before realizing it might encourage further enquiries. "And even if I did, I'm trying not to think or talk about them."

"And how's that working for you?" Cass offered a crooked smile that took the edge off their words.

"Abysmally."

They both cracked up laughing.

"That's not why you're here, though, and it is what I pay Min for."

"Fair enough. In that case, tonight I will be playing the part of supportive friend focused on celebrating your achievements and kindly not mentioning the state of your love life." Cass reached out their arms and enveloped her in a firm embrace. "I am so proud of you."

"Thank you." Hannah accepted the hug gladly and tried to blink back the tears that filled her eyes at the sentiment.

"So, how do you wanna celebrate? I could take you out for dinner if you're up to that."

"That could be nice."

It was tempting to say stay in and get a takeaway instead, but it might do her good to get out of her flat, and she'd be less likely to mope about you-know-who.

"What do you fancy? Italian?"

"Yes please."

Not that there were many options that they both liked or places they could tolerate. The cosy Italian tucked down a side street that they frequented had simple delicious food, with low lighting and well-distributed tables, so they could eat in relative peace.

"I'll book us a table while you put those in water." Cass pointed at the flowers she was clasping.

"Good plan."

Hannah headed to the kitchen, where she located a vase and appropriate scissors. She filled it with tepid water and the accompanying plant food, before she carefully unrolled the bouquet and set to work trimming the stems diagonally one by one over the paper wrapping so she didn't make a mess. The stems were firm, and the ends came away with a satisfying snap. She positioned each flower in the vase, losing herself in the arrangement like it was a game of Tetris.

Cass joined her when she was only halfway through.

"Table's booked for seven, so we have an hour. Time for a drink." Cass removed a wine bottle from their shoulder bag and waved it at her. "I've booked a taxi, so we can get a bit tipsy if we like."

"You've got it all thought out." Hannah looked down at the partly dissected bouquet. "You pour?"

"I'm on it."

Cass had spent enough time there to not need directions to the glasses or bottle opener. They poured two generous glasses and placed one on the counter next to Hannah.

"So, how are you feeling about the deal now it's all confirmed? When are you going to make the big announcement?"

"I'm feeling good. It wasn't something I'd planned on, but I think it'll be better for me on balance, and hopefully no one will be turned off by the sponsor." That was a thing she was still worried about, but only time would tell. "In terms of the announcement, I need to coordinate with Barnaby's as they're going to do a big press release."

"I doubt anyone will be seriously put off, and even if a small number are, you might get at least an equivalent boost through their publicity. And once your personal social media officer is in play."

"That's what I'm counting on. Though I can't believe I'm going to be responsible for someone else's job." That was not something she'd ever anticipated or wanted.

"I'm sure you'll be a great boss—honest and fair, and not focused on profit margins. Whoever gets the post will be lucky to have you, as well as the job."

"Thanks. Hopefully." Hannah continued to trim and arrange the stems, not having to worry about making eye contact, which Cass also did better without.

"Definitely."

They stayed in companionable silence as Hannah finished her arrangement, then tidied up the mess. Cass followed her into the lounge with both glasses of wine as Hannah brought the vase through to display, then plonked down in their usual armchair.

"Just popping to the bathroom. And I need to get changed as we're heading out." Hannah looked down at her comfy joggers and loose top that draped her braless chest. She could get away with it at home and around Cass, but it sadly might be considered indecent elsewhere.

"No worries. I'm good here." Cass didn't bother with any false assurance that she should head out as she was.

They pulled out their phone and nestled back in the chair with their wine. But when Hannah returned, they seemed less comfortable. Their mouth was turned down and their eyes were pinched as they stared at the screen.

"What's wrong?"

If their table wasn't available, she could cope with staying in instead. She just might remove her bra again.

"Umm." Cass seemed like they were going to explain then shut their mouth as if thinking better of it.

"What?" It must not be about the restaurant booking. "What's going on, is everyone okay?"

Cass's eyes darted to hers then back to their phone. "Hopefully?"

It sounded too much like a question.

"Seriously, Cass, you're worrying me now. I know we're supposed to be celebrating tonight, but if something has happened and you need to go—"

"No, it's not like that." They sighed. "I know you didn't want to talk about Drew, but…" They passed their phone to her.

It was open to a long chain of messages, containing sentiments and threats that made her nauseous without even knowing the cause. Then she scrolled up to see it was all in response to a throwaway line. Posted by Drew. It was all aimed at Drew.

"Oh God." She scrolled down again through the hateful messages that brought burning bile to her throat. "Why would they think that?"

Cass reached to take their phone back, but Hannah couldn't stop looking. "Stuff gets misinterpreted and overblown online all the time. Isn't that why you avoid it?"

"I know, but Drew clearly doesn't mean any harm."

And it wasn't like they were a celebrity with a big following. Or was this her fault, had she brought unpleasant public attention to Drew through the podcast? Had she exposed them to a wider audience that didn't understand or appreciate them? Their original post was a possibly jokey couple of lines relating to the difficulty being recognized in their gender due to their body shape in comparison to those fitting the slim stereotype. Maybe the wording could've sounded less judgemental, but it was Drew's experience, and they had a point. It wasn't like they were claiming to speak for everyone else, but their respondents clearly did not get that or want to. The comments included the standard dirty twist of any statement about being trans to make it seem anti-feminist.

"Well, they clearly don't know Drew like you do."

Hannah's eyes itched with unshed tears. Tears of fear and anger and sorrow as she imagined Drew having to read all that venom directed at them. She did know them better than that and knew that beneath their confident exterior they were extremely sensitive to what others thought. This would hurt them badly. Drew cared deeply about their community, maybe too deeply, as it didn't appear to care back. At least some of the hate was coming from fellow trans and queer people. Even if some of them had genuine issues with what Drew said, surely they could see that it didn't help that many people joined in to say the same thing in increasingly accusatory and outright spiteful ways.

"It'll be okay. It's not a doxing. No one's sharing or asking for anyone to find Drew's personal information. It'll be forgotten soon, and everyone will move on to piling onto someone else."

But Drew surely wouldn't forget. Unless this was normal for them and what they were quietly dealing with on a regular basis, unbeknown to her. She flicked through their earlier posts, but none had anywhere near that level of responses, shares, or negative feedback. It could be seen as evidence that she was right not to recommend Drew for the publicity job. It could be an opportunity to say I told you so. But she didn't want to say that. She wanted to comfort them and kiss better the wounds she knew this would be inflicting. What the playground rhyme said was wrong: Words could really hurt you. It wasn't physical abuse that had left her shattered, and she got the impression Drew could take a literal punch a lot easier than this.

"Hey, it's okay. They'll be okay." Cass slid over onto the sofa next to her and pulled her into a side hug.

She let her tears spill onto their shoulder; tears for Drew's pain and for the fact she wasn't there to help them through it. She should be there. Drew had supported her, and now it was her turn to prop them up. Maybe they could've phrased it better or thought it through, but they were only human and they didn't deserve this. They deserved all the support and love they offered other people. Maybe they'd given up on her after her final foolish outburst, but she couldn't give up on them—not without ensuring they knew that they deserved better than what the world was telling them.

❖

Drew wrapped their hands around their refreshed cup of tea to resist the urge to reach for their phone. Not that they could check it even if they wanted to, as Leigh had confiscated their phone, tablet, and laptop. She was right that it wouldn't do any good to keep watching the internet tearing them a new one, but it didn't feel good leaving people talking behind their back without at least trying to explain themself.

It would blow over if they let it...as they repeatedly told themself without entirely believing it. Their big mouth had got them into this mess, but it couldn't get them back out of it. At least not until everyone, including them, had calmed down a bit. They had already started planning their apology video in their head.

The dating show they had been half watching—whichever one it was—came to an end, and the countdown for the next episode began. They eyed the remote control that rested on the arm at the other end of the sofa, but it was just out of reach, and they had nothing better to do than stay curled up on the sofa feeling sorry for themself. Going outside, even just into the back garden to potter, felt too exposing. They hadn't been doxed still—Leigh was keeping a close eye out for any reference to their address, as were those friends who had strong enough stomachs to keep reading—but they felt like they were being watched, judged, and found lacking. They swung between being glad they weren't living alone and being horrified that they might have put Leigh at risk. It was another layer of guilt to add to the pile.

They still couldn't get their head around how their downfall had happened so quickly and colossally. Sure, maybe they shouldn't have been so brash and should have stopped to think how people might react before posting their thoughts, but the post was hardly out of character. However, their reach had grown following their involvement in the pod, so it was no longer just people in their little bubble. Which was what they had wanted, but...you know what they say.

Hannah was probably nursing a proud *I told you so* while they nursed their bruised ego. Maybe that wasn't totally fair, maybe she would take their side, but it wasn't like she would even find out. She was probably oblivious to the drama playing out under their name.

Maybe they should take the onslaught as a cue to step back from social media longer term to preserve their sanity and relative safety. But would it be worth it to lose contact with all their old friends and internet comrades who formed their virtual community? Before they'd been very strongly encouraged by Leigh to step back, they had noticed a few allies stepping up in their defence. Not enough to hold back the wave of bitter judgement that threatened to suffocate them whenever they glanced at their comments, though; rejection from the community they were supposed to be part of. In some ways it just reinforced their point that there wasn't space for people like them, but in that instance they would've preferred to be proved wrong.

They'd had the odd troll pop up before, but not enough to be a serious nuisance, and it had become second nature to block and report and move on. Reporting the comments didn't do anything, but blocking did delete the bile from their feed and prevent them giving in to the temptation to engage. The trolls weren't responding in good faith or really interested in anything Drew had to say, and replying probably just helped create more wank fodder. Drew might not be perfect, but at least they didn't get off on non-consensual online humiliation.

The doorbell rang, and they pulled up the hood of their hoodie. They did appreciate the concern of their friends, but they weren't exactly in a state to entertain and didn't want many people to see them at their most vulnerable. Footsteps thundered down the stairs as Leigh went to get it. She'd been able to work from home, so they didn't have to turn anyone away themself. Or risk answering it to a nosy neighbour or acquaintance who was more interested in the hot goss than their well-being. Leigh seemed to enjoy the chance to send those people packing.

They could hear Leigh giving her usual spiel. Though they couldn't hear the response, from Leigh's side it was clear the intruder didn't buy the *They aren't home* line, so Leigh had gone into *They aren't up to seeing anyone* territory. The door clicked shut again, and then the footsteps came their way, and Leigh slipped into the lounge carrying a gift bag sporting the face of a grumpy-looking cat. At least the image seemed appropriate to the mood. She held it out to Drew wordlessly and balanced on the arm of the sofa, draping a comforting arm around them.

The bag contained a bunch of CDs and a slim box. They lifted out one of the bulky cases. It wasn't music, but an audiobook in several parts. The title was by one of their favourite sapphic writers and was set in an animal rescue—exactly what they needed to distract them and help restore their faith in the world. It had been a while since the libraries stopped stocking hard copies of audiobooks and switched to apps, not that they ever stocked much in that genre, and it brought a small nostalgic smile. The box contained an old-school portable CD player. They hadn't realized they even made those any more. There was a postcard in the bag featuring another pampered grumpy cat ordering them to *Know you are worthy* and on the back was a simple unsigned note: *In case you want to listen outside of the car.* They couldn't be sure, but the handwriting seemed familiar, and who else would—

"You're right. The plaits are cute," Leigh whispered in their ear.

Drew almost headbutted her as they twisted round to face her.

"She's still on the doorstep if you want to see her. She seems to be waiting for proof of life. I can try to send her away again, or I can make myself scarce—it's up to you."

Drew looked back at the gift in their lap. Hannah had gone out of her way to put it all together and come to them. It was unlikely she'd made that effort to say *I told you so.* Or that she didn't want anything more to do with them. They flipped back to the front of the postcard and smiled. From anyone else the message might have seemed sickeningly cute, but Hannah could get away with it.

"You don't have to invite her in. At least not straight away. From the little you've told me, she can stand to be kept waiting." Leigh stood up and moved back giving them space. "Take your time to decide if you want to let her in."

Drew had the sense she wasn't just telling them to consider whether to physically let Hannah into the house. Could they trust her to be supportive given their last encounter? But then that had been when the roles were reversed. Maybe Hannah was also better at offering support than receiving it, and it was their turn to see if they could accept it.

"Okay. I'll see what she wants." They didn't have the energy to kid themself that they didn't want to see her.

Drew dragged themself up out of the deep well of the sofa.

"I'll be upstairs if you need me." Leigh gave them a quick but loving kiss and headed out of the room before them.

They made it to the front door and paused as Leigh's steps faded away. Were they really up to facing Hannah? There was only one way to find out. They fumbled the catch and got it down on the third attempt.

Hannah stood slightly back from the door with her hands in the pockets of a faded pair of dungarees.

"Hi." Drew hadn't decided what kind of welcome to give her.

"Hi," Hannah repeated. "I'm sorry to turn up unannounced, I know I hate that, but your phone seemed to be switched off and I was worried and I wanted to be here for you because you deserve to have people there for you, and you don't deserve any of that hatefulness. You deserve so much better. And better than I treated you. I'm sorry."

"Thank you." Drew stayed back, still waiting in case there was a *but* coming, trying to take in her rambling speech.

"I know you have your wife, and she's obviously lovely and looking after you, but I'm here too if you want me." Hannah held out her arms in an uncertain but clear gesture.

Did she really believe they deserved more kindness? How were they supposed to leave her just standing there, looking so open and cute, with her care for them practically radiating off her. She hadn't behaved perfectly, but neither had Drew, and maybe they both still deserved another chance. And hell, they'd missed her.

They held out their arms in return. "Come here."

Hannah practically launched herself into their embrace. They both stood there in the open doorway, which suddenly didn't seem such a threat, holding tight as if determined not to let go until any distance between them had melted away. It was funny—Drew had held Hannah completely naked many times, but it had never felt that intimate.

The tears they'd been holding back since their argument, since she'd walked away, since they'd seen the virtual world turn against them, started to escape. It was only when Hannah let out a loud sniffle that they realized she was crying too. They held her tighter.

"We should probably move out of the doorway if you don't want to attract more attention," Hannah murmured into their shoulder, without relinquishing her grip on them.

"Yeah, I've had enough of that. You want to come in?"

Hannah pulled back and studied their face. "Do you want me to?"

"Yes, I want you." Drew took her hands and gently pulled her across the threshold and shut the door behind her.

"Good, cos I want you too." Hannah pressed her forehead against theirs. "I'm so sorry. I never should have turned my back on you. I kept wanting to apologize but I was too stubborn and scared, and this just gave me the kick I needed."

Drew wanted to say they were sorry too, but before they could speak, Hannah's lips were on theirs and they lost the words in that moment of connection. There would be time for more apologies later. Right then, what they needed was to accept the affection she was offering and let themself be comforted.

A creak on the staircase reminded them they weren't alone, and Hannah pulled back.

"Sorry to interrupt. Just wanted to check you were okay, and his highness demanded to be let down." Leigh stayed at the top of the steps with a faint smile on her lips.

Pebbles was less subtle and rocketed down to join them, winding himself around both their legs with such vigour that Drew had to hold onto Hannah to ensure they both remained upright.

"I don't believe we've been properly introduced. I'm Leigh."

"Um, hi, Leigh. I'm Hannah." Hannah glanced up at her briefly before kneeling to fuss Pebbles.

"I know." Leigh walked down the stairs towards them. "You are welcome in, but…"

Drew tensed and felt Hannah respond in tandem.

"Drew is obviously fragile right now, even if they won't admit it, so if you upset them more, you won't be welcome."

"Noted," Hannah replied. Her tone and face were dead serious.

"Good." Leigh smiled and gave Drew's arm a squeeze as she slid past. "Now we've got that out of the way, let me make us another cuppa. Then I'll head back upstairs to finish work, with my headphones on, and leave them in your care."

"Thanks. I promise to look after them."

Drew looked between the two women, relieved to see no sign of a dominance battle about to take place, but still… "I'm not a child."

They were going to add that they could take care of themself, but that clearly wasn't true right at that moment.

Leigh had already moved out of earshot, but Hannah caught their grumble. "No, but even big, tough grown-ups need looking after sometimes."

"You're gonna make me cry again."

Drew turned away before they did and started to lead Hannah through to the lounge. Pebbles came with them. He definitely seemed to approve of Hannah, and they did say animals had good judgement.

Though maybe they needed to trust their own judgement and how right Hannah's hand felt in theirs, and not worry what anyone else thought. They were evidently never going to get everyone's approval, but that could be okay as long as they had the backing of those that truly mattered to them.

Chapter Twenty-four

Hannah sorted through the mounds of paper and tried to breathe. She'd underestimated quite how popular the job offer she'd created would be. It wasn't that she'd thought no one would want it—she'd guessed correctly that many online autistic advocates/activists/artists would jump at the opportunity. She just hadn't realized quite how many there would be. She almost regretted making the application process so easy.

This was why she did it, though. She wasn't looking for someone skilled at complex application forms—she wanted someone enthusiastic and dedicated like her who got what the podcast was about. She had something concrete to go on, having asked all applicants to put together samples of how they'd promote a few selected episodes, including one of Drew's, as she didn't want to risk hiring someone who would misrepresent them and other trans people further.

She needed a system if she was going to get anywhere. Hannah unfolded herself from where she was crouched on the floor surrounded by paper and retrieved some Post-its from the stationery drawer. There was one simple place to start: weeding out those who weren't queer and autistic. It had been explicit in the advert that these were requirements, but a number of respondents seemed to believe they weren't really mandatory. She wrote on the first two Post-its *Not LGBTQIA* and *Not autistic*, then added *Not provided examples*. Given how simple she'd made it, it didn't seem too strict to reject those who'd not completed the assignment.

It seemed like a good place to start, but as soon as she started looking at the applications again she got caught up reading each in depth. Skimming never was her strong point, so she gave in to the inevitable and added three more Post-its to the other side of her—*love at first sight*, *maybe*, and *not for this*. The last category made it easier than a simple *no good* as it felt less judgemental of their work. She wasn't saying that they weren't good enough, but that they weren't the right fit for her or the show.

Having established a system, she settled into a steady pace and was soon surrounded by six piles of paper rather than one large overflowing one. It wasn't until she accidentally took a slurp of fully cold tea that she noticed the cramping in her legs. She stumbled through to the kitchen to refresh her mug and risked checking her phone.

It was a good thing she did as it turned out even more time had passed than she thought. There was a message from Cass saying they were on their way and would be there in half an hour. Hannah was on the verge of rushing off to start tidying up when she noted there were in fact multiple messages from Cass including an ominous *I think you need to see this* and a link to a post.

Hannah groaned. *Please don't be another pile-on.* Drew was still recovering from the first wave. They definitely hadn't been their usual self when she'd visited, and it had been hard to see them that way, looking like a devoted puppy that had been kicked and couldn't understand why people were so cruel. But it had also given her a first real peek at their vulnerable side and the chance to reassure them she still loved them even in their weakest moments. Except she had been careful not to use the *L* word. It was still early days, especially given they hadn't spoken to each other for weeks beforehand. Hopefully her heartfelt apology was enough to give them an idea of the depth of her feelings for them.

She took a deep breath and pressed the link. It did take her to one of Drew's socials, but this time it was a video by them that had earned dozens of hearts and thumbs up. She let out the breath in a long sigh of relief. It didn't seem urgent but she pressed play, fuelled by curiosity and the desire to hear their voice, with the excuse that Cass might be wanting to talk about it when they arrived, so it could count as part of getting ready.

It was a simple frame featuring Drew sitting on what Hannah recognized as their living room sofa. They had clearly chosen not to bother with a fancy background, and the lighting was natural, not highlighting but also not detracting from the purple bags under their eyes.

"I want to start by apologizing to anyone who felt unseen or invalidated by my post the other day—I don't need to tell you which one." They chuckled, but not in their usual full-throated way. "That wasn't my intention, and I'm genuinely sorry to have caused anyone from our community pain. We have enough of that from the outside. I know I might act tough and use humour to deal with shit, but that doesn't mean I don't really care. I do. I care deeply, and it hurts to know I let you down.

"I will try to do better next time and think about the impact of how I say what I say. I wanted to make room for more of us within the narrowly recognized portrait of the trans and non-binary community, not push anyone out. So I'll try to do better. But I need you to as well.

"I know there were other non-binary people who felt genuinely rejected by my sentiment, but from the looks of it, there were also many more people who were just quick to jump in with vicious accusations without considering the validity of my point or personhood. I am a real person, as you can now see, and the wave of hate I received was hard to take. I bet it was also hard on those people who felt seen by my original post, and then witnessed this response to recognition of their existence. They deserve better than this. Please, help me make our wonderful queer community more inclusive, not less.

"And to those haters that don't want people like me to be part of our community or to even exist: walk away. You're right that this isn't the place for you. I won't be engaging with anyone speaking in bad faith or who could easily just google their *legitimate questions*, and I'm asking everyone else to do the same. Maybe ignoring the bullies won't make them go away completely, but unlike in real life, online we have the option to delete their words and not let them take anything from us."

Hannah was already choking up before she got to that point, but at the instruction to walk away, tears started to trickle down her cheeks. She caught them on the back of her hand, determined this time not to be one of the people to turn away.

"Thank you to everyone who has offered support and who recognized I'm just a human who fucks up sometimes. We all are. Let's not stop trying to create a place for us to belong in all our messy, queer glory.

"I also want to thank a special someone who probably won't even see this. Which probably makes it pointless, but I gotta take the chance. Thank you for not walking away forever and for reminding me that I don't need to be the strong one all the time. Thank you for making me feel good enough and reminding me I don't need to try to be perfect. Thank you for being completely you and reminding me it's okay to be me. Thank you for letting me in and for reminding me why I've kept my heart open. Because you are worth it too."

Okay, she was in danger of being a complete blubbering mess when Cass arrived. Which was silly as she couldn't even be sure that last part was for her. Drew didn't name her or reference anything about her to make it certain. But that could be Drew respecting she wouldn't want their audience to know. Cass had sent it to her…

Do you think that last part is for me? she typed out, then deleted it when she remembered they were driving over. She could ask them when they got there.

Or she could go straight to the source. Drew had risked putting themself out there at their most vulnerable, so shouldn't she risk getting it wrong? This was a situation where not saying anything just in case could mean missing out on something important.

She typed out a message with care, deleting more words than ended up in the final version. It also wasn't the time to stray from her direct approach.

*Hey. I saw your video *heart emoji* That was so brave of you. You truly are good enough and more, and worth opening my heart for. I just have to check: Who was that last part aimed at?*

She tucked her phone in her pocket after sending so she wouldn't keep staring at it waiting for their reply. She really did need to rush to get ready for Cass now. She started by heading to the bathroom and splashing cold water on her face, washing the tears away and hopefully preventing swollen eyes. Then she squirted cleaner round the toilet bowl, before heading back to the lounge to clear the piles of paper. Her phone buzzed in her pocket just as she regained her position amid the organized mess.

*Thank you, lovely *heart emoji* *smiley crying emoji* That last part was all for you x*

The confirmation brought such an intense rush of feeling that she had to flap some of it free. She kept rereading their message as if expecting it all to turn out to be a misunderstanding because how could it be her who brought that public outpouring of affection from someone? But it was for her, and when Cass arrived fifteen minutes later, she was still sitting there, rewatching and rereading and letting that sink in.

❖

The date was the result of negotiation. Drew had asked Hannah to go on a traditional dinner-then-a-movie date, going out to the cinema for once to make a bigger thing of it than just curling in front of the TV together at home. Hannah had said yes but argued that it should be the other way around, so they could discuss the movie over dinner. Drew had to concede she had a point, though they'd never struggled for something to talk about together.

Drew's early, or at least not late, streak had continued, and they sat with the car idling waiting for Hannah to appear, having reassured her there was no rush and they could wait. They checked their emails and were surprised to find one from the woman herself—sent ten minutes before. The subject line said it was a file share. Was it the promo for the soon-to-be relaunched pod? Hannah had been contributing to and waiting for it the past couple of weeks. But when they opened the email, it was several very large audio files, which combined would be way longer than even a full episode.

The passenger door opened before they had the chance to listen, and Hannah slid in.

"Hey, you." She leaned over and kissed them in a way that made them wish they were staying in.

"Hey," they replied once they'd come up for air.

Hannah put her seat belt on before they could suggest a change of plan. "Shall we go, and we can talk on the way."

"I guess we should." They leaned over for another kiss before reattaching their own belt and setting off.

It was a good thing they did as the traffic was bad. They really needed to remember rush hour was a thing. It did give Hannah the chance to catch them up on the latest developments with the pod.

"We've booked the interviews for next week. Gary and Anita are going to support, but it would be good to have someone else there so they can't outvote me. I know I handled it badly last time, so feel free to say no, but would you consider being the fourth member? It would be good to have someone else who's been involved in the original podcast, and I'd like to hear your thoughts."

"You want me to be part of the interview panel?"

Drew had to check they'd heard right given Hannah's determination that they not be involved in any decision-making previously.

"Yes. If you wouldn't mind. I can pay you and this time discuss how I want us to play it beforehand, and agree how it will work. But no pressure if it's not something you want to—"

"I'd be happy to help."

Drew reached over and squeezed her hand briefly, wishing they weren't driving and could show her how that made them feel. It might not be a big deal to someone else, but it was for Hannah. And them. There was a little voice in the back of their head questioning if it was asking for trouble and if they should stay well back, but they'd both agreed not to hold back any more.

For their date, they'd selected the smaller arthouse cinema with its bigger seats and lack of rowdy teenagers. Hannah suggested the back row. When they arrived and took their seats, there were only a few other people in there. Clearly Drew wasn't the only person who tended to stream at home instead. Which suited them just fine.

Hannah lifted the chair arm between their seats and snuggled into them. "This okay?"

"Of course." They put their arm around her and let themself take up space without having to worry about intruding on their neighbour.

But ten minutes into the film, Drew was seriously starting to regret going out. As they leaned in for another kiss, Drew wondered why it had seemed like a good idea. They were too old to be making out like that in the back row of the cinema, though this wasn't something that seemed to worry Hannah. The film, thankfully, wasn't one that required complete attention. It was an action-filled thriller, and by unspoken agreement they indulged in long drawn-out kisses during the long drawn-out action scenes.

Halfway through, Drew was ready to give up entirely. Hannah writhed in their arms, almost climbing into their lap as they kissed, and it was a fight not to let their hands explore her body. They did not want to get banned from the establishment.

"Wanna leave? This film isn't exactly grabbing me."

Hannah looked seriously conflicted. "So tempting, but I have to stay to the end unless it's offensively bad."

"Okay." Drew groaned.

Hannah nipped their lip, and they had to hold in a deeper groan.

"But we could head back to mine after instead of out for dinner. If you're not too hungry."

"Good idea. It's not food I'm craving."

They nibbled at her throat and felt her gasp against them and her fingers curl into their back.

In the end, they only made it as far as the car afterwards before they got carried away. Hannah clawed at their clothes, and their hand slipped under her top to graze her erect nipples.

"Depending how you feel about sex in public, you might want to take me home quickly."

Drew glanced around the gloomy car park. There wasn't anyone in sight, but... "We should get going."

Hannah sank back in her seat looking disappointed. *Was she being serious?* The idea of potentially being seen did give them a thrill, but not in the town centre car park where just anyone could come by. "Maybe another time, somewhere more...suitable."

Hannah let out a low chuckle and stroked their thigh. "I'll remember that."

Thankfully the traffic had died down, but the fifteen-minute drive still felt like forever to wait for her. Hannah went through their CDs and found one that did nothing to break the mood. The deep beat and seductive singer spurred them on.

Hannah didn't waste any time once they were back at her flat. As soon as she closed the door, she pressed Drew against the wall and kissed all the breath out of them. Then she undid their trousers and dropped to her knees to take them in her mouth. They finally let out a deep groan as she sucked them between teasing nips at their thighs, encouraging them to spread their legs wider.

"Can I sit down," Drew begged, not wanting her to stop but not sure they could stay standing.

"No." Hannah pressed them firmly against the wall and looked up at them with a wicked smile. "But you can lean on me."

They couldn't argue with that look and the firm command that made them even more turned on, if that was possible. The idea of insisting never crossed their mind. Drew would do whatever they could to please her when she looked at them that way. They steadied their hands on her shoulders and leaned back into the wall, thrusting their hips out more towards her. Hannah drove her tongue back between their thighs, and their knees shook as they pushed themself to stay upright until they climaxed.

Hannah stood and took them by the hand while they were still shuddering. "Now you can lie down."

She led them straight to her bedroom and gave them a gentle shove back onto the bed. "You know, we are going to have to talk about your submissive tendencies in the bedroom. Preferably soon."

She climbed on top of them and kissed them hard. They moaned into her mouth but couldn't think what to say when she pulled back.

"Not in a bad way. So I can take full advantage of them. If you want me to." She ran her hands up their arms and pinned their limbs to the bed beside them.

"I want you to."

It was something they'd never seriously considered before being with Hannah. They were used to being the masc one, which tended to bring expectations of taking the lead, whether they wanted to or not. Hannah seemed able to bring out a different side of them, the side that wanted to bow down before a strong woman and let her do what she wanted with them, without having to worry about how that power dynamic might end. It was a chance to let themself go and lose control, yet know they were safe.

"Good. Don't worry, I don't expect you to say much in this state." She gave them another more tender kiss. "Wait there while I go to the bathroom."

Even if they'd wanted to, Drew wasn't convinced they could stand up again yet. They stayed flopped on the bed, then pulled out their phone to check that the vibrating alert wasn't something they needed to respond to. It was just Pebbles's dinner alarm, a reminder to ensure someone attended to him and he didn't slaughter them in their sleep. They had warned Leigh not to wait up for them, so she would take care of it.

Out of habit, they flicked to their emails and came to the message from Hannah again. Clicking through, they saw the files were labelled with chapter titles. The first was simply labelled *Title and Dedication*. It was a much smaller file than the others and downloaded before Hannah returned, so they clicked play.

Hannah's voice drifted out of their phone announcing the title of a new romance novel by one of their favourite authors. Had she recorded the whole thing for them? They remembered bemoaning the lack of audio versions of her books, and Hannah must've taken note. A different flavour of heat flooded their body.

Hannah's voice continued, "This special recording is dedicated to a very special someone who deserves all the happy endings. This is for you, Drew. Thank you for reminding me of the joys of falling in love."

Drew's breath caught at the last word.

"You weren't supposed to listen to that until you got home." Hannah walked back into the room.

"Sorry." Drew held out their arms to her. "I couldn't resist."

Hannah crawled onto the bed and into their embrace. "I forgive you," she whispered between kisses.

"Thank you. And thank you for doing the recording for me. It means a lot."

The full recording was several hours, and it was likely she'd spent even longer to get it perfect.

"You're welcome." Hannah snuggled in closer. "So, what do you want to do now?"

Drew ran a hand down her arm and felt her delightful shiver. But they didn't just want an evening of intense sex. "I want to make love to you."

The phrase hovered between them for a moment, and Drew wondered if they had misjudged Hannah's readiness for it.

"I would love that," she whispered, tucking her hot face into their neck and clutching at their shirt.

"Good." They kissed her forehead, and she looked up into their eyes. "Because despite our best efforts, I've fallen in love with you."

Hannah smiled and her eyes took on a shimmering glow. "We tried, but"—she kissed them, then pulled back again to look at them—"I think I've fallen in love with you too."

"You think?" They raised an eyebrow.

"I know," she said, putting her hand to their cheek. "I love you."

"I love you too." Drew cupped her face in their hands before giving her a tender kiss.

"Now, are you going to remove all my clothes and make love to me, or do you want to talk more?"

"We can talk more after. I could stay over, and then there's no rush at all."

They ran their hands over her body, relishing the idea of taking her slowly and lovingly into the night.

Hannah gave a firm "Yes" before melting into their caresses.

Dinner out was clearly not going to happen. That could wait until they were past the stage in their relationship where they didn't want to be anywhere where they couldn't rip each other's clothes off. And Drew was in no rush to move past that stage any time soon. They looked forward to many more nights wrapped up in Hannah's embrace and following both their desires to find out what their connection could become.

EPILOGUE

It felt weird not being the one pushing the buttons. Hannah's fingers twitched as she watched the tech in the sound booth through the studio window. It was also weird to be in the same room as her guests while they recorded. But that wasn't bad weird. The studio was large enough, and they were spread out so not in each other's personal space. She occupied her hands with lining up the edges of her prompt cards, which she had laid out on the large desk, a definite improvement on her bedroom floor, while the music washed over her.

Phoebe was singing along to the backing track that played in her headphones. Hannah's own headset was temporarily slung around her neck, so she could enjoy her neighbour's voice without any static or the beat covering it. Phoebe didn't need the backing music to lift her voice—there was enough tone and soul in it to be all you needed. When Phoebe had finished, she looked to Hannah. Hannah gave her a double thumbs up and slipped her headphones back on.

A voice spoke in her ear. "I'm happy with that take if you are."

"Yes, I'm happy with it. She did great."

It felt wrong talking about Phoebe while she was in the room without her being able to hear everything. But Hannah appreciated that the studio had left her some control by not directing the guests, except when addressing everyone through the main speaker.

"You know, we could make this the official jingle if you wanted. She's a great talent and it helps the brand to have a unique intro," Gary added. He was tucked in the corner of the booth out of her eye line, and she'd forgotten for a moment he was even there.

She didn't mind his input, though. She had been thinking the exact same thing. It would be a shame to waste Phoebe's recording by only playing it once. She would need to see if they could pay Phoebe for her contribution, though, so they didn't take advantage of her.

"I agree. We can talk about it after."

This seemed to make Phoebe's smile wilt a little, which confused Hannah until she remembered Phoebe couldn't hear the other side of the conversation.

"It's all good," Hannah assured her. "We're ready to move on to recording the chat now. Is that okay, or do you need a break first?"

"I can do it now."

It had been a slow start being the first time recording in the studio. Hannah had been given a tour before she'd committed to recording there, but Phoebe had wanted to look around. It was Phoebe's first time making a studio recording too, and she seemed determined to make the most of the opportunity. Hopefully it wouldn't be her last, and one day she'd be back recording a whole album, rather than one little jingle. Maybe Hannah would be part of her story as the first person to involve her in a professional recording. Hannah had no real desire for fame and fortune herself but liked the idea of giving others a boost. Especially talented people like Phoebe who were less likely to be given a chance by the wider world.

"If everyone's ready, I'll count you in," the tech said.

"We're ready," Hannah said before remembering her other guest. The new set-up was clearly throwing her off. "If that's okay with you too."

Rebecca appeared much less at ease than Phoebe, who had seemed to recognize quickly this was somewhere she belonged. She had been chatty when they'd met outside and done the informal tour but had barely said a word since they sat down. Her pale skin seemed to have gotten even paler, and wispy strands of brown hair were escaping from what had started as a neat bun perched on the crown of her head.

Hopefully Drew hadn't coerced her into agreeing to take part. They had said Rebecca was flattered by the invitation and wanted to join Phoebe for the recording. They had also said she was keen to meet Hannah now that she knew about their relationship, a potentially awkward social situation Hannah had been putting off. She had no desire to become close friends with her metamours, but she did want to be allies. Meeting at the studio with others present for a specific activity took some of the pressure off. For Hannah, anyway. Rebecca looked like she thought the microphone was a coiled snake that could spring on her at any moment.

"Um, yes, I'm okay to start," Rebecca said with a light shake in her voice.

Maybe they should chat more first, though that didn't seem to be decreasing Rebecca's nerves. Perhaps she preferred to just get on and get it over with.

"We'll start with introductions, and I'll do a synopsis of the book. I will pass to Phoebe first, and then you can add anything you'd like."

"I can say who you are too if you want," Phoebe offered.

"Thanks. That might be best. You are better at public speaking than me." Rebecca gave a shaky laugh. It was a fair conclusion. Phoebe was an amateur actor as well as singer, so she was no stranger to speaking to an audience.

"It's okay, I got you." Phoebe seemed happy to take responsibility for Rebecca, which took more pressure off both Rebecca and Hannah.

Hannah had to admit, she had hoped Phoebe would act as a bit of a hinge for their interaction. She was proving a good ally, maybe even a friend. It could be nice to have a friend in her building to hang out with when she wanted company, especially given the as yet unfulfilled promise of more spare time to fill. She'd already popped in a couple of times to see Phoebe's new roommate, a mischievous kitten that provided plenty of entertainment and prompts for conversation.

"Excellent. We're lucky to have you with us." She smiled at Phoebe and hoped Phoebe didn't pick up on quite how much she meant it.

Of course, there was more to her connection with Phoebe than being friendly neighbours. Phoebe had known about Hannah's relationship with Drew before even Rebecca did, having put two and two together after noting Drew's regular visits to her flat, and given her attachment to several members of their polycule was considered an honorary sister to them all. A younger sister with a flair for the dramatic, but her heart seemed to be in the right place, and she'd only encouraged the welcome of Hannah into the network. She was someone Hannah could trust, or at least she was taking the risk that she could.

"As we talked about before, I'm happy for you to say how we

know each other, and that can help lead us into the themes of the book," Hannah reminded her.

It was a compromise. Hannah still didn't want to put herself out in public too much, but she could share some personal information where it was relevant and could help challenge assumptions. Especially with Phoebe there to happily hold the spotlight.

"Okay." Phoebe sat up straighter.

"Ready," Hannah confirmed to the sound tech and watched as he silently counted them in.

"Hello and welcome to an extra special episode of *Beyond the Books*. I'm your host, Matilda, and this month I'm coming to you from a recording studio where I'm sitting with this month's guests. To celebrate our new sponsorship deal with Barnaby's and access to this space, I have not one but two guests with me, one of whom you have already heard providing superb vocals for our jingle. I will let her introduce herself—over to you, Phoebe."

Phoebe leaned forward without hesitation and took the cue to give what was clearly a practised introduction. She was a natural entertainer, and Hannah felt herself start to relax as she absorbed Phoebe's enthusiasm.

It was very different to recording alone in her wardrobe back at home, but Hannah had moved on a lot since she'd started, and it was definitely time to put herself out there. She didn't have to share everything with the world, but she had nothing to hide and a lot she wanted to explore. She was ready. And it helped that she didn't have to do it all by herself.

It was a good thing Drew had managed to get to Hannah's early, as when they arrived there was more to handle than expected. They had offered to give Hannah a lift to the launch event so she didn't have to worry about getting hot and flustered on the bus beforehand. Then Phoebe had asked to come with them, so she could help and get there before the general public.

Having recorded the jingle for the new-look pod, Phoebe was officially part of the team and had been asked to give a live performance at the event, which had turned into a full vocal set once everyone realized what she was capable of. A couple of musicians, including Hannah's bestie Cass, would be accompanying her. At least with them performing, Drew wouldn't have to worry about being interrogated by Cass—Drew had met them a couple of times before, but they hadn't had the chance for a one-to-one conversation. They got the impression Cass was the protective type who would go to bat for their friend whenever needed. Close friends could be even harder to win around than parents, and more important given they tended to be around a lot more.

Drew hadn't met Hannah's parents yet, and though Hannah wasn't as close to her family of origin as Drew was to their mum, it was still an intimidating prospect. They were trying to worry less about what everyone thought of them, but surely anyone would be keen to impress the parents, and Hannah had confirmed they would be at the launch. Drew had flapped over what to wear, then settled on their standard checked shirt, their go-to as one of the few they'd found that fit them. Smart, but not unapproachable.

They buzzed through to Hannah's flat first. She answered the door without any trousers on, and they nearly suggested staying in, but this was a one-off event they shouldn't miss. It wouldn't be a good start to Hannah's business partnership to not show up because she was busy having sex. And Phoebe might dob them in if they claimed illness. Thankfully her flat didn't share a wall with Hannah's, but she was close enough to figure out what was going on—as they'd already discovered.

"Hey." Hannah drew them inside and shut the door on the security camera before giving them a warm kiss.

Drew reluctantly pulled back before they got too carried away and held out their gift. "Congratulations. I'm so proud of you."

Hannah blushed and took the gift bag with a smile, then peeped inside.

"You can open it now."

"Thank you." She put it on the hall table and pulled out the book bag with a gasp. "Oh, wow, it's beautiful. And so clever!"

It was a literal bookbag, hand-fashioned—not by them—from the cover of a hardback book with matching fabric lining and shoulder strap. They'd seen some at a craft fair and knew Hannah would love it.

"Yeah, the person who makes them is very talented. Just like you."

"And you're very sweet. Thank you, darling, I love it. And you." Hannah gave them a big hug and kissed them with feeling.

"I love you too," they said, hands cupped to her face.

They really were proud of her and completely besotted. Once they'd stopped holding back, it hadn't taken long for their feelings to burst into full bloom. They were still figuring out together how they wanted their relationship to work, but there was no longer any question that they both wanted it. They would find a way.

Drew let their hands drift down her body as they kissed again, grazing the bottom of her T-shirt and the edge of her underwear.

Hannah slapped their hand away. "Behave. We'll have time for that later. I need to get dressed and into professional podcaster mode."

"Mmm, if you have to. I'll go check if Phoebe's ready." If they hung around, they wouldn't be much help with getting dressed. Quite the opposite.

Phoebe was ready and waiting, along with three large boxes of cakes. She waved Drew into her flat with a finger to her lips. They followed her to the round tin, where she lifted the lid to reveal a large iced cake with a book and microphone for decoration under the name of the pod.

"Don't tell Hannah. Can we put it in the car without her seeing? At least the big one. She can see the little ones." Phoebe gestured to the other see-through containers.

"If we're quick. She's gonna love it. Nice work."

It made their own gift pale in comparison in terms of effort made, but this wasn't a competition. It was about supporting Hannah and showing how much she was appreciated. She might prefer not to spend much time socializing, but that didn't mean people didn't connect with and care about her. The only question was whether she realized that.

"Callum's coming with his parents, but not till after it starts. I think it's better to take it now."

"I agree. Let's do this before she comes out to join us." Drew scooped up the big cake box with care and got Phoebe to hold the doors. Between them, they got the cake safely secured and hidden in the boot before Hannah emerged.

"Is Becca coming?" Phoebe asked on their way back in.

"Not today. But she sends her best wishes."

Hannah had asked whether Rebecca should be personally invited and whether she'd want to come, but Drew had figured correctly that she'd be nervous about cramping their style. Especially given this was the first public event they were attending as a couple. Drew had agreed with her it might be best to give it a miss.

At least Rebecca had met Hannah and shown her support by guesting on the show. That seemed to be all Hannah wanted, and Drew could live with that—not every big occasion had to be a whole family affair. Hannah had been clear she had no intention of becoming a regular at the kitchen table, but she'd gotten along just fine with Drew's other partners when she was around. They didn't want her feeling that wasn't enough because it really was. It just wasn't what Drew was used to. But they hadn't been drawn to Hannah because they wanted more of what they already had. Each of their partners brought something unique to their life, and that was how they liked it.

By the time they'd picked up the final load from Phoebe's, Hannah was ready and waiting for them.

"What's in the boxes?" she asked.

"Cakes." Phoebe lifted the lid of the box of cupcakes Drew was holding. "I made them specially."

"Excellent. I always enjoy your baking. Thank you."

"You're welcome, neighbour." Phoebe beamed.

Phoebe had confided she figured she'd got lucky having Hannah as her immediate neighbour, which given some of the stories Drew had heard was definitely true. Not everyone who lived in the supported living flats was on their way up, sadly, and they had spotted the occasional emergency services intervention themself. It had sparked a worry or two about Hannah's well-being, but she clearly wasn't in that dark a place, and they would do their part to ensure she never ended up in the state her ex had left her in again.

"Shall we get going? We can't have the stars being late for the big day." Drew led the way.

It was a quiet Sunday in town, and they made it to the bookshop in plenty of time, plus were able to pull up right outside. Drew left everything in the car while they went to check the set-up and find a way to distract Hannah so they could sneak Phoebe's gift in without her seeing.

When they opened the door, they were greeted by a surprising amount of movement and faces. One group was erecting a makeshift stage in the far corner, and others were busy moving the portable displays to create more floor space and put out chairs.

Drew turned to Hannah. "You ready for this?"

"I think so." She was already pulling her earplugs out of her pocket and twisting them into position.

"I'm here if you need anything. Not that you need me, you got this, but if—"

"I'm glad you're here." Hannah slipped her hand into theirs and squeezed. "Let's do this together."

Hannah walked forward, still holding their hand, and one by one the others present noticed her and started heading her way. Hannah kept hold of Drew, seeming unconcerned about the conclusions anyone might draw or about being seen with a fat, visibly queer partner in public. That hadn't been the case with everyone they'd dated. They happily held on.

Hannah's phone buzzed, and she removed it from her pocket with her other hand. "My parents are on their way. They'll be here in half an hour."

"Okay."

Drew let out a slow breath. It would be fine, and their introduction to her family wasn't supposed to be the focus of the day.

"They'll love you. And even on the off chance that they don't, I still will." She stroked their knuckles with her thumb.

"You sure about that?" Drew gave her a sideways smile.

"I'm certain. I want to be with you. No matter what anyone else thinks."

"Good to know." Their vision clouded briefly with a film of happy tears.

Thankfully they were joined by some of the set-up crew, which gave their emotions the chance to settle down. Hannah didn't need them to be a blubbery mess. But she did need them there as her grip on their hand testified. And more than that, she wanted them by her side. Which was where they wanted to stay.

About the Author

Kit Meredith (they/them) lives in the middle of England in a home filled with craft materials and creations. After years of longing, they finally have a dog and cannot shut up about it. They are enjoying being the irresponsible fur-parent for once.

Kit is an extroverted introvert who enjoys connecting with people through the arts, including running local community groups focusing on LGBTQIA storytelling. Neurodivergent, polyamorous, and queer, they relish writing about characters who also live and love queerly.

They have had a range of short stories published in anthologies under other pen names. This is their second novel and can be read as a standalone or as part of their Poly Connections series. You can find out more and connect with them via their website. https://kitmeredithauthor.wordpress.com.

Books Available From Bold Strokes Books

An Extraordinary Passion by Kit Meredith. An autistic podcaster must decide whether to take a chance on her polyamorous guest and indulge their shared passion, despite her history. (978-1-63679-679-6)

Heart's Appraisal by Jo Hemmingwood. Andy and Hazel can't deny their attraction, but they'll never agree on the place they call home. (978-1-63679-856-1)

That's Amore by Georgia Beers. The romantic city of Rome should inspire Lily's passion for writing, if she can look away from Marina Troiani, her witty, smart, and unassumingly beautiful Italian tour guide. (978-1-63679-841-7)

Through Sky and Stars by Tessa Croft. Can Val and Nicole's love cross space and time to change the fate of humanity? (978-1-63679-862-2)

Uncomplicate It by Kel McCord. When an office attraction threatens her career, Hollis Reed's carefully laid plans demand revision. (978-1-63679-864-6)

The Unexpected Heiress by Cassidy Crane. When a cynical opportunist meets a shy but spirited heiress, the last thing she plans is for her heart to get involved. (978-1-63679-833-2)

Vanguard by Gun Brooke. Beth Wild, Subterranean freedom fighter, is in the crosshairs when she fights for her people and risks her heart for loving the exacting Celestial dissident leader, LaSierra Delmonte. (978-1-63679-818-9)

Wild Night Rising by Barbara Ann Wright. Riding Harleys instead of horses, the Wild Hunt of myth is once again unleashed upon the world. Their ousted leader and a fey cop must join forces to rein in the ride of terror. (978-1-63679-749-6)

A Thousand Tiny Promises by Morgan Lee Miller. When estranged childhood friends Audrey and Reid reunite to fulfill their best friend's dying wish, the last thing they expect is a journey toward healing their broken friendship and discovering a newfound love for each other. (978-1-63679-630-7)

Behold My Heart by Ronica Black. Alora Anders is a highly successful artist who's losing her vision. Devastated, she hires Bodie Banks, a young struggling sculptor, as a live-in assistant. Can Alora open her mind and her heart to accept Bodie into her life? (978-1-63679-810-3)

Fearless Hearts by Radclyffe. One wounded woman, one determined to protect her—and a summertime of risk, danger, and desire. (978-1-63679-837-0)

Stranger in the Sand by Renee Roman. Grace Langley is haunted by guilt. Fagan Shaw wishes she could remember her past. Will finding each other bring the closure they're looking for in order to have a brighter future? (978-1-63679-802-8)

The Nursing Home Hoax by Shelley Thrasher and Ann Faulkner. In this fresh take for grown-ups on the classic Nancy Drew series, crime-solving duo Taylor and Marilee investigate suspicious activity at a small East Texas nursing home. (978-1-63679-806-6)

The Rise and Fall of Conner Cody by Chelsey Lynford. A successful yet lonely Hollywood starlet must decide if she can let go of old wounds and accept a chance at family, friendship, and the love of a lifetime. (978-1-63679-739-7)

A Conflict of Interest by Morgan Adams. Tensions rise when a one-night stand becomes a major conflict of interest between an up-and-coming senior associate and a dedicated cardiac surgeon. (978-1-63679-870-7)

A Magnificent Disturbance by Lee Lynch. These everyday dykes and their friends will stop at nothing to see the women's clinic thrive and, in the process, their ideals, their wounds, and a steadfast allegiance to one another make them heroes. (978-1-63679-031-2)

Big Corpse on Campus by Karis Walsh. When University Police Officer Cappy Flannery investigates what looks like a clear-cut suicide, she discovers that the case—and her feelings for librarian Jazz—are more complicated than she expected. (978-1-63679-852-3)

Charity Case by Jean Copeland. Bad girl Lindsay Chase came home to Connecticut for a fresh start, but an old, risky habit provides the chance to save the day for her new love, Ellie. (978-1-63679-593-5)

Moments to Treasure by Ali Vali. Levi Montbard and Yasmine Hassani have found a vast Templar treasure, but there is much more to the story—and what is left to be found. (978-1-63679-473-0)

The Stolen Girl by Cari Hunter. Detective Inspector Jo Shaw is determined to prove she's fit for work after an injury that almost killed her, but a new case brings her up against people who will do anything to preserve their own interests, putting Jo—and those closest to her—directly in the line of fire. (978-1-63679-822-6)

Discovering Gold by Sam Ledel. In 1920s Colorado, a single mother and a rowdy cowgirl must set aside their fears and initial reservations about one another if they want to find love in the mining town each of them calls home. (978-1-63679-786-1)

Dream a Little Dream by Melissa Brayden. Savanna can't believe it when Dr. Kyle Remington, the woman who left her feeling like a fool, shows up in Dreamer's Bay. Life is too complicated for second chances. Or is it? (978-1-63679-839-4)

Goodbye Hello by Heather K O'Malley. With so much time apart and the challenges of a long-distance relationship, Kelly and Teresa's second chance at love may end just as awkwardly as the first. (978-1-63679-790-8)

Emma by the Sea by Sarah G. Levine. A delightful modern-day romance inspired by *Emma*, one of Jane Austen's most beloved novels. (978-1-63679-879-0)

One Measure of Love by Annie McDonald. Vancouver's hit competitive cooking show *Recipe for Success* has begun filming its second season, and two talented young chefs are desperate for more than a winning dish. (978-1-63679-827-1)

The Smallest Day by J.M. Redmann. The first bullet missed—can Micky Knight stop the second bullet from finding its target? (978-1-63679-854-7)

To Please Her by Elena Abbott. A spilled coffee leads Sabrina into a world of erotic BDSM that may just land her the love of her life. (978-1-63679-849-3)

Two Weddings and a Funeral by Claudia Parr. Stella and Theo have spent the last thirteen years pretending they can be just friends, but surely "just friends" don't make out every chance they get. (978-1-63679-820-2)

Firecamp by Jaycie Morrison. Going their separate ways seemed inevitable for two people as different as Fallon and Nora, while meeting up again is strictly coincidental. (978-1-63679-753-3)

Coming Up Clutch by Anna Gram. College softball star Kelly "Razor" Mitchell hung up her cleats early, but when former crush, now coach Ashton Sharpe shows up on her doorstep seven years later, beautiful as ever, Razor hopes the longing in her gaze has nothing to do with softball. (978-1-63679-817-2)

Fixed Up by Aurora Rey. When electrician Jack Barrow and artist Ellie Lancaster get stuck on a job site during a blizzard, close quarters send all sorts of sparks flying. (978-1-63679-788-5)

Stranded by Ronica Black. Can Abigail and Whitley overcome their personal hang-ups and stubbornness to survive not only Alaska but a dangerous stalker as well? (978-1-63679-761-8)

Whisk Me Away by Georgia Beers. Regan's a gorgeous flake. Ava, a beautiful untouchable ice queen. When they meet again at a retreat for up-and-coming pastry chefs, the competition, and the ovens, heat up. (978-1-63679-796-0)